The Storyteller Series, Book 2

The Storyteller's Quest

Patricia Srigley

WigglesWorth Press and SrigleyArts.com

Library and Archives Canada Cataloguing in Publication:
Please contact the publisher for this information

ISBN 978-0-9880081-4-4

Layout by WigglesWorth Press
Cover design by Patricia Srigley
Cover art by Patricia Srigley

Published by: WigglesWorth Press and SrigleyArts.com
Montreal, Quebec, Canada

Also available!

The Storyteller's Curse, Book 1
The Storyteller's Quest, Book 2
Fire-scape
Universe Idol
All Planetary Shipping
Scarecrow in the Graveyard
The April-May June Series
Deeply
One Crooked House

SRIG LEY ARTS .COM

Wiggles Worth Press

Contests

1. The Queen's Request

This little piggy went to see the queen
This little piggy stayed home in bed
This little piggy ate cakes and pies
This little piggy had none
And this little piggy said 'No No No'
All the way'away from home

-Bayerd the Storyteller, The Piggy's Quest

"A quest? Surely you jest," Bayerd drawled from the chair where he was lounging with his feet propped up, while his latest manservant tended to his toenails.

"No, I do not jest. Nor does Queen Hellenor. She summons you to attend her. She will tell you all about the quest herself." Kelp stood by the opened door of the luxurious tower rooms they had moved into after their nuptials, as if she expected Bayerd to jump to his feet like a little bunny and hop along to visit the queen that very moment.

He did not bestir himself. Instead, Bayerd reached for another pastry. His hand found nothing but an empty platter. Hadn't there been a dozen pastries on it when Irvette carried it in? Surely he hadn't eaten a dozen? No, Marsdale, his manservant, must have been sneaking pastries when Bayerd wasn't looking. Now he would have to order another dozen.

"A quest?" He chortled. "Ridiculous nonsense. You must have misunderstood your auntie, my love." He scanned for the handy handbell he used to bring the servants running.

"I did not misunderstand, dearest," Kelp said.

"Well, then she is rambling. She is getting on in years. Perhaps her mind is losing its sharpness. Like an old sword, it must be getting dull."

1

Bayerd spotted the handbell behind a bowl that was depressingly depleted of cheese curds or any other delectable nibbles. Perhaps Marsdale had had his sticky fingers in there as well. Bayerd picked up the bell and rang it energetically to summon Irvette.

Kelp marched across the room and yanked the bell right out of his hand. "My auntie's mind is not dull. It is as sharp as a freshly honed blade and she is waiting to tell you about your quest." She seemed to be speaking through gritted teeth. Perhaps she had a toothache. Bayerd hoped not. Kelp had lovely teeth for a royal—for anyone, and he would not wish her beauty to be marred by a gap-toothed smile.

"What sort of quest?" he inquired, to humour his wife, who had surely misunderstood the queen.

Kelp looked a bit shifty-eyed when she said, "Um … I'm not sure. Queen Hellenor hasn't said much to me. She will reveal the details to you herself. She wants to see you in her private quarters without delay, as I have already said, twice. Thrice now. Do get up."

Bayerd did not get up. He frowned. "Her private quarters? But they are located at the far end of the castle. If she wants to address me, shouldn't she come here?"

"She is the queen, Bayerd. You go to her, she does not come to you."

"Well, that doesn't seem right if she is the one who wishes to speak with me. And why would she want to send me on a quest now? It seems highly unlikely. I'm sure you've misunderstood. The anniversary of our nuptials is fast approaching. Hellenor wouldn't send me on a quest now. It might cause me to miss the grand celebration. I'm going to perform the tale of the night we met—the night I saved you from a herd of dragons."

"Again?"

"I haven't performed it for at least a month. High time the castle folk had a treat. Speaking of treats …" Bayerd tried to grab the handbell back.

Kelp was having none of it. She appeared to roll her eyes, but surely that was due to a fleck of dust or dirt. She must have gotten something in her eye, blown in through the tower window on the light breeze. And it sounded like she sighed, but that was undoubtedly the same warm summer breeze gusting in through that very same window.

For a year now, Bayerd had lived like a prince, and why shouldn't he live like a prince? He was a prince, although in truth, his title was an honorary one. He was lowborn and had lived a lowborn life until he and

Princess Kelp had met each other one starry night in the forest, the night he had saved her from dragons—or at least one dragon. And she may have lent him a helping hand. Although that particular tidbit was rarely mentioned, at least not by him, and the rest was history—a history he had embellished quite lavishly for the sake of his reputation as a professional storyteller, and formerly travelling troubadour.

Since then, they had lived in wedded bliss, which is not great fodder for tales. He hadn't scripted a new adventure since he had said 'I do', but his old stories were so wonderfully entertaining, and so well performed, that no-one ever complained when he hopped upon a tabletop to relive his glory days in words. Well, no-one complained except for Orson, Bayerd's good and true friend from the time before he was a prince. And since Orson was inclined to be broody, he complained about everything under the sun anyway, hence his words were without merit.

Bayerd turned a deaf ear whenever Orson started comparing Bayerd to a plump pampered pussycat or some such indolent creature. Orson was presently away from the castle on an errand for the queen. In truth, Bayerd did not mind the respite from his good and true friend's disparaging comments, which were clearly inspired by jealousy, since Orson had not been dubbed a prince and had not married the most beautiful princess in the land.

Queen Hellenor still ruled the Golden Kingdom, but she was getting older and creakier by the minute, so Kelp stood by her side at all official functions now. Soon enough, Kelp would rule the Golden Kingdom with her golden-haired husband cutting a dashing figure by her side. Bayerd looked forward to the day when he could wear a kingly crown, rather than the small princely one he now had to make-do with.

"Bayerd, Queen Hellenor is waiting. I will accompany you to hear what she has to say about this quest." Kelp tugged on his arm, trying to raise him up.

Bayerd glanced down at his toenails. The last one hadn't yet been trimmed and polished. "Oh, fine, if I must." He sighed dramatically, so she would know just how hard done by he was feeling. "But wait until my last toenail is polished. Mr. Pinky needs to look his best for the queen." This time, he saw Kelp roll her eyes heavenward, and he knew it didn't have a thing to do with dust.

"My aunt will not be examining your toenails, dearest, especially since I am sure you will wear your favourite golden jewel-encrusted slippers to her rooms."

Bayerd sniffed. "True enough, but I'll feel unbalanced if only nine of my ten toenails are in top form." Kelp rubbed her temple. "Have you another headache, sweetling?" he inquired.

"I do feel one coming on."

"You seem to be getting more and more headaches of late. Have you seen the castle physician?" Bayerd inquired.

She nodded. "He wants to bleed me, and that is not the cure for my headaches."

"I don't think that is the cure for anything other than blood poisoning. And has he said anything about why you've not conceived?" Bayerd asked. Kelp had been hoping to be blessed with a child in her belly by now, but it had not happened, and truth be told, that was fine by Bayerd. Children were whiney and sticky. He thought of them as a curse rather than a blessing, and he was a man who knew all about curses. A howling babe was a curse he could well do without.

Bayerd's attempt to distract Kelp with conversation long enough for Mr. Pinky to get polished was unsuccessful. "Marsdale, get out now," she snapped at his manservant.

The fellow should have checked with Bayerd before he hightailed it from the room, but he did not. He fled without even a glance in Bayerd's direction. "So much for loyalty. I think I'll have to replace him," Bayerd huffed, studying his unfinished toenail with regret.

"It is not proper to keep the queen waiting," Kelp said, nostrils flared and arms crossed. The frown line between her eyebrows was becoming a permanent fixture.

"Oh, I suppose it isn't. Although I'm sure you've quite misunderstood her about this quest business, or Hellenor is losing her marbles." Bayerd stuffed his toes into his golden jewel-encrusted slippers and rose. He stretched and donned his finest fur-trimmed cape before he sauntered over to Kelp's side and kissed her between the eyebrows. She grabbed his hand and started marching. He was towed along in her wake all the way to Hellenor's private rooms.

The queen's oversized guards, one on each side of her doorway, did not bar their entrance, proving they were expected. The queen's ladies whisked them inside without delay, and then made themselves scarce.

4

Hellenor was waiting on her upholstered couch, which was sagging with age, just like her face.

"Queen Hellenor," Bayerd said with a graceful bow that almost popped the button on his trousers. They had been let out twice by the tailor already, and there was no spare cloth in the seams to let them out a third time. His wardrobe had gotten uncomfortably snug over the winter. Perhaps it was time for a new wardrobe. Fashion was an ever-changing beast, and Bayerd certainly shouldn't be behind the times. The castle folk needed someone to hold in esteem in regards to what should and should not be worn.

"Bayerd, have a seat." Queen Hellenor waved a bejeweled hand at the opposite couch.

He sat and glanced around at the nearby tabletops. They were all disappointingly empty. "No tea? No pastries?" he inquired.

"Not this morning, Bayerd."

"Are you sure? Because my butler ate all my morning pastries, and I'm feeling rather peckish."

"I'm sure you can survive without pastries until the noonday meal," she said more crisply than was necessary.

"Well, so much for the social niceties," he muttered.

Kelp narrowed her eyes at him. "Listen. Don't speak!"

"Aren't you going to join me, sweetheart?" He patted the place beside him—close beside him.

"I would rather stand." Kelp looked at her aunt most beseechingly. "Pray continue, Auntie. Tell Bayerd why you have summoned him."

The queen inclined her head once, with regal aplomb. "Yes. Bayerd, I am sending you on a quest."

Bayerd chuckled. "Oh, I think you've made a little mistake there, Queen Hellenor. Surely you meant to summon someone else, not me. Perhaps it is Orson you want. He is a fine chap to send on a quest, what with his long strong sword arm, and he does so enjoy a good quest. Why, I'm sure he'll be back from his errand in a day or two. How about I send him to see you as soon as he turns up? And you can tell him all about this quest."

The queen's lips tightened, making them look as wrinkly as a dried prune. "I have not made a mistake, little or otherwise. I am sending you, Prince Bayerd, on a quest. You will leave the castle on the morrow, at first light."

Bayerd stopped smiling. "What? Leave? Tomorrow?" Panic wrapped around him like a dragon's tail, squeezing until he could barely draw breath. He had rarely ventured outside the castle walls this past year, since he had learned in the most painful ways imaginable, exactly how dangerous it was out there, what with the fire-breathing dragons, and hellcats running wild, and murderous men in miniature, and then there were the harpies. No man was safe from their clutching talons, their beaky lipless mouths, their scaly black-tipped breasts, and their unholy appetites.

"But … but…" he sputtered, "I'm not really in the mood for a quest. The dog days of summer are upon us, and travelling in the heat can make a man quite sweaty and overheated. Horses don't like it either, or dogs, I shouldn't think. Probably why they're called the dog days, because dogs don't like the heat any more than men. And of course it is much hotter outside the castle walls." Not to mention dangerous, but he didn't say that aloud. He did not want anyone, especially Kelp, to think him a coward. No, he was simply rambling, or ranting, or some unflattering combination of the two.

"Regardless," the queen's wrinkled lips pulled into a tight little smile, "you will do as I command. You will leave tomorrow on this most important quest."

"But Orson's not back yet. I can't go on a quest without Orson, now can I?" Everyone in the land knew that Bayerd was easy pickings without Orson's sword to protect him. And even Orson had not been able to protect him from what lurked outside the castle walls.

"This quest is not a dangerous one, so you will be fine without Orson," Kelp said, which was odd, since she had claimed to know nothing about the quest.

"But …but … our anniversary fete is fast approaching. I can't miss that. You wouldn't want me to miss that, would you, Kelpie?"

She did not reply and avoided his gaze.

The queen said, "The quest should not take more than a month, so you will be back in plenty of time for your anniversary fete. Perhaps you will even have some new tales to tell for the occasion." Her words sounded like a command masquerading as a hint. "You do know how I love a good story."

"Yes, Queen Hellenor, I do. Why, I could tell you one right now, if you like," Bayerd said, hoping to distract her from the silly quest business.

6

Alas, she was having none of it. "I will choose two of my royal guards to ride with you. That should suffice," she said.

Bayerd was fast running out of excuses to stay safely inside the castle walls. "But ... I have obligations here." It was a blatant falsehood and they all knew it.

"We will simply have to muddle along without you until you return," the queen said gently, but with final authority. A crook of her baby finger would see his head lopped off, so she could certainly order him on a quest. And if he didn't leave willingly, she could have him catapulted over the battlements in a fantastic bloody display that would end his quest before it even began.

He slumped, knowing when he was beaten. "Well ... I will leave tomorrow then. But two men? Perhaps I should take a hundred, just in case we encounter ... bandits or some such."

The queen glanced at Kelp before she said, "Four of my knights will ride with you."

Four didn't seem like nearly enough. "Perhaps fifty, in case we meet a whole band of murderous cutthroats."

The queen sighed. "Six and not a man more."

"Six? Are you sure six will be enough for this quest? Uh ... what is the quest?" he asked.

"Did you bear witness to the fire that streaked down from the heavens last evening?"

"Not with my own eyes, but Kelp saw it. She claimed the ground shook when the heaven fire impacted with the earth." He adjusted his vest, which was riding up, allowing several rolls of fat to loll out. "I was already abed, so I missed the excitement." In truth, he had been passed out from too much drink, to keep the nightmares of harpies at bay. It had become his nightly ritual.

"You have told tales about such fire coming down from the heavens," the queen stated.

"I've told a few such tales." Bayerd could guess where this was going. "T'is a precious piece of the heavens sent to earth dressed in a coat of flame. The crystal will have magical properties that will bless the lucky man who possesses it. Why, I once met a man who had charge of just such a magical rock -" Bayerd was about to launch into one of his most fantastical tales when Kelp cut him off.

"We have heard that tale, more than once, more than twice and more than thrice. Now listen to your queen," she ordered in her steeliest tone.

7

Queen Hellenor cleared her throat. "Bayerd, I charge you to find the spot where the heaven stone hit the earth. Find the stone and bring it back to me. Guard it with your life -"

"Perhaps not with his life, Auntie," Kelp cut in.

"Oh, well, not your life, Bayerd, but do your best to find it and get it back here to me. Return with this magical heaven stone and you will have completed your quest," the queen decreed.

The quest didn't sound too hazardous, except that it required venturing outside the castle walls. Yet with six of the queen's knights to protect him, Bayerd supposed he could manage it. And it's not like he had a choice. A royal command was just that—a command. Unless he feigned an illness. Yes, a sudden illness might well discharge him from the quest.

He rose and bowed. The button finally lost the battle to hold his trousers closed. It popped off and flew across the room to land in the queen's lap. Bayerd pretended he didn't notice. The queen pretended likewise.

He said, "As you wish, Queen Hellenor. I shall seek this heaven stone, I will find it and bring the precious gift to you. And I will guard it with my very life." He was lying through his teeth. He fully intended to wake up so very ill the next morning, he would not be able to crawl out of bed, let alone go on a quest.

Kelp tucked a hand under his elbow and turned him toward the door. "You leave tomorrow, Bayerd. You must pack, and arrange a horse that is steady and won't toss you off at every turn. You had best get to it."

He crossed the room, one hand discreetly holding his pants in place. He expected Kelp to accompany him, but she did not. He was herded right out the door, and that door closed behind him, rather hard, with Kelp on the opposite side.

"I'll return to our rooms and await you there," he called through the thick wood, ignoring the two oversized guards who were looking down at him with just a touch of smirk. He marched away, holding up his trousers and mulling things over.

Something was not right with his Kelp. Perhaps he should have noticed sooner, but he was a man and he had not. He usually had to be told things, and she had not told him that something was amiss. Yet in his heart, he suddenly knew there was.

All the way to the other end of the castle, and up the stairs to their tower rooms, he considered what he might have done or not done to irk his dear wife. He couldn't come up with a single thing and was still in the midst of packing, to appear as if he truly intended to go on his quest, when Kelp finally returned to their rooms three long hours later. He had all his outfits laid out on the bed, complete with matching slippers and accessories.

Kelp frowned fiercely. "What are you doing?"

"Packing, but I can shift the clothing if you wish to make better use of the bed." He winked in case she did not comprehend his words as he had insinuated them.

She sighed. "Bayerd, you don't need a new outfit for each and every day you will be gone. One change of clothing will suffice, I'm sure. That is how you used to travel."

"Yes, but that was before I was a prince. Things are quite different now, aren't they?"

"Yes, they are." There was a weary tone to her words and a melancholy expression on her face.

"Have I done something to upset you, my love?" he asked.

Kelp pondered his question for a minute that felt like an hour to Bayerd's heart, before she said, "No. It's not you, it's me."

He was not reassured. "But -"

"We shall speak when you return." She picked up a pair of leggings that had ended up on the floor.

"Speak about what? And why can't we discuss this now?" he asked.

"Because you have far too much to do to prepare for your quest. We will speak when you return to the castle. Now, you need to know your destination." She crossed to the window and pointed due west. "The heaven fire streaked to earth on the far side of that hill over yonder. It landed quite near the top."

Bayerd joined her at the window and squinted across the miles to where a line of high hills was bordered by thick forest, and closer to, plowed farmland. "The lowest roundest hill?" he guessed.

"No, the highest, pointiest hill. That one." Kelp adjusted her finger by several degrees.

"The craggy one with the tip that disappears into the mist? And has snow on its cap, even though it is summer?" Bayerd's voice rose in alarm until it sounded quite squeaky. It was not a voice a professional storyteller could take pride in, unless that storyteller was acting out a farcical tale with a frightened mouse in it. But at least Bayerd did not have to be afraid, since he was going to be far too ill to go on his quest.

"Yes, that hill." Kelp lowered her arm.

"But ... that is a mountain, my love, not a hill at all. It is quite far away, and ... and very high." It looked like the type of unforgiving landscape where flocks of harpies would roost.

To distract himself from thinking about harpies, he tried to judge the height of it. The hill, or mountain, jutted up from the horizon in a lopsided triangle. In profile, it resembled a misshapen nose. He had once heard another storyteller, whose voice hadn't been nearly as impressive as Bayerd's own, tell a chilling tale about a mountain called 'The Witch's Nose' and the vile creatures that inhabited its upper reaches. It was lucky that he was going to be too ill to go haring up the mountain that resembled just such a beaky snout, or he would have been quaking in his golden jewel-encrusted slippers.

Bayerd kept his thoughts focused and pretended, even to himself, that he was preparing to go on a quest. A sincere act now would make his sudden illness in the morning all the more believable. And what was a storyteller if not an actor? He threw himself into the role. "I've never travelled in that direction. I look forward to exploring the new lands," he declared, standing taller and thrusting out his chest, although alas, it was his belly that appeared larger.

Kelp shot him a suspicious glance. "Truly?"

He studied the mountain, jaw firmly set. "I doubt a carriage will make it up the steep slopes. I will need a string of packhorses to carry my wardrobe and other supplies, including a plentiful store of weapons. Do you know of anyone who has travelled up that mountain?"

"No, I know of no-one. But it is not so high as it looks, I'm sure." Kelp tilted her head and squinted at the mountain. "Or maybe it is as high as it looks. Regardless, the queen has consulted with Sir Gallant, the head of her guard, and they have chosen the men who will ride with you. You should go and meet them at the stables and arrange your horse."

"I'll take Blackie. She's my horse." Kelp had gifted him the beautiful steed soon after they had met.

"Yes, but she's a bit ... lively for you, and you have quite a distance to ride, and doubtless one or two steep slopes to ascend. Ask the stable master for a steady mount instead."

"I suppose that might not be a bad idea. I don't want to roll down that mountain. And I'll need a string of packhorses to carry my supplies. Clothes, food, perhaps some wine. Lots of weapons," he

10

caught her hand and kissed her fingers, "just in case we encounter an army of cutthroat bandits." Or a flock of depraved harpies.

She pulled her hand away. "You aren't going to war, my husband. You are going to retrieve a rock. Six men with their personal weapons will be more than enough of a troop to ride with you. Go and meet your men and arrange your horses. I'll pack for you. Maiga can help me."

"Are you sure?"

"Yes, Bayerd. Go. You have much to do in a very short time." She gave him a little push.

"Make sure my clothes are rolled smoothly so they don't wrinkle." Bayerd aimed a kiss at her lips and made contact with her cheek instead, when her head turned aside. He descended to the courtyard with a troubled heart.

The billet for the queen's guard was located beside the stables. A number of sweaty brawny knights were practicing their swordplay in the yard. He assessed them, wondering which ones had been chosen to accompany him on the quest he was going to be too sick to carry out. As large and muscular as they were, not one was quite as large and muscular as Orson, although they all seemed quite able with their swords.

Bayerd approached them, feeling much smaller all of the sudden, especially when one of the lummoxes fell back and knocked him on his ass. The swordplay stopped. "Sorry about that, Prince Bayerd," the offender said. He offered a hand to pull Bayerd to his feet. The hand would have swallowed Bayerd's whole, and probably crushed it as flat as a pancake, so he struggled up on his own.

He dusted dirt off the red velvet leggings he had donned to replace his button-less trousers, and said graciously, "No harm done." He had lost a golden slipper and stuffed his foot back into it, thinking he should have put on his boots to venture so near to the stables. Ah well, too late now. Since he had everyone's attention, he said, "I am here to acquaint myself with the six fine knights who have the honour of accompanying me on a most glorious and dangerous quest."

The men darted glances at each other before the lummox motioned toward the stone wall where four men lounged, playing cards. "Those four and …" He scanned the yard. "I think the other two are in the stables. I'll fetch them for you, shall I?"

"I would appreciate that, my good man."

11

In a couple of minutes, the chosen six formed a raggedy line before him. Bayerd took their measure. "What is your name?" he said to the tallest and brawniest of the six, whose hair was almost, but not quite, as dark and gleaming as Orson's.

"Sir Conquer is my name," the fellow said.

"You are charged to accompany me, Sir Conquer?"

"My queen bids me to go on this quest and I will do so with a brave heart. I will saddle up my mighty steed and ride like a champion into battle with naught but bravery in my heart. I will wield my sword bravely, until the ground runs red with the blood of my enemy. I will bravely stand alongside my fellows and -"

Knights! Too often they fancied themselves storytellers when their mouths were better suited to spitting out phlegm. Bayerd cut him off, saying, "This quest does not include a battle, Sir Conquer, but I'm sure your strong sword arm will come in handy outside these castle walls." If Bayerd truly had been going on the quest, he would have been dreading a month of listening to Sir Conquer wax poetic with his limited vocabulary.

The knight standing beside Sir Conquer had dimples. They weren't as deep as Orson's, but they were appealing nonetheless. "Your name?" Bayerd inquired.

"Sir Basher."

"Are you eager to ride on this quest, Sir Basher?"

"Eager isn't the word." Sir Basher left it at that.

Bayerd appreciated his brevity. "How's your sword arm?"

"Strong and able."

"Excellent. You'll do, Sir Basher," Bayerd said. Sir Basher nodded once. Perhaps the fellow was a bit too taciturn.

Bayerd moved to stand before the third knight in line. He had thinning brown hair and watery brown eyes and a narrow nose. He squinted as if he was nearsighted. Perhaps he needed spectacles. All in all, he was a rather nondescript fellow for a knight, and not quite as tall as the pair that flanked him. "Your name?"

"Sir Jabalot," the fellow declared.

"Sir Jabalot, is it?" Bayerd knew these men chose their own titles when knighted, and Jabalot was an interesting moniker. Creative. "Well, Jabalot, are you fit for a quest?"

"I'm fit for anything."

"How are your fighting skills?"

"Better than most." For some reason, he glanced pointedly at Sir Basher. Jabalot could have done with a dose of humility.

"Excellent," Bayerd said and moved a few steps to stand in front of knight number four. A wicked scar ran from his ear to his chin, decorating his jaw. His hair was liberally laced with gray and there was a stoop to his shoulders. He was rather old to be an active knight.

"And you are?" Bayerd said.

"Sir Gerald at your service, Prince Bayerd."

"You look like you have fought hard in battle." He motioned to the scar.

"Cut myself shaving," Gerald said with a straight face.

"Then I think we shall all let our beards grow on this quest," Bayerd declared, "so we will not be gravely wounded."

Sir Gerald nodded. "A wise precaution, Prince Bayerd."

He seemed like a no-nonsense type, and with a sense of humour to boot. His name suited him. Bayerd took a step to the right to meet the fifth of his men. His hair was as red and curly as a fool's wig. He wasn't as steady on his pins as the other knights and smelled strongly of ale. "Your name?"

"Sir Revel."

"How are you on a horse, Sir Revel?"

"I can usually hang on in a pinch," the fellow said with a silly grin.

"We have far to ride, so I hope you can." If he really had been going on his quest, Bayerd would have worried about both of them falling off their horses, all the way up the mountain and down again.

"Giddy up!" Revel cried, slapping his thigh a few times and galloping in place. Sir Gerald did not look amused and almost knocked the knight over with a well-placed elbow jab to the ribs.

Bayerd moved along to meet his sixth and final knight. His hair was almost as golden as Bayerd's and worn in a ponytail, as Bayerd often wore his. The fellow's clothes were fashionable, too. Not as fashionable as Bayerd's, but fashionable for a knight of the realm. He was the shortest and slightest of the six, and barely loomed over Bayerd at all.

"And what is your name, my fine fellow?" Bayerd said.

"Sir Swift."

"Greetings, Sir Swift. And are you?"

"Am I what?" Swift asked, a blank look in his blue eyes. One of the pupils was larger than the other, giving him a lopsided expression.

"Are you swift?"

"That's my name," the fellow said.

Perhaps he wasn't as swift as his moniker. Bayerd stepped back to survey the six men who had been chosen by the queen as his close companions for the next month. "Sir Conquer, Sir Basher, Sir Jabalot, Sir Gerald, Sir Revel and Sir Swift, I am pleased to have six such fine men to accompany me on this dangerous quest. I have no doubt that we will succeed in our mission to capture the heaven crystal and bring it to Queen Hellenor as a prize. Prepare your gear and polish up your weapons. Select a mount that is steady and strong. We will be climbing some slopes."

He felt bad lying to the six knights, who would be sorely disappointed when the quest was cancelled. He gazed over the battlements at the mountain, which seemed to jut up even higher than it had earlier. He thought he saw a shadow cutting through the mist near the top of the mountain and squinted. Harpy? Dragon? His imagination? He took a deep breath to calm his pounding heart and clasped his hands together to stop them from trembling. Even though he had no plans to scale it, the mountain terrified him.

"I would recommend an early night and a sound sleep. We will depart tomorrow at first light. Expect to be gone for a month or so." He stepped back and surveyed the dozens of knights who were watching him address his men. "I do hope the rest of you aren't too disappointed at not being chosen. I'm sure there will be another quest soon enough," he orated so all could hear.

The men returned to their swordplay, whispering amongst each other. Some hearty guffaws reached Bayerd's ears and he wondered what was funny. He hoped he wasn't the joke. And he didn't expect his advice for an early night would be heeded, not when the men faced a month away from the castle. They would likely indulge in revelry and turn up exhausted and hungover, which was neither here nor there. Once the quest was cancelled, they would not be riding anywhere on the morrow.

And Bayerd had his own plans—plans which involved his beautiful Kelp. He might not want children, but the process of creating them was another matter entirely. His bed had been a cool and lonely place of late, but surely Kelp would be amenable tonight, since she believed he would be departing for a month on a dangerous quest.

2. The Quest that Was

There once was a man newly wed
Who was afraid to leave his bed
Alas his poor wife
Suffered such strife
She whacked him over the head
— Bayerd the Storyteller, Limerick

When Bayerd returned to their rooms, Kelp wasn't there. His clothing was all neatly rolled and stacked, ready to travel with him. The hillock of multi-coloured tunics and matching hose looked like it was wrapped in a rainbow. If he had been going on a quest, he certainly would have looked his best.

Bayerd mulled over how to romance his wife on his supposedly final night in the castle. A private feast perhaps, and some wooing, followed by a bath for two? Kelp was half-mermaid and enjoyed bathing more than anyone in the land. Bayerd did, too, as long as it was with Kelp in their huge bathing tub that was almost a pool. How long had it been since he had shared an intimate bath with his wife? Far too long was the answer.

Inspired, he vigorously rang his handbell until Irvette arrived. He ordered her to trot on down to the kitchen and arrange for an array of delicacies to be delivered at eight o'clock sharp. At the same time, he ordered his manservant to round up a bunch of menials to fill the bathing tub to the brim with heated water.

When the sky darkened, the bath was ready. Dinner arrived at the appointed hour, and still Kelp did not appear. Bayerd consoled himself with wine, to drown his sorrows. When he'd had rather too much wine, he stripped and got in the tub to wait. He brought the jug of wine along, as well as the platters of delicacies. He floated those like boats—boats full of food that he nibbled. He was doubtless deep in his cups at that point.

Many of the platters sunk beneath the waves, until much of the dinner was floating around in the tub with him. He tried bobbing for food to pass the time, and almost drowned in but three feet of water. Only some desperate flailing about saved him from a most humiliating end.

To recover from his near-death experience, he drank more wine, until the jug was almost empty. When a buxom serving wench entered the chamber, probably to retrieve the dinner platters, Bayerd's eyeballs were every bit as drunk as he was, and he lost control of them. They stared in fascination at the twin mounds of flesh that roiled up and out of the wench's plunging neckline. The pillowy things jiggled when she walked. Bayerd had never before laid eyes on her, or her frighteningly large bosom.

"You're new," he said, with a slur even his drunken ears could hear.

"Aye, Prince Bayerd, I am." She surveyed the room. "No-one else about?"

"No, I'm all by my lonesome," Bayerd said morosely.

The wench strode about the room and took a peak into the bedchamber.

"What are you doing?" Bayerd asked.

"Just having a gander at how the other half lives." She darted into the bedchamber, out of sight.

"Hey, come back here." Bayerd would have gone after her, except for being wet and naked and too drunk to walk.

After a minute, she reappeared. "Merely having a little look-see," she said and approached the tub. The closer she got, the bigger her breasts looked, as if they were swelling before his eyes.

"You'll have to join me in here, if you're wanting your platters back," he joked, and leered. "Tits … I mean, t'is the only way to fetch the dishes. And the food. Tits … I mean, t'is floating. Have you ever bobbed for apples before?"

She peered into the tub. "I've never bobbed for apples, Prince Bayerd, but I've bobbed for chestnuts. And I see two lovely chestnuts down there in the water that I wouldn't mind tasting, in my mouth, if you know what I mean." Subtle she was not. She took the jug out of his hand and had a very long swig. She definitely emptied it of every drop, even the dregs.

Being a man whose needs had not been satisfied for some long time, Bayerd could not help but rise to the occasion, in spite of the cooling water.

16

"Oh, and what else do I see down there?" She bent over to have a closer look, exposing a great deal more of her mountainous chest. So much so in fact, that one of her breasts fell right out of her gown and dangled before him like a cow's udder. "Should I bob for a sausage as well, Prince Bayerd?" She licked her lips.

"Do you ... do you see a sausage down there?" he asked.

"Aye, I do. A lovely big one, and I've not had me dinner yet." She bent lower, to have a better look. She bent so low that Bayerd's face was about to be smothered by her wayward breast. All he would have to do was open his mouth, and her nipple would drop right in.

The outer door clicked opened and startled them both. With a little squawk, the serving wench overbalanced, no doubt weighted down by her breasts. She landed in the water on top of Bayerd, sending waves cresting over the side of the tub. Bayerd was pushed under and proceeded to drown. Flailing did no good when a hefty maiden with even heftier breasts was sitting atop him like an anvil.

When she finally stumbled from the tub, Bayerd popped up out of the water, sputtering and gasping for air. He blinked water from his eyes and saw that Kelp had finally turned up, and she did not look pleased. The serving wench stood beside the tub, dripping and tucking her breasts back where they belonged. The second one had managed to escape while she had been splashing about.

"Kelpie, my love, there you are. I've been waiting for you, in the bash—bath, with dinner," Bayerd slurred, motioning to all the floating food.

"Have you?" Kelp said with icy politeness. She fixed her cold gaze on the wet serving wench. "Get out." The girl scurried from the room as fast as her drenched skirts would allow, leaving a wash of water in her wake.

Kelp slammed the door after her and stalked toward the tub. She looked down at Bayerd, her face as grim as he had ever seen it. And yet sad, too. "You have sunk to a new low, husband," she said.

"I have, because I almost drowned. Is that what you mean?" Not only did he feel the fool, he sounded it as well.

"No, that is not what I mean." Her lips tightened and she turned her back on him. "It is fortunate you are going on a quest tomorrow, for it you weren't, I would summon a dragon to carry you off to the farthest reaches of the kingdom and drop you there." And Kelp could do it, for she had quite a way with dragons.

"But Kelpie, nothing happened."

She turned back around. "And if I had not entered when I did, would you be able to say the same?" Her beautiful brown eyes gazed pleadingly into his.

"Uh … no … I mean yes. I mean nothing would have happened, I'm quite sure." He was floundering, and it had nothing to do with the water.

Kelp sighed. "I am not quite so sure, in fact, I don't believe you."

"It only happened because … I am a man with needs and we have not lain together for some time."

"Perhaps you should ask yourself why that is, and if that grants you the right to dally with the serving wenches."

"But it's not my fault. You should have been here, with me. You're my wife, t'is your duty to lay with me." His ears heard the petulance in his tone. He sounded like a bloody spoilt royal, for god's sake. It was the same voice he had once used to mimic spoilt royals in the tales he told, and here he was starring in that role. Was that truly who he had become since his union with Kelp?

"Duty? Duty?" Her voice was pitched high enough to make his ears cringe. She planted her hands on her hips. "Well, let me tell you a hard truth, husband. That is all it has become—a duty, certainly not a pleasure. I will see you off on your quest tomorrow, but that is all I will do, unless I kill you in your sleep." Kelp spun on her heel and bolted from the chamber, slamming the door hard enough to shake their tower all the way down to its rock-solid foundation.

Bayerd did not go after her. He was half-drowned, spectacularly drunk, and his sausage had shriveled—he was in no condition to win his love's favour, especially when she wanted to kill him. He climbed out of the tub and his foot caught on the edge. He fell hard, landing on his face. He heard a small snap. It should have hurt, but he didn't feel a thing. He crawled across the floor and into his lonely bed.

He must have fallen instantly asleep, or he passed out (which was much more likely), because when he opened his eyes, it was morning. Rather late morning, judging by the bright sunlight outside. His nose was throbbing terribly.

Kelp's side of the bed was still empty. He hadn't expected otherwise. He touched the side where she should have lain and stroked Kelp's pillow, sad enough to shed a few manly tears. He could hear her

18

two ladies, Maiga and Irvette, bustling around in the adjacent room, setting out breakfast—or was it lunch?

It was time to set his ruse in motion, for he had no intention of going on his quest, especially after last night. It was now more important than ever that he stay in the castle. He had to set things right with Kelp.

Bayerd groaned weakly. No-one heard him. He groaned louder, still no-one turned up. He groaned very loudly. Still nothing.

He sat up and pulled on the leather riding trousers and the cotton tunic he had laid out the previous evening, before he had gotten into the wine. He stumbled out of the bedroom, the picture of weakness. Given the degree of his hangover, it was no act. He paused to lean on the doorjamb for support, as if it was the only thing holding him up, which it was.

Kelp was seated at their dining table. She glanced over with a face that was so cold, it could have been carved from ice, although she did look rather startled when her eyes came to rest on him. But only for a moment. "You've broken your nose again," she observed.

"Have I?" Bayerd felt his nose and cried out in pain. "Yes, it is crooked. I guess I have." He didn't try to straighten it. He was already in enough pain. He shoved away from the doorjamb and stumbled to the table where he flopped onto a chair. He coughed and said in an invalid's rasp, "I've slept too late. Why didn't you wake me?"

Kelp raised one eyebrow. "I tried."

"Ah." Bayerd's reputation for sleeping like the dead was justified. He had once slept through a dragon's attack, and gotten quite burnt as a result. And then there was the time he had slept through his own drowning, only to be saved by a wayward log. "I think I've slept late because I seem to be a little under the weather." He downplayed his faux illness, waiting for a show of Kelp's concern that would allow him to elaborate on just how gravely ill he was.

"A brisk ride will have you feeling as fit as a fiddle in no time, I'm sure, and there can be no finer day than this." Kelp shoved a platter in his direction. Bayerd could not deny the sunniness of the day and he didn't try. He slumped in his chair and scowled. "Eat quickly," Kelp prompted, "your men have been waiting for hours. And Maiga, hand my husband a damp rag so he can clean the blood off his face."

Maiga must have already intended to do so, because the cloth was in his hand almost instantly.

19

Bayerd gingerly wiped quite a bit of dried blood from beneath and around his nose. He was already feeling rather queasy, probably due to all the wine, so the sight of blood made his stomach clench. The nausea helped him to act sickly. "I don't think I can eat a bite. My stomach is churning. Is it very hot in here?" He dabbed at his forehead with the cloth and willed himself to sweat as if he had a fever. He couldn't quite manage it.

"Not really." Kelp motioned for Irvette to clear the table. "If you are not going to partake of the meal, I will see you off now."

Bayerd frowned at her. "But Kelp, I'm not well. I don't think I can go on my quest today. Maybe I'll be well enough tomorrow."

Kelp rose and looked down at him, was it piteously? He suddenly felt ashamed of himself. But not so ashamed that he was willing to go on a quest that would end in certain death when he fell off his horse and rolled down a mountain. Or worse, was abducted by a whole flock of harpies who would keep him prisoner to mate with them, over and over again, until he was nothing but a dried husk of a man.

He shivered and changed the subject. "I must apologize for last night. I was not myself."

"You were quite yourself, Bayerd, or at least, the man you have become—and that is the problem. You will leave today on your quest." She did not actually say 'or else', but she might as well have.

Bayerd watched the delicious breakfast depart without him having tasted a morsel. If he really was going on his quest, and he was starting to suspect that might be the case, he was going to miss the castle food, but he would miss Kelp more.

When he just kept sitting there in something of a stupor, Kelp said, "Time to go, husband. Stand up."

He sniffed. "But I'm not well enough to go."

"Perhaps this quest will cure you of what ails you." She pulled him to his feet. "Maiga, round up a few more servants to carry Bayerd's supplies down to the stables." And Bayerd knew they would carry him, too, if Kelp ordered it.

He was not being given any choice in the matter. He was being evicted from his home. But would he be allowed back? Perhaps he would only be welcomed back if he succeeded at his quest, and if Kelp forgave him.

Bayerd went into the bedchamber to gather his personal supplies. He was sitting on the edge of the bed when Kelp came in and sat down beside him. "Must I go?" he asked.

Kelp didn't even think about it. "Yes. This time away from the castle will be good for you."

"But I like it here. It's … comfortable." Bayerd had almost said 'safe'.

"There are more things in life than comfort. You used to enjoy a good adventure. I'll never forget the sight of you being carried off by a harpy, after the headsman almost took your head." She smiled reminiscently, and so sadly.

Bayerd shuddered. Kelp did not know of the intimate deed he had had to perform to appease the harpy and save his skin, Orson's hide, and Kelp herself, and that was one shameful secret he would take to his grave. Nightmares of harpies still plagued him, like a true sickness. There were no repulsive harpies inside the castle walls, but they lurked outside them, perhaps lying in wait for Bayerd. Perhaps waiting to shred his pants off again to get at what lay within.

He swallowed sickly. He wanted to crawl back into his luxurious bed and take Kelp with him. He wanted to huddle beneath the covers and never go on his quest, but that he could not do. His queen had commanded him to find the magical heaven rock, and there was no refusing such a command—especially when Kelp was evicting him from their tower.

She stood up and pulled him to his feet. She strapped his sword around his waist herself, and had a hard time buckling the belt over his protruding belly.

Kelp's ladies and half a dozen servants entered and filled their arms with Bayerd's wardrobe. Kelp escorted him down the stairs, out into the courtyard, and all the way to the stables, followed by the parade of servants, their arms loaded with patterned fabrics. He felt rather like he was being taken to meet the headsman again, to lose his head. He might not have minded that so much, given how it was throbbing like a battle drum.

"I've had the kitchen send packed rations to the stables already, for you and your six men," Kelp mentioned.

"Thank you. You will miss me, won't you, Kelp?"

"Mm," she murmured noncommittally and patted his arm as if he was her doddering grandfather.

21

At the stables, his six men were waiting, and each one looked sweatier and grumpier than the last. Even their six horses looked disgruntled, fully tacked and standing in the glaring sun, as was Bayerd's mount.

"First light you said. T'is nearly noon," Sir Basher ground out.

Sir Jabalot merely cast Bayerd a baleful glare. Sir Revel was slumped against a post, eyes closed as if he was asleep on his feet, like his big brown horse. Bayerd's own steed, a dark chestnut with distinctive white spots on her behind and nose, snorted wetly on his tunic in disgust.

He stepped back and used his sleeve to wipe horse snot off his chest. "I apologize for the delay. It was unavoidable. But we may depart as soon as my supplies are loaded." A couple of stable boys led out three packhorses and there was a general fuss while his wardrobe was tied onto their backs. He heard snickering from the surrounding knights. A hot wave of embarrassment washed over him. He looked like a bloody jester with his colourful motley and string of packhorses to carry enough clothes for a dozen men. At least Orson was not present to witness his foolishness and shame. Orson would never have let him hear the end of it.

He turned to Kelp, eyes downcast. "Perhaps it would have been wise to travel a bit lighter," he murmured.

"Perhaps it would," she said.

"I will miss you, my love. I will count the days until I return to your side." He pulled her to him and locked lips most improperly since they were not in the privacy of their bedchamber.

She allowed it, but her lips were still and cool. She pulled away first and murmured in his ear. "This is your quest, Bayerd. You are the leader of these men, not Sir Basher. Do not let him, or any of them, treat you with disrespect."

They were not the parting words he had been hoping for. Something along the lines of 'I will miss you' and 'be safe' and 'return swiftly' would have been more loving. Yet after last night when she had threatened to kill him, Kelp's coolness was not unwarranted.

Bayerd smiled valiantly, hoping to mask the growing ache in his chest. "Stay safe while I am away from your side, my love."

Kelp nodded. "You as well, Bayerd."

"This month will feel like a year to my heart," he added.

"Oh, I'm sure the time will pass quickly enough," Kelp said crisply.

A bit irked, he turned to his horse and tried to mount. The stable boy had to give him a boost. His mare was not particularly tall, but neither was he. At least she was old enough to be sedate, and wide-backed so he had more to sit on. Someone had named her Marigold, but he decided to call her Spot, which was not quite so girlish, and suited her far better since she had distinctive spots.

When he was settled in the saddle, he was handed the lead-line to his packhorses. At least they were tied together in a string, so he only had one additional strap of leather to worry about. He gathered his reins and looked around the courtyard. Few of the castle folk had turned up to see him off. Or perhaps they had come earlier and left in disgust when he was hours late for his own quest.

He spotted Queen Hellenor beside the castle. Shifra stood by her side, flanked closely by a pair of the queen's guards, probably to make sure Kelp's evil cousin didn't pull out some hidden dagger and stab Hellenor to death. Shifra was next in line to rule after Kelp, in spite of her best efforts to do away with Kelp and replace her as the crown princess.

Bayerd hadn't been aware that Shifra was visiting the castle. Since he rarely left his tower these days, perhaps there was a whole lot going on that he didn't know about. But her presence was puzzling. Shifra should be far far away. Queen Hellenor had all but banished her to the northernmost reaches of the Golden Kingdom, after Shifra had tried to murder Bayerd and Orson, and had murdered a common man who was their friend. Alas, Shifra did not get to go to prison, because there was no concrete proof that she had done the deed, and she was a royal. The ruling class was far less likely than common folk to see the inside of a prison.

So what was she doing here?

At least she was under the diligent eye of the queen's loyal guards, and Hellenor knew not to trust her one iota. Bayerd bowed his head to Hellenor. She gave him a reserved royal wave in return. He glared at Shifra. She smirked back, looking awfully pleased about something. Her smug expression sent a chill down his spine.

He gazed once more upon Kelp's beautiful face and said, "I did not know Shifra was visiting the castle."

"She is here because she wants to marry some northern baron. She petitions the queen for her blessing, or so she claims. I'm not sure I believe her."

23

"Beware of your cousin, Kelp. She may still be plotting against you," Bayerd said, quite unnecessarily.

"No doubt she is. Shifra has been plotting against me since the day she was born. I am well aware of my cousin's nature, Bayerd, as is Hellenor."

"Still, I don't like leaving you alone with Shifra in the castle. Perhaps I should delay my quest until she is gone," he suggested. Kelp's answer was to smack Spot smartly on the rump. The horse trotted forward, almost unseating Bayerd. He was summarily being sent on his quest.

Bayerd clung to the saddle and managed to make it over the drawbridge without falling into the churning water. It was a fortuitous start to the quest that it appeared he would be going on after all. Although the unease he felt at leaving Kelp alone with Shifra in the castle was a sincere one, and almost enough to make him forget his own fears.

3. And Then There Were Four

Six of one, half a dozen of the other
Be they doughnuts or armies
T'is all the same to the queen mother.

-Bayerd the Storyteller, Royal Appetites

Bayerd's six men rode behind him, sharing casual conversation with each other, but not with him. Well, they were all mad at him for leaving them standing all morning when they could have been sleeping. Conquer did more than his fair share of the talking, making liberal use of grandiose terms, even when he was referring to something as mundane as lacing up his boots. The fellow had no idea how words should be properly strung together, with the more dramatic ones rationed for best effect.

They rode through the afternoon on trails, cutting across farmland that showed the promise of a good harvest. With greater proximity, the mountain began to look more and more like a gigantic witch's nose. Bayerd tried to recall the details of the tale he had heard about a similar mountain, but it had been years ago, and he could not. And it was no matter. This mountain was not the one in the tale, which was surely fictitious anyway.

Bayerd kept them at a walk, since his head remained a tender thing. And he didn't want to fall off on the first day of his quest. There would be plenty of time to give the knights something more to laugh at than his wardrobe.

Late afternoon, they left the farmland behind and entered the forest proper. Weaving between trees slowed their pace and it felt like they made little progress. When the sun lowered and the forest got quite dusky, Bayerd said, "Look for a sheltered spot to make camp."

"About bloody time," Basher muttered. He was proving to be the surliest of the six.

They found a small clearing near a babbling brook and Bayerd reined in Spot. He all but fell off the horse. It had been a year since he had spent so long in the saddle and he couldn't feel his bottom at all. He rubbed it and said to Jabalot, "Gather some deadwood and start a fire."

Jabalot scowled in response, or perhaps he had not stopped scowling since they left the castle. At least he entered the forest, hopefully searching for deadwood and not just to relieve himself.

"Basher, see if you can shoot a few rabbits for dinner, or some birds. Any game will do," Bayerd said.

"We've got rations. No need to hunt yet," Basher said.

"Well, help Jabalot gather wood then."

"I wouldn't help Jabalot reattach his bloody head if it had been hacked off," Basher snarled and pulled a jug from the bulging pack strapped to his horse.

Bayerd considered the knight's words with a sinking heart. "There are hard feelings between the two of you?"

Basher snorted. "Hard feelings. That's calling a bear a mouse."

"Why didn't one of you tell me?"

"Not your ruddy business, is it?" Basher took a long swig and didn't offer Bayerd so much as a sip. Revel must have been inspired by the bottle. He pulled one out of his pack and took a long pull. Was drink all that the knights had packed?

Basher narrowed his eyes on Bayerd. "Duty to our queen comes first. We will do as we are charged and accept our punishment like the knights we are."

"Punishment?" Bayerd inquired, puzzled.

"Going on this silly quest. A month away from the comforts of the castle. Riding with you, listening to the same tired tales over and over. That's our punishment for our various wrongdoings. Didn't you know?" He swigged again.

"I did not." So riding with Bayerd was a chastisement. No wonder the other knights had laughed when Bayerd had told them not to feel bad because they hadn't been selected to ride on the quest. His cheeks heated with shame. He had never felt more like a lowly jester than he did at that moment.

"What did you do or not do to be sent on this quest?" he inquired, shifting the focus of the conversation onto Basher.

"Fighting, although I was only defending myself." Basher swigged again.

"From Jabalot?" Bayerd guessed.

"T'is thanks to him that we're both here." Basher glared at the surrounding trees as if they had rooted there with the sole purpose of vexing him.

"What is the cause of this grudge between the two of you?" Bayerd asked, hoping to make peace between the two men, and ensure a more amicable quest.

Basher smirked. "I slept with his wife."

"Ah, I see." So no peace then.

"Slept with her a lot. Gave her what Jabalot couldn't, in spite of his name." Basher's teeth flashed white in the dusky light and he drank again. Perhaps he was a drunkard as well as a rogue.

Bayerd winced. "Well, as long as you keep the peace between you, this private matter is not my concern."

"You would say that." The knight spat in the dirt, insultingly near to the tips of Bayerd's boots.

"What?"

"Oh, come on, you can't be that dense, can you?" He glanced around at the men who were unsaddling and rubbing down their horses. They were all ears and grinned as if they knew exactly what Basher was on about.

Bayerd scratched his ear where a mosquito had bitten him. "Dense about what, exactly?"

"The princess and your so-called friend, Orson. The whole castle knows, so you must know. Figured you were turning a blind eye, to preserve the scraps of dignity you've got left," Basher said, with too much relish.

"The whole castle knows what?" Bayerd was not usually clueless, but he couldn't fathom what Basher was saying.

The fellow exhaled gustily and handed Bayerd his bottle. "If you really don't know, t'is not my place to say. Have a drink and drown your sorrows."

"I cannot drown my sorrows if I don't know what those sorrows are. I command you to tell me." He grabbed the bottle and drank, feeling the need.

"Command? You couldn't command me to piss, little man." Basher grabbed the bottle back and marched toward the stream, in the opposite direction Jabalot had taken.

Clearly, Bayerd did not wear the mantle of authority as impressively as Queen Hellenor. He got busy unpacking his packhorses. He was still at it when Jabalot returned with an armload of broken branches. Bayerd nodded to the fellow, who had done his duty. "I hear there are some hard feelings between you and Basher," he said without preamble.

27

Jabalot dropped the sticks and gripped the hilt of his sword. "A feud between brothers is nobody else's business. Keep out of it."

"Brothers? You are brothers and he slept with your wife?" Bayerd cried, his tongue getting away from him.

The knight's sword slid from his scabbard faster than Bayerd's eyes could track it. He leapt back and hauled out his own weapon, not that he was any good with a blade, but still, it was better than standing like a lamb to be slaughtered. The other knights watched with amusement and not one moved to defend Bayerd from harm, although Gerald did edge closer to the action. Whether it was to help slay Bayerd himself or protect him was anyone's guess.

"He took advantage of her," Jabalot snarled, pointing the tip of his blade at Bayerd's still throbbing and swollen nose. "Not like Princess Kelp and your false friend. No-one is taking advantage of the other there. Both are eager and willing to shed their small clothes at the wink of an eye, aren't they?"

The sword dropped from Bayerd's hand as the news hit him with the force of a falling tree. "Kelp and ... and Orson?" he gasped. "No, it can't be true."

Jabalot snorted and lowered his sword so he could lean on it. "Surely you can't be so deaf, dumb, blind and stupid that you can't see what's going on right under your nose."

"No, you are wrong!" Bayerd cried.

"I suppose all those picnics they go on, just the two of them, are to enjoy nature, eh? The birds and the bees?" Jabalot insinuated sarcastically.

Bayerd felt like he was standing in quicksand, being pulled under. Kelp and Orson did go on a lot of picnics, alone, just the two of them. They always invited Bayerd, but he always declined, preferring the castle walls around him. "Picnics are merely picnics. Picnics are not evidence of anything untoward," he snapped.

Jabalot regarded him piteously and shook his head. "I hope you locked a chastity belt on your princess while you are away on your quest and Orson is back at the castle. Who do you think arranged the timing of that? Not Queen Hellenor, I say. Princess Kelp probably had her fingers in that pie, making sure Orson wasn't around when you were sent on this quest, then he'll turn up and la-dee-dah, they'll have a month together, rolling around in your bed."

"You are wrong. A magical stone came down from the heavens and landed on the mountain we ride toward. Kelp couldn't have arranged that," he declared.

"Did you see this stone burning a track across the sky?" Jabalot asked.

"No." Bayerd had been asleep, or perhaps passed out from drink.

"Nor did anyone, except Princess Kelp, I say."

Bayerd searched the faces of his men, hoping for a claim that at least one of them had witnessed the piece of heaven coming down to earth. Not one head nodded. They all shook.

"Kelp would no more betray me than I would betray her," Bayerd ground out, and when the significance of that statement hit him, he stumbled toward his packs, where he had laid them on the ground. He had almost betrayed Kelp just last night, hadn't he?

He groped around inside the pack sent from the kitchen and was delighted to feel a jug, because he needed a jug. He gripped it so tightly, the vessel should have shattered. He yanked it from the pack, removed the cork with his teeth and took a fortifying swig. It made him feel a little calmer.

Bayerd knew Jabalot was full of hot air. Basher, too. Kelp would never betray him in such a way, even though he had come within a nipple of betraying her. She had true integrity. And Orson—a man could not wish for a truer friend than Orson, even if he did bed more girls than a dozen randy dogs. Even if he was tall, dark and broodingly handsome with winsome dimples and an impressively long, strong sword arm—and sword. He would never betray Bayerd and Bayerd would stake his life on it.

After a few more fortifying gulps, he said, "If you, or any other man, speak ill of my wife or my good and true friend Orson, I will cut out your tongue." He glared at Jabalot. "Keep your peace with your brother on this quest, and do your duty as your queen has commanded."

Clutching his bottle, he headed upstream, angling away from Basher's tracks. He felt the need for solitude, and wine. A lot of wine. A creek's worth of wine. He toed off his boots and settled on the edge of the brook, with his feet soaking in the cold flow of water. He finished the whole damn jug in double-quick time. He didn't believe for even a heartbeat that Kelp and Orson had betrayed him, but it was upsetting to discover the whole castle judged that Bayerd was being cuckolded. And thought him a fool of the highest, or lowest, order.

29

Bayerd fell asleep by the creek, feet dangling in the water all night long. He awoke chilled to the bone, damp and stiff, bitten by bugs, hungover, and hence, in a foul mood. After he had relieved himself, and washed his face and hands in the cool creek, he filled the empty wine jug with icy water and drained it. Feeling slightly less like vomiting, he donned his footwear and stumbled back to the campsite.

The men were all asleep, rolled in their blankets in a circle around the dying coals. Although there only seemed to be five of them. One of the bedrolls was empty, yet he didn't see or hear anyone moving about. "Get up," Bayerd barked.

Jabalot proved to be the lightest sleeper. He leapt to his feet, a wicked dagger in hand. It wasn't very clean. Dried blood clung to it, probably from some previous battle, although it was a negligent knight who did not keep his blades polished and oiled against rust. And if anything was guaranteed to rust a blade, it was blood.

"Who is supposed to be on watch?" Bayerd demanded.

"On watch against what? Squirrels?" Revel quipped, his orange hair appearing from under his blanket.

"There should always be a man on watch. We are outside the castle walls where all manner of horrors lurk," Bayerd shot back, hoisting his pack off the ground.

Jabalot stretched and looked down at Bayerd. "We're not all afraid of our own shadows, little man. If you want someone on watch, do it yourself." He hitched up his trousers, turned his back on Bayerd, and farted loudly before he strutted into the trees.

Bayerd, who was usually glib of tongue, stood speechless. The fellow was beyond insolent. To malign Bayerd and pointedly fart in his general direction, then stride away without giving him a chance to retort, was a cutting insult. And to do so with Bayerd's men as witness was heaping insult upon injury. Bayerd was, at least by title, the man's better. He was also in charge of the quest.

Temper ruling, he started after Jabalot. He was stopped short by the sight of Sir Swift, shedding his blanket and rising to his feet. He was wearing Bayerd's clothing, and he had chosen one of Bayerd's favourite ensembles. The golden and black patterned cloth of the tunic gleamed under the morning sun, and the black tights clung to surprisingly shapely legs. The villain had even slept in the matching slippers with the big gold buckles. The outfit looked out of the place in the forest, but attractive nonetheless. Sir Swift wore it well. In truth, he wore it better than Bayerd with his recently acquired rolls of tummy and soft jiggly thighs.

"What the hell do you think you're doing?" Bayerd demanded of Swift.

"Getting up, as you bid me, Prince Bayerd." Swift bowed gracefully before him.

It was certainly preferable to a fart, but was the fellow clueless? Since Bayerd still had his sword in hand, he used it to point at Swift's chest. "You are wearing my clothes!"

Swift looked down and cried, "Egad, so I am. Lovely outfit, such rich fabric. How does the gold look with my golden hair?" He turned his head this way and that, tossing it like a frisky pony.

"They do complement each other," Bayerd answered automatically, then sputtered, "but … but why are you dressed as me?"

"I must have been sleepwalking and dressed in your fine clothes quite unawares." Swift's face was the picture of innocence, although with his one enlarged pupil, his gaze appeared lopsided.

The other knights did not trouble themselves to hide their amusement. Bayerd was less than a day into his quest and already he was fed up with being a laughingstock.

"Get out of them," he ordered, "or I will cut them off you." He thrust his sword threateningly.

"And ruin such a fine suit of clothing? That would be a foul crime, indeed," Swift declared, scanning the campsite. "But where are my clothes?"

"And where is Basher?" Sir Gerald said in his gravelly voice, rising stiffly to his feet. He had a hand on his back and trouble straightening.

"His horse is gone," Revel said. And so it was, although the fellow's bedroll was still on the ground.

"True. Perhaps he is watering it at the creek." Gerald bent with a groan to roll his blanket.

Jabalot returned then, his hair and face damp from washing in the stream. Even his blade was clean, glinting under the sun on what promised to be another fine day. "Did you see Basher by the water?" Bayerd asked him.

"I did not see him or anyone. Why? Is he missing?" Jabalot's lips twitched. Was he trying to contain a grin?

"Both he and his horse are gone, yet his bedroll is there." Bayerd motioned at it with his sword, which was coming in handy as a pointer, if not a weapon.

Jabalot shrugged. "Perhaps he rode ahead to scout the lay of the land."

"Without his bedroll?"

"Probably thought he would be back before we were up and about. He knows you call the shots, so he probably thought we'd all be sleeping until noon. I'm sure he'll turn up by then." Jabalot got to rolling up his own blanket, whistling a cheery tune. His demeanor was much more jovial than on the previous day. Then again, he hadn't been standing in the hot sun for hours, waiting for his tardy leader to turn up.

Bayerd took bread out of his pack. His sour stomach needed something to soak up all the wine he had drunk the night before. While he chewed, he watched Swift search the campsite from top to bottom for his clothing. The fellow was making quite a performance out of it, lifting the larger rocks and peering beneath them, as if his clothes might be found there. He even ventured into the surrounding vegetation and poked around in the brush. Bayerd knew exactly when the fellow gave up his search because he dramatically tossed his hands in the air and declared, "My clothes are gone. Not a trace, I say. All I've found is a large pool of blood. It looks fresh, so something must have made a kill there while we slept."

"And no man on watch? T'is lucky we aren't all dead in our bedrolls," Bayerd said with a pointed look at Revel.

"And my clothes are gone. Stolen, I say." Swift waved an arm around the campsite. "Not a thread left. You can look for yourself if you don't believe me. I'll have to wear these clothes, unless you've a desire to see me riding stark naked for the rest of the quest."

"I've no desire to see your buttocks, or any other part of you, slapping up and down in the saddle. Keep the clothes." Bayerd approached the smoldering remnants of the fire and tossed in a crust of bread that was green with mold, and stale to boot. Clearly, the kitchen had given them the leavings as rations, since they would be too far away from the castle to complain about the quality of the food.

He squinted at the coals when a bit of fabric caught his eye—charred fabric. Swift must have burnt his clothes so he could wear Bayerd's more princely garments. Bayerd was sorely tempted to confront the knight again, except he was quite sure Swift would glibly declare that

32

he must have burnt his clothing in his sleep. And how could a man argue against such malarkey?

Trying to ignore his pounding head and queasy stomach, Bayerd repacked his packhorses. At least he had one less suit of clothing to cart about. When they were ready to depart, Basher was still missing.

Bayerd paced around a bit, then decided to attempt to fill his role of leader. He led his horse to a boulder so he could mount without demeaning assistance. He looked down at the knights from his superior position. "We shall set off. Basher will be able to find us easily enough, since a trail left by nine horses is a trail that even a blind man can track."

The men mounted without protest and the horses trotted off eagerly. They were rested and watered. The day was still cool enough to be pleasant, especially when shaded by the woodland trees. The oppressive heat would come later, when the sun was high enough to shine through the canopy of branches. Perhaps Bayerd would call for a siesta then, if they had made decent progress.

All morning, they clattered through trees, following the stream against the current for the most part, as it was tracing in the right direction. Basher did not show his face and Bayerd did not see any signs of recent passage, not that he was a tracker. When the sun was just past its zenith, Bayerd called a halt. They ate some rations and napped in the cooler shade of the forest for several hours.

Still, Basher did not catch up with them, nor did they catch up with him. A thought struck Bayerd then, that perhaps Basher had abandoned the quest. Maybe he had ridden back to roll around in the hay with Jabalot's wife while Jabalot was far from home.

Jabalot clearly hadn't thought of that possibility because he was still in a genial mood without his traitorous brother around. All morning long, he had sung as he rode, and while his voice was not up to the professional standard of Bayerd's, he could carry a pleasing tune and knew a wide range of ballads, some that Bayerd had never heard. He had listened with a sharp ear and hummed along, committing the words and melodies to memory. Jabalot's singing also kept Conquer from talking nonstop, butchering the artistry of the wordsmith.

After the respite, they remounted and rode through the afternoon. Bayerd was rather surprised that all the dangers that lurked outside the castle hadn't banded together to attack him yet, but perhaps they were simply biding their time, plotting a spectacular ambush.

When they stopped to make camp at dusk, they were still in thick forest. Bayerd hadn't caught a glimpse of the mountain all day. He surveyed his men. "Who is the best archer amongst you?"

Jabalot said, "I am."

"Only in your swelled head," Revel shot back.

"Oh, and I suppose you fancy yourself the ablest archer here?" Jabalot said.

"There's no suppose about it."

The two knights faced each other, hands on their swords. Jabalot's cheerfulness had vanished in the blink of an eye. Bayerd sighed inwardly. His attempt to send one of the men to hunt dinner was not going as smoothly as he had foreseen. "How about you both go and hunt game. Whoever brings back the most catches will be considered the ablest archer," he proposed.

The pair turned to glare at him instead of each other. Jabalot said, "That is no true contest, since Lady Luck plays a major role. One man may encounter no game to shoot, while the other may find plenty."

"You'll require a target to know the truth of it," Gerald said.

"Yes, that would prove the matter, although the best archer does not always win the contest," Jabalot insinuated rather snidely.

It was a barely veiled dig. Bayerd couldn't shoot an arrow to save his life, as he had proven to the whole kingdom in his quest to earn the princess's love, yet he had won his archery match because a dragon had soared down from the sky to roast his opponent. Orson claimed that Bayerd couldn't hit the broad side of a castle if he was standing ten paces from it, and there was some truth in what he said. But Bayerd would not be participating in this contest, he would be overseeing it, so he would not disgrace himself anew. "Decide on a target and we'll have the matter settled," he said.

There was a short debate before the knights agreed on a skinny white birch tree. Gerald cut a cross into the bark with his dagger. The mark was at shoulder height and small enough to be challenging. They flipped a copper coin of the realm to decide on who would shoot first. Revel won the toss and picked up his bow. He tried to notch an arrow and dropped it. It took him three attempts to get an arrow loaded into the bow. He took careful aim, swayed a bit, and let it fly. The arrow missed the tree by a generous yard.

Jabalot hooted in laughter, then took his turn. As intently as he squinted at the tree, he missed it as well, although he came an inch or two closer than Revel. Revel elbowed him aside, stumbled, steadied himself, and after another lengthy loading with a repeatedly dropped arrow, he finally fired off a second shot. It didn't come any closer to the target than his first attempt.

"Tree moved," he snarled, taking a swig from the flask on his belt.

Jabalot made another attempt, squinting and blinking for about a minute before he released his arrow. It whizzed by the trunk with impressive speed, and no accuracy.

If Bayerd had been the type of man to belittle another, he would have taunted the inept archers with a few clever jests, but he held his tongue. He was the leader of the quest. It would be unseemly to mock his men, no matter that they mocked him.

Revel drank again, dropped and picked up the same arrow half a dozen times, and shot again. He missed again. Jabalot squinted, shot, and hit a different birch tree. Bayerd couldn't help but wonder what quality of knights Queen Hellenor had chosen to support him on his quest. Clearly, not her finest.

Bayerd could bear no more of the futile contest. He said, "Stop." Revel lowered the arrow he was aiming. Bayerd stepped in front of the unwounded tree. "Let's choose a larger target," he said.

With a wide grin, Revel aimed his arrow at Bayerd's middle. "How about your belly?" he said, as if it was a friendly jest. Bayerd certainly hoped it was. He had already endured the pain of enough arrows to last a lifetime, and he had a manly collection of scars to prove it.

"Very witty, Revel, although after this display, I'm not sure you could hit even that," Bayerd quipped back. Perhaps it was not the smartest idea to challenge a disgruntled man who was aiming an arrow at you, yet Bayerd couldn't resist. Before Revel could release his notched arrow, Bayerd strode over to the wide trunk on an ancient oak and patted a large knot. "That's your target. Aim at the center, and move ten paces closer." With hasty steps, he relocated himself to the rear of the two competitors.

Jabalot counted off ten paces, squinted, aimed, and let fly his arrow. It sailed to the left of the oak and one of the horses squealed and fell down. The men rushed over to investigate. All were relieved to find their steeds still alive. Bayerd gazed down at one of his packhorses, who had an arrow through her neck. She wasn't even twitching; she was quite dead. He felt a bit guilty about the part he had played in her demise by selecting a tree in sightline of the horses, but he had thought the trunk too wide to miss. The rest of the mounts must have been worried about their safety because they were snorting and pulling against their lines.

"Poor beastie." Bayerd crouched down and patted the warm, velvety neck of the horse. At least it had been a quick and merciful kill. And now there would be no need to hunt game. He stood up, brushed dirt off his knees, and said, "The contest is ended. Jabalot, it's your kill. Carve her up for dinner. Revel, go collect all the arrows. Gerald, see if you can calm the horses, and the rest of you can gather firewood, a lot of firewood. We have a rather large amount of meat to smoke." On the bright side, they would have full bellies for many days to come.

It took several hours of attending the fire to smoke all the best cuts of horse. The large fire kept away any predators that might have been drawn to the scent of blood. A lot of the horse meat got eaten as soon as it was removed from the heat, and it was with bulging middles that the men laid out their blankets in the dark. Bayerd set Gerald and Conquer to share the night's watch in turn, judging them to be the most dependable of his five remaining knights. Basher was clearly not coming back. No wonder he had left his bedroll behind. He knew he wouldn't be needing it.

Bayerd rolled up in his blanket, feeling quite satisfied with how the day had turned out, in spite of his dead horse and missing man. Bayerd thought his leadership skills were improving. The men had followed his latest orders without too much backtalk, and without any spitting or farting in his direction. Then again, maybe they had simply been quite famished and craving meat, so it had suited them to follow his directions. Regardless, it had been a promising day compared to the one that had come before.

Smiling, Bayerd fell deeply asleep. He awoke to the feel of sunshine on his face and the sound of birds chirping in song. He opened his eyes and blinked. Four figures were looming over him. He squinted up at the four faces. His knights were awake, dressed and kitted out for riding.

"We were quite sure you were dead," said Revel, his orange hair a halo around him, backlit as it was by the sun, which was rather high in the sky.

"We've already started digging the hole to bury you," Jabalot added.

"Well, you've wasted your effort. I'm entirely alive." Bayerd blinked the haze of sleep from his eyes and sat up. He focused on Sir Swift, who was no longer wearing black and gold. He was dressed in royal blue. His tunic was embroidered with orange stars—familiar orange stars.

Bayerd staggered up to face him. "Why are you dressed in another of my outfits?"

"Pissed myself last night," Swift declared without shame.

"You pissed in my black velvet leggings?" Bayerd snapped.

"And tunic. Must have drunk too much wine." He stroked a hand down his chest, "But you need not worry, I much prefer this outfit. Lovely stars, so bright and twinkly. And you wouldn't want me smelling of piss for the rest of the quest, now would you?"

Bayerd, who hadn't bothered to change since he had left the castle, wasn't alert enough to debate the matter. And he was short one packhorse. A lighter load would be a blessing. "Well … don't piss in that outfit." He surveyed the men. "Where is Conquer?"

They shared blank looks. Gerald shrugged. "He had the last watch. When I woke up, he wasn't in camp. I assumed he went to the creek to freshen up, water his horse, except he hasn't returned."

"And his horse is gone?"

Gerald nodded. "His kit is here, though, and his blanket."

"All of you, go and search for him while I pack up my kit," Bayerd said.

The four knights ambled in the direction of the creek. They really should have chosen different directions to cover more ground. Bayerd chewed a crust of stale moldy bread while he rolled up his blanket and stowed his remaining outfits onto the two packhorses. He saddled Spot and mounted her to lead the packhorses to the creek for watering. They had gone about twenty horse paces when the packhorses stopped dead. Spot bounded forward and Bayerd was yanked from the saddle by the tether wrapped around his fist. He landed hard on his back in something wet and sticky.

He sat up with a groan and looked at where he had come to ground. He was in the midst of a large pool of blood. Runoff from butchering the dead packhorse surely, but he would have expected it to have soaked into the ground overnight. Perhaps there had simply been too much blood to soak in. His horses didn't like the scent of the gore and pranced skittishly, almost trampling him.

"Settle down," he said, and struggled to his feet. His entire back was wet with blood. His outfit would never be fit to wear again.

He led the three horses away from the blood and tied them to a tree beside the creek. They drank thirstily. None of his men were in sight or sound. He appreciated the fact that no-one had witnessed his tumble off his horse. He stripped off his bloodied outfit and tossed it into the bushes. The skin on his back was tacky with blood, as was his ponytail, so he waded into the icy water and rinsed off thoroughly. He untied his hair, dunked his head and scrubbed his scalp all over.

Clean again, he dried off with one of his plain cotton shirts, then donned the least flashy of his more accessible outfits. The tunic was forest green and brown with a minimal amount of embroidery. The leggings were dark brown as well. He didn't bother with the matching scarf or slippers. Slippers were completely impractical for riding. Why he had even packed them was something of a mystery. He stepped back into his riding boots.

Presentable again, he led the horses back to the clearing. The men were waiting. Four, not five.

"No sign of Conquer," Gerald said.

"Not a trace," Jabalot concurred.

Swift looked him over from head to toe. "I don't like your outfit. It's without pattern, and so plain. The boots don't match at all."

Bayerd ignored the critique of his attire. "Conquer probably rode ahead to scout the territory. I'm sure we'll find him soon enough. Let's go."

They mounted and rode through more trees. The day remained fine and there was nothing to see but forest. Conquer did not show his face, and they didn't spot any recent hoof prints in the soft ground.

At sunset, they emerged from an edge of trees and the mountain loomed high in the sky before them, bookended by smaller and gentler hills. Their destination was noticeably closer, and looked much steeper and craggier. While he had a clear view, Bayerd scanned for the best path to start climbing the mountain. He thought the right side appeared more promising than the left, but neither side looked to have an already established trail.

The land directly ahead was gently sloped and less treed. The trees that did grow were smaller and scrubbier. It was the lowest of the foothills and they could see for quite a distance. There was no sign of Sir Conquer, nor any trace of his passage. Had he abandoned the quest as well?

Standing in the dark shadow of the mountain, Bayerd shivered as if a clammy snake had slithered through his guts. In only two days, he had lost two knights. And after the archery display, he was not impressed with two of his remaining four. One was a drunkard and he was starting to suspect the other was half-blind and couldn't see further than the tip of his own arrow. Sir Gerald was old and Sir Swift was quite loony. If they encountered danger, they would be incapable of making a stand. If they encountered danger, Bayerd might as well fall off his horse onto his sword and be done with it.

4. Tongues Will Wag Like Dogs' Tails

Six plucky knights sent on a quest
One fell off as they rode west
Alas, there was no doctor to attest
This man is dead, let him rest
Five plucky knights sent on a quest
One fell off as they rode west
Alas, there were no doctor to attest
This man is dead, let him rest.
(Repeat with four, three, two, one)
-Bayerd the Storyteller, Countdown

Orson knocked on Kelp's door and entered with a cocky stride. Kelp greeted him with a warm embrace. "You are back, Orson! It is so wonderful to see you." She kissed his cheek and he blushed. "Thank you for making yourself scarce this past week."

"Least I could do to help cure Bayerd of his cowardice," Orson said bluntly. "So, how did you get him outside the castle walls? Did you hold a sword to his throat?"

Kelp motioned for him to join her at the table where pastries and tea were set out. "Not a sword, although it did take a firm hand. Aunt Hellenor played her part and sent him on a simple quest. He did attempt to feign an illness so as not to go, but I nipped that in the bud." Her smiling eyes met his.

"Bayerd has never been sick a day in his life, except when he was poisoned or burnt or drowned or stabbed or shot with arrows," Orson declared.

"Yes, he is uncommonly healthy when he is not injured." She stopped smiling. "A serving wench tried to have her way with him the night before he left."

Orson laughed and smacked the table with his big palm. "Bayerd? Surely you jest."

Kelp grinned back. "I do not."

"Do share the details." Orson's eyes twinkled with merriment.

"He was in the bathing tub, and it looked like she was about to hop in there with him when I caught them. She was so shocked by my arrival that she fell into the water on top of him and almost drowned him. It was rather funny, I suppose, except I was so angry, I did not see the lighter side then. He looked quite terrified when I turned up, and I think I rescued him rather than caught him in a dalliance, but still … if I had not arrived when I did, I fear he may have given into temptation. He was quite drunk."

"When isn't he these days? Course he would have given into temptation. He's a man, or he used to be. All men are weak-willed where women are concerned, Princess. You do know that about men, don't you?" Orson raised an eyebrow.

"I suppose. I just thought Bayerd was different. I thought he was … mine, and mine alone." Kelp sighed sadly.

"If his head was screwed on straight, he would be. He's just not been himself since …" Orson bit his lip and turned red.

"Since what, Orson?" Kelp refilled both their teacups.

"Ah, just some of the bad stuff that happened when we were trying to save you, trying to get away from Darton. It upset Bayerd, and he's never gotten over it. It festers inside him. But I hope getting him out of the castle will help him find his nerve." Orson slurped once, draining the contents of the tiny cup.

"I admit, I did feel bad sending him away, yet it is for his own good."

Orson selected an apple tart. "And our good. He's driving us all crazy. Had to be done. If I had to listen to that ridiculous dragon tale one more time, and it getting taller with each telling, I was going to toss him into the moat and let him drown, I swear I was."

"I know. He gets steadily worse. Lately, he is loath to leave even our chambers, and when he does, he jumps at shadows. He must find his nerve again, or soon he will be too afraid to get out of bed." Kelp's lady approached with a fresh steaming pot of tea.

"Amen to that." Orson selected a blueberry pastry, having devoured the other in one bite.

Kelp leaned closer and brushed crumbs off his cheek. "It's funny, but I miss seeing his face already. And I don't even have his portrait to gaze upon. I can't find my favourite locket, the one that holds the

41

miniature of our wedding portrait." She smiled quite sadly. "Maybe he took it with him so he could gaze on my face while he is away. I just hope that serving wench didn't steal the locket when she was alone here with Bayerd. It was encrusted with rubies and very valuable."

"Did you have the girl's belongings searched?" Orson asked.

"I did, and there was no trace of my locket." Kelp gave a little shrug. "Perhaps Bayerd did take it with him."

"Maybe. Your face is a lot prettier than his. Although it's not like him to take things without asking, especially valuable things. Then again, he's not been himself."

"Too true." Kelp stirred her tea listlessly.

"I thought I spotted Shifra in the courtyard when I rode in," Orson mentioned to change the subject, since Kelp looked so sad, not that the topic of her murderous cousin was any better.

"She is visiting to arrange a marriage contract with some northern baron. Hellenor allowed her to come here and I can't say I am pleased. At least she is under guard whenever she is not locked in her tower. She should not be able to get up to any mischief."

Orson wasn't so sure. Shifra was sneaky and treacherous, and he had a rather gruesome scar across his chest to prove it. "So, what quest did you dream up to send Bayerd on?" Orson asked, to change the subject again.

Kelp leaned a bit closer. "I didn't have to dream one up at all, as it turned out."

"Do tell." Orson leaned closer, all ears.

"I couldn't sleep and I was standing by the window, right there." She pointed. "And lo and behold, a heaven stone burned a track across the sky and landed near the top of the biggest hill yonder. Bayerd has been charged to find the magical stone and return it to Queen Hellenor."

Orson got up and strolled over to the window, a half-eaten pastry in hand. "Which hill?"

Kelp joined him and pointed again. "That one."

Orson winced. "That is no hill, princess. That is a bloody mountain. Does the mountain have a name?"

"No, although in shape, it looks rather like a witch's nose, doesn't it?" She tilted her head, regarding it.

"It does." Orson sat down again, frowning. "I'm sure I've heard a tale about that mountain, not a good tale either. Something lives on that mountain, something that does not like men."

Kelp laughed and rejoined him at the table, smoothing her skirts around her. "A tale is simply a tale, Orson, as you and I know better than most. And I've never heard tell of anything disturbing about the hill, or mountain, not that anyone ever travels in that direction. There's nothing of import on the far side of the chain of hills—no sea, no farmland, no trade routes, no reason to go there at all."

Irvette was brushing crumbs off Orson's side of the table. She said, "Princess Kelp, I've heard rumours about that mountain myself."

"What have you heard?" Orson said, before Princess Kelp could ask.

"Men who travel there don't return. They are never seen again. That's why no-one knows anything about the mountain, and what lies beyond it."

Kelp smiled. "What a ridiculous notion. It's nothing more than a perfectly ordinary hill, or mountain if you insist. I wouldn't send my husband into true danger." She pushed the platter of pastries closer to Orson. "He wanted a hundred knights to ride with him. My aunt bargained him down to six and selected the most inept of her men. Four of the six have been assigned the quest as a punishment for one offence or another. In contrast to that lot, Bayerd should gain some confidence in himself and his abilities again."

Orson rubbed his jaw thoughtfully. "Tricky tactic, but perhaps some proper knights should have ridden with him, given where he is going."

"Oh, not you too, Orson! The only danger Bayerd will encounter will be falling off his horse, as he is wont to do anyway," Kelp cried.

Orson grimaced. "If he falls off on that slope, he could roll all the way down the bloody mountain."

Kelp cast him an exasperated look and picked up a sharp little knife to cut up an apple. Unlike most of her class, she did not fear fresh fruit.

Orson dropped the subject. Bayerd was already away from the castle, and there was no changing that. "So who did Queen Hellenor send with Bayerd?" he asked instead, curious. He hung around with the knights to practice his swordplay, and knew them all well. Queen Hellenor had wanted to knight him, but Orson had declined the offer. He liked the freedom to come and go as he pleased. He did not want to be restricted to the guards' quarters, and have to abide by their strict regime.

"Let's see. There was Sir Revel who has a problem with drink," Kelp said.

Orson chuckled. "He falls off his horse almost as much as Bayerd."

"And Sir Swift who took a severe blow to the head with a jousting pole in the spring tournament. He hasn't been the same since. He's not one of the men being punished."

Orson nodded. "I know him. He's right off his rocker now. Misnamed for sure, poor Sir Swift."

"It is rather sad, isn't it? He used to be such a bright fellow." Kelp handed Orson a slice of apple, speared on her knife. "And then there is Sir Gerald."

"Nothing wrong with him." Orson quite liked Sir Gerald.

"He is not being chastised either. He's steady enough, but getting on in years and his joints have stiffened sorely. His sword is no longer quick or strong, but I trust he will help Bayerd to keep the others in line. We didn't want Bayerd to be completely defenseless, I mean, his party could run into a bear in the forest, and there are wind storms at this time of year. And there is the occasional unsavoury character lurking in the outlying lands, isn't there?"

And then there was the mountain itself, but Orson didn't mention that again. "True enough. Who else?" He helped himself to another slice of apple. He was no gossip, but he did enjoy chatting with Kelp about the castle folk and their affairs.

She thought for a moment. "Oh, Sir Conquer. He's so lazy, he won't trouble himself to swat a fly if it is perched on his nose."

Orson chuckled. "The only thing about Conquer that isn't lazy is his tongue. He never shuts up. He'll drive Bayerd batty with his inane chattering, won't he?"

"Oh, I didn't know that about him."

"Who are the last two?" Orson prompted.

"The last two are brothers, Sir Basher and Sir Jabalot. They've been squabbling with each other lately, annoying all the other knights," Kelp said.

Orson winced. "Those two might not have been the best choice."

"Why ever not?"

"Basher was sleeping with Jabalot's wife, and there was no sleeping going on, if you know what I mean." He winked, to emphasize the point.

"Of course I know what you mean. I am not dense, Orson." She nibbled her bottom lip. "So there is true enmity between the brothers?"

"And just cause for it, at least on Jabalot's part." Orson had no chance to say more. A knock on the door interrupted their tea.

Irvette answered it. There was a brief conversation outside the door and she returned to them immediately, wringing her hands. "Princess Kelp, the stable master has requested your presence in the courtyard, without delay."

"Do you know why?" Kelp asked.

Eyes downcast, the servant said, "I would rather not say, mistress."

Kelp rose. "Tell me." It was an order.

With obvious reluctance, Irvette said, "A horse has just ridden into the courtyard, there's a body—a dead body—draped over its back."

Orson leapt up, knocking over his chair. "Bayerd is dead again?"

"Not Prince Bayerd, but one of the men who rode with him."

Irvette hastily stood aside when Kelp and Orson rushed for the door. They hurried down the many stone steps. At the bottom, Orson tucked Kelp's arm securely in the crook of his elbow. "It will be alright, Princess. It's not Bayerd." He patted her hand in comfort.

She gripped his arm tight. "Still, it is not a promising beginning to his little quest, is it?"

"Nope." Orson couldn't disagree with that.

They crossed the courtyard arm-in-arm. In the front of the stables, a body was laid out on the ground. From the neck down, it was covered by a horse blanket. It looked very insubstantial on the earth it was about to return to. The stable master and Gallant, Master of the Queen's Guard, stood beside it. Many knights ringed them at a respectful distance. The men parted, allowing Kelp and Orson to move unimpeded through their ranks.

"Looks like Sir Basher, in better days," Orson murmured to Kelp, when they were near enough that he could see the bruised and bloated face.

The stable master and Gallant bowed when Kelp approached. "Is the body that of Sir Basher?" she asked.

"That it is," Gallant confirmed. "And he's been most foully murdered. You'd best not look upon his corpse, Princess Kelp."

Kelp arched one eyebrow in his direction. "I am no swooning lady, Sir Gallant, and this man was one of my husband's knights. I will see the injury with my own eyes and know the truth of how he died."

Gallant nodded to the stable master. He lowered the blanket to the corpse's middle. "Looks like he was bashed on the head, had his throat cut, and he was beaten a bit. Well, you can probably see all that for yourself, Princess Kelp," Gallant said.

Kelp nodded. Orson studied what he could see of Sir Basher and swallowed hard. The man was a gruesome bloody sight to be sure. Someone had bashed his brains in, and sliced his throat so deeply, it was a miracle his head was still attached.

"How did he end up back at the castle?" Orson asked. A dead body did not normally stay in the saddle.

"He was draped over the horse and tied there. Horse aimed for home carrying her dead rider. Poor beastie was in quite a state when she arrived. I've got a boy tending her in the stable."

"Any damage under the blanket?" Orson asked.

"A few more stab wounds in … unmentionable areas," Gallant said with a wince. Orson could guess the location of those stab wounds, given that Basher had been sleeping where he shouldn't, without the sleeping part.

"Someone did not like Sir Basher." Orson put a steadying arm around Kelp. "But I'm sure Bayerd is fine. Basher's brother, Jabalot, probably killed him because he was sleeping with his wife. Any man worth his salt won't tolerate that behaviour."

A number of the knights muttered to each other under their breath. Kelp turned toward them. "What did you say?"

"Nothing," they all mumbled, staring at their muddy boots as if they had never seen such fascinating footwear before.

Hands on hips, she marched toward them. "I heard my husband's name mentioned and if he is in danger, I would know it. I will not be kept in the dark. What do you know about this murder?"

She waited, eyes narrowed on them. Not one man spoke a word, although one did flush redder than the others. Kelp strode over to him and looked up. "What is your name?"

"Sir Lance," he mumbled.

"Tell me what you said, Sir Lance, unless you need the rack to loosen your tongue as well as your joints."

The tall burly knight hunched like a whipped dog. "Princess, what I said has naught to do with this murder."

"Then what does it have to do with?" she asked.

"Nothing of import. I should have held my tongue. It's always flapping when it shouldn't." He swallowed hard, his Adam's apple bobbing up and down.

"Then flap it now. Repeat what you said."

"I can't. You'll have me beheaded. I'd rather be rack-tortured, even though I'm quite tall enough, thank you." He hunched his shoulder's more, as if trying to shrink into himself.

Kelp tapped her toe like a woodpecker's beak, hard and fast. "If I agree to forego the beheading, will you repeat what you said?"

"I'd really rather not."

Orson felt it was time to step in. He pulled Kelp aside and whispered in her ear, "Let me talk to him, man-to-man. He might have just been bad-mouthing Bayerd for being a coward. Many in the castle do these days, and he wouldn't repeat that to you, but he may to me."

Kelp rubbed her ear. "You've nearly deafened me."

"But I was whispering."

"You don't know how to whisper, Orson. Fine. You have two minutes to get the truth out of him, or I'll have him whipped until he talks. You can tell him that," she said, plenty loud enough for Sir Lance to hear her threat with his own ears.

Kelp moved away, granting them a modicum of privacy. Orson sidled closer to the knight and tossed an arm companionably over the fellow's shoulders. "Now, tell me what you said and I'll pass the information along, if it is something the princess should know," he said.

"Bloody hell, I shouldn't have got out of bed this morning."

Orson tried to reason with him. "Surely it can't be that bad, Lance. If you said Bayerd's a coward, you're not the only one. If you said he's a fool, well, I say that all the time. I say it to his face. I've even called him a jester to his face, although that really sets him off. If you said he dresses like a fop, well, he does these days. Looks bloody ridiculous strutting about in his fancy hats and peacock feathers, and his little slippers with the shiny buckles, and a bow on his ponytail, doesn't he?" The men all chuckled and nodded. Kelp cleared her throat, pointedly. Orson was getting sidetracked.

"It was none of those things. I only wish it was," Lance whispered. He really could whisper, Orson barely heard him.

He tried again. "If you said Bayerd's getting as fat as a Christmas hog, well, we can all see that when he waddles across the courtyard."

Still, Lance shook his head. Orson was stumped. "What else? You better tell me or it's the rack, or whipping. Maybe both with the temper the princess is in."

Lance sighed and seemed to deflate. "I said ... I said ... Bayerd tolerates that behaviour."

47

Orson was clueless. "Bayerd tolerates what behaviour?"

The knight beside Lance helped out. "Cuckolding."

"Princess Kelp is lying with another?" Orson gasped out rather loudly. Even he knew he hadn't whispered.

Kelp marched closer. "That is a vile lie! I am no adulteress. Why would you start such an awful rumour?"

"I didn't start it," Lance cried. "I only repeat what is common knowledge among the Royal Guard, and the knights, and the castle folk, and … and every other soul in the kingdom with ears and a tongue."

Kelp sputtered a bit, too outraged to speak.

Orson said, "Princess Kelp is no adulteress. I am her constant companion in the castle, and outside the castle now that Bayerd is too cowardly to venture past the battlements. I am always by her side, I stand in for her husband when he cannot perform his husbandly duties because of his condition, and I swear on my honour that Kelp is a true and loving wife."

Orson noticed Kelp gaping at him with a dropped jaw. Almost everyone wore the same incredulous expression. Orson mentally replayed his words in his head, and realized how they could have been misconstrued. "Me? Me? Everyone thinks I am lying with Princess Kelp behind my friend's back? Me?" he sputtered. His honour had never been so foully misjudged.

"I am true to my husband and only my husband. Orson and I are merely good friends, nothing more," Kelp cried angrily.

Orson surveyed the surrounding faces and knew no-one believed them. Everyone believed he and Kelp were having a lusty affair. Everyone was talking about it, including the knights, and Bayerd had ridden off with six knights. How long before he heard the talk and believed that his truest friend and wife were pleasuring each other behind his back? Perhaps he had already heard the rumour.

Kelp must have come to the same realization. She clapped a hand over her mouth and tears filled her eyes. A princess should never cry in front of her people, so she spun on her heel and strode for the castle. Orson would have followed her to offer comfort, but with so many eyes upon him, he could not. In everyone's mind, that would simply confirm the rumour as truth. Orson would simply have to wait until later that night, when no-one was about, then he would sneak into Kelp's chambers for a private word to discuss the matter. They needed to find a way to disprove the slanderous rumour.

5. When Mountains Grumble

Roses are red,

Violets are blue,

T'is how I feel,

When I'm without you.

-Bayerd the Storyteller, Blue Mood

Bayerd's third night away from the castle passed uneventfully. He assigned watch to Revel and Jabalot, since Gerald needed some sleep, and then he slept like a man who had been bashed on the head with a large rock. He awoke to find all four of his knights still present and accounted for, stuffing their faces with moldy bread, hard cheese, and smoked horse meat. A cool, damp wind had blown in overnight and they were huddled around a fire. Perhaps the change in clime was because they were closer to the mountain.

Swift was dressed in yet another of Bayerd's outfits. This one was green and silver with silver bells on the cuffs, which jingled wherever Swift moved. Bayerd wore his blanket like a shawl and went to sit by the fire. He grabbed the very last small and shriveled strip of horse meat left to them and said, "Swift, why are you wearing yet another of my outfits?"

The fellow gazed at Bayerd blankly. "These are my clothes, not yours. They have bells on them." He waved an arm around, causing the bells to jingle merrily. "I feel like a jester. If only I could juggle."

The knight wasn't merely mad, he was proving delusional as well. "What happened to the clothes you were wearing yesterday?" Bayerd was a tad curious about that.

"I was watering Mercury, my trusty steed, and I fell into the creek. T'is too cold to ride wet, so I changed. Isn't it lucky I brought so many clothes along with me?" He waved his jingling arm in the direction of the horses. The two packhorses were already laden with clothing. The outfit Swift had worn on the previous day was indeed wet; it was draped over a low tree branch to dry.

Bayerd glanced at Gerald and in a whisper asked, "Why does he think my clothes are his own?"

"He took a jousting pole to the head at the spring tournament. Hasn't been the same since," Gerald whispered back.

"Ah, well, that does explain things," Bayerd said. And this was one of the knights the queen had chosen to have his back? Was she trying to get him killed? She had always held Bayerd in esteem, but perhaps her opinion had changed of late, since he had changed.

He saddled Spot and mulled things over. In his heart, Bayerd knew he was no longer the bold, dashing hero Kelp had married, and perhaps he had never been that man, except in his own fertile imagination. But he hadn't been a cringing coward with a heart filled with fear, as he was now.

Maybe the queen wanted Kelp free to marry a more suitable royal, so was trying to get him killed off. That thought gave Bayerd momentary pause. Would she go so far as to order his death? Was one of his remaining four knights a secret assassin? And if so, which one? Swift could be faking his malady to put Bayerd off his guard, although the lopsided pupils said otherwise. And then there was Gerald. If Bayerd was any judge of a man's loyalty, Gerald would do whatever his queen ordered, including murdering her niece's rubbish husband, for the good of the realm.

Bayerd didn't think Revel was a likely assassin since he drank from morning until night from a flask that he kept refilling, and he had fallen out of his saddle thrice already, which was twice more than Bayerd. And what about Jabalot? He was a hard fellow to read, one moment surly, the next sunny, his temper prone to changing in the blink of an eye. Although he was half-blind, which would not be a desirable trait in a killer-for-hire. A half-blind assassin might well do away with the wrong target, or miss entirely.

Perhaps he was simply being paranoid, yet Bayerd studied the men and didn't trust one of them. If only Orson was by his side. Bayerd trusted Orson with his life, and he trusted Orson with his wife.

He slipped the bridle over Spot's head and said, "Let's go. I want to reach the lower slopes of the mountain by nightfall. We will make our ascent on the right side. It looks a tad gentler than the left, and not so littered with big boulders."

The fire was doused. Swift mounted and took charge of the packhorses, claiming them as his own. He rode off in the lead as if he

50

was also usurping Bayerd's title of prince and leader of the quest. He forgot the wet clothing he had hung up to dry. Bayerd didn't bother to fetch the garments. He had no desire to wear anything Swift had worn. The fellow had probably pissed in his sleep again, and that's why he had jumped in the creek fully dressed.

As delighted as Bayerd was to have another taking charge of the packhorses, which made for an easier ride for him, he did not appreciate Swift assuming his role as leader of the quest. That would not do. "Saddle your mounts and catch up with me," Bayerd said to the other knights, who had yet to tack their horses.

He mounted and set off at a canter to claim back his rightful place as leader. Spot seemed a bit surprised, since he usually did not ride her at speed.

As soon as Bayerd caught up with Swift, he urged Spot to pass the packhorses. They didn't care a fig, but Swift's horse did. It tried to bite Spot, who shied away rather sharply. Bayerd kept going straight, without his horse. He hit the rocky ground directly in Swift's path. There was no time to roll away. Bayerd simply wrapped his arms protectively around his head and hoped he wouldn't get trampled to death.

Swift's horse jumped him easily, as did the first packhorse. Maybe the second didn't see him, or it blamed Bayerd for the arrow through its friend's neck, because Bayerd took a direct blow to his face. Everything spun in circles for a time. When he managed to sit up, Swift was riding back toward him, chasing Spot. Bayerd cried out and dropped back to the ground. Spot leapt over him and kept on galloping. She was much faster than he had known.

Swift's mount skidded to a stop. "Looks like she got away," Swift said and dismounted. He was courteous enough to help Bayerd to his feet.

Alas, Bayerd's nose was gushing blood like a fountain. He staunched it with his sleeve since he didn't have anything else. Swift dug around in his pack until he produced a dirty rag. Bayerd shook his head, preferring his clean sleeve.

"That was quite a fall, my good man," Swift said, as if congratulating Bayerd for a job well done. He even slapped him on the back. "Glad to see you on your feet."

Bayerd sneezed, spraying an impressive amount of blood onto Swift's chest. The fellow looked surprised, then crestfallen. "Dang, you've ruined my tunic."

Bayerd sneezed again, adding more red.

"Well, that's torn it. I'll have to change." Swift headed for the packhorse.

Bayerd followed Swift since he needed to change, too. The front of his tunic was soaked with about a bucketful of blood, and wet enough to give him a chill—and get him killed. Reeking of blood when travelling through lands populated by wild beasties was a blatant invitation for them to come and dine on fresh meat.

He stopped beside the packhorse and shed his clothes, staunching his nose with the tunic he had just removed, until the blood slowed to a trickle. He felt his nose and was pleased to find it straight again. The horse had set it for him.

On the opposite side of the animal, Swift was quick to undress. At least he was getting rid of the annoying bells. Bayerd must have been drunk when he had the castle tailor sew such an outfit, with bells no less! Did he aspire to be a lowly jester? Or had he subconsciously realized that he was acting the part of one, and so should dress as one?

Swift untied the outfit on the very top of the packhorse. It was red and silky. Bayerd let him have it. He reached for the next one down, since it was the easiest to unpack. "What do you think you're doing?" Swift asked, slapping Bayerd's hand away as if he was a naughty child.

"I'm getting a dry suit of clothes. It's damn cold in this wind." Bayerd tried to yank the rolled bundle free.

Swift held on tight to the garments. "These are my clothes. Wear your own!"

"I don't have any other clothes," Bayerd said, shivering.

"Oh. Well in that case, I suppose I could lend you something to wear. I do seem to have a surplus of outfits with me. But you should ask, you shouldn't just help yourself. That's quite rude, you know. And a polite please wouldn't go amiss."

Bayerd didn't try to reason with him, since there is no reasoning with a madman. Madmen needed to be humoured and cajoled. He let go of the rolled outfit, which was too thin and silky to be warm anyway, and said, "Sir Swift, may I please borrow something to wear? Before I freeze my arse off?"

"Of course. I can't have one of my men freezing, now can I?" Swift took his sweet time examining the outfits on both packhorses before he selected a plain pair of leather riding trousers and a simple dark tunic and cotton shirt. The outfit didn't have a pattern on it. Bayerd couldn't remember packing it. Kelp must have slipped it into his luggage. Good lord, he missed her.

"You can wear this one. It is not to my liking at all. I can't think why I brought it along." Swift tossed the bundle of clothes at Bayerd, who felt like he was turning to ice, standing naked in the gusting wind. It seemed to be blowing a lot harder than it had only minutes ago.

The other knights cantered up and stared at Bayerd and Swift, both in a state of undress. "What's going on?" Gerald asked suspiciously.

Bayerd yanked on the trousers. "I fell off my horse and got a hoof in the face. There was a lot of blood, so we are changing."

Swift buttoned up the red silky tunic. "If you sneeze blood on me again, it won't even show," he declared, stroking the silky cloth on his chest.

"I don't suppose any of you caught my horse?" Bayerd asked, even though it was as plain as the swollen nose on his face that Spot was not with them.

"Didn't see her," Jabalot said, which was no surprise to Bayerd. He didn't think the fellow could see past his own eyelashes.

Gerald simply shook his head.

Revel said, "I might have seen a horse run by. Didn't know it was yours though, so I didn't chase it."

"How could you not recognize my horse? She has white spots on both the front and rear," Bayerd cried.

"You weren't on her. Could have been anyone's horse," Revel said.

Bayerd waved an arm around the wilderness. "With such distinctive markings? And do you see any other folk around here?"

"Just 'cause I don't see them, doesn't mean they're not there, or here, or here and there." Revel laughed uproariously, as if he had told or heard the funniest joke in the land.

Bayerd's head was starting to ache, and he didn't think it was because a hoof had kicked him in the face. The day was definitely getting off to a rockier beginning than the previous one. "I'll have to double up with one of you," he said.

They all looked at him askance, as if he had suggested sharing a bedroll rather than a mere horse. Gerald frowned. "I wouldn't ask a horse to carry such a burden as two men, not when we are travelling all day over rough terrain, and you're no lightweight, if you don't mind me saying so, Prince Bayerd. Why don't you shift your clothing to one of the packhorses and ride the other.

"T'is no longer my clothing. Swift has laid claim to it." Bayerd dabbed at his still leaking nose and assessed the shrinking amount of clothing. It was still far more than one man needed, or even two men needed, since two were now sharing the wardrobe. "I could abandon some of the clothing, and ride one of the packhorses," he decided.

Swift cried out as though in great pain. "No! We are not abandoning my clothes, they are as dear to me as children. They go where I go and I go where they go!" He threw himself in front of the packhorse, arms spread wide, as if to save the clothing from an enemy attack.

Jabalot pulled out his sword. "Want me to stab him?"

"No!" Bayerd stepped between them. "No need for that. We will take all the clothing. It can be arranged to fit on one of the packhorses, I'm sure."

Jabalot lowered his blade. "Have it your way, but if you want someone stabbed, I'm your man. Always happy to do some stabbing and jabbing." He sounded rather like an assassin.

"We will not be killing one of our own. We will not be killing any of our own," Bayerd said in his steeliest tone. Power resonated in the words and seemed to echo around them like war-drums for a moment. Jabalot blinked in surprise. It was a voice Bayerd often called up when telling his tales—or used to call up. He hadn't used the voice for a very long time, he suddenly realized. And it felt good to use it. It made him feel like the storyteller he once was.

He turned to Swift with a smile. "Stack as many of the clothes as you can on the smallest packhorse."

Swift got right to it, and he proved to be quite adept at arranging a load of clothing. He got them all to fit and tied them securely in place. They did not bother to pick up the two bloodied outfits. Those were abandoned where they lay, looking gruesome on the ground, as if a murder had been committed there, or perhaps two murders.

Bayerd mounted the packhorse and they set off again. The delay had cost them some travelling time, but they soon made up for that. As they approached the foothills, the ground was smooth and flat with little vegetation, so their pace was quick. The packhorse proved to be an acceptable mount. Her stride was even a little smoother than Spot's, which his throbbing nose appreciated. Alas, his belly was empty and the sensation gnawed at his innards. Since they were out of both rations and horse meat, Bayerd had no choice but to go hungry. And he couldn't recall the last time he'd been in such a state, although it would have been when he made his way as a storyteller and troubadour, with Orson by his side, in the days before he was a prince.

He studied his belly. It hung over his belt and bounced with every trot of his horse's hooves, up and down, up and down. When had it gotten quite so large? He scowled at it. Perhaps Kelp did not find him as attractive as she once had, wrapped as he was in fat, which would explain why their bed time had become as rare as a robin in winter.

They rode hard all day, taking only one short break. All of them wanted to find shelter before nightfall, and there was less and less shelter to be had as the slope of the foothill steepened. Game was scarcer, too. There would be some hungry days ahead, unless they shot another horse. Bayerd was loath to do that. He liked horses, and in spite of all the falling off, he liked riding. It was so much faster than walking.

Bayerd was aiming for a scrubby patch of trees backed by towering boulders, which must have tumbled down the side of the mountain at some point, when a cry went up behind him. He turned his horse and trotted back to where Revel was rolling around on the ground, clutching at his forearm. It was bent in the middle, in a place where no arm should ever bend. A sharp point of bone was sticking through the skin and Revel was bleeding rather profusely, as if there had not already been enough bloodshed that day.

"What's happened?" Bayerd asked, as if he couldn't guess.

Gerald dismounted stiffly. "He fell off. Landed on a rather pointy boulder. Alas, he's done fair damage to that arm."

Jabalot joined Gerald on the ground and said, "He's no use to us now. Doubt he'll be able to ride. Want me to cut his throat and put him out of his misery?"

"Of course not," Bayerd said. "He is no horse with a broken leg to be put down. He is a man who can be healed in time."

"We'll make camp over by those trees and boulders," Swift said, still fancying himself in charge.

Bayerd took a quick scan of the land and couldn't disagree. "It is the best shelter that is available to us," he confirmed. He dismounted and took the reins of the rider-less horses, while Gerald and Jabalot hauled Revel up and walked him to the chosen campsite. Revel's constant

55

drinking from his seemingly bottomless flask had not numbed the fellow's pain, if his screaming was anything to judge by.

Everyone pitched in to set up camp and take care of poor Revel. He was given more drink to help dull the pain, before Gerald yanked on his arm to set it straight, bandaged and splinted it. Revel passed out during the setting of the bone. He felt no more pain after that.

Swift found enough wood to start a fire. Bayerd located a thread of a creek. It was coming down from the mountain, behind the big boulders that backed their campsite. He took the horses in turn to water them. The water was fresh and as cold as ice. He had seen the snow on the mountain's peak with his own eyes. It was no wonder the water was frigid. Alas, the narrow run of water was not deep or wide enough to support fish.

They settled rather miserably around the small fire, with hungry growling bellies. There was little shelter from the cold wind. Revel kept moaning and groaning in his restless state of delirium. Before too long, they bedded down, huddled under their blankets.

In spite of all the discomfort, Bayerd slept like the dead. He awoke to rain pelting his face. Considering how thoroughly soaked he was, and given the fact that he was lying in a sizeable puddle, it had probably been raining hard for most of the night. Three of his men were clustered under a tree with a tent of branches over them. Revel was not amongst them, so he was probably lying down elsewhere.

Bayerd tossed off his sodden blanket and sloshed over to them. "Did you not think to wake me before I drowned?" he snapped.

Gerald simply cast him a weary glance. "We did try to wake you. I swear, you could sleep through the end of the world."

"Oh, well … fair enough. Where did you stash Revel?" he asked, not bothering to address the fact that Swift was now wearing his favourite auburn paisley waistcoat and burnt orange leggings, with the matching paisley scarf—and his favourite golden jewel-encrusted slippers. The clothing thief was managing to keep them dry, at least.

"My injured man is missing," said Swift.

"Missing? But Revel is in no fit shape to ride anywhere." Bayerd glanced at Gerald for answers. He trusted Gerald far more than any of the others.

"T'is true," Gerald said, a frown pulling at his scar, making it look deep and quite gruesome even through the fellow's heavy stubble. "I was the first awake and Revel was nowhere to be found."

"Let me guess, his horse is gone as well."

"No sign of him or his horse. And it's going to be impossible to track him in the heavy rain," Gerald confirmed. As if to prove the wetness of the day, a big cold drip landed on Bayerd's neck and meandered down his back under his clothing. He shivered hard.

"We're better off without him," Jabalot said, as callous as he ever was.

"But he is not better off without us." Bayerd scanned as far as his eye could see. There was no sign of a man or a horse. There was only a rather desolate wet landscape in every shade of gray imaginable. He narrowed his eyes on Jabalot. "You didn't take it upon yourself to dispose of the man, did you?"

As Jabalot vehemently denied doing any such thing, an ominous rumbling sounded from above, where the mountain loomed over them. It wasn't thunder and the noise was far too big to come from any animal. Not even an angry dragon could have achieved such volume. It seemed to come from the mountain itself, and Bayerd suddenly felt as small as an ant. And every bit as vulnerable.

He squinted up, trying to see through the curtain of mist. "What was that?"

Gerald, too, tilted his face toward the mountain. "Don't know, but it doesn't sound good, does it?"

"Not good at all. Time to pack the horses and get the hell away from this place," Bayerd said.

"I will do no such thing," Swift cried. "I am not going out in the rain to get my clothing wet!" He gestured at Bayerd's remaining outfits, which were stacked atop a blanket under the sheltering branches.

"As you wish, Swift." Bayerd was already as wet as a man could get; he left the shelter and started tacking his packhorse. Half of his knights had now mysteriously vanished, and he was pretty sure the mountain was about to tumble down on the rest of them. He wasn't going to stand around and wait for that to happen. Gerald and Jabalot ducked from beneath the branches carrying their saddles.

In no time, the three of them were ready to depart. The rumbling mountain was rumbling even louder, as if unhappy they were trespassing. The ground was also shaking underfoot. Bayerd mounted the packhorse and rode over to Swift. "Tack your horse and ride with us," he ordered. "It is not safe here."

"It is safe, and more importantly, it is dry." Swift planted his hands on his hips and tried to look down his nose at Bayerd. He couldn't manage it because Bayerd was astride a horse, and much taller than he would normally be. "You are the most troublesome of my men. I may have you beheaded when we return to the Golden Kingdom. Now be off with you." Swift flapped a dismissive hand before he turned his back on Bayerd and crossed his arms, stubbornly refusing to leave the makeshift shelter and get wet.

"Beheaded, is it? Well, if I am to be beheaded, I should at least deserve the punishment," Bayerd declared, his temper rising like a pot boiling over. He was normally a good-natured fellow, but even a good-natured fellow can be pushed too far. He hopped off his packhorse and helped himself to Swift's tack. He slapped the saddle onto the back of Swift's bigger mount. If the knight wasn't going to ride her, Bayerd would. If Swift fancied himself the leader of the quest and dressed as a prince, let him ride the prince's horse—and that was a packhorse.

"Catch up with us when it stops raining," Bayerd told Swift. He scrambled onto his new horse and started cantering. Swift's horse, Mercury, had a distinctive golden-brown coat with a black mane and tail. She was pretty and not overly large, and she proved to be obedient and smooth-gaited. Bayerd liked riding her at once. He might just claim her as his own for the rest of the quest, and it wouldn't make him a horse-thief. Unlike a lowborn man, a prince had the right to claim anything that he desired. And Swift had usurped all his clothes so he could usurp Mercury. It was a fair trade.

They hadn't gone more than several hundred yards when they discovered a split in one of the craggy rock faces. It appeared to lead into the bedrock of the mountain. It was wide enough for two men to ride abreast.

"That's worth investigating," Gerald said. They all dismounted. Gerald rooted around in his saddlebag until he located a torch.

Jabalot took his sword in hand. "Looks like good shelter if there are no bears or wildcats within."

Bayerd simply wished they had found the cave before the rain. Even though he didn't like caves in general, it would have kept them dry. As it was, it was going to take days to dry out their sodden blankets and saddles.

Gerald handed Bayerd his reins and crossed over the threshold into the cave to light the torch with his flint. It sizzled a bit with moisture before it caught and flared bright. He disappeared into the black gaping maw in the rock, with Jabalot close behind. Bayerd got to hold his horse, too, as if he had been summarily demoted to stable boy.

Bayerd did not mind. He preferred to stay outside in the rain with the horses, since he was already as wet as a drowned fish.

That opinion changed when the disturbing rumbling noise suddenly increased in volume. The ground shook harder underfoot. Small stones began to rain painfully down on him like hail. Bayerd hurried into the cave then, tugging all three horses with him. Inside, it was midnight black. Bayerd couldn't see Gerald's light at all. Had it gone out?

"Gerald! Jabalot! Where are you?" His voice echoed around him as if there were lots of Bayerd's, not merely one.

"Here," they called. Their echoing voices came from all directions. After a few moments, an edge of light appeared. It brightened as Gerald neared. "This isn't merely a cave, Prince Bayerd. The back wall narrows into a passage into the mountain," he called.

"Imagine that," Bayerd panted. He was having a bit of trouble breathing when he imagined the miles of rock and earth overhead, just waiting in anticipation to collapse and crush him.

"There is no way to tell how far it goes, of course, not without following it," Gerald said.

"Well, I don't think we'll do that. This quest is to find the heaven rock, and the last place it will be found is in the heart of a mountain. It will be found beneath a starry sky, or a sunny sky, or a cloudy sky, depending on when we find it." Bayerd turned toward the entrance, wanting nothing more than to get the heck out of there, but that was not to be.

The rumbling overhead increased one hundredfold. The horses reared and bucked. The walls shook and chunks of rock rained down around them. Bayerd was knocked to his knees so he could not run, which probably saved his life.

The terrible crashing assaulted them on all sides. It went on and on as if it would never end. Bayerd covered his head with his arms and tried not to whimper. He waited it out, pelted by pebbles, rather as if he was being stoned by a village of angry babies.

The crashing and rumbling lessened by degrees until it sounded like nothing more than sand running through a giant hourglass, if you were inside it. Bayerd took a shuddering breath and choked on thick dust. There was coughing and rustling around him, so he knew he was not the sole survivor. Mercury snorted and shook her head, dislodging rocks from her mane.

"Gerald, how fare you?" Bayerd croaked, his throat clogged by dust.

"Well enough, Prince Bayerd. And how fare you?" Gerald croaked back.

"Quite spectacularly, considering that a mountain has fallen down on my head."

"Doesn't anyone care to know if I'm still breathing?" demanded Jabalot.

"Are you still breathing, Sir Jabalot?" Bayerd asked.

"Aye, and I'm not flattened either. Now let's get the heck out of this hellish place."

"I'll see if I can light my torch. It's gone out," Gerald said, as if they couldn't see that for themselves.

A flint stone rasped several times and the torch flared to life. Gerald looked quite menacing with a mask of dirt stuck to the sweat and blood on his face. Jabalot looked about the same, with a red trickle running down from his forehead into his eye. The horses were all still standing, eyes flashing their whites. Bayerd patted Mercury on the nose. "It's all right, girl. We'll be out of here in no time," he crooned to calm her.

Gerald cleared his throat. "I fear you are lying to your horse, Prince Bayerd."

"Why would you say such a thing?"

"See that wall of boulders there?" Gerald motioned to it with the torch.

Bayerd got a sinking feeling in the pit of his stomach. "I do see it."

"That is the exit to this cave."

"Was the exit," Jabalot snapped, wiping blood out of his eye with his sleeve.

"You mean we're ... buried alive?" Bayerd gasped, panic filling him.

"Unless there is another exit," Gerald said, "I fear we are."

"I knew I should never have left the castle." Bayerd fought to breathe when the weight of those rock walls seemed to press in on him. "I'm a cursed man, you know. Trouble prefers me over all other men."

Jabalot spat on the ground in front of Bayerd's boots. "Are you the only man trapped in this cave then? Do we count for nothing?"

"Of course you count. You've misconstrued my words, for I fear my men are sharing my curse. Three have vanished and the rest are buried

60

alive." A last pebble came down from above and plunked onto Bayerd's head, as if to jar him to his senses. "Swift!" he cried. "Swift is out there. He can dig us out." Bayerd pressed against the rock, shouting, "Swift, Swift! Hear me, damn you. Swift!"

Gerald laid a hand on his shoulder. "Swift may have fared worse than us. He had no shelter when the rock came down."

"Probably crushed flat, probably nothing but a puddle of bloody pulp," Jabalot cut in.

"Oh, lord." Bayerd sank to the ground when his legs gave out. "We're doomed. I'll never see Kelp again. She'll never know my sad fate." Nor had they parted on the best of terms. The thought of never loving her again was too painful to bear. Would she pine for him and finish her life as a spinster? Or would she seek comfort in the arms of another, another who was tall, dark and brooding—like Orson? And what of Orson? With Bayerd out of the picture, would he feel any loyalty to a dead friend?

Bayerd's hands clenched into fists. No! He would not give into despair. Fear had been his master for long enough. The worst had just happened. He was buried alive, facing a slow death by starvation, dehydration, or suffocation if the horses breathed up all the air. There was nothing worse that could happen, hence, there was no longer anything to fear—well, except for Kelp believing him dead. Clearly, there was only one course of action left to him. He had to bravely get the hell out from under the mountain, or die trying.

Bayerd stood up with resolution. "Let's see if we can dig ourselves out." He began shifting the rocks that were small enough to shift. As soon as he moved one, it was replaced by two. He kept excavating and his men soon joined him.

The three of them worked at the wall of rock until the size of their cave was reduced by half. All they were doing was making it smaller by filling the space with rocks and inviting more inside. And one of the horses had pooped. Bayerd had buried the poop beneath rock so as not to step in the patty, but that did not stop it from stinking. And too many of the boulders were simply too big to budge.

Gerald finally sighed and stretched his stiff back. "Prince Bayerd, I fear this is a futile waste of our time. There is simply too much rock, it could be a mile deep. And there is no way in hell we can move the larger of these boulders. Perhaps we should seek another egress before our torch burns away and we are without light."

61

"Do you think there is another way out?" Bayerd asked, hopefully.

"The passage at the back of the cave is not blocked. It could cut right through the mountain to the other side," Gerald said.

Bayerd recalled the vast base of the gigantic mountain. "That would be quite a trek."

"Would you rather stay here and rot? Until we are naught but bones?" Gerald asked.

"No, I would not. How many torches do we have?" he said,

They each checked their packs. Jabalot had brought two, and Gerald found a second in the bottom of his pack. Bayerd hadn't thought to bring any, but when he checked Swift's saddlebag, he found three. It was a treasure-trove given their dire straits. Bayerd also found a wine bottle filled with water, and a wine bottle filled with wine. Bayerd was going to richly reward the loony fellow, if he hadn't been crushed to death, and if Bayerd ever saw him again.

Their spirits a little higher, they entered the passage and set off into the heart of the mountain.

6. Another One Bites the Dust

T'was at the good queen's behest
The brave prince was sent on a quest
And with him, her champions best
Six knights and one prince rode west
They rode hard, they rode without rest
Until naught but one was left
Alas, I do not jest
Which one? Can you not guess?

-Bayerd the Storyteller, Survivor's Tale

Orson tiptoed into Kelp's dark bedchamber. He'd had to wait for everyone to bed down before he could talk with the princess in private. Now, finally, the whole castle was quiet. He reached her bed and gripped her shoulder to shake her awake—at least he thought it was her shoulder. As soon as his big hand closed around soft boneless flesh, he realized his mistake. He released her breast, but not quickly enough to stop her from shrieking.

"Shush, Princess," Orson whispered, or thought he whispered. "T'is only me, Orson."

"What the devil are you doing?" Kelp snapped.

"I want to talk about … the rumour." He sat down on the edge of her bed, or what he thought was the edge of her bed, until the rounded curve of her hip shifted beneath him. Off balance, he tumbled backwards on top of Kelp. She thrashed about, trying to dislodge him, and merely got them both tangled in her blankets.

"Stop squirming," Orson growled.

"Get off me," Kelp hissed.

"I will if you stop squirming!"

"Stop shouting!"

"I'm not shouting," Orson shouted.

Two bodies dashed into the room carrying lanterns. Orson froze. Kelp stopped thrashing about.

"Princess Kelp? I thought I spotted an intruder sneaking into your bedchamber, and then I heard a ruckus. Is all well?" Maiga asked.

Orson sat up, tossing the blanket off his face, which felt as redhot as coals. Kelp sat up beside him, her nightdress in disarray. She shifted it to cover an exposed breast. She had a birthmark beside her nipple. Orson hadn't known she had a birthmark there, and he shouldn't know it. He looked away and saw her ladies' expressions. He knew the situation looked bad for him—very bad.

Maiga's eyes were wide, as were Irvette's, standing by her side. Their mouths' were agape, yet no sound came out. The ladies were backed by two guards, who gawked at the bed. Orson didn't know quite how to explain the scene, so he mumbled, "Uh … I fell on the princess, quite by accident, and then I couldn't get up."

The ladies backed for the door, taking the guards with them. The petite, dark-haired Irvette looked very disappointed in them, while the red-haired Maiga simply said, "Sorry to have interrupted your evening." She even closed the door to grant them the privacy to carry on.

Kelp disentangled her feet from the covers and used them to shove Orson off her bed whilst clutching the blanket to her chest. "Orson, what in Hades are you doing here? In the middle of the night?"

"I just wanted to talk about … the affair everyone thinks we're having," he said lamely.

"Well, if they didn't believe we were having an affair before, they certainly will now. In fact, I think we are having an affair now that we've rolled around in my bed together in the middle of the night." She dropped her head into her hands.

"Don't cry, Princess. We'll explain it to Bayerd when he gets back."

"And what if he never comes back? What if I have sent him into danger with treacherous men? What if I have sent him to his death?" she sobbed. "I know he was driving me crazy, but I do love him, and I miss him. I didn't think I would, yet I do."

Orson sat down on the very edge of the bed and put a comforting arm around her shoulders. "He'll come back safe and sound, Princess. You know Bayerd, he has nine lives."

"Nine lives that he has already used up, and then some," she said, eyes tearing up.

Orson sighed and pressed her against his side comfortingly. "He'll be home before you know it, and I bet you a bag of gold coins, he brings the heaven stone with him."

Kelp sniffed and laughed weakly, in spite of the tears. "You are a dear, Orson. I don't know what I would do without you. Alas, we will have to be more circumspect from now on. No more picnics unless we take my ladies and a few guards along as chaperones."

"I'm hoping Bayerd will accompany us as well, when he comes home cured of his cowardice."

Kelp leaned her head against his shoulder and said, "I do look forward to that."

There was a brisk knock at the door and it was flung opened before they could part. Irvette, Maiga, and a knight that Orson recognized as Sir Stalwart, stood outside. Orson removed his arm from around Kelp, He stood up, feeling as guilty as a villain even though he was no such thing.

"What now?" Kelp asked, head held high.

"There's another body," Maiga blurted, while Irvette simply glared. Orson seemed to be the target of her censure.

"On horseback," Sir Stalwart added. "We've just lowered the drawbridge to bring the horse across."

"Is it Bayerd?" Orson asked.

"The man looks too tall and slender, but he appears to be one of Prince Bayerd's party. We'll know more when we get the body off the horse."

"Orson, go with the guard. I will dress and be down directly," Kelp said.

Orson went, glad to get the hell out of her bedchamber. Sir Stalwart held his tongue until they were at the bottom of the spiraling stone steps, then he leaned in close. "You're a bold one, Orson, I'll give you that. I like my head too much to dare bedding a royal, but if I was going to bed a royal, it would be Princess Kelp. Shame she's wasted on one such as Bayerd. No pleasure for her in that match, eh? Guess that's why she's taken you into her bed. You do have quite a reputation for satisfying the ladies. They gossip, you know, when they think no men are listening."

Orson clenched his hands into fists, yet kept them at his side. As much as he wanted to punch Stalwart in the nose, it would only make matters worse. "I am not bedding the princess. I wouldn't betray my friend, and Bayerd is man enough to satisfy his wife." At least he used to be. Orson wasn't so sure anymore. If his friend had lost his courage, perhaps he was no longer a man in other vital ways.

They crossed the courtyard as a sweaty lathered horse was led up to the stables, a body draped over its back. It was definitely not Bayerd, unless he had been stretched an extra foot on a rack in the days since he had left the castle.

"Tied to the saddle, just like the first body—just like Basher," Sir Stalwart commented.

Sir Gallant had been rousted from his bed, along with about half a dozen knights, all in hastily donned clothing. Many lanterns were lit, awaiting the horse with its burden. Gallant himself cut the body free and lowered it to the ground. "It's Sir Conquer," he said, "and he's been murdered."

That much was obvious. Dried blood caked his head and throat. But unlike Basher, his body had not been stabbed multiple times.

Kelp and her two ladies appeared in the circle of light. "T'is Conquer," Orson told her. "Murdered, like Basher."

Kelp looked down and nodded, her face as grim as Orson had ever seen it. "I fear Bayerd is in grave danger," she said softly, as if to herself. Tears filled her eyes and hung on the lashes like dew drops. How could anyone gaze upon her face and doubt her love for her husband?

"I fear the same," Orson said, the stench of the murdered knight thick in his nostrils.

Kelp addressed Orson, her face set. "We will ride after Bayerd at first light. We can ride a lot faster than him, what with his ..." her voice caught, "his propensity to fall off his horse. We can catch up, I know we can."

Gallant cleared his throat. "The two of you going off alone together ... t'is not seemly. You must take a few of my knights along, and one of your ladies, Princess Kelp."

She glared at him, every inch the royal ruler. "We are not going to go alone. Of course I will take some knights, but not enough to slow us down. And I can't take one of my ladies. A carriage is a hindrance I will not accept."

Irvette stepped forward. "I can ride, Princess Kelp, I can ride like a man. I grew up riding with my brothers. I will accompany you."

Kelp clasped Irvette's hands. "If these murdered knights are any true sign, it will be a dangerous journey, Irvette."

"I understand that, Princess Kelp, but my place is by your side. I will accompany you."

Orson had never seen this side of the mousey Irvette. It made him look at her anew. In the flickering lantern light, with her cheeks flushed and eyes sparkling, she was an animated vision. The last time he had bedded Irvette had been before Bayerd had wed Kelp, so perhaps it was time to bed her again. And that would prove that he was not bedding the princess, wouldn't it?

"Thank you, Irvette," said Kelp. "That's settled then. We'll leave at first light."

Gallant nodded. "I'll have the horses ready, and the supplies, and four knights. I'll choose four of my best, not like the sorry lot I sent with your husband. Now, try and get some rest before your journey, for I fear it will be a grueling one. Prince Bayerd's party has three days lead time."

"At Bayerd's pace, that's only about a day," Orson said, quite unconcerned.

The advice was wise regardless, but they did not have a chance to follow it. They were still standing thus when the sound of wings overhead reached Orson's ears. 'Dragon' was his first thought. Before he could react, a much smaller body landed near him.

Everyone froze in place and stared at the hideously ugly bird woman. Orson tried not to gag on the fetid reek that emanated from her. Her eyes were wide with fear, showing their whites in flashes. Her feathery hair was patchy and she looked to be molting. Her black claws clutched at the dirty pack she had strapped around her chest, hiding one of her scaly, black-tipped nipples.

"Harpy, is that you?" he asked. To him, all harpies looked and smelled alike, so he really had no idea if this was the harpy that had saved his life, and Bayerd's, and then demanded a terrible toll to carry them to safety.

She cawed and removed a large squirming bundle from the pack. She held it out to Orson and took a step toward him, shrieking shrilly. He heard the slide of weapons and said to the nearby knights, "She's no threat. Leave her be. Keep those swords sheathed."

He took a step to meet her. "Harpy, do you want to give that to me? Do you want me to take it?"

She cawed and tossed it at him. He caught the bundle and before he could see what it was, she had launched back into the night sky. She disappeared into the darkness with a powerful flap of her wings.

"What is it, Orson?" Kelp asked.

"Don't know, but it's moving." He almost dropped it, except a happy little gurgling sound stopped him. "It can't be," he gasped. With a sinking feeling in his gut, he unwrapped the tattered man's tunic that was doubling as a swaddling blanket. Inside was a babe, more than six months in age if Orson was any judge. It had blonde curly locks and sky-blue eyes, and wore a crown that was much too large for its small head. Orson recognized the crown. It had belonged to the harpy that had saved them. As more of the blanket fell away, Orson knew it was a boy child. And given the colour of the curls and eyes, he knew whose boy child it was.

His friend was well and truly cursed.

"Orson, why did she give you a baby?" Kelp asked.

"T'is mine," Orson declared rashly, his mouth faster than his brain.

Kelp took a good look at the babe, who smiled angelically up at her. Her eyes narrowed. "Funny, but he doesn't look at all like you." Her voice dropped to a whisper. "He looks rather like someone else I know. Didn't a harpy save your life, and Bayerd's, more than a year ago, was it not?"

"Might have been," Orson said, most reluctantly.

Kelp motioned everyone back—everyone except Orson. The enthralled audience had been edging closer and closer to get a look at what Orson held.

And Kelp was too sharp for her own good. Orson normally liked that about her. "There was a toll to pay for saving our lives," he muttered, adding, "I was unable to pay it. I was gravely wounded at the time and … and … she's a harpy." He shuddered, feeling sick all over again when he thought back to that time.

"Bayerd paid the toll." It wasn't even a question.

"He did. Couldn't believe he managed it, but he was desperate. He knew your life depended on our making it back to the castle. If we hadn't, you would have lost your head. He did it for you, Princess."

"Oh, my poor Bayerd. No wonder he is so traumatized, to have a harpy force herself upon him. A harpy! I'm surprised he didn't join the religious brothers again." She bit her lip in distress. "He never told me."

"Too ashamed," Orson said. And what man wouldn't be?

68

"There is no shame in doing what must be done to save the lives of your friends. And this is the result?" She reached out to take the babe from Orson, removing the crown when it slipped down over the babe's head. "Why has the harpy placed the crown upon his head?"

Orson couldn't even begin to guess, unless the harpy thought it would ensure that the child be treated as befit a king. Kelp couldn't seem to take her eyes off the little fellow. "He's quite beautiful, isn't he? With those golden blonde curls and such blue eyes. He's perfect, except for being filthy. How could a harpy produce such a child?"

Orson knew more than he liked about harpies and said, "Girl babies are born pure harpy. Boy babies are born pure men. Boy babies are normally killed at birth, by their mothers. That's why harpies must mate with men, for no such thing as a male harpy exists. I wonder why Harpy let this little one live?"

Kelp lifted the child to her shoulder protectively. "Murder one's own child? How awful, how tragic. Orson, Irvette, come with me." She strode toward the castle with the baby, leaving a most curious cluster of knights and castle folk gossiping in her wake.

***

The roosters hadn't even crowed when Kelp, Orson and Irvette met up with the four guards selected to ride with them. Stalwart was one of them. Gallant claimed that Sir Stalwart was a skilled tracker, and they would need just such a man to find Bayerd.

Their party galloped over the moat as the sun cleared the horizon. Kelp was so worried about Bayerd that she completely forgot to worry about leaving the queen alone with Shifra, and Orson didn't spare the matter a single thought. Kelp should have worried, and Orson should have spared the matter a great many sober thoughts.

While they were away from the castle, Maiga would tend the baby brought by the harpy. Orson had gotten up early to play with the little fellow before they left. He was quite enthralled by the child and wanted to name him Little Bayerd.

Kelp had vetoed that idea, saying the christening could wait, and that Bayerd should have a say, him being the father and all.

They rode hard for several hours, until the horses were sweaty and lathered. Irvette rode every bit as well as she had claimed and did not slow them down. In truth, Orson had a hard time keeping pace with her, and he did try. The way her curvy bottom bounced in rhythm with the saddle, well, it was a sight to behold, so he tried to hold the spot to her rear.

They stopped for lunch beside a river and gave the horses a much needed breather. The day was hot and it would have been nice to nap. Alas, there was no time to spare. Orson felt a sense of urgency pulsing through him that was probably second only to Kelp's.

When she called, "Mount up! Let's ride," Orson tightened the girth on his saddle and tried to bridle his horse. Silver tossed her head and neighed.

"What is it, Silver?" he said.

An answering neigh had them all turning their heads as a brown spotted horse trotted into sight, fully tacked, but without a rider in the saddle. Kelp gasped and clapped a hand over her mouth. The horse trotted right up to them as if they were all good friends.

"That's Marigold, Bayerd's horse. The one he rode on his quest," Kelp cried.

"Horse is probably heading for home then. Bayerd must have fallen off just around the bend." Orson grinned happily. "We'll find him."

They set off, extra horse in tow and Stalwart in the lead, following its faint hoof prints in reverse.

Bayerd was not right around the bend in the path, or the next bend, or the one after that. They rode all day long and did not find Bayerd or his men. At dusk, the horse's tracks led them to the cold ashy remains of a fire near a stream.

Orson glanced around the clearing and said, "This is the kind of spot Bayerd likes. This is where he and his men camped on their second night. Wouldn't have made it this far on the first day, not with Bayerd riding a horse, and you said they got off to a late start?"

"Bayerd slept in. They left at noon," Kelp said, studying the campsite as if it might offer up clues as to what had become of Bayerd.

Orson nodded as if that confirmed it. "So, this is where they stopped on their second night. We're already a day ahead in catching them. And since Bayerd is no longer riding, but walking, we'll find him in a tick, mark my words."

"He could be riding one of his packhorses," Kelp said. She had already told Orson about the three packhorses Bayerd had needed to carry all his clothing.

"Aye, true enough. Well, we'll camp here for the night," Orson said.

Everyone dismounted and stretched weary muscles. A fire was lit and the horses were tended to. They had plenty of rations and ate well before bedding down. Orson was tired enough to sleep, yet darted glances at Irvette, hoping to catch her eye. Her long dark hair looked soft and shiny in the firelight, and Orson had an urge to stroke it. A little romp in the bushes would probably do them both a world of good.

Irvette avoided his roving eye and bedded down close beside the princess. Alas, she was probably too tired to romp. She was used to lounging about the castle, not riding hard all day. Orson told himself there were more nights to come and rolled up in his blanket. Sleep came quickly. There is nothing like a gently crackling fire and fresh forest air to lull a man into pleasant dreams.

The morning brought clouds and the promise of rain. As soon as they were in the saddle, Stalwart led them to the creek, so they could follow the clear tracks of Bayerd and his surviving men.

Orson was passing some tangled vegetation when a heap of cloth in the bushes caught his eye. He dismounted and picked it up, then wished he hadn't. It was one of Bayerd's patterned tunics, and the back was thoroughly blood-soaked. They had found Bayerd's horse and now the bloody clothes, yet there was still no trace of the man himself.

Kelp approached at a trot and Orson quickly hid the bloody garment behind his back.

"Orson, what have you got there?" she asked.

"Nothing. Nothing at all."

Kelp stopped and everyone else reined in their horses. "Orson, show me what you have behind your back."

He dropped the tunic and flashed his hands. "Naught but these two hands, Princess Kelp."

"What did you just drop?" She tried to peer around him.

"Nothing. Nothing at all." Orson kicked backwards, trying to send the garment into the creek.

"Must I dismount and fetch the thing myself?" Kelp arched an eyebrow at him.

He sighed. "I'd rather you didn't see what it is. Please don't look, keep riding."

"After a statement like that, I will only think the very worst. Show me what you found," she ordered in her steeliest tone.

"T'is merely clothing." He gave an exaggerated shrug.

"You are trying my patience most sorely, Orson, and we are wasting valuable time. Show me!"

He reached behind and lifted the tunic into sight. Of course Kelp recognized it at once. She cried, "Bayerd's tunic, the one he was wearing when he left the castle. Is that blood?"

"A bit," Orson said, trying to keep the worst of the stain hidden.

"That is not a bit, that is as much blood as a man's body holds," Kelp sobbed. "First his horse, now his bloody clothing. He's dead, isn't he, just like the other two men."

"T'is only clothes, Princess. Doesn't mean anything without a body inside them. If you think about it, the fact that Bayerd is not inside these clothes means that he is still alive. He couldn't take them off if he was dead, now could he?"

Kelp drew in a shuddering breath and nodded once. "I suppose there is some twisted logic to that."

Orson tossed the bloody tunic back in the bushes. "We'll keep riding. We'll find him. We haven't come across any more bodies and that is a good sign, isn't it?"

As if to prove Orson wrong, a horse trotted into sight. A body was draped over the saddle, just like the previous two.

"T'is Sir Revel," Stalwart gasped. "I'd know that ridiculous ginger hair anywhere." He urged his horse forward to catch the reins of Revel's horse, which seemed quite content to be caught. Everyone gathered around as Sir Revel was cut free from the saddle and laid on the ground.

"Neck is sliced deep, almost clean through, just like the others," Orson said. "And he's soaking wet."

"It often rains over mountains while it remains dry in the lower lands," Stalwart said.

Kelp crouched beside the body. "Look at his arm. It is wounded, yet bandaged. They must have been attacked at some point."

"And now Bayerd's lost half his knights, and he's worse than useless with a blade. I think we should make haste." Orson pulled Kelp to her feet. "We can bury Sir Revel on our return journey, if his body hasn't been dragged away and eaten by the beasties."

Kelp nodded in agreement. Without saying a word, she remounted.

With yet another horse in tow, they cantered forward, following Sir Stalwart who was tracking the passage of Revel's horse now. It was a fresh trail and easier to follow. It more or less mirrored the route taken by Bayerd and his men.

They rode hard all day and the sun did not show its face. Late afternoon, they found the third campsite. There was no doubt it was Bayerd's because one of his outfits was tangled in the bushes near the charcoal remains of a fire. As soon as they dismounted, Orson pulled it free. "He's left a perfectly good suit of clothing behind. That's not like Bayerd."

"He does take pride in his wardrobe. Yet, finding it here, it proves he is still alive, doesn't it?" Kelp gazed beseechingly at Orson.

"Course it does. Alive and well, I'd say, since these garments are unbloodied."

Kelp frowned deeply. "Perhaps we should keep riding. There is still an hour or more of daylight left."

"No point in wasting good daylight," Orson agreed. He tossed the clothes back into the bushes and vaulted back on his horse.

They weren't even out of sight of the campsite when they found more evidence of disaster. Stalwart, in the lead, spotted the bloody garments on the ground first. He stopped and pointed, as if everyone could not see the bright patterns and rusty red smears on the earth for themselves.

Orson dismounted to investigate. He picked up the bloodiest of the tunics. "Bayerd's, awful lot of blood, but on the front this time." He checked out the other tunic. "Also Bayerd's. Less blood. Why would Bayerd be wearing two sets of clothing?"

"Maybe he was cold and wore two layers," Kelp said, her voice thready and strained.

"Still no body inside the clothing, Princess. That means he is still alive, probably. Although he won't have much blood left in him." Orson pulled a face.

"And the way he is going through clothing, it is indeed fortunate he packed so many outfits." Kelp was putting on a brave face, proving herself every inch a princess. "Unless I find Bayerd's clothes with his dead body inside them, I will believe him alive," she declared.

They set off again, but it soon became too difficult to track the trail across the rocky ground in the waning light, so they stopped and made camp. There were still enough rations to keep them from going hungry, and they sat around the fire and ate them. Kelp was pale and very quiet. In spite of her avowal to the contrary, she was gravely worried. She didn't eat a bite, passed her rations to Orson and curled up in her blanket.

"She's thinking the worst," Orson murmured to Irvette, making a true effort to speak quietly.

"She is. And guilt gnaws at her." Irvette lowered her long lashes to gaze at the fire.

"Guilt?" Orson said.

"She sent Prince Bayerd on this quest. She sent him up this mountain without realizing it is considered a cursed place by many of the common folk. If Prince Bayerd dies on the quest, she will blame herself," Irvette whispered near his ear. Her breath was warm, tickling him and inspiring lust.

"Irvette, would you care to take a little stroll with me." Orson added a bit of a leer so she would know he did not really want to go for a walk.

She turned to gaze directly at him. "I have already taken a *stroll* with you, Orson, and have no desire to do so again."

Orson was left quite speechless. Girls never refused him. They almost lined up to lay with him. Had he not pleased Irvette when he bedded her? It was highly unlikely, but perhaps he had drunk too much wine that night. "Did you not enjoy *strolling* with me?" he asked.

She gave a little shrug. "It was fine."

"Fine? That's all? Fine? Are you sure you're remembering me? Not some other bloke? Because I have quite a reputation for pleasing the ladies, you know." Orson nodded emphatically to emphasize the point.

Irvette glared at him with such ferocity, he was glad she did not carry a sword. "You are the only man I have ever lain with, you village idiot, and it meant not a thing to you. And now you are sharing Princess Kelp's bed, and betraying your friend," she hissed angrily.

"I am not sharing Kelp's bed. I wouldn't."

"I am not a stupid girl, Orson. I saw you abed together the night before we left the castle. Until then, I did not credit the gossip as truth, but after what I saw with my own two eyes, my opinion has changed." She gave a little sniff of disdain.

Orson shook his head in denial. "I already explained that. I fell on Kelp and couldn't get up."

"Shush, you are shouting." Irvette rose and gazed down at him for a moment, her eyes hidden by shadow, then she turned her back and went to bed down beside Princess Kelp.

Orson scowled after her. Clearly he would have to clear this matter up, then bed her again so she would recall what a wonderfully pleasurable experience it was to lie naked with him. But he would have to wait until tomorrow night, since she was clearly not in a receptive mood.

He rolled up in his blanket and closed his eyes. He fell asleep with great hope in his heart that he would bed Irvette before another day had passed. If Orson truly was the only man she had ever lain with, she was long overdue to lie with him again. And they would find Bayerd, alive and well, the very next day—it would be a great day all round.

He could not have been more wrong; perhaps he was the village idiot.

***

The morning brought thicker clouds and a chilly breeze, or the air was simply cooler in the higher altitudes in the shade of the mountain. They set off without delay and rode through a landscape that was increasingly barren, rocky and steep. Orson rested his hand on his bow and kept a sharp eye for game. He was the first to spot a massive tumble of rocks that had come down from the mountain, obliterating the faint tracks they were following—Bayerd's tracks. At the edge of the rockslide, he also caught a glimpse of some patterned fabric. Yet another of Bayerd's ridiculous costumes?

Orson cantered ahead of the others and found a whole collection of clothing in disarray, littering the ground at the edge of the rockslide. All Bayerd's, without a doubt. He hopped off Silver and grinned at the others when they caught up. "Looks like Bayerd has lost all his clothes. We'll probably find him buck naked on the other side of this rockslide."

No-one grinned back. They were all looking at something else amid the clothing. Bayerd's favourite golden jewel-encrusted slippers, Orson realized, and there were feet inside them, feet attached to legs. The ankles and calves were all he could see of Bayerd. The rest of his friend was covered in a heap of large and even larger boulders.

Kelp slid off her horse and fell to her knees beside the slippers. She laid a hand on the ankle. "He's very cold." She sounded surprised, as if she had expected to find warm flesh, as if Bayerd had merely been playing possum under tons of rock.

75

Orson rushed over and began hauling rocks off Bayerd's legs. He kept at it like a madman until the thighs were exposed, and then he stopped. His friend was quite crushed. His body was broken beyond repair, not to mention stone-cold dead, with a wash of blood caked into the dirt beneath it. This was no stained tunic. What lay beneath the weight of the rock would undoubtedly be naught but bloody pulp. Kelp did not need to see that.

She hadn't moved. She sat on the ground holding one of the golden slippers as if she was carved from stone herself. "He really is dead this time, isn't he?" She looked up at Orson, her face white and still enough to be a mime's mask.

"He is." Orson sat down beside her on the cold stone, the smell of death strong in the air. He put an arm around her and pulled her close, and to hell with what anyone thought of that.

Stalwart said quietly, "I will see if there is any sign of Gerald or Jabalot or Swift, although if they are under all this rock, I doubt we will ever lay eyes on their remains."

All the knights got to work, sifting through the rubble and climbing around the rockslide. They did not find any trace of the three missing knights, and they probably never would. The earth had already taken care of burying their bodies.

Orson held Kelp, and stroked her hair. When he tried to move her away from Bayerd's body, she finally started to cry, and then she wouldn't stop. Orson picked her up and carried her around the rockslide to where a copse of scrubby trees still stood, undamaged by the devastation.

Irvette followed, leading their horses. "Looks like a good place to make camp," she said and began to gather deadwood. Quite a bit had come down the mountain with the boulders. She soon had a roaring fire burning.

The heat did not seem to touch Kelp, who began to shiver so hard, her teeth chattered. Orson wrapped a blanket around her and lay beside her, hugging her tight against his chest, trying to hold her together when it felt like she might break apart. Their grief united them in an intimate way.

Bayerd had been Orson's lifetime companion and the truest friend a man could know. He had made Orson both laugh and pull his hair out in frustration. Life had never been dull with Bayerd as his friend. Orson's life would be a much emptier place now. His grief was no small thing.

Perhaps holding Kelp was also keeping him in one piece. He could only imagine her pain, to lose the man she loved and had promised to share a lifetime with. To be widowed so young was tragic. Bayerd's son would never know him, and Bayerd would never know he had sired a beautiful little boy, with a harpy of all creatures.

When the sun rose, he would bury his friend's body deeper in rock and then they would ride home. They would probably never know who had slit the throats of the three knights, but at least they knew Bayerd's tragic fate. They would not be left to wonder if he had lived or died.

Orson made a private vow that he would devote his life to raising Bayerd's son, and tell him all about his father, except for his last year of cowardice. If Kelp also wanted to be a part of the lad's life, they could raise him together. Suddenly, he found his eyes flowing with tears. It wasn't in the least bit manly, yet he could not stop them.

He must have fallen asleep at some point, but not soundly. He awoke from a restless doze to a quiet campsite and a dying fire. His sword was also digging into his hip, since he had neglected to remove it. Orson rose without disturbing Princess Kelp or anyone else.

The men had collected quite a stack of wood. Orson added a generous amount to keep the animals at bay since there was no man on watch—or the man who should be on watch had fallen asleep. Orson would fill that role once he had heeded the call of nature.

The moon was high and three-quarters full, casting enough light for a man to see where he stepped. Orson left the campsite and veered away from the piled rock that was a grave, perhaps haunted by his friend's restless spirit. Floundering in his sorrow, he walked farther than he intended. After he had relieved himself, he fully intended to head back to the campsite and keep watch, except he spotted a flickering light. Was it an uncommonly large firefly? Unlikely since it seemed to be coming from inside the mountain? But how could that be?

Orson did have a bit of a tendency to be a curious fellow on occasion, and he walked toward the flickering light, hand on the pommel of his sword, just in case. He discovered a crack in the rock base of the mountain, barely wide enough for him to squeeze through if he turned sideways. He turned sideways and squeezed through, following the mysterious flickering light that danced ahead of him.

Orson kept going and going, and the crack in the mountain proved to be a passage. It widened until Orson could walk comfortably. Perhaps too comfortably. He was striding confidently along when the ground disappeared from beneath his feet. He fell quite a long way before he landed hard enough to drive all the air from his lungs and all the thoughts from his head. He succumbed to a darkness that was darker even than the inside of the mountain.

7. Horses Don't Hiss and Snakes Aren't Furry

There was a young dandy who dressed
His physique in the stylish best
Until he did fatten
And split seams of satin
Now he is mostly undressed
-Bayerd the Storyteller, Limerick

Bayerd kept putting one foot in front of the other, feeling his way in the dark. They had been walking for what felt like eons and were forced to ration the torches for brief periods at a time. All three men were tormented by thirst, having bypassed hunger long ago. They were bone-weary and disoriented, but at least the tunnel hadn't come to a dead end, sealing their fate and becoming their grave. Although it was the grave for other poor souls. They had tripped over so many skeletons, Bayerd had lost count. The deeper they went under the mountain, the more plentiful the boney fellows became.

It proved quite impossible to judge time and distance when there was no light, and nothing to mark their bearings except bones. The tunnel narrowed gradually until the horses had a tight squeeze in spots. The men took turns leading the way, since it was the most treacherous role. The lead man was the one most likely to whack his head on low rocks, or collide with the wall if the tunnel angled sharply, or step off into space if the ground dropped away. The lead man ended up with enough bumps and bruises to feel like he had been the loser in a drunken brawl, so it was only fair that they took it in turns.

At the moment, it was Bayerd's turn to lead the way. He knew that he was, literally, on his last legs. Gerald, too, was failing. His body was older and more worn. It was remarkable that he was still upright. Bayerd attributed that to the strength of the man's spirit.

Bayerd trailed his fingers along the rock wall and shuffled carefully along in the pitch blackness. When the top of his head scraped rock, he tugged Mercury's head lower and called back, "You'll have to duck here."

Both men said, "Aye," and he knew they were both still on their feet.

He kept moving forward, feeling like he was going nowhere at all. His mind wandered, absently weaving the events of his quest into a tale of adventure—a tale that would keep an audience on the edge of its bench. If he survived, he vowed to himself that he would script a fantastic tale about his quest. And it was high time that he scripted a brand new tale. He had been resting on his laurels. He could see that now with his eyes newly opened.

Perhaps another hour passed before he bumped into something. He blinked, coming out of his stupor. He might have been sleepwalking. What had he bumped into? It hadn't felt like rock. It had felt softer, furrier. Disoriented, he thought he had bumped into a horse's rump. Except wasn't he in the lead? And then he heard a low hiss. Horses did not hiss and snakes weren't furry, so what had he encountered? Bayerd was quite sure it was nothing good.

He stumbled back, fumbling with the flint stone to light the remnants of the last torch. The flint sparked twice before it caught. Bayerd held it in front of him like a shield, blinded by the light after so many hours of profound darkness. A large black silhouette danced before him. No, that was a shadow on the tunnel wall, but a shadow cast by what or whom? A rather high-pitched cry escaped his lips when someone said, "Greetings, trespassers."

Not a bear or wildcat then, since such animals had never been known to speak. "Greetings," Bayerd gasped in return. Before his eyes could adjust to the light and see who was in the tunnel with them, the torch died. It was spent.

"Who's there?" Jabalot demanded from behind.

"I don't know!" Bayerd cried.

"You are ssseeking passage through our tunnel?" the stranger's voice asked. It was not low or high, but pitched somewhere in the middle. There was a hissy quality to the words, as well as a rhythmic cadence that was unusual, as if it was keeping time with beating wings, or perhaps the speaker's own heartbeat.

"We are, although seeking passage out of your tunnel would be a more accurate statement," Bayerd replied. "There was a rockslide at the other end and we were trapped in this passage. You claim it as your own?"

"It is our tunnel. No-one leavesss unless we let them out."

Bayerd sighed. "But you let them in for free?"

"Of courssse."

"I suppose there is a hefty toll to pay to leave your tunnel?" Bayerd could have said 'to live', but he did not want to offend the person who was the master of their fate.

"Yesss." The voice trailed off in a menacing hiss.

"Can we at least discuss this in the light, so I can see who it is that I bargain with?" he asked.

"Follow me," the tunnel-dweller said, as if there was more than one direction to take.

They started walking again and before long, the darkness was not quite so dark. It lightened by degrees, allowing their eyes to adjust. The air grew fresher, too, making Bayerd realize just how stale it had been in the depths.

When they stumbled out of the tunnel, he found himself in an enormous space, the likes of which he had never seen, and he had done his fair share of travelling. It was an even greater surprise because he had expected to step into the out-of-doors, not an oversized room in what appeared to be an exotic palace of some foreign sort.

Polished crystal walls enclosed a vast dome-shaped room, punctured by about a dozen arched doorways, each the same as the last. Only three of the doorways had symbols carved above them, identifying them in some way that Bayerd couldn't decipher. The symbols were not ones he recognized. He glanced behind and noted that they had exited through an identical doorway, one without a symbol.

Subdued sunlight beamed in through a large round opening in the center of the domed ceiling, and a ceiling is not where windows are normally found. There was only one piece of furniture. It was in the center of the room, and it was round, too. The circular stone bench was carved with intricate designs and overlaid with thick fur covers. It was hollow in the center, surrounding a firepit of low flame and glowing coal. Anyone who sat on that seat would be warm and toasty.

In-between the doorways, a network of crystal basins were carved into the walls, or perhaps it was just one very long wall, since it was a circular room. A steady trickle of water ran from the highest basins down to the lowest, almost like rain. A tracery of broad-leafed vines clung to the areas around the basins, like nature's curtains.

"This room is quite fantastic. The other side of the mountain is very different," he rasped. Bayerd's throat was so parched, he couldn't even swallow, so speaking was not easy. The water tempted him in the worst way, but he had not yet been offered water. He also hadn't yet introduced himself properly.

"Other ssside of the mountain." Their guide chuckled and shed a furry cape, turning to face them.

Bayerd stared at the stranger. A female, he realized, wearing a simple shift that was scandalously brief, stopping at mid-thigh. And she was short, almost as short as a jester, and uncommonly muscular for a woman. Her skin was as pale as a larva, and rather scaly. Her eyes were an eerie pink. Her hair was as fine as cobweb, and just as colourless.

"Greetings," he said, dumbstruck by her appearance. He had never heard even one tale about such beings who looked half man and half ... what? Snake? Fish? Lizard?

She smiled and her face somehow remained lineless while the scales bracketing her mouth and surrounding her eyes overlapped each other, compacting most efficiently. Her exposed teeth were as pointy as a snake's fangs. "It has been some time since we discovered a man in our tunnelsss, and to find three in one fell swoop. Quite unexpected. You've even brought your horsesss to visit. I'm sure they've left a mess of poop in our tunnelsss."

Bayerd cleared his throat as best he could. "Not as much as one might expect since they've had no hay to eat for days. And the tunnels were not pristine to begin with, littered as they are with the bones of the dead." Bayerd attempted a disarming smile and declared, "I am Prince Bayerd from the Golden Kingdom, and you are?"

"Rianth of the Second Order. Ssso, not just a man, but a prince of the outer realm. Should I bow before you?" Everything she said sounded like a hissing chant in her rhythmic cadence.

"You are not one of my subjects, so no, I don't think a bow is in order." No-one bowed to Bayerd in his own kingdom anyway, but he didn't mention that.

Rianth approached the fire and hissed into it. As if she had sent a message through the flame, more of her kind filed through one of the arched doorways—the one marked with a spiral symbol overhead. Compact scaly men and women, all wearing simple shifts with short pleated skirts, moved to encircle Bayerd and his last two knights.

82

Gerald was stooped like an old man, leaning against his horse for support. The horses were swaying on their hooves.

"My men need to sit down, perhaps drink some water if you have water to spare," Bayerd said, licking his cracked lips. "The horses are quite thirsty, too, I'm sure."

Another woman who looked a lot like their guide, except scalier, stepped forward. "I am Suth of the First Order, and water you may have. We would not refuse to share what we have in plenty." Suth motioned to the basins in a 'help yourself' gesture.

Bayerd assisted Gerald to walk to the nearest basin, followed by the man's horse. The pair sucked water noisily, sharing the same basin. Jabalot and his horse didn't hesitate to find their own basin. When Gerald seemed steady, Bayerd moved to a nearby basin with Mercury and they drank greedily. The water was cool and pure. Water had never tasted so sweet. Why did men crave wine when they could drink water instead? Bayerd gulped until his stomach bulged, and even then it did not seem like enough water to quench his thirst.

He stopped drinking when Mercury backed away from the water, tugging on the reins. If his horse had had enough to drink, Bayerd should be satisfied, too.

Suth was waiting, very close—too close. She said, "We will take care of the horsesss for you. Our monarch will bargain with you over the toll to be paid for passage through our tunnelsss."

Bayerd gave his reins over to her. She handed them to another. All the horses were led out through the arched doorway identified with the symbol of a wavy line to identify it.

"Rianth will show you the way," Suth said.

Rianth nodded once. "Accompany me."

Flanked by his knights, Bayerd followed Rianth through the last remaining archway with a symbol over it. This one looked like three interwoven flames. They found themselves in another tunnel. It was blessedly short—they could see light at the end of it.

Gerald murmured, "I don't have a good feeling about this."

Jabalot said, "Do you think we'll ever see our horses again?"

"We are being treated with courtesy. Show our hosts the proper respect," Bayerd whispered back.

The tunnel turned into shallow stairs, carved into the rock beneath their feet. They tromped down, down, down, and ended up in a much smaller room that had roughhewn stone walls. The air was hazy with a pungently sweet-scented smoke. The window was again in the ceiling, casting a dim light down from above, made all the dimmer by the mistiness of the room.

Only three of the scaly people were in this room, sitting in what looked like a grand sunken fireplace that was cut into both the wall and the ground. They were all women, each crowned with a high pile of the fine cobwebby hair. He could see their necks and heads, while their bodies were concealed under fur, in the shallow pit of the fireplace. The haze rose from there, further obscuring the bodies of the three women. Their heads were at least three times larger than the others of their kind. Their necks were uncommonly long, not in a swan-like graceful way, but in a squirmy serpentine way. Their mouths were too wide and inclined to protrude, as did their jaws.

Gentle heat emanated from the nook, dispelling the dank chill that seemed to seep in from the tunnel. Rianth extended surprisingly graceful arms toward the trio. She cupped her hands and held them there as if begging.

The central woman leaned forward and blew into the cupped hands. A small cluster of flames appeared and burned in Rianth's hands as if there was kindling there. All three women spoke at the same time in a strange hissing tongue that Bayerd could not understand.

Rianth understood and replied, "I have captured three men in the tunnelsss, and three horses. One man is a prince of the Golden Kingdom in the outer realm. He is their leader and will ssspeak for them." The flame kept burning in her hands, yet Rianth showed no sign of distress.

More hissing came from the three women.

"Captured?" Bayerd mouthed. He hadn't felt captured. He had felt almost like a guest, at least until that moment.

Rianth turned to Bayerd, still holding the flames in her cupped hands "The Tri-Alanth will bargain with you. You must hold the flame to hear her."

"Huh?"

"You cannot understand her wordsss unless you hold the flame," she hissed.

"Which one is the Tri-Alanth?" he asked, delaying. He did not want to hold fire. Fire was hot, fire burnt flesh, as Bayerd knew better than most men after his close encounter with a dragon.

"They all are the Tri-Alanth. Do not extinguish the flame until a bargain has been agreed upon. If you do, there will be no bargain at all. You will forfeit your right to exit the tunnelsss, if you extinguish the flame before a bargain is ssstruck."

"You mean we would have to stay here forever?" Bayerd said.

"Yesss."

He gulped. "But ... that flame looks hot."

"It isss."

Bayerd stuck a finger into the flames she held and jerked it out. "Ouch. But ... aren't you getting burnt?"

"I do not burn." She proffered her scaly hands, holding that crackling flame.

Did she expect Bayerd to simply take it? He linked his hands behind his back. "But I do burn."

"Then you should ssstrike your bargain quickly."

"What sort of bargain? What toll do most travelers pay?" Gerald asked.

"It is alwaysss different." She tried to hand Bayerd the flame again.

He kept his hands linked behind his back like a child. "Wait, I'm not ready. I must confer with my men." Bayerd turned to face them. "We have little to bargain with, unless one of you has a stash of coins or some other riches on your person."

Both shook their heads.

"Well ... I'm not eager to hold fire."

Gerald slapped him on the back. "Then bargain quickly, as Rianth advised, and pray we have something they want, or I fear we will be sent back into the tunnel to die like all those other poor souls whose bones we trod upon."

Bayerd would have preferred more encouraging words. He returned to Rianth. "If you act as translator, I won't need to hold the flame."

She shook her head. "I cannot ssspeak for you. You must ssstrike your own bargain."

"Let's get this over with then." He reached out, his hands cupped as hers were. She deposited the little ball of flames into them. It continued to burn there, every bit as hot as he had expected. No, hotter. He cursed and fell to his knees. "What toll?" he gasped, sweat running down his face.

The three women spoke as one. "Ten yearsss each digging in the tunnelsss." The words were still spoken in a hissing tongue, but now he understood them.

"What? Ah! Damn."

"Ten yearsss each digging in the tunnelsss."

"I heard you. That is no bargain, that is a death sentence." Bayerd shifted the flame to his left hand and blew on his right. It was so red and blistered, he might as well have stuck it into a dragon's mouth.

"You can offer one man for thirty years and two will be free to leave," the Tri-Alanth hissed.

"Ah! No, I can't leave a man behind."

"Choose yourself and your men will go free."

"No!" Bayerd cried.

"You can counter bargain," Rianth said.

"Ouch, ouch, ouch. One man for one year. Me." He tried to blow on his screaming left hand. It only made the flame hotter. The experience was as bad as when Darton the Dark had tortured him with redhot coals after he had been poisoned. He had almost forgotten about that, or blocked out the painful memory.

"One man for twenty years."

"Three horses," Bayerd screamed in agony and writhed.

"Done," the Tri-Alanth said.

Bayerd couldn't believe his ears. "What?"

"The bargain is ssstruck. We have great need of horses. We would have accepted one." All three large heads chuckled rather nastily.

Rianth scooped the flame out of his hand before he had the wits to extinguish it himself. He collapsed to the ground. Since he was down there anyway, he rolled around a bit, whimpering. It felt like both his palms still burned. Well, fire was like that. The pain of a burn did not ease nearly as quickly as the pain of an arrow puncture or a sword slash, as he knew from experience.

Gerald helped him to his feet by yanking on his elbow. "Come put your hands in the water. It will cut the pain." He led Bayerd over to a wall-basin with a running stream of water, just like in the larger chamber. Bayerd plunged his hands in, trying not to sob. He did not want his two remaining knights to think him a crybaby as well as a fool and a coward.

"So, we're without horses now?" Gerald said. "What did they offer first?"

"Ten years for each of us, digging in the tunnels." Bayerd did not volunteer the information that the Tri-Alanth would have accepted one horse instead of three. He didn't want to appear more the sucker than he already felt.

"Horses aren't such a bad deal then. I'm sure you'll replace mine when we get back to the castle." Gerald winked.

"Do not doubt it. You will have your choice of the finest horse in the royal stables." He leaned his forehead against the cool stone. The wall helped him to stay upright. "But I fear our quest will now take much longer than planned."

"At least we won't be trapped in these cursed tunnels. I can't wait to get the hell out of here," Jabalot snapped. Without a doubt, they all felt the same.

Rianth escorted them back to the large round chamber. Not a soul was there now. "Farewell men of the outer realm," she said, and turned to leave.

"Farewell," Bayerd said, having trouble focusing on anything other than screaming pain of his hands.

"Wait!" Gerald said. "We need the packs that were on our horses, and our bedrolls and weapons. They were not part of the bargain, only the horses were. "

Rianth smiled and nodded. "That isss true. I will return with your property shortly." She headed for one of the arched doorways marked by a symbol.

"Hold on," Jabalot called after her. "We'll trade the tack for some rations and half a dozen torches. We haven't eaten in days and have no need for saddles now that we are without horses."

She considered that for a moment, nodded and went on her way.

While they waited, they drank more water and Bayerd soaked his hands. He even dipped his whole head in the water to wash away the saltiness of sweat. Gerald and Jabalot settled on the round bench. Bayerd soon headed that way, pacing before them because he was in too much agony to sit still.

"Odd place, isn't it," Gerald said.

"Bloody weird," Jabalot concurred. "I wonder why no man has ever returned to our kingdom from the other side of this mountain."

Bayerd blinked at him. "What are you talking about?"

"I've heard tell of it. Any man who crosses over this mountain is never seen again. That's why men don't come here. Never. T'is a curse place."

Gerald snorted. "That's nothing but a tall tale. Men don't come here because there's no reason to come here, nothing to gain. What fool would climb a mountain simply because it is there?"

"How do you explain all the bones in the tunnels then?" Jabalot retorted.

Gerald didn't have an answer for that, and his brow furrowed into deep worry lines.

"The tunnel-dwellers are letting us exit their tunnels," Bayerd said, "so we will return from the heart of the mountain, won't we?"

On cue, Rianth and Suth arrived with two men, each carrying an armload of packs, bedrolls and weapons. They lowered them onto the bench along with six torches.

"And rations?" Gerald asked.

"A sack of food isss being prepared. I will fetch it." Rianth and Suth left together, with the men.

Alone again, they organized their supplies. Gerald took a look at Bayerd's hands and tut-tutted. "You won't be able to use them for days. Let me wrap them. I've got some salve here that I use on my horse. It should stop the blisters from splitting apart when they start to dry out."

Bayerd nodded. "Thank you, Gerald. My hands would appreciate it more than they can say."

Gerald applied salve and Bayerd did his best not to scream. The strips of cloth Gerald wrapped atop the salve felt like sandpaper. Even with the wraps, Bayerd couldn't bear to use his hands, so Gerald organized Bayerd's supplies. He filled the two empty wine jugs to the brim with water.

The food arrived and it was a small sack indeed. Suth handed it to Bayerd, who received it with his forearms. "Thank you, Suth. Can you show us the way out now?"

"You are free to leave, but I cannot show you the way. That was not part of the bargain. Choose any doorway except for the three that are marked as our private quartersss. One of the other doorways will lead you out." Her face was expressionless enough to prove that she was wholly uncaring of their fate. "You have until thisss room darkens to make your choice, and to depart. If you passs this way again, it will require a second toll to attempt to leave."

"Trickery," Jabalot cried and grabbed for his sword. The fire hissed angrily behind him.

"Stop," Bayerd commanded Jabalot, his voice echoing like thunder around the domed chamber. It halted everyone in their tracks. Into the stillness, Bayerd said softly, "There is no need for bloodshed."

"Leave before the room darkensss," Suth hissed at them. She hurriedly departed through the same marked doorway that she had just used. Jabalot scowled after her, hand still gripping his pommel as if he might yank his blade out and give chase.

"Jabalot, Gerald, have a look through each of the unmarked archways. See if you can tell which one leads outside," Bayerd said, to distract Jabalot from violence. There were ten unmarked archways.

Jabalot circled one half of the room and Gerald circled the other. Bayerd waited on the round bench, his hands cradled in his lap. Fatigue was settling heavily upon him, as if the pain in his hands was sapping the dregs of his meager strength.

He could hear the fire crackling behind him. Perhaps because his body was rocking in pain, he noticed that the fire's snapping and crackling also had a rhythm, and its hissing sounded like the Tri-Alanth's tongue when he could not understand it—when he was not holding a flame.

Between them, Gerard and Jabalot stepped through every archway. When they reported back to Bayerd, he knew by their expressions that they did not bring glad tidings.

"Not one of them presents itself as a doorway to the outside world. They all lead into tunnels. I fear we are still deep in the mountain," Gerald said. "Probably only halfway through. I suspect we are in the very heart of the mountain."

"That must be why the light and water come from above. There must be fissures in the mountain, or they have dug tunnels going up," Bayerd said. Or they had had their prisoners do it for them. Every man who ever explored the mountain had probably found a tunnel that tempted him, a tunnel that he was curious to explore, perhaps dreaming of a vein of gold or a cache of precious gems. And then he spent the rest of his life paying for it with a shovel, since most men would not have brought their horses along. Only the rockslide had forced Bayerd and his men to take their horses into the heart of the mountain with them.

And the tunnel-dwellers did have their own code of honour. They did not steal, instead they made bargains. Tricky, yet honest bargains.

"We'll simply have to find the right tunnel to get out of the mountain," Bayerd said. "We have a one in ten chance."

"One in nine." Gerald sat down beside him and pointed. "That's the tunnel we arrived through. T'was directly opposite the tunnel with that flame symbol. And it smells of horse poop."

"One in nine." Bayerd sighed.

"Aye." Jabalot rubbed his chin, which now sprouted stubble long enough to be called a beard. "I could use my sword, convince one of them scaly folk to tell us which tunnel to take. A few stabs and they'll be spilling the beans along with their guts."

Bayerd shifted on the seat when the fire at his back felt hotter all of the sudden. And was it his imagination, or did the hissing flames sound angry? "Calm yourself, Jabalot. We will use our minds rather than our swords to solve this puzzle."

"Let's eat while we decide on a tunnel," Gerald said. "I've been too long without food." He opened the sack. Bayerd was expecting hard cheese and bread and dried meat, perhaps a few apples. He couldn't have been more wrong.

"Worms? Grubs? Beetles? And not even cooked?" Jabalot snapped. "What sort of food is this?"

"Probably what they dine on." Gerald helped himself to a worm. He did not chew it and swallowed hard when he gulped it down whole. "I've eaten worse in the battlefield," he said.

Jabalot shook his head when Gerald offered him a choice of worm or grub "It's all yours, old man. Unless Bayerd here is hankering for a grub or two."

"No, thank you." Pain had robbed Bayerd of his appetite, and he did not have the use of his hands to eat. He could not abide having one of his men hand feed him like a babe-in-arms.

While Gerard choked down more of the worms and grubs, Bayerd studied the archways, trying to guess which one might lead them directly out of the mountain. If the tunnel back to their side of the mountain hadn't been blocked, he probably would have headed home with his tail between his legs and to hell with the quest. But it was blocked, so they had to keep going—probably straight through the mountain to the far side.

He rose and circled the room, stepping inside each tunnel and listening hard, and sniffing the air. If they were only halfway through the mountain, they would have days of walking before they knew if they had taken the correct tunnel, or condemned themselves to die in some dead end passage.

The tunnels provided no clues and he returned to his men. Gerald was looking a mite queasy, and Jabalot simply looked hungry. Bayerd sat down between them and found himself rocking again, this time in rhythm with the beat he could hear in the flames.

"I do think I have figured out which passage is the one we seek," he said, to test an idea that was taking root in his mind. On cue, the hissing in the flames increased in volume.

"Which one?" Gerald asked.

"Let me think on it awhile longer," he said.

His back to the flames, he touched a burnt finger to his lips, signaling his men to keep silent. He looked down at his hands with regret and unwound the strip of cloth on the left one. Gerald raised an eyebrow in a silent question. Bayerd attempted a cocky grin. His face did not cooperate.

"How did you enjoy your supper, Sir Gerald?" he asked.

Gerald was savvy enough to realize that Bayerd wanted him to fill the air with words. "The worms were too gritty, while the larvae were too mushy. And the beetles, well, they were simply too crunchy. I have little legs stuck between my teeth. And everything needed some spice. Even though I ate a meal prepared for three men, my stomach still rumbles with hunger, as you can probably hear."

He continued on with the inane chatter. All the while, Bayerd was busy tying the cloth strip around his finger, so it would dangle down. When it was in place, he stood up and clumsily lifted his pack with his wrists. He fumbled it in the direction of the fire and said, "My hands are useless. I'm all thumbs." The end of the strip dropped into the fire and caught.

He fumbled the pack onto the bench and flicked the burning end of the strip back at the same time. He caught it with his left hand, holding the flame.

The pain was double what it had been the first time. He sat down hard, cupping the flame, hiding it from the main fire as if the fire had eyes. "I think our exit is the first passage to the left of the left of the doorway we arrived through." As hard as he tried to speak normally, he had to talk through gritted teeth to control the pain.

"Men from the outer realm are such fools," said three hissing voices behind him, coming from the flames themselves.

He had been right! The fire had a voice, the same three voices as the Tri-Alanth, three voices that always spoke as one. And it was confirmed that the passage to the immediate left of the marked doors was not the escape route they sought. "Which passage do you think it is, Gerald," he choked out.

"Uh, the one to the right of the tunnel that brought us here," he said.

"Wrong again," cackled the flames, in laughter.

"Jabalot, what's your guess?"

"Uh …"

"Quickly," Bayerd snapped. The smell of his burning flesh was making him sick.

"The one to the right of their marked doorways," he said.

The flames laughed snidely.

Bayerd glanced desperately at Gerald, who said, "No, t'is the one to the left of those doors."

The flames stopped laughing. "They don't know it is truth. They merely guess wildly," hissed the flames.

That was proof enough for Bayerd. He fell off the bench and pressed his palm against the damp earthen floor, extinguishing the cursed flames. He vomited up water when pain twisted his guts, wringing out the only thing in his stomach.

He could not hear what the flames said about that. Normal hissing and crackling were all he could hear. Gerald hauled him up and his two men sort of carry/dragged him to a basin. His hand was plunged into the cool water and the relief was not enough. He hung between them, sweating enough to soak through his clothes.

"Do you know which tunnel to take?" Gerald whispered in his ear. Bayerd nodded, and dunked his head at the same time. Gerald squeezed his arm. "Then I think we should depart without delay."

Bayerd nodded again, and dunked again. He rinsed his mouth, drank a bit, and felt capable of speech. "Grant me another minute and we'll be on our way." He breathed through the pain and when he could stand on his own two feet, he again filled his stomach with water. It would have to sustain him for a very long time, he knew.

He staggered toward the tunnel that would lead them out of the mountain. Gerald and Jabalot gathered their gear in passing, and followed Bayerd into the tunnel to the left of the mountain-dwellers marked doorways.

Behind him, Bayerd could hear the angry hissing of the flames as it reached a crescendo, complete with explosive popping sparks that shot into the air like mini fireworks.

Gerald lit a torch with his flint and took the lead. He set a quick pace that Bayerd struggled to match. Jabalot brought up the rear and he kept his sword in hand—a wise precaution. He kept shoving Bayerd to move it along with his other hand.

Once again, they walked through the darkness and dank earth. They were able to move much faster without the hindrance of the horses. The new tunnel was littered with as many bones as the previous one. They walked until they couldn't put one foot in front of the other, and then they fell down. They slept like that, sprawled in the dirt. And when they awoke, they drank a ration of water and resumed walking. Their water eventually ran out, but the torches held. They were superior to the torches Bayerd was accustomed to. They burned longer, cleaner and brighter.

After what must have been several days, Bayerd began to doubt himself. And he began to ramble with delirium. "Left. Is that my left or your left? Maybe it was the right, if your left was my right. It was hard to think when my hand was on fire, you know. Poor Mercury, such a nice horse, doomed to the underground. Swift will never forgive me. He's probably worn all my clothes by now, and pissed in them."

Jabalot told him to shut up. Gerald told Jabalot to shut up. Bayerd said, "Am I seeing double? Or is that a fork in the tunnel?"

8. The Man with No Memories

Bones be white
Skulls see black
And not a thing more
For eyes they lack
Skulls must look forward
For they can't look back

-Bayerd the Storyteller, Skull-duggery

The man awoke to darkness. He did not know who he was or where he was. He knew very little, in fact, except that he was lost in a dark maze and his head hurt. He got to his feet and started walking. When a strange light appeared in the distance, he followed it since it was the only thing that seemed to exist in the black tunnels that he wandered.

The man kept following the light, getting hungrier and thirstier, and praying it would guide him out of the underground. He stepped on more and more bones of men, crunching them beneath his boots. He knew they were the bones of men because he had picked some up and had a good old grope. He had felt long leg bones, and skulls, and ribcages. Some bones still had dried bits of flesh and muscle clinging stubbornly. He wasn't starved enough to gnaw on those. He was a man, not a wild dog. He knew that much.

He was lucky enough to find a torch, still clutched in a boney hand. He used a flint stone he found in his pocket to spark it to life, and then he had light. It took some time for his eyes to adjust, and when he could see, the tunnel was pretty much as it had felt beneath his hands. The walls were damp roughhewn gray stone and packed clay, and a fair number of bones littered the ground. Just how many poor souls had found their final resting place in the strange underground maze? Too many to count was the answer.

The man kept moving forward, no longer following the mysterious light which had not guided him out, or to food, or water, or other men. He followed his own torch light, and when he came to a fork in the path, he took the one that branched off to the right because the mysterious light kept following the main artery to the left.

There were fewer skeletons in the smaller passage. One had a bottle beside it. He shook it and liquid sloshed inside. Water? Drinkable water perhaps? He uncorked it and sniffed. It smelled like water, rather stale water, but beggars can't be choosers. He took a cautious little sip and it was stale water. It still tasted delicious. He drank half of what was in the bottle and saved the rest, in case it took him a long time to find his way out of the maze, or chance upon more water.

A few times, he thought he heard rustling in the tunnels. When that happened, he quickly extinguished his torch and went in the other direction. He did not want to meet what lived down in the depths. If he did, he would probably end up just as skeletal as all the other boney fellows that kept him company.

9. A Diamond for Your Thoughts

I held the fire
For it was my turn
Oh, my flesh did char
And my guts did churn
And boil and bubble
And turn, turn, turn
Like meat on a spit
Yet I did not burn

-Bayerd the Storyteller, One of Nine Lives

It was a fork in the tunnel. No doubt about it. Bayerd, Gerald and Jabalot stood like rooted trees and simply gaped at it. Tears might have been shed. The tunnel split into two passages, and each branch looked identical to the other.

"We'll never leave this cursed place. Never," Jabalot moaned. "No wonder no man has ever returned from this mountain. They all reside down here as skeletons."

Gerald lowered the torch he was holding and said, "Isn't that tunnel a little brighter?" He pointed to the left branch.

It did seem to be. "Let's go have a look-see," Bayerd said, stumbling into the passage first. A dozen paces proved it—there was light up ahead. Sunlight—it had to be sunlight. They had found their way back to the outside world!

They walked faster and faster, laughing like loons. They began to run and shout with joy. The passage curved gently. Bayerd dashed around it, and then he stopped. Jabalot slammed into him. Gerald slammed into them both, knocking Bayerd to his knees.

Not one of them said a word. Their disappointment was so profound, it was as pain. It was worse even than the pain of Bayerd's burnt hands, or the pain of torture. He sank lower, until his legs were folded beneath him, and he gazed at the dead end of the passage. The source of the light was no brilliant sun, it was but a small fire that crackled in a circle of stones, mocking them.

"The other branch must lead to the outer world," Gerald said, his voice expressionless. "At least we have wasted little time. We haven't travelled down this one any distance at all." He was certainly proving himself an optimist. He turned around. "Let's go back. The other passage will surely take us home."

Bayerd tried to dredge up the energy to stand. Before he could, Jabalot said, "What's that sparkling in the wall? Is that a gem?" He stumbled over to where the passage ended and pulled out his sword. He scraped at earth that was so hard-packed, it could have been rock. In a minute, he cried out in triumph and turned, holding up what appeared to be a large glittering diamond.

"Can't be real," Gerald said and took a closer look. He even scratched it across one of the empty wine jugs they still carried in case they found more water. It left a deep scratch in the glass.

"See, it is a diamond, a beauty. I bet these walls are laced with gemstones." Jabalot stuffed the diamond into his pouch and returned to the wall, using his sword to dig again.

"Jabalot, diamonds will not feed us, and we cannot drink diamonds. We must return to the main passage and continue our trek, whilst we still have the strength to do so," Bayerd said, finally finding his feet.

Gerald approached the wall near the fire, empty wine jug still in hand. "There's a dribble of water leaching out of the crack in the rock here. Perhaps it is even drinkable." He scratched a shallow trough with his sword to direct the wetness and propped the wine bottle against the crack to catch the water. "Let's stay long enough to see if the water is potable."

"I wouldn't mind a little drink," Bayerd said, licking lips that felt like old cracked leather. He sat down against the wall to watch the bottle fill, drip by excruciatingly slow drip.

Gerald joined Jabalot, digging at the wall with his sword. By the time the bottle was full, which was a very long time indeed, Gerald had found an impressive, blood-red ruby.

They tested the water and it proved pure and crisp. They each drank a third of the bottle and propped it up to refill it. Gerald and Jabalot kept excavating the tunnel wall. Jabalot found the next gem, a dark green emerald. The bottle was full again, so they drank again. The bottle was returned to the wall until Gerald found a huge blue sapphire.

97

Bayerd simply watched, his hands unable to hold a sword or any digging implement at all. His job was to keep charge of the water. He heated one bottle over the fire and they drank the water hot, just for a change. When their thirst had been fully slaked, Bayerd corked a full jug and started filling the second. Periodically, he napped. Gerald and Jabalot took turns sleeping in shifts. And they found more gems. And they drank more water. Their repetitive actions took on a rhythmic beat that was mirrored by the crackling flames. The beat lulled Bayerd into a dreamlike stupor that was quite pleasant indeed.

10. Bayerd the Skull

Skull is a very happy chap
His bald head is ideal
To wear a jaunty cap
He never stops grinning
From ear to ear
Though he has none
So he cannot hear
He speaks no evil
For he has no tongue
The songs in his head
Must remain unsung
He sees no evil
For he has no eyes
Not a tear flows
When he laughs
Until he cries.

-Bayerd the Storyteller, My Friend the Skull

The man who did not know who he was, finished his water, and lucked upon another torch, which allowed him to search for more water as he journeyed through what felt like an entire underground land. He might have gotten a bit delirious, because he took to carrying a skull around with him. He christened it 'Bayerd', although he knew not why. They had lengthy conversations that were quite nonsensical. Bayerd was a rather silly skull who liked to tell silly tales.

When the man napped, he kept Bayerd the Skull safely tucked under his arm, like a child's ragdoll, although the skull was hard rather than soft. And then one day, the man noticed that the tunnel wasn't quite so dark. He was so tormented by thirst that he couldn't even swallow or spare the tears of joy that sprang to his eyes. He tried to walk faster and fell to his knees. He got up, and leaning on his sword as if it was a cane, he stumbled forward. The bright light dazzled his eyes and the air smelled fresh and breezy. He took one more step and felt sunshine kiss his face.

He had escaped the black maze!

A panoramic view of foothills delighted his eyes. The sky was bright blue with puffy cottony clouds. He was quite sure they were the most beautiful clouds he had ever seen and he knew what clouds were, even though he couldn't recall ever having seen clouds before. His personal memories were limited to his time in the black maze.

The man breathed deeply, cleansing his lungs of stale tunnel air. He smiled up at the sun. When he heard the gurgle of water, he laughed aloud and traced the sound to a bright babbling brook that flowed down through the foothills where he had ended up. He fell to his knees and drank deeply. When his thirst was finally quenched, he dunked his whole head in the creek. The water was icy cold and invigorating.

He dunked Bayerd the Skull in the water, too, in case his tunnel companion was thirsty. He certainly needed a wash. When he lifted Bayerd the Skull out of the creek, he did seem brighter and happier. "Well, my friend, we have survived to live another day," the man who couldn't remember his own name declared.

Bayerd agreed wholeheartedly, and grinned as widely as he ever did.

11. Beneath a Rock and a Hard Place

There once was a young man from Elsewhere
Whose mind was as blank as it was bare
He spent all his time
Thinking in rhyme
His thoughts going entirely nowhere
-Bayerd the Storyteller, Limerick

Bayerd awoke from a nap, stood up and stretched. His pants fell off. He pulled them back up without thinking too much about it. He tightened his belt a couple of notches to hold his pants in place, and scratched his face. It was rather hairy. His stubble had grown into a full beard. It was reminiscent of the time when he had awoken from more than a month of sleep, after being shot with a poisoned arrow by Musspish. And then he realized something else. He had used his hands to fasten his belt and scratch his face. He unwrapped the cloth bandages and studied his palms. They were scarred by fire, especially the left one, yet they were fully healed.

His heart began to beat faster—faster than the drum-like beat of the flames. 'How long have we been here?' he thought, wary to speak aloud. Both water bottles were full. He automatically lifted one to drink when a thought struck him—could the water be laced with magic? It did have a sweet taste that curbed the appetite to be sure.

Gerald was the one digging for gems while Jabalot napped. Bayerd approached Gerald. "Gerald, how many gems have you got in your pouch?" he asked in a whisper, beside the man's ear. Gerald blinked as though coming awake. He had a beard, too, yet it did not hide the gauntness of his face. How had Bayerd not noticed the man's changed appearance before now?

"Don't know," Gerald said, his voice rusty from disuse.

"Let me count them for you." Bayerd took Gerald's pouch and sat down beside the sleeping Jabalot. Gerald kept digging at the wall.

With a pickpocket's light fingers, Bayerd removed Jabalot's pouch from his belt. He emptied both pouches of their cache of gems. Two piles of riches glittered on the dirty ground—more than he had expected and more than he had feared. He tallied them up. Jabalot had seventy-eight. Gerald had seventy-two. He put the gems back in their respective pouches, mulling things over.

They found about one gem per filled bottle of water. So that would mean they had been excavating the tunnel for one hundred and fifty bottles of water, but was that one hundred and fifty hours? Or days? Or some length of time in-between. The bottle filled a drip at a time, which was a very slow rate indeed.

The end of the passage was about five feet further from the fire than when they had arrived. Had the two men truly excavated five feet of hard packed tunnel? With naught but their swords? And only water to sustain them?

Bayerd darted a glance at the fire. Why did it never go out? What fueled it? Was it the earth and rock the men dumped into it at regular intervals, from their digging? Although rock and dirt did not normally burn. The smoke that came off the fire was not normal either, or they would have been coughing and choking. Maybe there was magic in the hazy smoke rather than laced in the water. And the rhythmic beat—was it not the same as the one he had heard in the fire in the round room?

As if coming truly awake for the first time in weeks, Bayerd realized the truth of it. There was some strange magic at work here, and they were its victims, or targets. He needed to learn more about the scaly people if he and his men were to escape, and he could only think of one awful way to eavesdrop. It had worked once, so it should work again, which was really too bad. His hands had finally healed.

Acting as if he was still none the wiser, Bayerd wrapped one of the strips of cloth back around his finger, leaving a dangling end. He dampened his palm to cool it, which might help a bit, and he left the water bottles close at hand.

As prepared as he could be, he scooped up a handful of rocky debris from around Gerald's feet. The man's mindless scraping echoed the beat of the flames exactly. Bayerd carried the leavings to the fire and dropped them in, making sure the dangling bandage caught like a wick. He sat down beside the bottles, his back hiding his actions from the flames.

Promising himself it would be the last time he ever willingly held fire again, he dropped the burning end of the cloth strip into his left palm. The rhythm in the flames was instantly translated into words—a chant of, "Dig, dig, dig, dig, dig." His palm stung as if he was holding a handful of angry wasps, but Bayerd gritted his teeth and endured the pain. Overtop the repetitive chant, the flames hissed, "We will get ten feet of tunnel out of this lot before they drop dead … as greedy as every other outer realm man … they will dig themselves to death … they will pay us for their burial with a cache of precious gems … they will pay us to lick their bones clean."

Bayerd squirmed in agony and bit his lip until it bled. His theory was proved true. They were being mesmerized, but he was learning nothing of import, at least nothing worth the price he paid in pain. Curse the Tri-Alanth for their foul magic, never forcing, but preying upon man's greedy nature to ensure his own downfall. He wanted to leap to his feet and shout at the flames, confront them for their underhanded spellwork, but he knew that would endanger him and his men.

He was about to pour water on his palm and douse the unbearable heat when the flame voices said, "The tall, strong man in the tunnels remains elusive … such a waste, he would be a good digger."

Bayerd could not stand the pain one second longer and splashed water onto his palm. He fought to contain a scream that would have done a banshee proud. The water steamed on his flesh and he felt no ease. He poured more water. When he could think past the pain, he staggered up, slung his pack over his shoulder and strapped on his sword with his one good hand. He couldn't wait to get the hell out of the hellish tunnels.

He strolled up to Gerald as if he had all the time in the world and tapped him on the shoulder. "We are under a spell. We have to leave now," he whispered.

Gerald kept digging. Bayerd shook his arm. "Come with me," he ordered quietly, but in a tone dressed in iron.

Gerald blinked. "What?"

Judging that Gerald was too spellbound to think rationally, Bayerd whispered, "I've discovered a much richer vein of gems. I will show you, come with me."

"Yes, yes, yes," Gerald said, chanting in rhythm, like the flames.

Bayerd gathered the man's equipment and shoved it into Gerald's arms, then he nudged Jabalot with his toe, rather hard. Some might have called it a kick. Jabalot jerked awake saying, "I didn't kill anyone." He cleared his throat and blinked. "I mean … is it my turn to dig?"

"Yes." Bayerd crouched down beside him and whispered, "I have found a much better spot to dig, ten times as many gems. Pick up your gear and I'll show you where it is."

Jabalot stumbled up and gathered his supplies. The fire hissed louder. It realized something was amiss. Bayerd lit his torch with a flint stone, not daring to get close to the magic fire. "Time to get the hell out of here," he muttered, and herded his men ahead of him. They were not inclined to move quickly. The fire grew large behind them.

"Run if you ever want to see daylight again," he growled.

"Huh?" said Jabalot, coming to a standstill.

Bayerd pulled out his sword and jabbed the fellow in the back. "Run or I will cut you down," he roared in a voice that seemed to shake the very tunnel walls.

"Well, no need to get snippy," Jabalot said and began trotting.

"Faster!"

"But you have the torch," Gerald called back from the lead position. "I'm as blind as a bat and cannot see where I step."

"Here," Bayerd shouted and tossed him the torch.

Gerald caught it and they moved a lot faster. When they reached the fork, Jabalot said, "Where is that vein of gems?"

"Down the right branch, the one we should have taken in the first place. Now hurry!"

Jabalot scowled. "Why? I'm sure the gemstones aren't going anywhere."

Bayerd raised his sword again. "I am the leader of this misbegotten quest. Run or I will run you through!"

They ran until they could run no more, then they walked briskly, then they merely walked and walked and walked. At some point, Gerald and Jabalot came completely out of their trance and asked how long they had been in the tunnels. Bayerd had no answer, except, "I don't know."

They kept walking. Finally, when Bayerd had lost all hope of ever escaping, Gerald called, "I think I see light up ahead."

"Pray let it be sunlight," Bayerd moaned. If it was not, he would surely succumb to madness, if he wasn't mad already.

But it was sunlight. The three men stumbled out of the tunnel's entrance into a world of blinding sunlight and crisp air and blue, blue sky. They turned their faces up to the sun like spring flowers, and they smiled. They had reached the far side of the mountain. After all they had endured, they were still alive. Surely the rest of the quest would be child's play in comparison to what they had already endured.

"Never thought I would breathe fresh air again," Gerald said. His skin was pasty and papery, and he looked to have lost a stone in weight. Jabalot was nearly skeletal. Bayerd was not quite as wasted as his two men, probably because he'd had a larger store of fat to survive on. Yet all of their clothes hung on their frames, and all of them had unkempt beards. They certainly did not resemble a prince of the realm and two knights, but rather a trio of beggars who had fallen on hard times.

"I wonder how long we were in that damned mountain," Jabalot mused, scratching at his beard.

"It is hard to judge, but I have surely missed the celebration of my first wedding anniversary," Bayerd realized. "The passage of time was skewed by magic. Those scaly folk, they have magic and they do not use it for good."

"How do you know?"

Bayerd raised his freshly burnt palm. "I eavesdropped again."

Gerald studied the blistered, scarred flesh for a moment, then looked directly into Bayerd's eyes. "You are not the fool or the coward that the kingdom judges you to be, Prince Bayerd." He bowed down on one knee. "I declare myself your knight in spirit as well as in name. My sword is yours to command."

"Well, thank you, Sir Gerald, and a finer knight I have yet to meet." Bayerd cleared his throat, overcome with emotion. He pulled the knight to his feet when Gerald lacked the strength to stand.

Jabalot scowled at them both in turn. "I don't know about you two, but I'm starved. If I don't eat soon, I'm going to swoon like a lady."

"Yes, we need to hunt. At least we still have our weapons, if not our horses." Bayerd studied the land where they had ended up. They were on the lower slopes of the mountain and still had some descending to do to reach the base. They had an expansive view of the lowlands, which were not nearly as lush as those in the Golden Kingdom.

Bayerd turned to gaze up at the mountain. Even from this side, it looked like a witch's nose. And in the clear light of the sunny day, a raw scar in the earth was visible, quite near the top, where something had cut a deep and wide swatch through the trees and vegetation that clung there, and melted the snow that painted the upper reaches white.

He knew at once that the heaven stone had left that mark. Just how big was this magical crystal that the queen wanted him to fetch for her?

"Gerald, do you see that long track cut into the mountaintop." He pointed.

"Aye, looks as if a giant's plow has tried to farm the side."

Jabalot squinted. "I don't see anything." A truer statement had rarely been uttered. Bayerd had forgotten how nearsighted the fellow was, since seeing further that your own nose hadn't been necessary or possible in the tunnels.

"What of it?" Gerald prompted.

"I think it is where we will find the heaven stone we seek. We may yet succeed at this quest."

Jabalot snorted. "Forget the bleeding quest. Let's just go home."

Bayerd wanted nothing more and nothing less, except for maybe a good meal. Alas, the quest had become something more to him than finding the crystal. Succeeding at his quest would prove he was a man again, not the cowering shadow of a man that he had been for the past year. If he abandoned the quest, he was not worthy of Kelp, and might again become that spineless creature. If he succeeded, he could return to her as a hero, a man brave enough to face down any foe, a man who did not have polished toenails and far too many silly clothes.

"No, a man does not abandon a quest. We shall not return to the castle until we have captured our prize, a precious piece of the heavens to present to Queen Hellenor," Bayerd declared in his most resolute, inspiring voice, the one he used in tales when he acted the part of a battle-scarred warrior inspiring his men to rally against a superior foe.

Jabalot snorted. He was not inspired. "If we traipse up that mountain, those scaly folk are just going to capture us again."

"I don't think they will," Bayerd said. "They do seem to have their own code of honour. They did not drag us into their tunnels, we went willingly. And they did not force us to dig, our greed played a role there, and our stupidity. It is quite likely that their magic only works inside their mountain, and we shall avoid that cursed place."

Gerald nodded. "And if we have the misfortune to meet up with them again, we now have a better understanding of their nature. We will not be so susceptible to their trickery."

"I pray we do not meet them again," Bayerd said with heartfelt emotion.

Jabalot sighed. "Well, if we are going to succeed at this stupid quest, we must stay alive, and to stay alive, we must eat. No rock from the heavens is going to feed us."

"True enough." Bayerd knew a good suggestion when he heard one. "But since we have to hunt, we'll hunt in the right direction." The slash in the mountain was to the north, and up of course, way way up. "We'll keep moving north on this slope in search of game, and keep an eye out for a suitable climbing path up to the heaven stone."

Bayerd started walking and discovered exactly how weak his legs were when they almost collapsed beneath him. At least the route they took was neither uphill nor downhill. They moved along the foothill, listening for game. Jabalot spotted a small patch of berries and gobbled them all up without sharing one.

"If I shoot a deer, you will not taste a succulent morsel," Gerald told him matter-of-factly.

"Likewise," Jabalot said.

"Well, I hope someone will share with me since my hand is too burnt to hold a bow," Bayerd mentioned.

Jabalot hooted with laughter. "Burnt hand or not, you couldn't shoot an arrow to save your life, as I witnessed with my own eyes when you were in that contest against Musspish."

"With your own eyes? Then you saw nothing. And that was a long time ago, perhaps I have improved. Now sheath your tongue and step lightly, we don't want to scare away any game." Bayerd's stomach felt as empty as a shriveled husk. The belt he wore was five notches tighter than when he had left the castle, and soon to be six if they did not eat.

They moved along, quiet and watchful, until Gerald held up a warning hand and soundlessly notched an arrow. Jabalot took his cue from Gerald and notched his own arrow. Bayerd hadn't heard or seen a thing worth shooting. He did his part by standing still, so as not to snap a branch and scare away any potential dinner.

Gerald crept forth around a large round boulder. Jabalot did the same on the opposite side of the rock. Both fellows disappeared from sight and all was quiet for a time. Bayerd got a bit curious, standing still and not moving a muscle, especially when he thought he heard faint gasps and grunts. And was that the clang of metal? Was there danger on the other side of the boulder? Did his men need his help?

Bayerd started to move around Gerald's side of the boulder, then he had a better idea. He should make his approach from an unexpected direction, just in case he was walking into an ambush. He backed up several steps and stuck his toe in a crack in the boulder. The lump of rock loomed only a foot or so taller than he was, yet in his weakened condition, he had to strain to haul himself up. He found a second crack with his other toe and managed to boost himself higher. He sort of slithered atop the boulder on his belly, like a snake. It rocked a bit, but it was such a big boulder, its weight should keep it steady. He kept slithering until he had a clear view of the other side, and a most peculiar sight.

Jabalot and Gerald had dropped their bows and now had swords in hand. They were battling, but not with any foe. It was each other they fought. And since the two men were in an equally debilitated condition, their swordplay resembled that of two drunken ancients feuding over the last mug of ale.

"If I carry out my orders now, we won't have to scale a mountain on a fool's errand. We can go back to the castle if you'll ally with me in this," Jabalot said, and thrust with his blade. He could not hold it aloft and it dropped, stabbing nothing but dirt, although it did come close to chopping off Gerald's toe.

Bayerd rose to stand on the boulder, towering over the men. "I am most curious, Sir Jabalot, what are your orders in regards to this quest?" he demanded in his most forceful tone.

Both men turned to gape at him. He crossed his arms and waited for an answer, planted there atop the boulder, and then it shifted in a downward direction. He lurched in that direction and his own shifting weight made the boulder tilt and roll a bit more, and then a lot more. The rock was rounder than he had realized, and perched precariously on an incline, it seemed.

"I think you better jump down from there," Gerald called, stepping quickly to get out of the boulder's path.

Jabalot moved too, in the opposite direction. At least the boulder had stopped his men from fighting. And Bayerd wanted to get the hell off the boulder, but he was so off-balance, the only direction in which he could jump was slightly downhill, and the boulder was heading that way in lurching fits and starts. If he jumped, he would be crushed, so he found himself high-stepping in place, trying to stay on top rather than be tossed into the boulder's path and flattened. The further the rock travelled, the faster and more uncontrollably it rolled. Soon, Bayerd was almost dancing a jig atop it, frantically scanning for a safe place to leap to, one that wouldn't see him pulverized into bloody pulp.

The boulder rolled faster still, steadily downhill, crushing saplings and lesser rocks, all without slowing down. When it pitched to the left, Bayerd took his chance. He leapt off the boulder in that direction, using the stone's momentum to toss him. He flew through the air, not forward or to the side, but somewhere between the two. He landed hard, and might have lain there groaning if not for the boulder. It kept wobbling and heaving toward him as if he had a red target painted on his tunic.

He staggered to his feet and started running. The boulder stayed on his heels, getting closer and closer to crushing him like a bug. He ran faster still, drawing on some inner reserve that must be stored inside men for such times as when they must run for their lives.

His legs pounding like a blacksmith's hammer, he scanned desperately for a safe path. Alas, the clearest path that let him stay just ahead of the crushing weight was the same one the boulder was set on taking. It was the path of least resistance. And then he spotted a depression in the ground that was, perhaps, deep enough to be called a hole. Was it deep enough to shelter him? Yet too small for the boulder to drop into? Only one way to find out. Bayerd leapt headfirst into the hollow and tried to make himself as flat as possible.

The cursed boulder rumbled over him—and stopped. The depression must have acted like a cup that it had sunk into, and that was trap enough to stop it. It also turned Bayerd's sanctuary into a prison—a very small prison indeed, with barely enough space to turn over.

After a fair bit of squirming, Bayerd managed to wriggle onto his back, face up instead of face down, and yet he wasn't any better off. Perhaps he was worse off. He was nose-to-rock, as it were. The boulder was right in his face, squashing his nose a bit. He pushed on it and might as well have tried to shift a fat and fully grown dragon, if one had been sitting on him.

There was a small crack of light on one side of the depression, where the boulder did not completely seal the hole. He heard footsteps approaching. Before he could shout for help, Gerald said, "That's the end of poor Prince Bayerd. Flattened by a boulder. Guess he truly was cursed."

Bayerd opened his mouth to declare himself still alive, when Jabalot chuckled and said, "T'is a blessing, to be sure. Now we can go directly back to the castle, my mission accomplished, and forget this quest for fools. We've both gemstones enough to live as rich as kings for the rest of our days."

Bayerd would have asked Jabalot what mission he had accomplished, since they had yet to find the heaven stone, if he hadn't been compressed under the rock with the worms and beetles, one of which was crawling down his tunic. And if he eavesdropped, he might learn more than by asking questions.

The large beetle seemed intent on relocating to his trousers. Bayerd squirmed and thrashed around a bit and missed a vital bit of their conversation. That conversation ended when his men were interrupted by a most unexpected newcomer. Bayerd would have recognized the voice anywhere and anytime, for it was as familiar to him as his own.

12. The Man who would Not Die

The boulder was big
As round as a ball
Rolled right over me
Squashed flat, I did fall
Looked like the end
Hence, a shock to all
When out from under
That rock, I did crawl

-Bayerd the Storyteller, One of Nine Lives

The man who still did not know who he was, was panting when he finally arrived at the place where he had seen a skinny blonde fellow dancing a jig atop a rolling boulder as it careened down the foothill. He skidded to a stop and there was the round boulder, no longer on the move. Beside it were two men who were in sorry shape to be sure.

"Well met my good fellows! Well met I say!" The man was so overcome to have found companionship that he set down Bayerd the Skull and barreled toward them. He pulled them into a bear hug, one skinny fellow in each arm. He only released them when they began to squirm like restless puppies. He beamed at them and they stared back, with such startled expressions, they might have been facing a ghost.

The older of the two said, "Orson, how did you come to be here of all places? And in such a state?"

"Orson?" the man said. "Why do you call me that?"

"Because that is your name," the old fellow said.

"Is it? Do you know me?"

"Aye, quite well. And you know me, Gerald, and you know Jabalot." The older fellow, who was apparently called Gerald, pointed at the other man, who was not looking at all happy.

111

"Do I? Truth be told, I can't seem to recall much of anything, but it is nice to have a name. Orson, you say?"

"Yes, Orson." Gerald patted him on the shoulder and smiled most kindly, crinkling the skin around his eyes. He seemed like an agreeable old fellow indeed.

Orson looked around. "But what happened to the skinny blonde chap who was dancing a jig atop that boulder?" He pointed at the thing.

With a heavy sigh, Gerald looked down at the base of the round rock. "Prince Bayerd, he was your friend, and I like to think he had become my friend as well. I am sad to say he has found his final resting place beneath that stone."

Bayerd. The name was familiar, but only because Orson had christened his good friend the skull by the same moniker. Orson frowned. "You mean he got himself crushed to death right before I got here? Well, that's very disturbing since he was my friend, although I can't remember him." Distraught, he picked up Bayerd the Skull and hugged it to his chest. It comforted him, as it always did.

"Those closest to him claimed he did not die," the man called Jabalot said. "Yet Bayerd has still ended up crushed to death by a rock, hasn't he? T'is quite a gravestone our false prince has to mark his final resting place." He gave the big stone a hearty slap, or a bit of a shove. The stone must have been balanced on the tipping point, because it shifted. Ever so slowly, it began to roll downhill.

Orson stared down, expecting to see a gory sight. Instead, the skinny blonde fellow smiled up at him from a muddy hole. Orson turned to Jabalot. "Those closest to him must be right. He does not die."

The blonde fellow, Bayerd, struggled out of the hole and wrapped his arms around Orson in a tight hug. He wasn't very tall, and he didn't let go. He said, "I am alive, and fully intent on staying that way. Why don't you remember anything?" He finally released Orson from the unmanly embrace. "And why are you holding a skull?"

Orson hugged the skull tighter. "He's my friend. I can't remember much of anything. I was lost in a dark maze for a very long time. I do remember that, but nothing that came before. T'was as if I was born into the black tunnels as a fully grown man."

"Did you meet any scaly folk during that time?" the small blond fellow, Bayerd, asked.

"Not a single one."

"Well, they were looking for you, I think. You were lucky to elude them."

"Yes, I do believe I was," Orson agreed.

"We, too, spent some time in the dark maze. It is beneath that mountain." Bayerd pointed.

Orson nodded, he knew that much. He glanced up at the pointy mountain that resembled a witch's nose in profile and said, "I've been camping over by the stream, since I didn't know where else to go. I'm lost, and I didn't want to go back into the maze."

"Wise choice. We did meet the inhabitants of the mountain. The scaly folk aren't the friendliest sort. They took our horses and delayed us for a time. We have just escaped ourselves." Bayerd smiled at Orson, his sky blue eyes crinkling into half-moons, as if he was truly delighted to see him. He even stepped forward to hug him again.

Orson stepped back. "Enough hugging, it's not very manly, is it? And you don't smell so good."

"I'm sure I don't." Bayerd just kept smiling at Orson, the foolish grin stuck on his face.

"Why don't we catch up on each other's news later," Gerald said. "Night will be falling shortly. We need food and a fire." The four men were starved enough to eat each other if they did not find game.

They all looked around, as if game might be standing there waiting to offer itself up. Bayerd spotted a splotch of red along the latest path of destruction left by the boulder. He motioned toward it and said, "This rock did not crush some other poor soul, did it?"

Gerald squinted in the direction of Bayerd's pointing finger. "Let us hope not," he said, "unless it is someone who has scales for skin."

The four men started downhill to investigate. As they got closer, they could see that something had indeed not escaped the boulder's crushing weight, but at least it was something with fur and horns and hooves. They all stopped beside it and looked down at the partially flattened carcass of a mountain goat. "I guess we will not go hungry tonight after all," Bayerd said.

Gerald chuckled. "Perhaps your weapon of choice should be a boulder rather than an arrow, for your boulder has caught our dinner."

"A boulder is a fair bit larger than the tip of an arrow, much harder to miss with it," Bayerd agreed, showing himself to be a humble fellow.

"Least your boulder only spoiled half of the meat," Jabalot said in a disgruntled tone. Orson didn't think he liked Jabalot.

113

"It did not spoil any of the meat, merely tenderized it since this does look like an old goat. And since I am a one-handed man again, you can skin and butcher it," Bayerd told Jabalot.

"I'll get wood and start a fire going," Gerald said.

"I can help. Why do you only have the use of one hand?" Orson asked Bayerd.

Bayerd held up a fire-scarred and freshly burnt and blistered palm. "T'is a long and twisted tale, my good and true friend, Orson. And I will be delighted to tell it to you once we have full bellies and a crackling fire to warm our cockles."

"Do I like hearing tales?" Orson asked.

"You most certainly do," Bayerd said. "And I have many tales to tell. They will all be new to you."

Jabalot and Gerald got rather pained expressions on their faces, as if they had both developed cramps in their guts. Perhaps they had, since they looked as starved as Orson felt.

13. A Man by Any Other Name is Still a Fool

What a strange beast!
Like the air you breathe
You cannot live without it
A dying man in dungeon chains
Craves it over sweet water
In memory, it will never fade
A sharply honed blade
To cut a cruel wound
That will never heal
A four-lettered, burden of a beast
-Bayerd the Storyteller, Unfinished ramblings on Love

Bayerd's contribution to their survival efforts was to scout for a good spot to camp, one that was not too far from the crushed mountain goat. He selected a level, sheltered patch of ground that was big enough for four men, and near a small creek. He kicked the area clear of pebbles and weeds with his boots. Orson stayed nearby, as if afraid to let Bayerd out of his sight. He gathered kindling awkwardly, keeping a tight hold on the skull he was carrying like a child's ragdoll.

Bayerd was very worried that Orson had lost his wits as well as his memories. He was as gaunt and hairy as the rest of them, so clearly, he had not had an easy time of it crossing under the mountain. He had been alone and without supplies. It was a miracle his friend had survived at all, but perhaps his mind had been permanently damaged.

Gerald walked up carrying an armful of broken boughs. They helped him to build the fire. Jabalot soon turned up with strips of raw meat to be smoked. They all helped with that task.

By the time darkness fell, they had a decent store of smoked goat and full bellies for the first time in many weeks. Gerald had even scavenged some edible roots. They had roasted those, to accompany the meat. Once sated, they filled Orson in on his past, trying to restore his memories.

And Bayerd also told Orson about their own time in the mountain tunnels, and the scaly folk who wielded magic, although the story was very off-the-cuff. He had not yet had time to script his adventure into a polished tale. That would come later, when he was home again.

Alas, Orson didn't have anything to report at all. He had no recall of Kelp or the Golden Kingdom. He had no idea how he had ended up in the tunnels. His mind remained stubbornly blank, except for his newest memories.

When the fire was nothing but coals, the four men fell into an exhausted sleep. It was the first proper rest that any of them had enjoyed in a very long time. Bayerd wasn't the only man who slept like the dead that night.

He awoke to the sun warming his face and no hunger gnawing at his belly. He felt a sense of wellbeing that was marred only by the fact that Kelp was so very far away. He yearned to hold her cuddled against his side. He ached to go home to her, yet he knew in his heart that he could not return to the Golden Kingdom empty-handed. He simply had too much to atone for.

As if the castle walls had blinded him to the truth, now that he was outside them, he could see clearly again. He had been an embarrassment to Kelp, cringing in his luxurious rooms instead of standing strongly by her side. He must redeem himself, and succeeding at his quest would be the first step to reaffirming his manhood, and earning his place by her side. Yet, after seeing that yellow-streaked side of him, did Kelp still love him?

For once, he was the first awake. He rose silently. Orson had no bedroll and was curled up on the ground, hugging his skull. Gerald was snoring softly; Jabalot was snoring loudly.

Bayerd laid his blanket over Orson and tiptoed away. He yawned and stretched and his pants fell off. He pulled them back up and tightened his belt yet another notch. He wondered if he should grant his men a day of rest before they began the climb up the mountain to retrieve the heaven stone. Lord knows, they did need it. Mulling things over, he headed for the creek.

As Orson had said, he was less than fresh. He stripped down and had a bath in the icy water. He used his sharply honed sword to shave off his beard and he tied his hair back. It had grown at least an inch since he had left the castle.

When he got back to the campsite, Orson was awake. He had revived the fire and was sitting in its warmth, huddled under Bayerd's blanket and talking to the skull. He was even feeding it little bites of goat, which were promptly falling back out through the hole where a man's neck would normally be.

"Good morning, Orson." Bayerd sat down beside him.

"Who are you?" Orson asked, which set alarm bells clanging in Bayerd's head.

"Your good and true friend, Bayerd."

Orson squinted at him. "The prince fellow I met yesterday? But you don't look like him."

"I cleaned up. No beard." Bayerd rubbed his smooth jaw.

"Ah, that explains it then," Orson said.

"Did you sleep well?" Bayerd helped himself to a strip of goat.

Orson said, "Yes, I did. And you, Prince Bayerd?"

"You don't call me that. We have known each other since we were lads. You call me Bayerd, and sometimes you call me a fool, and on rare occasions you call me a jester, which I do not appreciate. But you never call me Prince Bayerd, nor do I wish you to."

Orson nodded. "As you wish, Prince Bayerd."

"Just Bayerd, like your skull. Not prince," he repeated.

"As you wish, Bayerd."

"And did your skull, who happens to have the same name as me, sleep well?" Bayerd asked.

"Aye, Bayerd slept like the dead. He always does, you know." Orson fed the skull another bite of goat.

"Does he?" Alas, Orson did not even see the pun in his words.

"And now that he's had a bite to eat, he's in fine form," Orson continued, patting the skull fondly on the top of the head.

Bayerd frowned and tossed a broken bough on the fire. He wanted his friend Orson back, not this empty shell of a man who made polite and inane conversation. And wasted precious food on a skull when there were four starving men within spitting distance. Not only did he miss Orson's companionship, he also needed someone he trusted fully. He wanted to discuss the possibility that maybe, just maybe, Jabalot's orders in regards to the quest had been to make sure Bayerd did not return to the Golden Kingdom—ever. If that was the case, Jabalot might still attempt to assassinate him, if an opportunity presented itself.

Orson's protection, as well as his input, would have come in handy. But perhaps Orson's memories would return now that the friends were reunited. Maybe he merely needed a bit more time to recover from his ordeal.

Chewing on another strip of goat, Bayerd pointed up to the top of the mountain. "Orson, I have been sent on a quest to find a heaven stone that came down on the mountain. See the mark, near the summit?"

Orson squinted and nodded. "I see it." He turned his skull so its hollow eye sockets were facing the mountain. "Bayerd can see it, too," he added.

"He must have keen eyesight," Bayerd said, dryly, since the skull had no eyeballs to speak of.

"Oh, he does indeed." Orson smiled like a proud papa.

Bayerd sighed. "I am convinced that the heaven stone impacted there, so I must scale the mountain to retrieve it. Only then can we go home to the Golden Kingdom. Do you feel well enough to make the climb?"

Orson frowned, gazing upward. "It will not be an easy climb. Looks cold up there, what with all the snow and ice."

"I'm sure it is cold," Bayerd agreed. It felt like he was talking to a child.

"But I don't want to stay down here, not alone with only Bayerd for company." Orson meant the skull, and his eyes were wide with terror. "I don't want to be alone ever again. I can make the climb. A bit more food and my legs will be strong enough. "

"As you wish, Orson. I was hoping you would travel with me. So today we will eat this delicious feast of tough old goat, and we will nap like cats, and tomorrow we will start the ascent." It was decided.

So the four men did nap away much of the morning, after which, Orson and Jabalot hunted for game. Gerald followed the stream and found a pond where fish were plentiful. They each had a whole fish for lunch, along with some edible roots and fresh picked greens. They washed thoroughly in the pond and drank the pure water, and napped again in the sunshine. It was an idyllic day after the oppressive tunnels.

There were rabbits for dinner, with a dessert of partridge and blueberries, and more game and fish to smoke for their travelling rations. They bedded down early, knowing what the morning would bring.

They awoke to soggy skies. Bayerd hoped it wasn't an omen of things to come. They packed their meager gear and set off earlier than planned because of the rain.

Bayerd led the way, upward. He set a reasonable pace, which was not too fast. He kept an eye out for scaly folk, in case they popped out of some hidden nook in the mountain.

The morning's hike was not taxing as the slope was gentle. They stopped for lunch, ate cold meat, and napped. Mid-afternoon, they started climbing again. The slope grew ever-steeper and challenged their weakened legs. They had to stop again after only several hours. They ate, and took the time to build a branch shelter when rain started to spit down on them in earnest.

The four men and one skull slept side-by-side, in close proximity in the close quarters, for the sake of dryness. They shared the three blankets between them, and shared body warmth. Bayerd felt safe with Orson by his side, even though Orson was not yet himself. Lying in the makeshift shelter, he told Orson tales from their childhood. He was hoping to jar loose his friend's memories. Alas, it did not seem to help.

In the coming days, the men made slow progress. The sky remained dismal, and Bayerd spent a lot of time looking up. It had dawned on him that Kelp should have sent dragons seeking him, considering how long he had been gone, but the few dragons he did spot were at a great distance. None flew near the mountain and Kelp knew that had been his destination. So why hadn't she sent even one dragon to search for him? Unless she did not want him back. It was a depressing thought, so he tried not to think it at all.

There was little food to be had. It also grew steadily colder, until they wore their blankets as coats. There were only three blankets, so one of them was always cold. It was impossible for two men to share one blanket, given the rough terrain and steep narrow trails.

Eventually, the clouds blew away, allowing the sunshine to warm them. Their strenuous climb also helped to keep their bodies heated.

Whenever Bayerd had the breath to spare, he told Orson more tales from their past. Alas, it did not help Orson to recall a thing, but at least his friend was learning who he was, and where he came from.

It took longer than Bayerd expected to reach the uppermost slopes of the mountain, where the terrain was steep and icy enough to have them slipping down as much as they were climbing up. Luckily, they had some lengths of rope in their supplies to aid them when they had to scale cliff faces or cross over dangerous cracks that probably led straight down into the heart of the mountain—and the scaly folk who skulked within.

Finally, midafternoon on their fifteenth day of climbing, they reached their destination—the scar in the mountain where Bayerd believed the heaven stone had crashed to earth. Cheers went up from all four men.

The plowed track had looked short from below, but proved to be quite long. The furrow cut into the mountain at a depth of several feet, going neither up nor down, but sideways, as if it had tried to carve the cap off the mountain. It was also much wider than expected, at about six feet.

Again, Bayerd worried about just how large the heaven stone was. Judging by the track, it was certainly too big for him to put in his pocket and carry home. Regardless, he wasn't going to abandon his quest without gazing upon the heaven stone. And perhaps the impact with the mountain had broken it into pieces. Surely a piece of the heaven stone would do as a prize for Queen Hellenor.

Bayerd examined the track through the icy ground. He could easily tell in which direction the heaven stone had travelled, for the dragged streaks of debris all went to the right.

"Almost there," Bayerd said, grinning at the small group, and a sadder-looking trio was hard to imagine. In truth, they looked worse than when they had escaped the mountain, being that much thinner, hairier and raggedy. Regardless, they grinned back, white teeth flashing in ruddy, wind-burned and frostbitten faces.

"Let's go find this heaven stone," Bayerd said, "and hope it is broken or cracked into pieces, for if it is as big as this trench indicates, it is not a heaven stone we can carry."

They stepped down into the trough to follow it to the stone. It was easy walking along the cleared path, especially since there was no more climbing.

After a quarter mile or so, Bayerd could see the end of the track, although there was no stone resting there, nor were there broken fragments of a stone. He squinted against the bright sun and walked to where the furrow ended quite abruptly. He looked down into a fissure that cut into the mountain like a stab wound. It had not been caused by the heaven stone, yet it appeared to have swallowed it up.

"No," he cried and dropped to his knees so he could look down into the crevice. He could see nothing but blackness. The heaven stone had fallen into the cursed mountain. Had the scaly folk made off with his treasure?

Gerald crouched beside him in the snow. "It's fallen into the mountain," he said flatly.

Orson crouched on his other side. "I can't see anything. I wonder if this crack connects to that awful maze." He held his skull so it could look down into the crack too, saying, "Have a good look, Bayerd. Do you see anything down there?"

The skull did not answer. It never did, unless Orson heard its voice in his head.

"We've made this bloody torturous climb for nothing," Jabalot snapped, voicing what they were all thinking.

"There was no way to know that from below." Bayerd stood up and dusted snow off his knees. "And it was not for nothing, for now we know where the heaven stone has ended up."

"No, we don't," Jabalot countered. "All we know is that it's inside a bloody big mountain, so it could still be anywhere. And it doesn't matter now, does it? It's not like we're going to go back in there to find a stupid chunk of rock."

"Yes, we are," Bayerd said. "Our quest leads us back inside the mountain, so that is where we shall go to find the heaven stone."

All three men and the skull gaped at him. Even the skull thought he was bonkers. But Bayerd would not be swayed. To win Kelp back, he must succeed at his quest—and he would, unless he died trying.

"Only a fool would go back in that mountain," Jabalot said.

"Or a man on a quest," Bayerd countered.

Jabalot stepped close, put an arm around Bayerd's shoulders and murmured, "You do not die easily, so you are not an easy man to kill."

"What?" said Bayerd, unsure why Jabalot would be saying such a thing at that moment.

"And after all our time together, I regret that I have to do this, but orders are orders, and I'm not going back into that cursed mountain," Jabalot said, and gave him a hard shove into the black fissure.

In spite of Jabalot's words, Bayerd wasn't expecting it. He flew backwards into the crack in the mountain that had claimed the heaven stone. He dropped through the air, screaming, and then he hit rock. It was steeply angled and he bounced off it and kept falling, but it was still rock—and as hard as rock. After several more painful bounces, he began to slide, almost as fast as he had been falling.

The steep angle of the rock passage lessened by degrees. He slid slower and slower, until he finally came to rest in the dark, in the mountain, and alone. It was almost too much to bear. No, it was too much to bear. Bayerd struggled to hold onto the scraps of his sanity, and then something very large slammed into him, coming down from above.

He slid a bit more, along with whoever had fallen into him. "Who has joined me in this hellish place?" Bayerd asked.

"Me and Bayerd," Orson said. "We have come to support you. Well, we didn't really have a choice. That Jabalot fellow pushed us in. I don't think I like him."

There was the sound of screaming from overhead. A third and fourth body came down together, slamming into Bayerd and Orson. In a tangle, the four reunited men slid further into the mountain.

"Gerald and Jabalot, I presume," said Bayerd.

He was answered with a string of curses from Jabalot, and a bark of laughter from Gerald.

"Tell me, how do you both come to be down here? Orson is a most curious fellow and he is dying to know," Bayerd said.

"Jabalot tried to shove me in, too. I brought him down with me." Satisfaction laced Gerald's words.

"Well done, Gerald. Jabalot, who sent you on this quest to assassinate me? Or was killing me off your own bright idea?"

"Wasn't my idea," Jabalot said. "And like I told you on the top of the mountain, I didn't really want to kill you anymore, but -"

"Orders are orders," Bayerd cut in. "Tell me then, who sent you to assassinate me?" He was even more curious about that, than how he was going to get the hell out of the mountain for a second time.

"Suppose it won't hurt to tell you now, since I don't expect we'll ever leave this place," Jabalot said, "although I give you fair warning, you're going to wish you never knew the truth of it."

"Once I have heard the name, I will decide that for myself," Bayerd said.

Jabalot snorted. "As you wish. It was Princess Kelp."

"No! You lie!" Bayerd cried out.

"Why would I lie? We're all going to die down here, just a matter of time. No point in lying, is there? I'm sorry your wife wants you dead, but there you have it."

"You lie," Bayerd repeated weakly. He tried to yank his leg out from under some part of someone. That someone who was oddly still and slack. "Orson, you're awfully quiet. How fare you?" he asked.

He didn't receive an answer. "Did one of you clunk Orson on the head when you fell on us?" he asked the conscious men, preferring to focus on that, rather than his wife hiring an assassin to kill him off.

"I hit something pretty hard with my boot heel," Gerald said. "Thought it was that damn skull, but maybe it was Orson's hard head."

Bayerd groped his friend's head. There was indeed a lump as large as a chicken's egg sprouting over Orson's left ear. He slapped Orson's cheek several times, trying to rouse him.

When one of their remaining torches flared to life, it was a relief to be able to see. Gerald held the torch closer. Orson's face was pale and still, as if in deep, restful slumber. Bayerd slapped his friend several more times, even harder, until Orson's thick lashes fluttered. He opened his dark brown eyes and stared up at Bayerd blankly for a moment before he said, "Orson, there you are. I had a devil of a time finding you in this maze, but now we are reunited."

Bayerd frowned at him. "I'm not Orson. You are Orson."

Orson laughed, sat up, and slapped Bayerd on the back. "Stop being ridiculous, Orson. It is not the time or place."

Bayerd shared a deeply concerned glance with Gerald. "If I am Orson, and you are not Orson, pray tell me, who are you?"

"Have you lost your marbles, man? I am Bayerd, troubadour and storyteller extraordinaire, and your lifelong friend."

"And I'm Orson?" Bayerd asked in disbelief.

"And have been since birth. So, we must find a way out of this maze, and find the heaven stone. A tall order, I know, but I will succeed at my quest." He rubbed his burgeoning lump and winced. "The heaven stone would have kept falling, taking the path of least resistance, so I say we do the same." Orson struggled to his feet, plucked the torch out of Gerald's hand, and started half-walking and half-sliding down the passage. He didn't even pick up his skull.

Bayerd sat dumbstruck for a moment before he shrugged and said, "Follow Orson, I mean, follow Bayerd." He could not fault his friend's plan, only the name he called himself. He scooped up the skull before

123

he set off. It seemed wrong to abandon Orson's friend after all they had been through together.

Gerald and Jabalot followed him. Well, there really wasn't anywhere else to go. Climbing up and out of the mountain would have been impossible, whilst climbing down into the mountain was easy. They were sheltered from the elements and the air seemed warm after so much freezing. The steep passage gradually leveled out until it was as if they descended a gently spiraling slope. The ceiling of the passage was even high enough for them to walk upright in places.

Orson kept them entertained with one tale after another. Bayerd knew all the tales by heart, since they were his own, but to hear another speak them was a novel experience. And Orson did have an impressive voice, it being both deep and melodious. Not as impressive as Bayerd's own, but acceptable nonetheless. And now that Orson believed himself the storyteller, he spoke with wit, humour and confidence, traits he sorely lacked when he was himself.

Gerald and Jabalot certainly seemed to enjoy Orson's versions of the tales and resentment grew in Bayerd's heart. Being a storyteller of great renown was his claim to fame, the only one he truly had since he was not a great fighter or very tall or overly manly. For Orson to simply usurp his role, and with such apparent ease, was galling. He whispered to the skull he held cradled in his arm, "As if being uncommonly tall, strong and manly weren't enough, now he has to be the storyteller, too. I wonder if another blow to the head would put things right?"

The skull had no answer, so Bayerd edged closer to Gerald. "Do you think if we gave Orson another whack on the head, he would remember his true name and nature?" he asked quietly.

Gerald mulled that over for a minute. "Might work, but might be dangerous. What if he's knocked senseless? We need all of us as fit as we can be, for when we run into those scaly folk."

The man did make a valid point. Bayerd sighed and kept walking. And Orson as Bayerd started telling a new tale, one that Bayerd had not scripted, or even heard before. In a voice laced with sorrow, Orson spoke of a beautiful princess who was named after seaweed. "Her heart was quite broken," he said with regret, "because she believed her true love dead. With her own eyes, she had seen his golden slippers, still on his cold dead feet, protruding out from under a mountain of fallen rock."

"Swift?" Bayerd gasped. "Kelp thinks I am dead because she found Swift's body, dressed in my clothes?"

"Stop interrupting my tale," Orson snapped. "And she thinks I am dead. I am her husband. What is wrong with you, Orson? Why do you keep thinking you are me? Why, next, you will claim that you bedded a harpy and fathered a beautiful little boy, with sunny curls and sky-blue eyes. My wife is quite taken with the little lad, you know."

Bayerd's jaw dropped and he had a hard time snapping it shut, giving Jabalot time to howl with laughter and crow, "You bedded a harpy?"

"I did no such thing," Bayerd lied.

"Of course he didn't. I did," Orson declared, "to save Princess Kelp from the noose, and to save the life of my good and true friend, Orson, when he was gravely wounded by Shifra."

Bayerd groaned long and loud, as if he was being rack-tortured right there in the mountain. Some secrets were never meant to be spilled, and that one topped the list. "So Kelp knows about the harpy? And there is a babe?" he cried, since there seemed no more point in lying any longer.

"Aye, the truth will out, man. And I can feel no shame."

Orson might feel no shame in his role as imposter, but Bayerd was drowning in it. To be known as the man who had lain with a harpy—ye gods, he could never show his face in the Golden Kingdom again. Even accomplishing his quest wouldn't erase that disgrace. Especially not when there was a child as a living, squalling, growing reminder. There simply was no salvation from sharing his seed with a harpy. And Kelp knew—that was even worse than the whole damn kingdom knowing.

Orson kept running off at the mouth. Bayerd trudged behind him, shoulders hunched, hugging the skull for comfort. Bleakness settled over him like a heavy mantle as they descended deeper and deeper into the heart of the mountain.

He was so sunk in despair that he was not heeding Orson's words, not until he heard Kelp's name again. "What did you say?" he asked Orson.

"I said I miss holding Kelp in my arms, I miss gazing upon her beautiful face, I miss kissing that little moon-shaped birthmark on her breast. I miss everything about her."

Bayerd's heart felt like it stopped beating. "You've seen her birthmark? You've kissed it … but how?"

"I am her husband, of course I have seen her birthmark, and kissed it too many times to count."

"You've seen her ... unclothed? You've laid hands on her?" Bayerd gasped.

"Husbands are permitted to see their wives naked, Orson, and touch them," Orson said, in a most patronizing tone.

Bayerd could not argue with that, except that Orson was not her husband, so how had he seen Kelp naked? There was only one explanation, one that Bayerd had, until now, stubbornly refused to believe. Yet, in light of this latest evidence, he could no longer deny the truth—Orson and Kelp were lovers. No wonder Kelp had hired an assassin to kill him off. No wonder there were no dragons searching for him. It all made perfect sense now—except for Orson's presence in the mountain.

"Told you they were rutting," Jabalot said smugly. "Probably why she wants you dead."

"And now she believes I am dead," Bayerd said, his heart so broken, it was a cruel jest that it continued to beat. Orson and Kelp ... Kelp and Orson ... he truly wished for the mercy of death then, and clearly, it was a blessing that Kelp believed him dead. Now that he knew the truth of it, that Orson and Kelp were lovers, and that she had ordered his assassination, he could never go home again. Add to that the harpy. Even if, by some miracle, he did escape the mountain for a second time, only shame and death were waiting for him in the Golden Kingdom.

Bayerd was so immersed in his misery that he didn't notice the ground getting steadily steeper. He tripped and his feet went out from under him. He landed on his ass and began to slide. He managed to slow his descent by digging his fingers and heels into the ground. He came to a stop and his men caught up, moving with care, using their swords as canes.

"Is that a trace of smoke I smell," Gerald said quietly.

Bayerd sniffed and there was indeed smoke in the air. "Perhaps we are close to the base of the mountain and the scaly folks' fire," he said, utterly uncaring about what the future held for him.

"I suspect we are," Gerald said, in a whisper now.

"Lead the way, Orson," Orson said to Bayerd, his whisper much too loud. "You have the strongest sword arm of all of us."

Jabalot chuckled at such a ridiculous claim. Even Gerald laughed, although he tried to turn it into a cough. Bayerd was not fooled. And if

126

Orson's statement had been true, he might have been tempted to run Orson through with his sword. Then again, maybe not. After the business with the buxom wench, which was really just the icing on the cake, Bayerd could understand why Kelp would want him dead, and why she had sought solace in Orson's arms. But was he a noble enough man to wish his two dearest companions to be happy? No, he wasn't, not when it meant them being happy together whilst naked. As hard as he might wish to be self-sacrificing, he wasn't able to be that virtuous, not even close.

Orson pressed against the tunnel wall and waved Jabalot and Gerald to squeeze by him. Believing himself Bayerd, he was playing the role of coward.

Bayerd knew he had been a shrinking shadow of a man for the past year. And in the time before he was a prince, he tended to hide beneath tables when fists were flying and swords were slashing. But he was no longer that coward, to let his men face danger in his place—as he hoped he had already proven on his misbegotten quest.

Ah well, perhaps it was time to prove it again. He had no future to speak of anyway, and nothing to lose except his cursed life. He pulled out his much smaller sword and surveyed his men. "I will lead if you will follow."

"Rather you than me." Jabalot slapped Bayerd heartily on the back, in a man-to-man kind of way, almost sending Bayerd sliding again. Only his sword saved him when he tripped over it and landed on his knees.

"Are you trying to do away with me here and now?" he snapped, struggling up.

"Of course not. T'was merely an accident. Forgot how small and light you are, now that you're not as fat as a hog. And I have no need to kill you now, do I? No way in bleeding hell we'll find our way out of this mountain a second time."

"Well, thank you for those most heartening words, Sir Jabalot." Bayerd saluted the fellow and started moving. Gerald followed him, then Jabalot; Orson brought up the rear.

Bayerd started edging down the slippery slope. In a couple of dozen paces, he came to a branching passage. It was smaller than the one they traversed. He decided they should stick to their larger tunnel and he kept going. Soon, he could see a faint glow coming from somewhere ahead. He turned sideways and kept descending, digging the edges of his boots into the ground. A few more cautious paces and he could see the end of the sloping tunnel. He inched toward it and peered down through the hole.

Directly below him was the large chamber with the round firepit, surrounded by its circular fur-covered bench. The hole he peered through was very high up indeed, being located at the highest point of the domed ceiling the scaly folk had carved out of the mountain, or had had hundreds of men carve out for them, before those men breathed their last.

The chamber was empty of scaly folk. The ropes they carried might have gotten them down safely, except Bayerd did not want to be seen by the fire, which might have eyes as well as ears. He whispered, "Let us climb back to that branching passage and see where it goes."

His men nodded and started climbing. At least the other passage was close. When they reached it, Orson motioned everyone ahead of him again. Bayerd took the lead.

The smaller passage was every bit as slippery and steeply angled as the previous one. They moved with care until Bayerd thought he heard voices, and the tunnel brightened. He paused and touched his fingers to his lips, signaling silence. Gerald snuffed out the torch he had relit.

Bayerd gripped the skull tight and his sword tighter, and stepped forth. Alas, perhaps the passage was only meant to direct light downward, for the floor of it crumbled beneath even his reduced weight, and then he was falling like the cursed man he was.

14. Finders Keepers

I fell down a mountain
And did not die
Thought I might
Since I can't fly
Landed on my head
With a mighty cry
T'was rockhard rock
Yet, I did not die

-Bayerd the Storyteller, One of Nine Lives

The distance to the ground was not nearly as great as in the domed chamber, and not great enough to kill Bayerd, but he landed so hard, he saw a heaven's worth of exploding stars. He was lying there trying to breathe, rather afraid to open his eyes and see where he had ended up, when something as heavy as a horse landed atop him. He screamed in pain, sure that every last one of his ribs had broken inward.

"Sorry about that." Orson shoved on Bayerd's ribs to leverage himself off his human cushion. Bayerd screamed even louder. "Thought we were supposed to be quiet," Orson said, "although I suppose it doesn't matter now." He sounded terrified.

Bayerd cracked his eyelids opened to have a look. A sea of faces ringed them—hostile, scaly faces.

"Look who hasss returned," one of them said and stepped forth. Bayerd recognized Suth's hissing voice.

"We missed your hospitality so much, we decided to come back for more," Bayerd groaned, in too much agony to talk properly. He extended his hand to Orson, who gripped it and yanked Bayerd to his feet.

Bayerd screamed and cradled his middle. "I wanted was a gentle helping hand, not manhandling," he said through gritted teeth.

"Sorry about that, Orson," Orson said, darting fearful glances at their audience and sticking close to Bayerd's side.

"Have you changed your name?" Suth asked.

"I have not. My formerly good friend here has changed it for me. He is suffering from a case of confusion," Bayerd said.

"Ssso the big one is not right in the head?" Suth said snidely, sideling forward.

"He's fine. He's just had a difficult time of it lately, as well as more than one hard blow to his uncommonly hard head." Bayerd bent down to pick up the skull he had dropped in his fall. The pain did seem to be easing already, so perhaps his ribs were merely cracked, not broken.

All the scaly folk were watching him with their full attention, so he tucked the skull under his arm, gave it a reassuring pat on the head, and kept talking. "We found our way out of your tunnels, and amassed quite a fortune along the way. The bargain we struck certainly worked in our favour," he said, to remind Suth that they would not be so easy to fool this time around.

"And yet, here you are in our tunnelsss again, and not just in our tunnelsss, but in our private quartersss. That is called trespassing."

Bayerd shrugged with exaggerated unconcern. "There were no signs posting this as private territory, so it is merely a mistake, not trespassing."

"Ssstill," Suth said, "it will require another bargain for you to leave our tunnelsss, if you can." She smiled smugly, her scales compacting around her mouth until some of them disappeared completely.

"We did it once, we can certainly do it again. And perhaps we can increase the stakes," Bayerd suggested.

"In what way?" Suth looked as curious as Orson at his worst.

Before Bayerd could answer, Orson elbowed him aside, in the ribs. "It is my quest, I will bargain."

"No, you won't," said the true Bayerd, cradling his aching side.

Orson scowled. "But it is my quest."

"Orson ... or Bayerd," Bayerd felt ridiculous calling Orson by his own name. "You whacked your head and have no memories of these people or their ways, so I should be the one to bargain."

"But you told me all about them," Orson whispered loudly enough to be heard by all.

"Hearing a tale is not the same thing as experiencing it firsthand."

130

Suth interrupted at that point. "I think I would rather bargain with the big Bayerd, not the sssmall one."

The small Bayerd spun to face her. "You have no say in this matter," he ground out.

"But I do," Orson said, "and I will be the one to bargain."

"No, you won't."

"Yes, I will."

"No, you won't."

"Yes, I will."

They might have kept arguing pointlessly if a body hadn't tumbled down from above. Orson was directly below and automatically extended his arms. He caught Gerald quite handily and set the older man on his feet.

Bayerd said, "How fare you, Gerald?"

"Well enough, since I did not hit the ground. Jabalot gave me a little shove."

"Did he now?" Bayerd glanced up, but could see no sign of the pushy fellow.

"I was having a bit of an eavesdrop up there," Gerald continued, turning to Orson. "There is wisdom in what Bayerd—I mean Orson says." They were all getting rather confused.

"There is?" Orson said, in a permanent state of confusion.

"Yes. A leader delegates tasks to his men, does he not? Let your friend set the terms and you, as leader, will have final say to agree or disagree."

Orson mulled that over for a moment. "I suppose that is acceptable," he said rather grudgingly, "as long as I have the final say."

Bayerd got back to business, as if he had not been so rudely interrupted by Orson. He turned to Suth. "We returned to the mountain searching for something, something I think you may have in your possession." He and Suth studied each other with narrowed eyes.

"And what might that sssomething be?" Suth asked.

"The stone that came down from the heavens and hit the top of this mountain, then fell down into its cold heart -"

"Ah, that ssstone. Finders, keepersss," she hissed, confirming what Bayerd suspected—that the scaly folk had possession of the stone.

"True, but I rather have my heart set on acquiring that heaven stone, for my queen." Bayerd's voice was as hard as iron, yet soft, as if that iron was cloaked in velvet.

131

"Then I suggest we bargain for the ssstone," Suth said.

"And passage through your tunnels," Bayerd reminded her, lest she forget.

"For three men or four men?" She glanced up toward the ceiling.

"Passage for three men." The fourth was now on his own, since the fourth seemed set on killing not just Bayerd, but Gerald and Orson as well.

She inclined her head. "Passage for three men it is. Are you sssure you want to bargain for the heaven ssstone as well?"

Bayerd thought about holding hellfire, yet again, and swallowed hard. "Quite sure, as long as the heaven stone is small enough to be carried about by a man."

"It is sssmall enough to be swallowed by a man, being no larger than a sssnail," Suth said.

Bayerd frowned. "Truly? But I saw the scar it left on the top of your mountain. That was not caused by something as small as a snail."

"It came to earth in a large ball of ice, ice that has sssince melted," she explained.

"I see. Then I will be bargaining for the heaven stone as well." Even though he had no plans to return to the Golden Kingdom, he would see his remaining knight, Sir Gerald, home safely. Gerald could present the heaven stone to Queen Hellenor in his place.

He wasn't sure what to do about Orson. He certainly did not want to send the fellow back into Kelp's arms. The thought of them together was unbearable. Yet, should he not wish for the happiness of the two people he loved most in the world? In spite of their treachery? He was trying hard to come to terms with that hard truth, yet it was no easy task.

Suth said, "I will take you to the Tri-Alanth to bargain for your passage home."

"Wonderful," Bayerd said with false bravado. He followed Suth with all the enthusiasm of a man destined to face the headsman, as he had already done once in his lifetime. And Gerald and Orson followed him, Orson staying close on his heels. The circle of scaly folk was ten deep. They parted to make way for them, all hissing quietly. It sounded like they were in a nest of angry snakes.

Suth led them through the large outer chamber with its circle of fire and down the same shorter passage as last time. Perhaps the Tri-Alanth never left her own chamber, because she was waiting for them in the exact same spot, the misty recessed pit that was sunk into both the wall and the floor.

As before, the central of the three women blew fire into Suth's palm. She hissed something that Bayerd could not understand, and smiled at Bayerd quite gruesomely, revealing fangs that were as long as carrots. Her sisters smiled, too, their fangs every bit as long.

Bayerd felt rather faint and took several deep breaths, fortifying himself for the pain that was to come. There was a bit of back and forth hissing conversation between Suth and the Tri-Alanth before Suth addressed Bayerd. "I have made your intention known, that you wish to bargain for passage through our tunnelsss and for the heaven ssstone."

"Well, I thank you for that." Bayerd hoped it would make his own conversation with the Tri-Alanth a few burn blisters shorter.

"Are you ready to proceed?" Suth extended the flame.

"Let me consult with my men first," Bayerd said.

Before he could draw Gerald and Orson to the far side of the room for a bit of private conversation, Orson said, "Look here, Orson, I don't mean to be petty, but they aren't your men. They are my men. I should be the one to bargain now that the terms have been established, since it is my quest."

"Fine," Bayerd snapped, thinking about Orson and Kelp together. "You do the bargaining." Let Orson experience the pain of fire in his place. "So, what do we have to bargain with, aside from our lives?" he said, to help Orson along.

With a rueful grin, Gerald patted the pouch affixed to his belt. "A king's ransom in gemstones."

"Are you offering your fortune?" Bayerd asked.

"Better to be a poor man than a rich corpse." Gerald placed the pouch in Bayerd's hands. "I think it is why Jabalot took off. He did not want to share his wealth."

Orson snatched the sack out of Bayerd's hand and scowled at Gerald. Bayerd waved an arm toward the Tri-Alanth. "Have at it, Big Bayerd, and let us hope that the Tri-Alanth values gemstone as much as horses. Just don't bargain away our lives." He gave Orson a shove in the direction of the fire.

Orson approached Suth and said, "I am ready to bargain." She beckoned him closer and extended the flame.

Orson backed away from it. "What are you doing?"

"You must hold the flame to bargain."

Orson had not been present at the last bargaining session. He either didn't remember hearing about this detail of the transactions, or he had forgotten it. He had taken a second blow to his head, and now called himself by a different name.

"I'm not going to hold fire," he declared. "Fire is hot. It hurts, it does, and I am something of a coward, in case you didn't know. Scared of my own shadow, I am, and scared of lots of other things. Scared of just about everything really, including fire."

He hid his hands behind his back and turned to Bayerd. "Orson, I think you should do the bargaining after all, seeing as how you are so much tougher and braver than me."

Bayerd hugged the skull that was his namesake and shook his head. "It is not my quest, Big Bayerd, so I am not the one to bargain. You said so yourself."

"Yes, well, I've changed my mind. And as leader of this quest, I can change my mind as many times as I want. And you must obey my command, now get over here and hold the fire."

Bayerd narrowed his eyes on his traitorous friend, his temper flaring. "No," he said.

Gerald nudged him. "You may not wish to hear it, but I would rather you struck the bargain. It is not just fire that the bargainer holds in his hands, it is also my life."

The aged knight certainly had a lot of faith in him. It warmed Bayerd's heart. "You are right, as always, Sir Gerald. I may not appreciate your words, but I will heed them. In truth, I wasn't at ease with Orson striking the bargain." He had simply been angry and resentful enough to let him do it. Avoiding pain had also been a bonus.

Bayerd stepped forward, hands extended to accept the flame. He tipped it into his left palm, and it was every bit as hot as he remembered. Before the Tri-Alanth could speak, he gasped out, "A pouch full of gemstones for the heaven stone and passage through your tunnels."

The three heads laughed as one. "A fair bargain," the middle head hissed.

"What? You agree?" Bayerd cried, not quite able to believe his ears.

"We agree. You may leave through our tunnels, carrying the heaven stone."

"And you'll show us which passage will take us back home, to our side of the mountain," Bayerd gasped, falling to his knees and wishing he had the inner fortitude to sever off his own hand with his sword, to stop the agony.

"And we will show you which tunnel will lead you back to your side of the mountain," the Tri-Alanth agreed.

It seemed suspiciously easy. Sweat ran into Bayerd's eyes as he tried to make sense of the words when his brain could process nothing but pain. "We can leave, with the heaven stone?" he cried out.

"That is the bargain."

"Done, deal!" He placed his palm against the cool damp ground, extinguishing the flames. He fell down, rocking back and forth, unable to contain a keening cry.

Gerald and Orson hauled him up and dragged him over to the basin. His palm was held under the flow. He cursed when even that caused agony. "Never again. I will never hold fire again," he moaned.

"What bargain did you strike?" Gerald asked.

"An odd bargain, to be sure." Bayerd leaned against the wall, keeping his palm under the cool water. "For your pouch of gems, we can all leave with the heaven stone, and they'll even show us which tunnel will take us home."

"That does seem like a bargain in our favour. I wouldn't have expected that," Gerald said skeptically.

Orson said, even more uncertainly, "Why would they offer a bargain that benefits us?"

"Aye," Gerald growled. "Especially when we got away once. To me, these folks seem like the type to nurture their resentment and make it grow, and perhaps seek revenge."

"They do, don't they?" Bayerd was no more at ease with the bargain that his men. Could revenge be what the mountain dwellers sought? Had he been played for a fool?

"Are you ready to leave with the heaven ssstone?" Suth said, breaking into his thoughts.

"Yes, of course." Bayerd shoved away from the wall. As soon as his hand left the coolness of the water, it felt a hundred degrees hotter. He took a deep breath, and nodded resolutely to Gerald and Orson. "We'll take the heaven stone and take our leave."

Suth's smile spread widely across her face, and it was not a nice smile. "Right this way, Prince Bayerd."

Orson frowned in confusion. "Why does everyone think you are me?"

"It is a long and twisted tale," Bayerd said. "And I am going to enlighten you, as soon as we are out of this black-hearted mountain."

"And I'd be delighted to hear it, I think. But I thought I was the storyteller."

The Tri-Alanth hissed loudly, and Suth said, "It isss time. Follow me."

They followed her, and with each step, Bayerd felt more doomed. The bargain had sounded so good when his hand was on fire, but now that it no longer burned, he suspected more of their trickery.

Suth led them back to the large central chamber with the domed roof. It was crowded wall-to-wall with the mountain's inhabitants, probably every last one of them. They were all seated, facing the fire.

A clear pathway cut through their number, all the way to the fire. Suth stopped and pointed like an arrow at the path through her people. "Approach the flamesss."

"Where is the heaven stone?" Bayerd didn't see it anywhere.

"How eager you are." She just kept pointing so Bayerd walked toward the fire. And he walked alone. Suth barred Orson and Gerald from following, even though Orson started whining again about it being his quest.

Bayerd stopped before the fire and still didn't see the heaven stone. When three heads rose up out of the flames, he almost screamed. So the Tri-Alanth did leave her small chamber after all, by travelling through fire of all things! The heads kept rising, and their necks were so much longer than he had expected. In fact, their necks were as long as any fully-grown dragon's.

"I will not hold fire again. If you want to address me, you may do so in my tongue," he declared.

The Tri-Alanth did not answer him in words. The middle head bent down toward Bayerd and hissed, hatefully, disdainfully, vengefully. It was truly quite extraordinary how much loathing could be expressed by one little hiss.

Bayerd took a hasty step back, and almost bumped into Suth. Well, she was as short as a jester, so it was easy to overlook her. "The heaven ssstone is there." She pointed to a spot to the left of the fire. Bayerd squinted and spotted a small glowing ember, no bigger than a hummingbird's egg. It looked rather like a coal that the fire had spat out, simply sitting there on the ground.

"Are you sure that is the heaven stone?" Bayerd said. "It looks more like an ember from the fire."

Suth nodded. "I am sssure."

"So, I just pick it up and we can leave?"

"Yesss, pick it up … if you can," she hissed.

Bayerd frowned. "It looks a bit hot."

Something wasn't right, he just wasn't sure what. He walked over to the little stone and crouched down, studying it. On closer inspection, it did not look like an ember. It was a facetted crystal, and the glow it emitted flashed with a rainbow of colours, not just orange and red and yellow. There were blues and greens and even purples pulsing inside it.

He tentatively prodded it with his finger. It was cold rather than hot. The contact sent a strange tingling vibration up his arm. He donned his leather riding glove before he tried to pick it up with his unburnt right hand. It proved surprisingly heavy and his fingers slid off when he tried to lift it. He got a tighter grip and tried again. The thing didn't budge. It might have been as heavy as the gigantic boulder that had almost crushed him.

Bayerd tried once more, pulling on the stone with all his strength. It did not lift. He lost his grip and he fell on his ass. All around him, scaly folk tittered. He stood up and glanced around for Suth. She was waiting by the fire. He approached her and said, "I think we'll leave without the heaven stone. Which tunnel will take us home?"

"That was not the bargain. The bargain was that you could leave with the ssstone," she reminded him.

"Ah … but not without the stone," Bayerd said, clueing in.

"Exactly."

He worried his lip. "The stone is heavier than it looks."

"It isss uncommonly heavy, isn't it?" Suth smiled with satisfaction.

"But perhaps there is still a way to lift it," Bayerd said, thinking aloud.

"You have until sssunset to leave, after that, you will start digging in the tunnelsss." Suth settled on the round bench, biding her time.

"When does the sun set?" he asked. He didn't have a clue.

"In about an hour or ssso."

It was not very long. Bayerd beckoned Orson and Gerald to join him by the stone, and no-one stopped them. "Stone too heavy to lift?" Gerald said.

"Yes, and we must find a way to carry it, as we cannot leave here without it. Any ideas?"

"It doesn't look that heavy." Orson crouched down and tried to lift it. Of course he couldn't. "It made my hand feel all funny and shivery," he said, rubbing his fingers against his tunic.

Gerald put on his riding glove and had a try, too. "Bloody hell, the thing is heavier than my horse."

"So how does a man lift a horse?" Bayerd asked.

"He doesn't." Gerald crossed his arms and scowled.

Bayerd kicked the stone and hurt his toe. The scaly folk tittered again. They seemed to be enjoying the show. Well, all men enjoyed a good show. If Bayerd was about to be sent into the tunnels to dig until he died, surely he should be allowed a final, farewell performance.

15. Dragon's Breath

Had I but known t'was the last touch

Had I but known t'was the last kiss

Had I but known

Had I but known t'was the last look

Had I but known t'was the last smile

Had I but known

-Bayerd the Storyteller, Regret

Bayerd leapt up onto the seat of the round bench. He stepped nimbly along on it, circling the fire, making eye-contact with his audience. "I've a tale to tell before I enter your tunnels, never to be seen again, my tongue forever silenced," he declared, granting his voice free rein. The vast domed chamber had lovely acoustics. His voice boomed up and out, as big as the mountain's heart.

The Tri-Alanth watched him as though mesmerized. Not one of the three heads took their eyes off him.

"It is a tale of love. A grand and foolish love between a princess and a fool," he orated, placing a hand over his heart, to identify himself as the fool.

Before he could proceed with the improvised tale, Orson shouted, "Hey there, enough of that." He lumbered over and stepped up onto the bench with Bayerd.

"What do you think you're doing?" Bayerd demanded, although he could guess.

"What do you think you're doing?" Orson shot back. "I am the storyteller, not you. If a tale is to be told, I'll be doing the telling, not you." Orson poked Bayerd in the chest with his oversized sausage of a finger, almost knocking Bayerd right off the bench. It was the last straw!

Bayerd glared at his friend resentfully, fury rising up in him. He did not even try to tamp it down. "Is it not enough that you, my very best friend, bed my wife while I am risking my life on a quest for our queen?" he cried, advancing toward Orson.

All around them, the scaly folk gasped.

Orson merely looked perplexed. "You're not married, Orson."

"I am not Orson. You are Orson. You are not the storyteller. I am the storyteller. I am Bayerd the Storyteller."

Orson shook his head. "No, I think you're confused there, Orson. You are good at some stuff, like fighting and pleasing the ladies." He winked. "But you are no storyteller, and you have no wife. I am wed to the beautiful Princess Kelp, and let me tell you, once a man has known her love," he winked again, "he'll want for no other woman."

Bayerd howled in outrage and took his sword in hand. "Perhaps today I will be able to wield a blade with skill, for honour guides my hand. Defend yourself!"

"I'm not going to fight you, Orson." Orson raised both hands in a gesture of surrender. "We're friends, and you know I can't fight worth a damn. You'd kill me with the first stab."

"Defend yourself or I will kill you now!" Bayerd waved his sword around in Orson's general direction, although in truth, he couldn't bring himself to stab his friend unless his friend defended himself. Bayerd's aim was a bit off and his blade caught Orson in the forearm. Bayerd kept his blade sharply honed and even the trifling contact sliced Orson's flesh and drew blood.

Orson's jaw dropped. "You stabbed me," he gasped.

"I barely scratched you," Bayerd said. "Take your sword in hand before I draw blood worth whining about."

"As you wish, Orson." Orson took his sword in hand and raised it as if he knew how to use it, which he did when he was himself. Perhaps his muscles remembered what his brain did not.

Bayerd's anger was still ruling him and he slashed with his sword, making contact with Orson's blade. The ringing clang of metal echoed across the chamber. The scaly folk leaned forward in anticipation of a better show than they had been expecting. Even the Tri-Alanth leaned closer.

Bayerd slashed again with his sword. Orson returned the favour. His slash was so much more powerful and accurate than Bayerd's. Bayerd had to fall back, almost right off the bench. Orson kept coming, slashing and stabbing with his much longer and stronger blade, and arm.

Bayerd kept retreating around the bench. He had never had occasion to battle Orson before. He had only witnessed other poor souls attempting the feat, and it was a terrifying experience to be on the pointy end of Orson's big sword. It was akin to battling a rampaging bear, if a bear could hold a sword. But Bayerd had his honour to defend. Orson had slept with his wife, and tried to usurp Bayerd's role as storyteller and quest leader. A man could only take so much maltreatment before he snapped.

They kept fighting, with Orson advancing and Bayerd retreating. Orson's blade drew blood once, twice and thrice, before Bayerd did fall off the bench. At least he landed on his feet. Orson leapt down, the point of his blade leading the way. Bayerd barely managed to block his next thrust. He tripped backwards, completely unbalanced. He fell with his sword in hand. The tip of his blade hit the ground and there was an explosive bang and a brilliant flash of light, as bright as the sun itself. Bayerd was temporarily blinded, and when he could see again, his sword was sparking, its tip pressed against the heaven stone.

"No more fighting," he shouted at Orson, who lowered the blade he was still waving lethally about.

"I'm a better fighter than I realized, and you're really not very good," Orson said, sheathing his sword.

"That is because you are Orson, and I am Bayerd," Bayerd said absently, scrutinizing the tip of his sword where it was pressed against the heaven stone. He let go of the hilt and the weapon stood at attention, all by itself. Bayerd circled his sword, balanced on its tip, cozying up to the little heaven stone. He had never seen a sword do that.

He gripped the hilt of his sword and pulled. Did the stone move? Bayerd tugged harder, but it was as if his blade was stuck fast to the heaven stone, as if to a giant magnet. Perhaps the heaven stone wasn't so much heavy, as magnetized to the ground. Who knew how much metal lay under this mountain.

Bayerd stopped pulling and began pushing the tip of his sword under the heaven stone. He leaned on it with all his weight and wiggled it a bit, digging the tip into the ground under the glowing crystal.

All of the sudden, it slid fully beneath the heaven stone, perhaps breaking its contact with whatever metal it had been stuck to. Bayerd grinned and raised his sword triumphantly, the stone affixed to the tip.

His audience gasped in dismay, as well they might. He bowed to them. "Either I am a much stronger man than I appear, or the stone is

141

not nearly as heavy as we believed. In truth, it feels as light as a feather." He tossed his sword to his other hand, to rub it in. Alas, in his triumph, he had completely forgotten about his burnt palm.

Bayerd dropped his sword with a cry of pain. It hit the ground, and the stone was again stuck to the earth. Clearly, deliberately taunting the Tri-Alanth was a bad idea, in more ways than one. But he had been unable to resist a bit of gloating after so much hardship and strife.

The Tri-Alanth hissed angrily. All three heads were so furious, sparks shot out of their mouths.

Orson was the one to lift the sword and the heaven stone, shaking his head at Bayerd. Bayerd snatched his sword out of Orson's hand, saying, "That's my sword."

The Tri-Alanth hissed again, producing a shower of sparks. Bayerd turned to her, brushing sparks off his shoulders. "A bargain is a bargain," he said. "It is time for you to show us which tunnel will take us home, and we shall leave, carrying the heaven stone."

Suth was the one to point to the archway that would lead them back to their side of the mountain. "And there are no forks in the tunnel?" Bayerd asked.

"Always bear left," Suth said grudgingly.

"Well, I thank you for your hospitality." Bayerd bowed around, spun on his heel, and strode quickly away, carrying the heaven stone on his sword.

Before Orson and Gerald could fall into step behind him, the Tri-Alanth lunged out of her fire in a cascade of sizzling sparks. It wasn't merely her three necks that kept getting longer. Her body came out too, and it was a gigantic and terrifying blend of snake and dragon. She was as massive as any dragon, yet shaped more like a fat snake with legs, and the three long necks and three heads of course. She had wings too. They were extraordinarily long, and tucked tight against her sinewy body.

Bayerd planted his feet wide and faced her. "We struck a bargain," he thundered, his voice almost shaking the stone walls.

All three heads opened their mouths and blasted fire, trying to roast him alive. Bayerd was surrounded by her kinfolk, yet she did not seem to care that they might be harmed as well. Or perhaps they did not burn like a man from the outer-realm.

He turned and ran. He managed three steps before one of the long necks wrapped around him like a true snake and picked him up off the ground. One of the heads sank its fangs into his hand—the one that held his sword. He screamed and lost his grip on it. It clattered to the ground and the Tri-Alanth tossed him carelessly to the earth. Three heads loomed over him. Two were smiling maliciously; the middle one held his sword firmly in her mouth.

Bayerd staggered to his feet, scanning for Orson and Gerald. They were being held at bay by a crowd of scaly folk. Orson had his sword in hand, but he wasn't swinging it. His eyes were on Bayerd, trying to communicate something. Bayerd only realized what that was when Orson suddenly tossed his sword toward Bayerd, hilt first. In Orson's confused mind, he must have still believed that Bayerd was Orson, and could catch a blade in flight without losing a hand, and then wield it with skill to defeat the Tri-Alanth.

He cursed and tried to catch the hilt with his fang-bitten hand, rather than his burnt hand. Amazingly, he managed to knock it out of the air without amputating even one of his fingers. He scooped the sword up and raised it to defend himself from the Tri-Alanth. He had forgotten quite how heavy Orson's sword was compared to his own. It took every muscle he had to hold it aloft in his two injured hands.

The Tri-Alanth attacked, weaving around, jabbing at him with the sword she held clenched in her mouth. She fought as well as any knight, and far better than the six knights who had shared Bayerd's quest. His pitiful defense lasted less than a minute before her blade was true. It stabbed so deeply into his chest, the tip almost came out his back. Orson's sword slipped from his suddenly numb fingers. He sank to his knees, his very own sword still impaled in his chest.

Before he was in the least prepared, the Tri-Alanth yanked the blade out. Strangely, there was no wrenching pain or gushing fluids. He looked down and frowned. His tunic was cut opened, and the sword had, without a doubt, impaled him, so where was the fountain of blood?

The Tri-Alanth dropped his sword with a clatter, and all three monstrous heads gave anguished cries, their eyes on his sword. The heaven stone was no longer glowing on its tip. So where was it?

An alarming thought struck Bayerd. He parted his torn tunic to see his wound. Over his heart, there was a raised red and black scar, but it looked as healed as if it had been cauterized, rather than freshly inflicted. And his heart seemed to be glowing. No, it was glowing. He cried out in dismay. No sound came out, only a stream of fire. He slammed his mouth shut and the fire died. His mouth should have been burnt, yet the fire hadn't felt hot to him. It had felt pleasantly cool.

The Tri-Alanth fell back at the sight of fire coming out of his mouth, but she didn't stay back. She arched her necks and lunged toward him, perhaps to gut him and claim back the heaven stone.

"Stay back," he bellowed, and again no words came out, only a thick stream of fire that was so hot, it was more blue than orange. It stopped her in her slithering tracks.

"How are you doing that?" she hissed, and Bayerd understood her words perfectly. T'was as if he held fire in his palm again. Perhaps it was the magical stone that now resided inside him that made it possible.

"You understand me? You hear my words?" Bayerd said, in flames. He really couldn't manage a man's speech any longer. His true voice was lost to him.

"I do," she hissed back at him.

"Then heed my words. Our bargain stands. I am leaving with my men, and taking the heaven stone with me. Since it is now inside me, I am not about to leave it behind, am I?" His attempt at more than one short sentence resulted in a longer stream of blazing fire.

"Perhaps we can make another bargain, a new bargain," she proposed.

"Oh, I'm quite happy with the old bargain, and you have proven yourself untrustworthy." Bayerd noticed Orson and Gerald watching his flaming display with astonished eyes. Did they think he had been changed into some sort of dragon-man? Well, perhaps he had.

"The heaven stone inside you should be mine. It creates fire, and fire is my realm. The stone is meant for me. That is why it came down on my mountain. That is why it breathes fire like me."

"Such a happenstance is called chance," Bayerd said.

"No, it is called fate," she hissed.

"If you believe in fate, then the heaven stone is fated to be mine, since it has found a home in me," Bayerd countered.

"Your flame is impressive." The Tri-Alanth edged closer, all three of her long necks undulating like dancing snakes. "It is most attractive, most stimulating. I would like one taste of your flame, then I will let you and your men leave, alive. That is the new bargain."

"You want to taste my fire? That is all you ask to let us leave?" Bayerd said uncertainly. He was so focused on the middle head, which was doing all the talking, so he was completely taken aback when the

144

two other heads lunged at him, one from each side. Before he could dodge away, two necks wrapped around him. One even pushed between his thighs and rubbed him intimately.

The middle head got right up in his face, so close, he could see the fine network of hair that coated her scales. "I do not agree to the bargain," Bayerd shouted, blasting flame directly at her. She did not back off, but darted in, locking lips with him, taking his fire inside her. It was an unholy invasion.

He cursed and fought to be free of her lips, and the two necks that squeezed him. He wasn't strong enough and had to endure the invasive kiss. Her tongue darted into his mouth and snaked down his throat making him gag. He realized he was endangered in a new way. Was she trying to retrieve the stone by burrowing down to his heart through his throat? And just how long was her tongue? She breathed fire into his mouth, mingling her flames with his. Her fire no longer felt hot to him.

The other head was getting much too intimate with his crotch, and Bayerd hated to think what another snake tongue might do down there. He dropped to his knees and managed to yank one arm free of a coiled neck, almost dislocating his shoulder in the process. He groped around and felt the hilt of a sword. It felt familiar. His sword, not Orson's. In one motion, he jerked it up and slashed the neck of the dominant Tri-Alanth, the one that was choking him with her tongue.

She screamed fire and her tongue retracted. Her mouth went slack and her head dropped at his feet, completely severed from her neck—no longer attached to her sisters. He hadn't been trying to cut off her head, but his blade hadn't met much resistance. Perhaps she lacked proper bones.

A wash of blood soaked Bayerd, as if a bucketful of it had been tossed in his face. The necks that still trapped him tightened cruelly, trying to crush him. Fangs impaled his thigh, alarmingly close to his manhood. He slashed at a second neck, the one that was attempting to neuter him. He severed that head off, too. More blood soaked his pants, a mixture of both his own and the Tri-Alanth's. The remaining head darted around behind his back where he could not reach it, and sank fangs into his shoulder.

Bayerd tried to reach over his shoulder with his sword. He could not generate any force that way, nor could he see where her neck was. A flash of movement caught his eye and the fangs withdrew from his shoulder. He heard a thud. Another head hitting the dirt? The body of the Tri-Alanth collapsed to the earth.

There was a heartbeat of frozen stillness before Orson said, "Run!"

Orson was there, his sword in hand. The third head lolled at his feet. It was still attached to the neck, but quite unawares. Orson must have whacked it on the head, rather than messily severing it from its neck. Regardless, he might have just saved Bayard's life.

Gerald raced up to them, his blade raised overhead, intent on chopping off the last head. Before he could swing his blade, a wave of scaly folk rushed them.

"Run," Orson repeated, taking the lead, aiming for the tunnel that would take them home. Bayerd tripped over a neck and staggered when he tried to follow. Gerald grabbed his wrist and yanked, almost dislocating Bayerd's injured shoulder.

Together, the three men ran for their lives into the tunnel, knocking scaly folk aside like pins, clearing a path as they went. They were pursued into the tunnel by a mob of them. Alas, it was too dark to see, and therefore too dark to flee. Gerald had managed to snag a torch and he shoved it into Bayerd's hand saying, "Light it."

Bayerd blew fire-breath onto the thing and it flared bright. Gerald grabbed it back and took the lead. The scaly folk were soon left behind. Their short legs did not allow for speed.

The three men ran until their legs gave out, listening for any sound of pursuit. There was no breath to waste on words, not that Bayerd could talk. His voice had been replaced by fire.

When Gerald slowed to a walk, Bayerd could have kissed him. He was aching from head to toe and bleeding from more wounds than a butchered pig. "Bless you, Gerald," he gasped, in his profound relief forgetting about his affliction.

Orson slapped at his sleeve where it had caught fire and bellowed, "No talking, Bayerd, not a bloody word!"

"You know who I am!" Bayerd cried, setting Orson's other sleeve alight.

Once those flames had been extinguished, he hugged his friend until he remembered that Orson had betrayed him, then he shoved Orson away and glared. He ached to demand that Orson explain himself now that he was himself again. Sadly, Bayerd couldn't speak a word that any man could understand.

Gerald said, "Keep moving, t'is not the time for talk. And Bayerd, unless we need your fire to light our way, keep your mouth shut."

Bayerd nodded and Gerald set the pace. They walked as briskly as they could for as long as they could, then they stumbled along until they dropped with exhaustion. Gerald suggested one of them remain awake, and offered to take the first watch.

Sleep came instantly for Bayerd, who had lost so much blood, he felt more ghostly spirit than man. He had also lost the skull in the scuffle, and rather missed his boney namesake.

Orson shook Bayerd awake at some point, to take his turn on watch. Groggy with sleep, Bayerd said, "Leave me be." He set Orson's trousers on fire. Orson's shouting woke up Gerald, who suggested they resume their journey. The torch had been spent so Bayerd had to take the lead position, blasting his fire periodically so they could see their way.

As before, the days blended into each other in a chain of fatigue, hunger and dehydration. Twice they encountered branches in the path, and they bore left. When they spotted light at the end of the tunnel, Gerald gave a hoarse cry of joy, Orson cheered, and Bayerd laughed, which set Orson's hair on fire.

Once the flames were snuffed, they exited the mountain. There before them, silhouetted brilliantly against the setting sun, was the Golden Kingdom in all its glowing glory.

16. Homeward Bound

Oh, clear, clean, sparkling water
You have no equal or rival
Be you guzzled cool or hotter
Vital nectar for survival

Oh, water flowing in a river
Plentiful with silver fishes
Still you are my lifelong giver
Delicious fishes on my dishes

Oh, water raining from the sky
See the seeds grow into wheat
Quenching the land, cracked and dry
Wheat to bake the bread I eat

-Bayerd the Storyteller, Ode to Water

The three men simply stood like statues, gazing upon the glorious sight of the Golden Kingdom as though dumbstruck. "Home has never looked so good," Gerald said hoarsely.

"Aye, I may take a page out of Bayerd's book and never leave the castle again," declared Orson, slapping the older man on the back. Both kept their distance from Bayerd, what with his propensity to set them ablaze.

Bayerd gazed at the beautiful golden towers of Kelp's kingdom and his eyes glazed over with unshed tears. His heart ached to see Kelp, to hold her, to beg her forgiveness for the thoughtless coward of a man he had been. He just wanted to go home, except he no longer had a home. Or a lover.

Was it any wonder Kelp had taken Orson into her bed? No, it truly wasn't. She had deserved so much better than Bayerd and she had found it in Orson, who was strong and handsome, and noble and true. Except for betraying his best friend, Orson was a man you would be proud to call a friend. Bayerd had an urge to tell Orson that he understood his friend's actions, even if he could not forgive them. Kelp was so lovely, he didn't understand how other men could resist her. Alas, he no longer had a voice.

Bayerd bit his lip, trying to control his emotions. He had a good look at Gerald and Orson in the bright light of day. It was hard to imagine a sorrier sight. Both were far too thin and filthy, with gaunt, hairy faces, wearing clothing that a ragman wouldn't have deigned to pick out of the trash. Bayerd had accidentally set Orson ablaze so many times, his friend looked like he had been in a barn fire, trying to rescue the horses, which was just the valiant sort of thing he would do.

As if he felt Bayerd's scrutiny, Orson turned to him with a grin, then his face fell. "Good lord, Bayerd, you're bloody covered in blood. Guess that three-headed monster lady that was trying to have her way with you bled all over you. You do attract the oddest ladies." His brow furrowed. "Do you know, you fighting that monster is the first thing I can remember since I wandered into that mountain passage, yet clearly much time has passed and we've had a bloody hard time of it." He rubbed the top of his head. "That snake monster gave me a good whack on the head, and then I remembered who I was, but not a thing that came before."

Gerald approached Bayerd so warily, Bayerd might have been a specter from beyond the grave. "And you got stabbed through the heart, yet you did not die." He shifted Bayerd's torn tunic and studied the scar over Bayerd's heart. There were two there, now, the first having been inflicted by Kelp's nasty northern cousin when the lout had been set on marrying her. "I think you truly do not die," Gerald said in awe. "And now the heaven stone glows inside your heart."

Bayerd nodded with resignation. It did, and it would probably be stuck inside him until the day he did truly die, if he was still a mortal man with that magical stone squatting inside him.

Orson had been doing some hard thinking. His brow furrowed even deeper. "Kelp thinks you're dead, did you know? Someone else must have been wearing your golden slippers when they got crushed to death by tons of falling rock."

Bayerd nodded. Orson was missing a large slice of his memories, and perhaps that was for the best.

"That would have been Sir Swift," Gerald told him. "He had taken to wearing Prince Bayerd's wardrobe as if it was his own."

Bayerd sighed and glanced down at the disgusting rags he wore now, the only clothes left to him. He saw that Orson had spoken nothing but the truth. He was bloody red from head to toe. The Tri-Alanth's blood covered most of him, and added to that, a generous measure of his own. He hadn't yet tended to his wounds and the deepest of them were still leaking. His bitten shoulder and leg were damp from oozing punctures. And then there were the shallow sword slashes on his ribs, arm and shoulder—cuts that Orson didn't remember inflicting. The only wound that hadn't bled was the one over his heart, and that is the one that should have been a fountain of blood, and not merely because of the stabbing.

He could not go home again for so many reasons, yet still, he ached to gaze upon Kelp's beauty one last time, and he ached to complete his quest, for it was all he had left now. He had lost his storyteller's voice, he had lost Kelp to Orson, and he had lost his lifelong friend to betrayal. He had even lost his home, since the Golden Kingdom was Kelp's native land, not his.

The quest was all he had to cling to, paired with the burning desire to prove he was no longer a coward. Alas, the heaven stone could not be presented to Queen Hellenor without him, since it resided in his chest. Yet if he returned home, he would cause Kelp nothing but fresh heartache. She already believed him dead. Far better to let her go on believing it, and disappear into the night, even if it meant giving up on his quest. He knew that was the right course of action for him.

But before he parted company with Orson and Gerald, he had to communicate an important message. He needed to make sure they would hold their tongues about the fact that he was still a living breathing man. They needed to affirm his death, rather than dispute it.

Without horses, the walk to the Golden Kingdom would take days. He could remain with them for a few more nights, enjoy their companionship, and when it was time to leave, he would somehow pantomime his important message—that he would not be going home with them, and must remain dead to the Golden Kingdom.

Orson's next words shocked Bayerd out of his reverie. "And Basher and Conquer and Revel, they're all dead, too. Throats cut so deep, their heads were almost severed off."

"What?" Bayerd gasped.

Luckily, Orson was far enough away to be spared any more burning. The same could not be said for the little patch of daisies near Bayerd's boots. He stomped out the flames before they could spread, and waited for Gerald to ask the questions he could not.

Gerald said, "Dead? Murdered? How do you know?"

"Why, two turned up at the castle, gruesomely murdered and tied to their horses. That's why we were trying to catch up with you. And we came across Revel in the same state, tied to his horse, as we rode toward the mountain. And Sir Swift crushed under a mountain of rock. This was a cursed quest to be sure." Orson's brow furrowed in confusion, as it so often did. "Hey, where's Jabalot? Is he dead, too?"

"No, at least, he wasn't, but he might be by now. He is still in the mountain, and has most likely been captured by those nasty little mountain dwellers. Prince Bayerd returns to the Golden Kingdom with only one of his six knights—me." Gerald scratched at his unkempt beard and glanced at Bayerd. "I suspect Jabalot was the one who killed your knights. No, don't you say a word!"

Bayerd hadn't been about to talk. He was learning to quell the natural impulse. He simply nodded in agreement and pointed to the golden towers of the queen's castle, indicating that they should start walking. He, too, suspected Jabalot of doing the killing, but since Jabalot probably numbered amongst the dead in the mountain's tunnels now, it was neither here nor there. Of the six knights who had ridden with him, he was glad it was Gerald who had survived. He liked Gerald the best of all his knights. And he could do one thing to reward Gerald's loyalty. The Tri-Alanth hadn't had a chance to claim the pouch of gemstones that were part of the bargain, and it was now tied to Bayerd's belt. He removed the pouch and pressed it into Gerald's hands.

Gerald grinned. "My gems! I'll be the richest man in the kingdom. I thank you, Prince Bayerd."

Bayerd nodded and touched his heart, trying to communicate his gratitude for Gerald's loyalty.

Orson sighed gustily. "Gems are fine and all, but we need water and food before we start hiking. I hear running water just over there."

151

They were all dying for a drink—truly dying. They stumbled toward the sound of flowing water, and came across a decent-sized creek. They fell to their knees and drank like horses, their lips in the water.

When their thirst was slaked, Bayerd waded in, wearing his rags. He ducked under, sluicing blood off his skin and hair and clothing. The water turned red around him. He rinsed his wounds thoroughly, hoping they wouldn't fester. When he waded out, the air felt much colder and he shivered. Perhaps he should have endured his filth a little longer, in favour of dryness and warmth, especially with night coming on.

Orson said, "I think I'll look around for some game while there's still a bit of light."

"It might not be wise to make camp this close to the mountain," Gerald said. "We should keep moving and find a safer location. We can hunt game in the morning. What are a few short hours when we've been without so much as a morsel for days?"

He made a good point. They started hiking in the direction of the Golden Kingdom, the shining towers a beacon to them. Bayerd became quite chilled, in spite of the exertion of walking. He no longer had any fat on his frame to keep him insulated from the cold, and their packs and blankets had been left behind in the mountain, along with the skull. All they had left to them were their swords.

When it got truly dark, they stopped. They dared not light a fire, which could lead the scaly folk straight to them, if they still gave chase.

Orson assigned Bayerd the first watch, probably to avoid getting set on fire again. As tired as he was, Bayerd managed to stay awake for half the night because he was shivering too much to relax. The cold had seeped all the way into his bones. His thoughts tormented him as well, and he felt no inclination to close his eyes.

When the moon was lowering out of the sky, he awoke Orson to take the next watch. He did manage several hours of slumber, filled with dreams of all his happiest moments with Kelp. The memories were still fresh in his head when he opened his eyes. They were bittersweet memories now that he had lost her love.

A burning fire and the smell of cooking meat welcomed him back to the waking world. The sun was surprisingly high. No-one had tried to wake him—probably too scared, or if they had tried, he had slept through the attempt.

He sat up and stretched, and took a look around. Only Gerald was there, sitting in the fire's warmth, tending to the cooking. Bayerd made a trip into the trees to heed the call of nature, and returned to sit with Gerald. He eyed the cooking meat. It was scrawny—whatever it was.

"Quail," Gerald said. "Orson's off trying to catch something else, something bigger. Well, that one little bird won't feed three starving men, will it?"

Bayerd shook his head. It would only whet their appetites. He'd had to tighten his belt yet another notch, just that morning. He was every bit as scrawny as the poor quail that sizzled over the fire.

Gerald made eye contact and said, "It must be difficult, losing your voice."

Bayerd nodded morosely.

"And learning that your closest companion is bedding your bride." He exhaled and shook his head. "Well, you've handled yourself very well, all things considered. Better than most."

Bayerd shrugged. What choice did he have? As much as he wished it, he couldn't travel back in time and be a braver man, or a better husband. He had made his own bed, and now he had to lie in it. And that would be a cold, empty bed.

He could no longer make his way as a storyteller, but perhaps he could make his way as a fire-starter, or join a company of travelling freaks. Men who had a few coins to spare might toss them in his direction to see him blast fire out of his mouth like an honest-to-goodness dragon-man.

His future was a bleak thing indeed. And he wouldn't even have Orson by his side. He had come to accept that Orson should stay with Kelp. In spite of their betrayal of him, in his heart, Bayerd did want the two people he loved most to be happy, even if it was with each other and not him. It had not been an easy truth to come to accept, but in the end, his desire for their happiness had eroded away the anger and resentment he was feeling. Or most of the anger and resentment he was feeling.

Neither he nor Gerald stirred when they heard a rustling of branches. Both assumed it was Orson. Both hoped he was returning with more game. Both were wrong.

Jabalot burst out of the bushes and dropped to his knees, panting hard. "Thank heavens I found you," he cried.

Bayerd was so startled to see the man, that he said, "You're alive?" The stream of fire that came out of his mouth was aimed as much at the ground as Jabalot, so it only burnt the villain's knees. In truth, Bayerd wouldn't have minded burning more of the man who had tried to kill him, and may well have killed three of his knights.

Jabalot leapt up in fear, slapping out the flames that smoldered on his pants. "Don't burn me alive, I've only just found you."

Gerald was Bayerd's voice. He said, "How did you escape the mountain?"

"I was watching from that hole in the dome and saw what happened down below, and I saw which tunnel you took. When the room emptied, I climbed down on the ropes, well, only partway down since the ropes weren't long enough. Had to jump the rest of the way, but I didn't break my leg. Then I followed the tunnel out of that damn mountain."

"Are the scaly folk still after us?" Gerald asked.

"No, they gave up the chase pretty quick. Well, they had to take care of that three-headed monster, didn't they? She is their leader. They tossed the two severed heads into their round fire-pit, if you can believe that, and then about a hundred of her kin dragged her huge carcass into that same fire. I'm not sure if she was dead. Anyway, I escaped. Is that for me?" He pointed to the sizzling meat.

"Hands off," Gerald growled at Jabalot. "None of us have eaten yet and we're hoping Orson has found more game."

Bayerd was less concerned about his stomach, which had gone so long without food, it had given up all hope of getting any. He was more concerned with the killing of his three knights. He elbowed Gerald and drew a finger across his throat, in a not so subtle message for Gerald to question Jabalot about the murders.

His message was misconstrued. Jabalot cried, "You want to behead me? You want me killed? After all we've been through together?"

Bayerd rolled his eyes heavenward, then shook his head. Not having a voice was proving quite maddening. He pointed to Gerald, indicating the message was for him to pass along to Jabalot. Again, he must not have been clear enough. Jabalot freed his sword and pointed it at Gerald, saying, "Don't know why Bayerd wants you dead, but I'll have to do it, have to follow orders."

Of course Gerald unsheathed his sword. "You will not be killing me, assassin. You've done enough killing."

Jabalot gazed at him shiftily. "What are you talking about?"

"Orson's memories have returned to him. He told us that Basher, Conquer and Revel were murdered. All dead by your hand, and you almost killed me twice over, shoving me off of great heights," Gerald

154

declared, raising his blade threateningly. "But I refuse to join my fellow knights in the grave. And Prince Bayerd was not ordering my death, I think he wants to know why you murdered his three knights."

"I did no such thing, well, not really." Jabalot lowered his blade. He dug the tip into the ground sheepishly. "I might have killed Basher on purpose, but I couldn't abide my brother sleeping with my wife. I mean, men, or most men," he darted a glance at Bayerd, "can't abide that, can they?"

Gerald lowered his blade. "Fair enough, but what about Conquer and Revel?"

In Bayerd's opinion, Gerald should have kept his blade at the ready. All the men had been killed in the same fashion, and tied to their horses in the same way. Ergo, they had been killed by the same man. Jabalot had admitted to killing Basher, therefore, logic dictated that he had also killed Conquer and Revel. Gerald didn't seem to see that connection, and Bayerd had no voice to point it out to him. Nor was it something he could communicate with a nod or a shake of his head, or a shrug, or a wink of his eye.

Jabalot hummed and hawed a bit before he said, "Well, I suppose it could be said that I killed Conquer, but only by accident."

"Slitting the man's throat was an accident?" Gerald said with the perfect amount of skepticism.

"It was dark you see, and there was a rustling in the bushes. I thought it was Prince Bayerd returning to camp. His was the only empty bedroll, at least that I could see."

Since Jabalot was half-blind, the explanation was more than plausible.

Jabalot continued. "So I slit his throat, as I was charged to do, only it wasn't Prince Bayerd. It was Conquer, probably just coming back from taking a piss or something."

Bayerd shuddered. If he had not fallen into a drunken stupor at the creek, and had returned to camp, he would be the dead one, not Conquer.

"Anyway," Jabalot went on, "since I didn't mean to kill him, and I didn't want to get in trouble for that little slip of the knife, I tied Conquer to his horse, like I did my brother, and sent him on his way."

Gerald snorted. "And Revel?"

"Uh … I didn't mean to kill him either."

Bayerd raised one eyebrow inquiringly.

"I didn't," Jabalot declared insistently. "I was trying to kill you again. You really are a hard man to kill."

Gerald rubbed his bristled chin. "And how did you end up mistaking Revel for Prince Bayerd? His hair is orange."

"It was dark, you see, and I saw a shadowy figure stumbling around, didn't expect Revel to be on his feet, him being injured and all. I figured Prince Bayerd had gotten into the wine and was staggering about. Seemed like a good time to kill him so we wouldn't have to climb that damn mountain, so I slit his throat, only it wasn't Prince Bayerd, it was Revel."

"And you tied him on his horse and sent him on his way," Gerald assumed.

"That I did. Anyway, I didn't mean to kill him, so it was an accident. Murdering doesn't really count if it's an accident," Jabalot said, whining a touch, then he got an inspired look on his face. "I've got proof, you know, proof that I was only following orders." He dug around in his pouch, which was filled to the brim with gemstones. When he didn't find what he was looking for, he dug around in his pockets until he produced a ruby-encrusted locket on a thick gold chain. Bayerd knew that locket. It had often adorned Kelp's swan-like neck.

"Princess Kelp gave me this in payment," he said. "All I had to do was make sure you did not return from your quest. Is that proof enough for you?"

Alas, it was undeniable proof. Bayerd extended a hand and wiggled his fingers. Jabalot handed the jewelry over. Bayerd opened it and saw the miniature wedding portrait that Kelp had commissioned. As small as the painting was, they looked blissfully happy together. And they had been, for a short time, before Bayerd turned into an ass. He closed the locket and put the chain around his own neck. Now, he would have a picture of Kelp, always.

Jabalot protested. In answer, Bayerd pointed at the vast fortune in the man's pouch. Jabalot grimaced. "Oh, I suppose one little locket is neither here nor there, now that I am as rich as a king."

Orson interrupted them then, strolling into the campsite with a dead deer draped over his shoulders. His eyes widened when he spotted Jabalot. He tossed off the deer. "What are you doing here?" he asked curiously. Orson's memories were so fractured and compromised, Bayerd wasn't sure what he recalled about Jabalot.

"Reuniting with my prince." Jabalot shoved his sword into his sheath and raised both hands in a gesture of surrender. "Do you need help carving up that deer?"

Orson looked to Bayerd for guidance, and Bayerd could only shrug and point to the deer. He was hungry and they could sort things out after they had filled their bellies, as long as Jabalot didn't kill anyone in the meantime. When you are starving, food takes precedence over talk, even if it is talk of murder.

"Eating it is," Orson declared. "Uh, Bayerd, why don't you blast fire at the beastie, burn off its fur and cook the meat at the same time? We'd have food in our bellies that much faster."

"Come on, Bayerd. We're starving," Jabalot said plaintively.

They were. Bayerd approached the deer and began talking, aiming his fire at the carcass. He knew he would not be understood, yet he felt the need to get certain things off his chest. He said, "Orson, I know you've been getting naked with my wife behind my back, and while it breaks my heart. I am trying to come to terms with it. I understand how and why it happened. I was an embarrassment to Kelp, and I wasn't there for you either, huddled as I was in my quarters. I pushed the two of you together, and now that I have lost my voice, I can no longer be a husband to Kelp, and I don't want her to be alone, and well, I do want both of you to be happy, but you'll have to stop your womanizing. I don't want you betraying Kelp, the way you both betrayed me." Bayerd had to stop to take a breath. "When I disappear into the night, I hope you will tell Kelp, and Queen Hellenor, and every soul in the Golden Kingdom, that I succeeded at my quest. And you are not to say that I live still. I must remain a dead man, so Kelp can move on and be happy. I will take solace in the fact that you will stay by Kelp's side, and make her happy in a way that I did not and no longer can, now that I am as much dragon as man. My voice was the only worthy thing about me— running off at the mouth was my only talent. Now all that comes out is fire and more damn fire." His voice faltered and he had to clear his throat. The deer was quite furless by then, and the meat was sizzling. Laced as it was with blue flames, Bayerd's fire was proving a great deal hotter than a regular campfire.

He looked at Orson, trying to communicate with his eyes what his voice couldn't any longer. "I will know that you are happy and have a home, for you deserve a home after our long years of wandering the countryside. Whilst that is an adventurous life for a young man, an

157

older man needs a home and hearth, and a family. A place where he is respected and loved. It is what most men dream about. And your home will be a palace with the most beautiful woman in the land as your wife. What better life can there be than that?" It was the life that Bayerd, in his foolishness, had tossed away.

Bayerd kept flaming at the mouth until Orson said, "I think that's quite enough fire, Bayerd. Time to shut up." The deer was starting to look overcooked. It was ready to eat in an unbelievably short time.

All four men pulled out their daggers and sliced off the juicy, succulent meat, although Bayerd and Gerald kept a wary eye on Jabalot's blade in case it went astray.

After they ate, the sun was almost at high noon. They wanted nothing more than to nap, but Gerald vetoed that idea. "Safer to keep moving," he said. "I don't want to die in the shadow of this cursed mountain." He shot a dark glance Jabalot's way.

Bayerd nodded and struggled wearily to his feet. He started walking, eyes on the Golden Kingdom. He would spend this last day with Orson and Gerald, then he would communicate his farewell message somehow, and disappear into the night, never to be seen or heard from again. Jabalot would be pleased, since his mission to see that Bayerd never returned to the castle would have been accomplished, after a fashion.

They walked all day, and the kingdom didn't look one inch closer as the sun set behind it. They really could have used some horses. The dank clothes Bayerd had had to wear seemed to have given him a chill. He began to sneeze and cough, which proved to be highly dangerous. Great blasts of fire shot out of his mouth whenever he did. Orson got lit on fire twice. After that, no-one would go near Bayerd. He had to walk in the lead position and simply try not to set the forest ablaze.

When they could see the moon and stars rather than the sun, they stopped walking. Orson went to round up kindling and Gerald said, "We'll take turns on watch. Jabalot, you can sleep through the night."

"Still don't trust me? I keep telling you, I only meant to kill my brother, and he deserved it. And I had royal orders to kill Bayerd, the others just got in the way. I didn't want to kill them. They weren't sleeping with my wife, were they?"

"I don't know, maybe they were," Gerald snapped. They were all grouchy with fatigue.

Jabalot yanked out his blade. "Don't you call my wife a trollop. She only slept with me and my brother, no other. And with my brother dead, she'll be faithful to me."

Gerald pulled out his blade, too.

Before things escalated into bloodshed, Bayerd sneezed a stream of fire between the two men. They both leapt back. Swords were sheathed and cooler heads prevailed, thanks to Bayerd's fiery intervention.

Orson returned at that moment, his arms loaded with broken boughs. "Don't start the fire without the wood," he said, dropping the load at Bayerd's boots. Bayerd obliged and started it blazing. The men ate left over deer meat and began yawning.

"Bayerd, do you want first watch?" Gerald asked.

Bayerd nodded. The castle was still some days away. He could stay with his companions for one more day. It was no easy thing to leave them, for he knew once he did, he would miss them terribly, except for Jabalot.

He paced while the rest of the men settled for the night and fell asleep quickly. They were all exhausted. Bayerd was too, but he kept pacing. He did not want to accidentally fall asleep and have Jabalot slay him or anyone else. Once before, he had fallen asleep on watch, which had led to the death of a friend—and ultimately mating with a harpy.

Bayerd took a peek under his torn tunic and his heart glowed in the darkness, as if it was filled with fireflies. He kept hoping that the heaven stone would be extinguished, from being inside him so long, yet its glow did not seem at all diminished.

The moon moved across the sky, and he kept watch over his remaining men. He made sure the lump that was Jabalot didn't move from under his blanket. He was the only one who still had a blanket and pack, and being Jabalot, he certainly hadn't offered to share.

When Bayerd woke Orson to take the next watch, he did not bed down. Instead, he sat with his friend in the low light of the small fire he had kept burning with his breath. Orson gave him a long troubled look and said, "Since the fire's got your tongue, it's left to me to do the talking, isn't it. There are still some things I haven't told you, Bayerd."

Bayerd nodded for him to continue. Was Orson going to confess his betrayal while they had this moment of privacy? It had to be weighing heavily on him, for Orson was at heart a most noble fellow.

Instead Orson said, "Remember that harpy that had her way with you? Well, she turned up before I left the castle, with a babe—your babe." Bayerd nodded with resignation. Orson said, "Did I already tell you about the babe?" Bayerd nodded again.

"Huh. Sure wish I could remember what I have and haven't told you." He gazed into the flames moodily. Was he wondering if he had already confessed to Bayerd that he had stolen Kelp's affections? Did he know that Kelp had hired Jabalot to assassinate Bayerd? No, Orson would never have allowed that. He must be in the dark about Kelp's darkest actions.

Even if he'd had his voice, Bayerd wouldn't have enlightened Orson about Kelp's hired assassin. Better for his friend to think highly of his new love. And in his heart of hearts, Bayerd knew he deserved Kelp's harshest judgment, and therefore he could not fault her actions—much.

"I have to admit, I miss hearing your voice, even if it is only telling the same tired tale for the hundredth time," Orson continued. "After this quest, if you had your voice, you would have some grand new tales to tell, wouldn't you? Maybe your best tales yet." Orson poked at the fire with a stick. "Bet you've already scripted them in your head."

In truth, even though he never would be able to tell it, Bayerd had been scripting an epic tale of his quest—a dramatic, yet farcical account of all that had gone wrong, whilst still presenting himself as the hero of the tale. He nodded his admission to Orson.

"Figured as much. Well, maybe when we get back to the castle, and you have a quill and ink, you can record the tale. Some other storyteller could perform it, if it is a worthy tale. Lots of good storytellers around looking for new material."

Bayerd glared at Orson, not in the least bit heartened by the words. The thought of another storyteller performing his tales made jealousy rear its ugly head. He didn't want anyone performing his tale, save himself.

"What? Don't you like that idea?" Orson asked, clueless.

Bayerd shook his head emphatically.

"Fine then, I'll keep my ideas to myself since you think they stink. Maybe you should get some sleep. I think you're grumpy, although it's hard to tell since you can't talk. But you look grumpy."

Before Bayerd succumbed to temptation and set Orson on fire, on purpose, he went to bed.

17. When is a Man a Dragon?

There once was a man who breathed fire
Folks came from afar to admire
He started to sneeze
And burnt all their knees
Now that poor fellow's had to retire

-Bayerd the Storyteller, Limerick

The next day was a repeat of the one that had come before. The men ate well enough and breathed fresh air and walked at a manageable pace. Bayerd's cold seemed to be waning. He only sneezed a few times, and didn't set anyone ablaze. Jabalot didn't try to kill anyone, not even once.

Midafternoon, they crossed a trail that led toward the kingdom. It allowed them to pick up the pace. Bayerd realized he would have to take his leave that evening, and felt depressed inside. As much as he would miss Orson and Gerald, he knew he would pine for Kelp for the rest of his days.

Without warning, he sneezed and turned a mulberry bush into a crackling fire. As they were all stomping it out, they heard the beat of approaching hooves. Four knights appeared, cantering down the path toward them. They must have been patrolling the outlying farmland. The smoke would have drawn their notice. As soon as they spotted the ragtag men, they pulled out their swords.

Gerald stomped out a last cinder and grinned at them. "Is that how you welcome your long lost prince home? With swords rather than bowing before him?" He tilted his head in Bayerd's direction, seeming to enjoy the moment.

All four knights, who looked very familiar to Bayerd even though he could not recall their names, gaped at Gerald, then at Bayerd. "But … do you mean Prince Bayerd? Why, he's dead," said the first one.

"And he's fat," said the second.

"And fancy of dress, like a woman, with ribbons in his hair and bows on his toes," said the third.

"And he never shuts up, does he? That fellow hasn't uttered a single word," said the fourth.

Bayerd wanted to burn them rather badly, but he controlled himself. Alas, his plan to remain dead had been thwarted by the untimely arrival of these knights.

"Although that one looks like Sir Gerald, only years older and starved," said the first knight to his mates.

"And that other one looks like Jabalot, only skinnier and as filthy as a rabid raccoon," said the second.

"And the tall one is as tall as Orson, you know, the fellow who was bedding Princess Kelp before he disappeared without a trace," said the third.

The fourth one didn't have a chance to add anything. Orson gave a bellow of rage and pulled out his sword. "I would never betray my friend," he shouted. "And Princess Kelp is no farmer's daughter to roll around in the hay just for the pleasure of it, no matter how great that pleasure might be."

"Liar," Bayerd burst out, glaring at Orson. The fire that spewed out of his mouth travelled much further than usual, perhaps because he was so enraged. It shot at least twenty yards, terrifying the horses, and the knights astride them. Orson leapt aside and only his boots got scorched. The horses reared up and the knights fought to control them.

Bayerd bit his tongue and glared at his friend. He had come to terms with Orson being with Kelp, sort of, but to have his formerly truest friend lie to his face with such conviction—that was rubbing salt in a raw wound. Since he couldn't shout at Orson, and didn't want to battle him, since Orson was by far the superior swordsman, and he was too enraged to do nothing at all, he charged Orson.

Orson watched him come, a confused expression on his face. "What do you think you're doing, Bayerd? You don't believe their gossip, do you?" He looked hurt right before Bayerd slammed into him. It was just lucky that Orson had lowered his blade or Bayerd surely would have skewered himself on it. They both landed hard on the rocky ground and rolled around for a bit before Orson shoved Bayerd off and staggered to his feet. Bayerd stumbled up and tried to punch Orson. Orson blocked every swing with ease.

"Would you stop this before you hurt yourself," Orson shouted, grabbing both of Bayerd's fists and holding them in place. As hard as Bayerd tried, he could not free himself.

"You know, that one fights like Prince Bayerd, with no ability or skill whatsoever," said the first knight.

"Maybe he's not dead after all. I have heard tell that he does not die," said the second knight.

"But what's with the fire? I've never before seen a man shoot fire out of his mouth like a dragon," said the third knight.

The fourth didn't have a chance to say anything. Orson must have thought their fight was over. He released Bayerd's hands. Bayerd drew back and punched him in the nose. Orson returned the favour, with a bigger, harder and much more forceful fist. It was the last thing Bayerd remembered before he woke up as he crossed over a very familiar drawbridge, robbed of his chance to disappear into the sunset.

Alas, he was draped over the ass end of a horse as if he was a corpse, not a returning hero who had succeeded at his quest. It was simply demeaning. And he was quite sure his nose was broken, yet again. It throbbed and was full of dried blood, which made it tingle in the most irritating way. With no more warning than that tingle, he sneezed quite violently.

Flames shot out of his nose and mouth. At least he didn't light anything on fire, but he spooked the horse. It squealed and danced around on the slippery drawbridge. Its rider tried to calm it. The horse was having none of that. It bucked wildly and reared up, and bucked again.

Bayerd was tossed right off the horse. He flew up into the sky like a bird before he dropped a rather long way. He hit the water with a tremendous splash and sank all the way to the bottom of the moat, wondering if anyone would or could react quickly enough to save him. And he had to wonder if he wanted them to do any such thing.

It was dark in the depths and all he could see was his glowing heart, visible through the slash in his tunic. As he grew faint from lack of air, so too did the glow. It grew so dim, he could barely see it. Or he was dying and losing his sight. Even his thoughts lost their cohesion and turned quite nonsensical. He imagined the magical stone inside him pushing to get out, pushing against his flesh to be free, as if he should birth it back into the world somehow.

163

When a hand clamped onto his wrist and tugged, he thought it was a Mer, one of Kelp's watery kin. He tried to speak to them, and no fire came out of his mouth. Well of course fire couldn't burn under water. He laughed and accidentally breathed in water, and with it, dark nothingness.

He revived on the shore of the moat, spewing water rather than fire from his lungs. He was surrounded by so many of the castle folk, he could see naught but legs. There was a cacophony of voices, all talking at once. He deciphered snatches of conversation that seemed very disjointed.

One woman said, "It does look like him, before he got fat." Another man said, "I knew he could not die." Yet another said, "He looks more dead than alive, if you ask me." Then a loud, commanding voice said, "Make way for the queen."

Several nearby men pulled him to his feet. A man should never present himself to his queen whilst prostate on the ground. Only the churchmen liked people to prostrate themselves at their feet.

The crowd parted, but Queen Hellenor was not the one to approach. The one who was wearing the crown was the last person who should have been wearing it.

Shifra sashayed up to Bayerd and looked down at him, her eyes narrowed in confusion. He probably looked just as confused, and the questions that bubbled up inside him had to remain unasked, even though he wouldn't have minded turning Shifra into a pile of ash.

She said, "Good lord, is that you, Bayerd? Still alive?"

He glared at her, which she took for a yes. He yearned to ask about the fate of his beloved wife, since Shifra wearing the crown could only mean one thing—that both Hellenor and Kelp were dead.

Before he could die of a broken heart and join his wife in Death's kingdom, he spotted Kelp, alive and moving slowly toward him. Her lovely face was as pale as paper and her eyes were opened so wide, she truly might have been meeting his ghost, rather than her flesh and blood husband. He lost his heart to her all over again, and it broke anew when he remembered that she was no longer his love. Orson had claimed her.

He could not even greet her, at least not with words, so he bowed down onto one knee before her like a common man, which was the truth of it. He was no more royal than a pig in a sty, even though he had masqueraded as a prince for the most humiliating year of his life.

Kelp bit her lip and frowned in confusion. "Bayerd, is it … you?" He nodded and looked up at her, his eyes drinking in her beauty. "You are not … dead?" He shook his head. She reached down to touch his face, stroking his cheekbone and the hollow beneath it. His heart broke even more. "You've clearly had a difficult quest." Her words ended in a ragged sob.

He nodded. There was no denying it had been difficult. She gripped his hands and drew him to stand, then frowned and turned his rough palms up, studying the burn scars and healing fang punctures. "Oh, your poor hands." She kissed each of his palms, tears spilling over her lashes. "Why don't you speak? Are you so angry with me for sending you on this awful quest that you will not speak to me?"

Bayerd could only shake his head.

Kelp frowned deeper and glanced around. "And Orson, he is not dead either?"

It felt like she cut him with a whip, rather than her words. Bayerd yanked his hands from hers and stepped back. And where was Orson? Bayerd wanted to punch him in the nose again. He looked around and spotted his friend moving through the crowd toward them.

"Kelp, there you are. I found Bayerd, or he found me. He's not really dead, and neither am I." Orson reached them, a smile stretched across his face. He gripped both of Kelp's hands. "It is so good to be home. We had a terrible time in the mountain, although I can't remember most of it." Orson would have kept running off at the mouth except he spotted Shifra, wearing Hellenor's crown. "Hey, what's she doing wearing Hellenor's crown?" he demanded.

Shifra stepped forth. "Kneel before your queen."

"You're no more a queen than I am. Where is Queen Hellenor?" Orson looked all around as if Hellenor might be rubbing elbows with her subjects, and allowing Shifra to sully the crown by wearing it on her evil head. Bayerd was simply glad that Orson had asked the key question, since Bayerd couldn't. And Orson's curiosity would be no small thing.

Shifra nodded to some hovering guards and one of them kicked Orson in the knee, hard enough to make him drop where he stood. Bayerd protested. Luckily he shouted at the guard, not Orson, so the blast of fire that came out of him targeted the right fellow.

Everyone gasped and fell back, except for the guard who was going up in flames. He leapt into the moat.

"What … how?" Kelp said, shocked eyes on Bayerd.

Orson bounded to his feet. "Bayerd, he lost his voice, can't talk anymore, not without lighting everything on fire." As far as explanations went, Orson's was sorely lacking. Bayerd rolled his eyes heavenward, silently appealing to the saints for patience. At least the guards were hanging back, afraid to approach.

"Orson, what are you babbling about?" Kelp demanded shortly. She did not sound very loving toward her newly returned lover. Bayerd almost laughed. He stopped himself just in time.

"I'm talking about Bayerd's condition. He's like a dragon now. He can't talk, only fire comes out of his mouth. He's already lit me on fire at least a dozen times. It's why my clothes are all burnt, and my hair is burnt off, and see all these red patches, they're my healing burns from Bayerd setting me on fire." Orson's voice dropped to a whisper that could be heard clear across the moat. "You have to be real careful around him, and he's been grumpy, too. Suppose I can't blame him, since he's lost his voice and that's all he was good for. At least we won't have to listen to the same old tales over and over."

Kelp held up a regal hand, silencing Orson. Bayerd would have kissed her, if he still had that right. She turned to Bayerd and gazed deep into his eyes. "Is this ridiculous tale true?" she asked. He nodded once and her eyes filled with tears. "You've lost your beautiful voice?" He nodded again.

"Well, at least you are alive, although you're nothing but skin and bone. I almost didn't know you." Kelp embraced him even though he was dripping with foul moat water. It almost killed him, but he stepped out of her embrace.

"Kelp, where is Hellenor?" Orson asked again, while Shifra had a whispered consultation with her guards, and one went running across the courtyard as if on a most important errand. Bayerd recognized her former men—loyal to her, not Hellenor. How had she managed to take over the castle?

"I don't know where Hellenor is, although Shifra claims she is alive," Kelp whispered back. "When I returned to the castle from the mountain, Shifra was wearing the crown and Hellenor was nowhere to be found. Shifra claims to be holding her prisoner, and threatens to torture and kill her if I do not cooperate, so I have been cooperating. I abdicated my right to rule so she won't kill Hellenor." Her voice dropped lower still, and she spoke quickly, knowing her time to

166

communicate was limited. "I've done my best to find Hellenor, but I haven't managed it. Shifra's guards follow me everywhere. I have no freedom. I know she wants to kill me, but doesn't dare. That would result in a rebellion against her, and she knows it."

Kelp had no chance to say more. Shifra and her guards had apparently decided that Bayerd was too dangerous to let wander about the castle, now that fire was his weapon, and they had decided on a course of action.

A dozen men moved to surround him. They pointed a dozen swords at him, Kelp and Orson. Bayerd was sorely tempted to make a stand and burn them all, until he spotted the archers on the battlements. Too many of them were pointing notched arrows at Bayerd. He wasn't sure his fire could burn that many arrows before they pierced his flesh, or Kelp's flesh.

Orson did not need instructions, which was a good thing since Bayerd couldn't issue any. Ignoring Kelp's protests, Orson put a strong arm around her and moved her away from Bayerd, out of harm's way. Bayerd nodded his thanks and dropped to his knees, hands behind his back in the prisoner's pose, even though his mouth was now his weapon, not his hands.

Shifra stepped closer, but not too close. "I must say, I am surprised to see you alive. That trick with fire is very entertaining. I'm sure I can put it to good use." She smiled spitefully. The guard she had sent running trotted up to her, winded, holding something metallic in his hands.

He handed the pear-shaped object to Shifra, and Bayerd's heart sank. He recognized the torture device—a choke pear, or as it was more commonly called, a 'pear of anguish'. He felt anguished just looking at it. He had already endured torture at the hands of Kelp's nasty cousin and a deranged bishop. Was that not enough for one man? Especially when that one man was not a criminal?

Kelp cried out as though she was already experiencing the pain he was about to. He met her gaze and shook his head. Tears were flowing down her cheeks in rivers. He offered her a brave smile while he still could, although his lips trembled in a less-than-heroic way.

Shifra nudged him with the tip of her slipper. She did like being the center of attention. She fondled the pear and said, "Do you know what this little device is for?"

He nodded wearily.

"It will stopper your fire so it can only burn inside you. Open your mouth."

He did, before she began spouting threats. She had the upper hand, and everyone in the castle knew it.

"Wider," she said, when the fat end of the pear couldn't fit between his teeth. He strained his jaw and she forced it in, loosening his front tooth in the process. Alas, that was not the end of it. The device did so much more than that. Shifra turned a small key and the four segments of the pear sprang opened in his mouth, stretching his fragile flesh until it felt like it would tear apart, like worn cloth. The device was now locked inside him, unless one had the key to crank the pear closed again, which alas, he did not.

He groaned, unable to keep silent in his pain. And Shifra wasn't quite right about the torture device stopping his fire. When the pathway out of his mouth was blocked, the stream of fire shot from his nose. His nostrils naturally aimed downward, so the fire merely singed Shifra's slippers. When he tipped his head back, to aim a little higher, one of her guards banged him on the back of the head with a hard fist. His head dropped forward until his chin touched his chest.

"Hold him," Shifra snapped. She stepped close and grabbed his recently broken nose, plugging it. She held him like that until a metal clamp was produced and screwed onto his poor nose, blocking it completely, and that was chained around his head and locked there with a padlock. At that point, it was all Bayerd could do to get enough air into his body to keep from passing out. He relaxed, trying to calm himself, so he would need less air.

All around him, the castle folk murmured and muttered in distress. Kelp's sobs were the loudest in the courtyard, along with Orson's attempts to comfort her. Orson would look after her, Bayerd knew, and he felt both appreciative and enraged, all at the same time.

"Put him in the deepest dungeon cell, until I decide what to do with him," Shifra ordered.

Before they could manhandle him, Bayerd stumbled to his feet and started walking, his boot heels sounding as hollow as his heart. He veered right, toward the entrance to the dungeon. He would do his best to cooperate, so Kelp and Orson would remain unscathed.

A line of knights stood at attention when he walked by them, blood and drool running down his chin in a stream, mixing with the filthy water of the moat and looking all the more plentiful for it. He saw sympathy and compassion in their eyes. These would be Hellenor's men, forced to accept Shifra as their queen, because she was holding their true queen hostage. He nodded to them and, to a man, they did the same in return.

Bayerd descended roughhewn stone steps. It was a long way down. The air grew increasingly dank and putrid. The odor of those prisoners who had sickened and died below ground never left the morbid place. Shifra's guards kept prodding him to move faster. The steps led into a long stone passage with many doors on each side, and one thick wooden door with an impressive iron padlock at the very end.

"For the most special prisoners," one of the guards taunted as he unlocked it. On the other side of the door, was another long corridor. This one angled downward and probably led straight to hell. Bayerd felt like he was already in hell, so his final destination didn't worry him overly much.

At the end of that stone tunnel, there was yet another door, this one of forged iron. It was unlocked and Bayerd was shoved into the dark space. He tripped and landed on his knees. The door clanked closed and the lock ground shut, metal scraping against metal. He might have given into despair if a familiar voice hadn't spoken from out of the darkness.

18. Dungeons and Dragons

Oh, crackling sizzling fizzing fire
Both curse and blessing, are you not?
Seeking to burn high and higher
Razing trees or boiling a pot

Birthed to life by dragon's breath
Lightest touch, a forever scar
Tightest clutch, a gift of death
Oh, what a godlike force you are

Fire, shall you never be sated?
With your greedy appetite
Or like man, are you fated
To wreck and ruin all in sight

-Bayerd the Storyteller, Ode to Fire

"Bayerd, is that truly you?" Queen Hellenor's voice was unmistakable. So she was alive and being held prisoner in her very own dungeon. Shifra was a bold, unconscionable woman, even among royals.

Bayerd nodded, which was silly, since the cell was unlit and the queen couldn't see him any more than he could see her.

"It looked like you, in the flash of light from outside, but you as you once were, not you as you were when I last saw you. And do you have some sort of gag in your mouth? Is that why you can't speak?"

Why he couldn't speak had as much to do with his condition as the torture device, which was no mere gag, but of course he couldn't say

170

any of that. Bayerd crawled in the direction of the queen's voice. The floor was cold, hard stone. It was not even lined with straw as a courtesy to the rightful queen.

His questing hands felt her skirts, tucked around her knees. He stopped crawling. Hellenor, in turn, felt his arms up to his shoulder, and then his face, and her hands found the metal end of the choke pear jutting from his mouth.

She gave a cry of dismay before she said, "Such a nasty little invention. It is you, Bayerd?"

He nodded once and she could feel his answer. His struggle to breathe sounded like a dying man's last gasps at life, and she tsk-tsked. "Lay your head in my lap and we shall talk, as much as we are able." She guided his head down onto her padded thighs, and he collapsed there.

He had made it home from his quest, only to end up in the dungeon, with his head in the queen's lap. Never could he have come up with a tale as pathetic and ridiculous as what he was enduring.

Hellenor wiped away his tears in a most motherly fashion. "Aren't we a pair," she said with a sigh. "So, you have come home alive, only to find Shifra wearing my crown."

He nodded.

"Is Kelp ... well?" Clearly, she did not want to speak the word 'dead'.

Bayerd nodded more emphatically and took the queen's hand to squeeze it, offering what little comfort he could.

"Well, that is something." The queen squeezed his hand in return, then ran her fingers through his matted hair, combing out tangles. "Tell me, did you succeed at your quest?"

Bayerd nodded again. He shifted from his side onto his back. He parted the torn cloth of his filthy, still damp tunic, so the queen could see his glowing heart.

She gasped and touched the spot. "What is that? Surely not the heaven stone that you were to bring back to me?" He nodded. Hellenor actually chuckled. "Trust you, Bayerd, to succeed at your quest in a most original fashion. When we escape this dungeon, I will hear the tale of your quest, and I will do so sitting on my throne, wearing my crown. That is a royal command, so it must be obeyed."

171

Bayerd nodded, impressed with how resilient the queen was proving to be. The warm lap and gentle fingers stroking through his hair must have lulled him to sleep. He was profoundly exhausted.

He awoke what felt like hours later, and the queen slept too, snoring with surprising volume. He sat up, moving cautiously so as not to disturb her. The respite should have done him the world of good, and yet he felt chilled. Breathing remained an ongoing struggle that sapped his strength.

Without warning, he sneezed once, twice and thrice. Perhaps wearing his damp clothing in the dank dungeon had brought on another cold, or he had never truly gotten over his previous illness, because he seemed to be sickening now. With each violent sneeze, licks of flame found their way around the metallic pear, and past the nose clamp.

Of course, his sneezing awoke the queen. He sneezed again, and again. The tongues of flame he produced were enough to see by, in brief flashes like lightning. In the corner of the surprisingly large cell, there was an old wooden crate, perhaps to be used as a rudimentary chair, or table.

Bayerd crawled over to it and kicked it until it broke apart. He piled the wood and when his next bout of sneezing gripped him, he aimed his small flames at a few splintered bits. It took about a dozen sneezes before the kindling caught. He piled larger pieces atop them and soon had a small campfire. He could see, and the warmth was heavenly. Most of the smoke rose and was drawn out through the small barred window in the cell door, so the air did not become too tainted.

The queen crawled closer and Bayerd could now see that she had a ball and chain locked to her ankle. She held her hands before the flames to warm them and took a good look at Bayerd. "So, there is fire inside you?"

He nodded, sneezed and edged closer to the warmth of the campfire to dry out his clothes. He tapped his glowing chest pointedly.

"Because the heaven stone is inside you?" she stated. He nodded. "Is that why Shifra has you so trussed up?" She motioned to the gear on his face. He nodded again.

Hellenor leaned closer and studied the two locked mechanisms. "Let's see if we can't do something to make you more comfortable." She felt around her person until she produced a small, jeweled pin. She used the pointy end as a key, and fiddled with the locking mechanism on the choke pear. Every time he felt a sneeze coming on, he turned his head and covered his mouth so as not to burn her. She tried really hard and didn't give up until Bayerd shook his head.

"Perhaps the other lock will be less secure," Hellenor suggested. She went to work on the padlock keeping his nose clamp in place. Perhaps all the practice on the first lock had honed her lock-picking skills, or the padlock was a less sophisticated device, because after about ten minutes, the padlock clicked open, releasing the chain.

Bayerd was quick to unclamp his nose and toss the metal into the corner. His nose throbbed something awful when circulation was restored to it, but it felt perfectly straight, so perhaps the clamp had done a good job of setting it. And he could breathe so much better. He applauded softly, trying to communicate his admiration and appreciation.

"You are most welcome, Bayerd. Now if only we could get the choke pear out of your mouth, you would be a great deal more comfortable, I'm sure."

He nodded and sneezed again. Without the clamp to block it, the stream of fire that shot out of his nose was definitely dragon-worthy. It sizzled clear across the cell and hit the far wall, which was luckily hewn from stone, so it did not go up in flames. Alas, some of the fire found the edge of the queen's skirt and it began to smolder. Bayerd leapt up and stomped out the flames with his boots, so the queen hardly got burnt at all, although she was flustered.

"Well, I can see why Shifra has dammed your face. You are quite dangerous now, aren't you? Perhaps we can use that to our advantage, if we can liberate you from the second device." The queen tapped her chin thoughtfully.

Bayerd turned away quickly when he felt another sneeze coming on. He stood in the corner and succumbed to a bout of sneezing. And that's when he noticed something interesting. Now that he had more air, the fire was burning a lot hotter inside him, and the flames seemed to be softening the metal segments of the choke pear inside his mouth.

When he finished sneezing, he kept blowing fire into his mouth deliberately. The metal of the choke pear began to soften, maybe it was even melting a bit. Bayerd tightened his jaw around the metal, and employed his tongue and teeth to press it smaller, while continuing to direct fire into his mouth. When the malleable segments of the pear had been reshaped to close, the 'pear of agony' was small enough for him to pull out of his mouth, although he almost had to break his jaw to do so.

"Well done, Bayerd, well done," the queen said, beaming at him.

He nodded and grinned, as his mouth complained about all the abuse it had endured, and readjusted to its normal size and shape.

"Can you speak now?" Hellenor asked.

Bayerd shook his head regretfully, sneezed a few more times, then returned to sit with her beside their little fire.

"Instead of your voice, you now speak in flames?" Hellenor asked.

He nodded. And now that he knew his fire could melt forged metal, and he could breathe unhindered again, he was hopeful that he could liberate them from the cell—both of them.

He pointed to Hellenor's ball and chain, and mimed ripping it apart with his bare hands.

"I don't think you're strong enough to break chain, but maybe your fire can melt the links," she said.

It was what he had intended. She edged away as far as the chain would allow.

In flames that he aimed at the chain, Bayerd said, "It is my honour to serve you, Queen Hellenor, and I will do all that I can to restore you to your throne, once it has been scrubbed clean of Shifra's filth. Perhaps her new home could be this cell, although it is far better than she deserves."

The metal was quick to soften, melt and drip. Queen Hellenor gave a few strong tugs and the chain links parted, freeing her from the heavy metal cannon ball, and leaving her with a thick metal band around her ankle that could never be called jewelry.

"Now what, Bayerd?" Hellenor asked.

He shrugged and tapped his temple, miming that he was still working on a plan. Hellenor relaxed back against the wall, near enough to the fire to be warmed. She said, "A queen's life is spent plotting, you know. We shall come up with a plan together, and our chance of success will be so much greater."

He nodded deeply. He had always had great respect for Hellenor's mind. And as far as royals went, she even had integrity.

So they discussed their options and how best to proceed, although it was not easy now that Bayerd was a mute. Queen Hellenor certainly proved herself a clever strategist, and surprisingly sneaky. They had the bare bones of a skeleton plot in place when they heard approaching footsteps. They weren't nearly ready to act. Bayerd shot Hellenor a panicked glance and picked up the cursed choke pear. He forced it back into his mouth. From the outside, it was impossible to tell that the thing was not cranked opened, and immovable.

Hellenor shoved the clamp back onto his nose, and wound the chain around his head. It was not nearly as tight as it had been. She slid the padlock in place, but did not click it into the locked position. Queen Hellenor barely had time to sit beside her ball and chain, and reposition the chain to look like it was still in one piece, before the door opened. The band of light that flooded inside seemed overly bright.

"You there," said one of Shifra's men, pointing at Bayerd. "Get your arse over here. The queen wants to see you."

Bayerd tilted his head toward Hellenor, the rightful queen, and cocked one eyebrow insolently.

"Do you really want me to come in there and get you?" the guard asked, his voice liberally laced with threat.

In answer, Bayerd limped toward the door. He shared a last look with Queen Hellenor and winked before he left the cell.

Bayerd was escorted up the long flight of steps. Although it was not as hard to breathe as it had been, he got quite winded. Climbing requires more energy than descending. He began to see stars and stumble like a drunk. It was a relief to reach level ground and step out into the fresh air of the courtyard.

As he approached the castle proper, he squinted up at the window of the tower rooms he had shared with Kelp, not so long ago. His eyes were still adjusting to the brightness of the day, and watering as if he was crying, which he most certainly was not. He could still make out her hazy silhouette, framed in the arched opening with Orson behind her, holding a squirming babe—Bayerd's son. The three of them looked the rosy picture of a cozy family until Kelp spotted him. Even from a distance and with watery eyes, he could tell her face fell.

He dropped his gaze, ashamed of his status as a downtrodden, filthy prisoner. In his indulgent daydreams, he had imagined returning from his quest as a shining hero on a prancing white steed—although where his newfound ability to stay on a horse, and the white steed, had come from was a mystery. Unlike a tale told aloud, private daydreams did not have to be logical; they simply served to comfort in trying times.

Bayerd was shoved toward the castle's main door, to go and meet the false queen, dreading what she had in store for him.

19. The Show Must Burn On

I painted love with hungry oranges,
bleeding reds and contented yellows
I drew love with smooth lines,
endless curlicues and uncontrolled scribbles
I wrote love with an excess of adjectives,
glorious flamboyance, and minute detail
I saw love with a blind man's gaze,
wearing rosy glasses, with closed eyes.

-Bayerd the Storyteller, Of Love

Shifra had made herself right at home on Hellenor's ornate throne in the grand hall. The vast room echoed with emptiness since she was the only one in it—well, aside from half a dozen of her guards, and a couple more outside the door, probably to make sure they would not be interrupted.

Bayerd approached and stood planted before her. He did not bow down on one knee as protocol demanded. He simply could not kowtow before the evil woman. Shifra didn't care, probably because there were no castle folk about to witness his defiance.

She yawned in his general direction. "Finally," she drawled and took a long look at him. "I don't know what my cousin sees in you, I really don't."

Bayerd had often wondered the same himself, even before he had turned into the kingdom's biggest ass. Well, whatever Kelp had seen in him, she saw it no longer.

"There will be a banquet tonight. My subjects are getting … restless, and I've been quite bored. Being queen isn't nearly as much fun as I thought it would be, so I'm going to spice things up—provide some entertainment—and that will be you."

He raised one eyebrow inquiringly, since he no longer had a voice with which to entertain.

176

"That thing you do with fire, I want you to make a show of it. Tonight, you will be my jester, and you will play with fire."

It was the final humiliation, exactly as Shifra intended. He motioned to the devices on his face and raised his hands in a questioning gesture.

"Oh, I'll take those off so you can perform, but you're going to have to behave, or else Kelpie will pay the price. She is going to sit right beside me, and I'll have a dagger—a very sharp dagger—at her back during your performance. Understand?"

He bobbed his head. How could he not?

"And you are not to breathe a word to anyone about your cellmate. Oh, you can't, can you?" Shifra tittered at her own little joke. "I have a costume all picked out for you, and since you smell like the moat, you are to bathe before the performance. I don't want to lose my appetite, now do I?"

She flicked a hand, as though he was a pesky fly that she was shooing away. The guard at his back grabbed him by the scruff of the neck and started dragging him toward the door. A second guard joined them. Apparently one was not enough.

"Oh, and don't try to escape," Shifra called. "I have several of my most loyal servants guarding Kelp's tower. If you try anything, they have their instructions. Kelp will be the one to suffer."

Bayerd went along like a lamb, thinking hard. The plot he had been concocting with Queen Hellenor had not foreseen Shifra forcing him to perform as a jester before a crowd, with fire no less. Alas, now both Kelp and Queen Hellenor were being held hostage, in their own way, so he would have to act with the utmost stealth.

One of the problems with plots is that they can't anticipate all happenstances, or how others will react to unfolding and unexpected events. Sometimes the best plan is simply to be smarter, quicker and cleverer than those you aim to defeat. And Bayerd was good at thinking on his feet—he was a storyteller after all. A storyteller fosters an agile and creative mind. His best advantage was that Shifra did not know he could remove the choke pear and nose-clamp himself, and that would be at the most opportune moment.

The guards escorted him to a small room near the kitchen. A tub of cold water waited, and a bar of the harsh lye soap the kitchen staff used to wash pots. This would be no luxurious soaking. Regardless, he was looking forward to finally washing away the lingering stench of moat water, monster blood and rancid smoke.

A jester's costume was dangling from a hook. The diamond pattern was a garish purple and yellow. The ridiculously large lace trim at the neck, wrists and ankles was a rusty red—the colour of dried blood. The garment appeared too small, so it must have been borrowed from a real jester. Simply looking at the thing made Bayerd feel dispirited.

"Into the tub," the taller guard said.

Still thinking hard about how to escape, and free Queen Hellenor without getting Kelp or anyone else killed, Bayerd stripped off his grubby tunic. There were gasps from his two guards when his new wounds were exposed. The one across his heart looked like a fatal injury, to be sure. No wonder he was getting a firmly established reputation as someone who did not die. And the glow in his heart was certainly worth a second look. Men did not normally glow, in fact, men never glowed. And the light was still beaming as brightly as before he had fallen into the moat and drowned.

He hesitated to remove more, and motioned the guards toward the door. "Not supposed to leave you alone," said the taller one. Bayerd pointed to the sturdy lock on the solid door—a lock that could be locked from the outside.

"I don't really want to see his naked arse," said the shorter guard.

"Do you think I do?" said the taller guard.

"I didn't say that."

"Let's lock him in, then we can nip over to the dining hall and have a nibble of cheese and a mug of ale. We missed lunch and I'm quite starved. We'll be back before he's dry behind the ears." The taller guard was far from starved, he had a well-padded frame. Bayerd, on the other hand, truly couldn't remember when he had last eaten, although he knew it was before the damn choke pear was shoved into his mouth.

The shorter guard was quick to agree, and after warning Bayerd to be clean and dressed like a jester when they returned, they took their leave. The lock clicked into place and Bayerd was blessedly alone.

He waited a good three minutes before he removed the choke pear and nose-clamp. He donned his tunic for lack of anything cleaner to wear—the jester costume was not an option. He would rather parade around buck naked than wear such motley, when given a choice.

All sounded quiet outside the room. He blew a stream of fire at the lock, softening the metal until he could force the door ajar. No-one witnessed his escape. He closed the door again, as if he was still locked inside.

The smell of food drew him to the kitchen. A starving man was of little use to anyone, and Bayerd knew he would need his strength to defeat Shifra.

The barn-sized room was a hive of activity, as usual. As soon as he stepped into its humid heat, the spitboys stopped turning the spits and the dishwashers stopped scrubbing the pots and the cooks stopped chopping and stirring and kneading. In fact, every one of the fifty or so kitchen staff froze as if turned to stone. A stick of a woman approached with a huge gap-toothed grin, her trusty wooden spoon in hand. "Prince Bayerd? That really you? Back again from the dead?" she cried.

He nodded to Mrs. Baker and bowed before the ruler of the kitchen kingdom. She had saved his life on one occasion, when he'd had an appointment with the headsman, and she had gotten him as burnt as an overcooked biscuit in the process.

"I heard tell that you can shoot fire out of your mouth like a dragon now that you've escaped from hell and brought the hellfire back to the land of the living inside you. That true?"

Ah, so that was how the gossip was transforming his tale. He nodded again, since he really couldn't explain that he had not been to hell and back, although in truth, it felt like he had. And he could shoot fire out of his mouth, which was what Mrs. Baker was asking.

"You'd be right handy to have around my kitchen then. A couple of my fires aren't burning hot enough. Can you give them a blast of hellfire?"

Bayerd nodded. She herded him to the back of the kitchen where the spitboys were sweating in the heat. The fires looked plenty hot. Bayerd suspected that Mrs. Baker merely wanted a little show. He stood before the fires and said, "If it is more fire you want, more fire you shall have. I just hope you will feed me, as I am quite starved and the food smells delectable, as always." The fire that shot out of his mouth wasn't aimed quite right and some wayward flames set an unlucky spitboy's vest ablaze. A handy bucket of water was tossed over the lad before any real harm was done.

"Enough of that then," Mrs. Baker declared, latching onto Bayerd's arm and tugging him toward the door. He dragged his heels and mimed eating.

"Yes, we do have a lot of food to prepare in a very short time, for the banquet tonight," she said.

He managed to snag a couple of warm biscuits off a tray, as well as another item that might come in very handy. Mrs. Baker said, "Course you're hungry, should have realized. You're barely half the man you used to be." She cackled in laughter, filled a sack with more biscuits, a cold sausage, and a lump of hard cheese, and pressed it into his hand. He kissed her cheek in gratitude, pointed a finger at himself, then held his index finger before his lips, miming 'shh'.

"Course we won't tell that evil imposter queen that you were here. You just get her off the throne," Mrs. Baker said, proving herself more quick-witted than most other folk he had tried to communicate with.

He laid a hand over his heart and nodded.

"Then you better stop shillyshallying around my kitchen and get to it." She smacked him on the bottom with her wooden spoon and ejected him from her kitchen kingdom.

Bayerd hurried back to his makeshift prison room, and shut himself in. He savoured the fresh buttery baking, chewy cheese and spicy meat, whilst he mulled over his next best move. He decided that he should cooperate with Shifra for the moment, stay alert, and be ready to act when opportunity presented itself. Perhaps it was not the cleverest of plans, but it was the safest in regards to his loved ones.

He finished every last crumb of the food. Feeling somewhat rejuvenated, he blasted his fiery breath at the tub, heating it until it was steaming nicely. He stripped, sank into the water up to his neck, and soaped off the lingering slime of the polluted moat. He cleansed his many wounds as best he could, before he ducked under and washed his hair with soap. He even shaved his face with the sharp little paring knife he had palmed when pilfering biscuits. Although as it turned out, there had been no need to pilfer it. Mrs. Baker would have gifted him the biggest, sharpest blade in her kitchen, if it was intended to slit Shifra's throat.

Clean and with a full belly, he left the water and dried off. He faced the cursed jester's costume and stopped feeling at all restored. With gritted teeth, he put the damn thing on, and it was such a tight fit, several seams split. He had just replaced the choke pear and nose-clamp, and hidden the knife in his boot, when the guards returned, smelling strongly of ale.

"I was a bit worried 'cause that lock doesn't seem to be locking quite right," said the shorter guard, "but here you are, right where we left you."

"And don't you look a treat," said the taller guard.

Scowling as fiercely as he could with the half-melted choke pear stretching his mouth, Bayerd gestured at the costume with irate hands. The smallness of it made it look all the more ridiculous. The arms and legs were so short, the lace trim encircled Bayerd's forearms and calves, rather than his wrists and ankles. He ached to burn the costume right off his skin. And he might do just that—when the opportune moment presented itself. In case he did burn off his costume, he bundled up his leather trousers and tucked them under his arm to take along. The guards did not protest, or perhaps they didn't even notice. They did seem more than a little tipsy.

"I'm looking forward to the fire-show," confided the shorter guard, and there was no sarcasm in his tone.

"Do you know, I am too," said the taller guard, adding, "I wish there was a dragon costume, so he could dress up like a dragon."

Bayerd wished the same. He would much rather dress as a dragon than a fool.

They turned to Bayerd. "You'll make it good show, won't you? Even though you don't have a dragon costume?" said the shorter one.

"A really good show," added the taller one.

Bayerd nodded. When preforming, he always did his best. He bowed with a flourish, and a great deal of hand twirling, as if to prove the point.

Before they left the room, the taller guard took a ring of keys out of his vest to free Bayerd's face for the show. Bayerd jerked the keys out of the fellow's hand and undid the locks himself. He did not want the guards to realize he had sabotaged both devices. He removed them and dropped them into the shorter guard's hands. The choke pear was coated in spittle and the fellow grimaced with distaste. He tossed both devices into the tub.

Bayerd filled his lungs with air, and instantly felt more at ease. He grinned, now that he could, and tucked the keys back into the guard's vest. The guard said, "Thank you."

Bookended by his escort, Bayerd made the trek to the grand hall, praying the night would end triumphantly for him, rather than in his bloody death.

20. Return of the Jester

There once was a jester and fool
Who stood on his hands on a stool
He fell on his head
And ended up dead
Now that poor foolish fool is a ghoul
-Bayerd the Storyteller, Limerick

he grand hall was so crowded with castle folk, there was barely room for one more body. The news of Bayerd's rebirth from hell, and the fire-show he was to perform, must have spread throughout the castle like a rampant case of lice.

A great rowdy cheer went up at his appearance. Shifra sat on Hellenor's throne, and she did not cheer. It would have been quite un-regal behaviour. She did allow herself an indulgent little smile, though.

Kelp sat close beside her, a prisoner even though she wore no visible bonds. A hulk with an apish demeanor, and one long eyebrow where he should have had two, stood directly behind her. His hand was hidden by her chair, no doubt holding a razor-sharp dagger. Kelp's jaw was set and her eyes burned with defiance. Even though the odds were stacked against them, she had not given up.

Orson and Gerald sat together at the table nearest the head-table, and Jabalot was with them, so he must have finished spilling his guts to the castle torturer, figuratively if not literally. His presence at the banquet proved that he had been judged innocent of murder. Well, carrying out a sovereign's orders is no crime, quite the opposite. For Jabalot to be a free man rather than a hanged one, Kelp must have testified on his behalf, and confirmed that she had given the assassination order.

Bayerd had told himself he understood the motivation behind Kelp's actions, she was a royal after all; assassination was a way of life for the ruling class. He had been an embarrassment of a husband, one she needed to replace with someone more suitable. In understanding Kelp's actions, he could accept them, but that did not mean it was an easy thing to do. And truth be told, in spite of all the evidence to the contrary, a stubborn corner of Bayerd's heart had clung to the faint hope that his wife was innocent of plotting his demise, and that Jabalot had simply been a convincing liar, or mistaken, and had somehow gotten his hands on Kelp's locket. Now, that beautiful little kernel of hope was dead, and he felt rather dead inside, too.

He walked alone up to the head-table. His escort had stopped just inside the door. Bayerd came to a stop before Shifra, and deftly tossed his trousers beneath the table. The room fell silent. As much as he was playing at being cooperative and defeated, he could not bring himself to bow before her as if she was his rightful queen.

"Have you forgotten to bow before your queen, jester?" Shifra said, her voice pitched too high to be her normal tone. Was she trying to impersonate Queen Hellenor, as well as replace her?

He shook his head, jaw clenched tight, so he wouldn't give into temptation and fry her where she sat, which would surely have gotten Kelp stabbed in the back, and more than a little burnt.

"I'm sure your dear wife wishes for you to bow before me, since she has abdicated so I can rule. You do want that, don't you Kelpie?" Shifra simpered.

Bayerd did not meet his wife's gaze. He was too humiliated by his foolish appearance. "You should bow, Bayerd. I do not wish to see you beaten into submission," Kelp said softly.

To spare her, and himself, unnecessary pain, he bowed down on one knee before Shifra. And he felt he had made his point, that the false queen was no queen to him.

"So, you were successful, and have brought the heaven stone back to the Golden Kingdom," Shifra said, still in the annoyingly snooty voice. He nodded once. "And in exchange for the stone, you have lost your voice, and can now breathe fire like a dragon."

It was as much statement as question. Bayerd nodded again. His vocabulary, such as it was, was pathetically limited.

"You will perform for me—for us." Shifra waved an arm in the direction of the restless crowd. "You shall do so after the meal. For now, show me, the heaven stone."

Bayerd frowned. Did she not realize it squatted inside him? He undid the ties of his costume and parted the cloth down to his navel, fully exposing his scarred and glowing heart. It was a sight to behold, one that had a number of the nearest maidens swooning, and several men.

Kelp inhaled sharply and bit her lip in distress. He touched the spot where the glow was brightest and could not stop himself from gazing at her beautiful face. In spite of everything, his love for her was probably glowing in his eyes, just as brightly as the heaven stone glowed in his heart.

Shifra gasped, "Oh my word. The stone truly is inside you, and so bright. Come closer." He stepped as near as he could with the table between them. She leaned over the wood and studied his chest, then jabbed the brightest spot with her fingernail. "You have succeeded at your quest in a most peculiar way. But succeed you did, against all odds," she drawled, looking into his eyes. Was she insinuating something?

"But your quest is not complete until you present me with the heaven stone." Shifra glanced maliciously at Kelp. "It will have to be cut out of him."

"You will do no such thing," Kelp cried angrily. "My husband has endured enough hardship on his quest without coming home to be carved opened."

"Isn't it too bad for you that I, as queen, rule absolutely. My word is law and I want my heaven stone." She lounged back on the throne, her posture too saggy to be regal. "Oh, do sit down, Bayerd. I'm not going to have you sliced opened here and now. I have a banquet to enjoy, and a great desire to see my jester perform with fire. Since you can't talk anymore, a fire-show is the least you can do to entertain me, before you're carved open from stem to stern."

To delay being carved opened, Bayerd aimed for the empty chair beside Kelp. Shifra said, "Not there, sit beside me. You shall be my jester king—king for a day." She pointed to the empty throne beside her, on the side away from Kelp.

Bayerd trudged toward it, keeping his eyes downcast, deeply mortified. It was bad enough to present himself as a jester, but to be seen as Shifra's pet jester—that was even worse. He perched on the edge of his seat, near enough to Shifra to make his skin crawl as if it was infested with spiders.

Platters of food were carried in by a host of servants. In spite of his earlier snack, he was quite starved and simply glad his mouth was free to eat. He devoured one delicious course after another, and sipped wine, while he mulled over what sort of fire-show he should perform. He studied the everyday objects on the table, assessing which would make

184

good props, based on whether or not they burned—and how hotly. And he wondered which might be used to rid the kingdom of Shifra, without Kelp paying the ultimate price with her life.

Regardless of how the evening unfolded, whether Shifra killed him to get the heaven stone, or he managed to rescue Hellenor and disappear into the night, he did want to gift Kelp with a last memory of him that would be worth remembering. He used to thrive on being the focus of all eyes, when he had a voice. He had traded that voice for a bizarre talent with fire, yet he could still put on a show. He drank more wine, until he remembered how overindulging had contributed to his downward spiral into idiocy. He switched to water. After weeks of being tormented by thirst, water still tasted like nectar.

Everyone seemed to eat more quickly than usual, as if eager to get to the climax of the evening. Bayerd supposed most folks would enjoy watching a man breathe fire, especially if it was done with flare.

When the platters had been cleared away and the cups refilled, Shifra cleared her throat pointedly. Bayerd took that as his signal to perform. He rose to his feet and leapt up onto the table in one motion.

Shifra cast him a withering glance. "Sit down, jester. First the court must hear an account of your quest from those who can speak."

He should have realized it wasn't his turn. He had performed at enough banquets to know that there was a protocol to be followed when a man returned from a quest. Bayerd hopped off the table and slunk back to his chair with reddened cheeks.

Orson, Gerald and Jabalot rose when Shifra motioned them to approach. Now that he was himself again, Orson did not enjoy being the center of attention. He shuffled forward with hunched shoulders. Gerald, on the other hand, seemed to take it all in stride, looking as at ease as if he was in his own quarters. And Jabalot simply squinted around nearsightedly. He probably couldn't even see Shifra sitting right there in front of him.

All three bowed before their false queen. Shifra said, "Entertain me. Tell me all about the quest to find the heaven stone."

Orson elbowed Gerald, probably to go first. "Well, let's see," said Gerald. "We left the castle, lost three of our knights, got trapped inside the mountain by falling rock that killed Sir Swift. Found a maze, met some small scaly folk, bargained our way out of the mountain, although leaving it took some time and effort, climbed the mountain, fell back into the mountain, found the heaven stone, Prince Bayerd cut some heads off a three-headed giant lizard monster - "

Bayerd dropped his head on the table with a loud thud, stopping Gerald in mid-sentence. He could stand no more of Gerald's butchering the tale of his glorious quest. He stood up, pointed to Orson and used his hands to mimic big flapping lips, wanting Orson to take over the telling of the tale, since he could remember what had happened from that point on. And surely he could not do a worse job of it than Gerald.

"You want a roasted duck to eat? Haven't you had enough dinner? You don't want to get fat again, do you? " Orson said.

Bayerd tossed both hands into the air with exasperation. Kelp said, "I think he wants you to tell the rest of the tale, Orson."

"Me, really? Well, I've never thought of myself as a storyteller, but since Bayerd is a mute now, guess I could give it a shot."

Bayerd gestured for Orson to proceed with the telling. In his head, he had finished scripting his exciting fire-show, and he wanted to get to it. Once it was out of the way, he could focus on rescuing Queen Hellenor and Kelp from the evil Shifra.

"Alright, then. Let's see," said Orson, rubbing his bristled jaw. "Well, we were in this big round room in the mountain, surrounded by scaly folk who were no bigger than jesters, but scalier of course, and the three-headed monster had her three snake necks wrapped around Bayerd, and it wasn't so much that she was attacking him, it was more like she was trying to ... to ..." Orson's cheeks reddened and he cleared his throat. "You know, she wanted to ... have her way with him, like the harpy did."

Bayerd covered his face with his hands, as mortified as a man can get without dying of shame. There was absolutely no reason to bring the harpy into the tale of the quest. None!

Alas, Orson wasn't finished. "And Bayerd, he only bedded the harpy to save my life, and save Princess Kelp from having her head chopped off. Most men couldn't have managed it, well, you know what harpies look like now that they've visited the castle, but that was the price he had to pay." Orson shuddered from head to toe. Bayerd surged to his feet to leap over the table and strangle Orson.

"Sit," Shifra ordered, as if he was her lapdog. He flung himself back into his chair, for Kelp's sake. He didn't want her to get stabbed, not even a little bit.

"Orson, you are supposed to be telling us about the quest, not the past," Kelp reminded him.

Shifra simply laughed cruelly. "Oh, I think I want to hear more about your husband and this harpy. Was he cheating on you with the harpy?"

Orson must have finally realized that the harpy was a topic best avoided, and he shot Bayerd a sheepish look. "Sorry, guess I got a little sidetracked there. Uh, let's see, where was I? Oh, yes, the three-headed monster was trying to have her way with Bayerd, and with three heads, well, I'm sure you can imagine, you can do more things with three heads than if you only have one head. So one head was kissing Bayerd, and another head was … uh … lower down." Orson blushed again. "And Bayerd, he fell over. Probably fainted, he does that a lot."

Bayerd hadn't fainted, he had dropped to his knees to get his hand on his sword, but he couldn't say that. He couldn't say a bloody word.

"Anyway, Bayerd must have spotted his sword, after he fainted, and he picked it up and he cut off the head that was kissing him. I couldn't believe he managed it. And then he cut off the head that was … down there, lower down. But he couldn't reach the third head. It hid behind his back, so I snuck up behind Bayerd and bonked it on the head, knocking it out."

When Bayerd had mentally scripted the valiant tale of his quest, Orson's minor contribution had not been included. He scowled in annoyance.

"I guess I saved his life," Orson said modestly, usurping the role of hero as his own. "Then we ran for our lives, into the tunnel that would take us home. The scaly folk chased us, but they couldn't catch up with their short little legs. Even Bayerd was able to outrun them. Took us days to escape that mountain, days without food or water, but at least we had each other."

It was the first properly worded thing Orson had said, in his account of things, and the audience banged their cups in appreciation.

When they fell quiet again, Orson added, "Jabalot caught up with us and we found our way home, and here we are. Oh, and I forgot to say Bayerd got stabbed in the heart by the three-headed monster, and the heaven stone is now stuck inside him, so he succeeded at his quest, brought the heaven stone home in his innards. That's why he breathes fire and can't talk anymore." Orson stopped speaking abruptly, with no proper conclusion to his version of the quest—what he remembered of it.

Shifra yawned and said, "It certainly doesn't sound like much of a quest. Return to your seats. Jester, I am ready to be entertained. I will see you breathe fire now."

Bayerd wasn't really in the mood to perform a fire-show any longer. He was feeling far too miserable and degraded, but he did want to give the castle folk, and Kelp, a fresh and spectacular memory of him, one that would last long after he'd been killed or had run off—depending on how things turned out in the end. It would be a tale that Kelp could tell his son when the lad was older, for if Bayerd did survive to run away from home, he would not be taking the babe with him. Children were nothing but a hindrance, and if he had charge of the child, he would probably set him on fire, or drop him off a horse onto his little head. The son he had yet to meet deserved better than that.

A babe should have a secure home, and a mother and father—things that Bayerd had never known. Kelp would be a warm and loving mother, and Orson would fill the role of father. In spite of everything, Bayerd could think of no better man to raise his son. Bayerd simply had to get Hellenor back on her throne for the Golden Kingdom to be a wonderful place again, and he was hopeful that maybe, just maybe, his fire-show could be the vehicle to do just that—as well as serve as his final, spectacular, farewell performance.

Trying to forget that he wore a jester's motley, and hoping his audience would grant him the honour of doing likewise, he rose and leapt onto the tabletop for a second time.

21. Burning Man, and Woman

I burned alive
And I did not die
Went up in smoke
Up, up to the sky
Golden curls char black
How I wanted to cry
Alas, I could not
My eyes were too dry

-Bayerd the Storyteller, One of Nine Lives

As Bayerd had scripted in his head, he extended both his arms wide, as if he was trying to embrace the whole world. He stood like that, unmoving, until every last onlooker in the packed hall sat still and quiet, eyes on him. When the mounting suspense reached its climax, he tilted his head back and roared with abandon. The flames that shot out touched the rafters high overhead. He stopped roaring because he did not want his final performance to include burning down the castle.

His audience gasped as one. Most in the kingdom had not yet seen him breathe fire, and had probably been imagining a candle's flame or something equally small—not a thick, sizzling stream of blue fire that would have done a dragon proud.

Bayerd strode from one end of the table to the other, then back to the middle, letting the suspense build anew. Along the way, he collected three serving trays, dumping their contents loudly and messily to the floor. They were round and made of wood, and all three were sticky with drink and cooking oil. When Bayerd breathed fire on them, they caught at once and burned bright and hot. Bayerd tossed one, two, then three trays high, spinning through the air. He juggled them like a jester, for that was his new role. He was a storyteller and troubadour no longer.

Again, the castle folk gasped and cheered and banged their cups enthusiastically. He was handling burning trays with no sign of pain or suffering. He juggled until he missed one of the trays. Luckily it landed on the stone floor, not on someone's head. Although he wouldn't have minded one little bit if it landed on Shifra's head.

For his next trick, he hopped down to the floor and ripped one of the stitched banners off the wall. He waved the cloth around over his head in a showy display, before he laid it, smooth and unwrinkled, in the open space between the raised head-table and the first long table where Orson sat with Gerald and Jabalot. All three were watching the show with enthralled expressions. Orson had never looked so enthralled when he watched Bayerd tell a tale, and it galled.

Bayerd motioned a serving wench over, one who was carrying a vessel of oil to refill the lamps that were burning low. She came forward eagerly, perhaps wanting to be part of the display. Bayerd lifted the vessel off her tray and motioned her back. He did not want his show marred by burning the wench, or any other innocent party.

He walked all around the banner, pouring a steady stream of lamp oil along its edge. When the vessel was empty, he tossed it aside and leapt into the middle of the rectangle. The crowd screamed encouragement. Bayerd grinned like a rogue. This time when he breathed fire, he pursed his lips, as if whistling. The stream of flames he produced was smaller, and more manageable. Already, he was learning how to control his fire.

He aimed the stream at the hemmed edge, and turned in a circle, lighting up the entire border of the yards of cloth. Burning hot and bright, the blaze spread inward to where he stood. He was a bit worried about his costume going up in flames before he wanted it to, but since his leather trousers were handy, he would not be left bare-assed if that happened. And he suspected his hair, like the rest of him, did not burn since it hadn't yet.

When the flames reached him and he was bathed in them, he bounded in circles, knees high, as if trying to avoid getting burnt alive.

The audience applauded in appreciation, and laughed at his playacting. The banner did not burn for long, and only some of the lace trim on his costume burned, which Bayerd made a show of slapping out. He kicked away the last of the burning scraps of banner with his boots. The flames had been low enough to avoid setting his costume alight, which was good. He needed his costume for the finale. And it was almost time for that finale. He couldn't wait to turn the garish motley to ash.

In preparation for what he hoped would be his most spectacular trick yet, Bayerd approached Orson and Gerald's table. A pitcher of water sat there and he handed it to Orson. He leaned forward and pointed to his head, signaling that Orson should pour it over his hair. It was less a precaution, since he was quite sure his hair was as fireproof as his skin, and more a buildup to the climax of his show, which should not be sprung on his audience too quickly. The suspense needed to build again.

Orson said, "If you're thirsty, there's a glass right there."

Gerald took the pitcher out of Orson's hand and poured it over Bayerd's head, soaking his hair. Bayerd stood upright, flipping his hair back. It had grown unfashionably long on his quest, which made it very flippable.

With a peacock's strut, he detoured by the head-table and retrieved his trousers, then continued on toward the hall's main fireplace, which was the size of a small bedroom, or perhaps a pantry. It was filled with glowing coals—not burning logs. Someone had neglected their duty and forgotten to add wood.

There was a stack of logs beside the fire. Bayerd set his pants down and tossed in half a dozen of the largest. He pointed at the tinder and his audience yelled and hollered their encouragement, getting quite raucous.

Grinning, Bayerd shouted in flame, "If it is fire you want, fire you shall have. And not only fire, but a burning man, and a burning man is not a man you will ever forget!"

His blue fire set the logs burning like a pyre. Bayerd stuck his leg into the blazing hearth and yanked it out again. His audience cheered and shouted for him to do it again. He glanced over at Kelp, who was worrying her lower lip. She shook her head. Bayerd blew her a kiss before he stepped fully into the hearth and the blazing fire that now filled it.

It was a strange place to be, surrounded on all sides by dancing flames that were as tall as he was. He could hear the shouting of the castle folk as if from a great distance. When he tripped over a log and fell into the fire on his ass, he thrashed around a bit as if he really was burning, making the clumsy accident part of his show. Someone in the audience began to scream hysterically in fright.

His show was supposed to be entertaining, not distressing, so he found his feet and leapt out of the hearth. His jester's costume was going up in flames, as he had intended, and that gave him immense satisfaction. Before it was completely burned away, he yanked off his boots, jumping around on one foot then the other. The little kitchen knife, his only weapon, skittered under a table, but that was no matter. It was such a paltry weapon, it probably wouldn't have been of any use anyway, especially in his hand.

He pulled on his leather trousers in the same way, farcically, over the charred remnants that were all that was left of the jester's motley.

Now that he would not be left fully exposed before the entire court, he strode toward Kelp, the last of his costume turning to ash while he wore it.

He reached the head-table, still smoldering a bit, and bowed before Kelp, not Shifra. Kelp clapped her hands appreciatively, commending his performance. Bayerd hoped she knew it was dedicated to her. He touched his heart, then turned to the cheering crowd, who was most generous in showing its appreciation. He bowed to them, too, and scooped a cup of hard liquor off the table. He blew fire on it and drank down the flaming liquid, feeling no pain at all.

The castle folk kept cheering, shouting for an encore. Bayerd wondered if he was a better fire-breather than a storyteller, then dismissed the thought. It was simply the novelty of his act that had the audience so enthralled. And he had no idea what to do for an encore. He hadn't scripted an encore. What could he do that would top his finale? Anything lesser would be anticlimactic, and that would never do.

Unless he doused himself with lamp oil before he stepped into the fireplace one more time. Yes, that would be even more spectacular than what he had already done.

He scanned the room for more lamp oil. There was a vessel of it at the very end of the head-table. He strutted toward it, and lifted it high. The crowd chanted, "Yes, yes, yes."

He lowered the vessel to his neck and poured it down his bare chest and over both shoulders. The serving girl, who had provided him with the first container of lamp oil, dashed up and took the vessel out of his hand. She poured it down his back for him.

He kissed her hand in thanks and strode toward the fireplace. The fire had lowered and he shouted into it, "I am your master and it is time to burn high again. It is time to serve me." His stream of flames turned the fire into a contained inferno. Bayerd paced away from it, then spun around and dashed toward the fireplace. Without even slowing down, he leapt into the flames. The lamp oil caught immediately, and fire spread across his bare skin.

Bayerd bounded out of the fire wearing a cloak of flames that burned high off his body, off his very skin, sizzling hotly. The crowd gasped and cried out in fear. More than one lady screamed hysterically. Surely his latest display wasn't that much more frightening than what had come before? And then something landed with a thunk at Bayerd's feet. He looked down, and there before him was a singed head.

For a shocked second, he thought he had overdone things, and that his own head had burnt right off his shoulders and dropped to the ground at his feet. And then a second crispy head landed beside the first. The two severed heads of the Tri-Alanth stared up at him accusingly with their blackened eyeballs. Bayerd spun around to face the fireplace, terrified of what he would see there.

He was right to be terrified. A familiar head on a sinewy neck curled out of the flames, followed by a long thick body. The two headless necks were no longer headless. Ugly baby heads were growing there, whining and mewling in a most annoying pitch.

Behind Bayerd, benches toppled as the castle folk fled for the doors. The Tri-Alanth blasted a wall of fire at them, barring their way, while the baby heads produced only sparks. Everyone retreated, pressing against the far wall. A few of the braver souls dashed here and there, dousing the small fires that her flames had ignited.

"Do not harm my people," Bayerd shouted in flames, stepping in front of her fire, blocking it from targeting the crowd behind him. "Your quarrel is with me, not with them." Their two streams of flame intermingled into one.

"I have no sistersss because of you, only squalling babes that never shut up," she screeched. "You decapitated my sisters and stole my heaven stone, the stone that whispered to me of all the fires in the heavens, and the great fire in the sky that warms our land. The stone that whispered all the wonders of the universe into my ear, and now instead I have to listen to squalling babes day and night. I will burn your people to ash for your crimes."

"You did not honour our bargain," Bayerd said as coldly as he could with a mouthful of flames. "Your sisters attacked me. I was merely defending myself. That is no crime."

He glanced around, trying to spot Kelp. She stood with Orson and Gerald, behind their table. The two men were ready to protect her if need be, although it looked like they were arguing about something. The guard that had held the knife at her back was nowhere near Kelp, who was watching Bayerd with pleading eyes. He wanted to tell her that he was no longer a coward and would not let her or her people come to harm, but without his voice, he could not. He only hoped she could read that pledge in his eyes. Events did seem to be unfolding in a way that, with a little luck, could be manipulated to work to Bayerd's advantage—if the Tri-Alanth didn't kill him first.

Shifra kept sitting on her throne, watching. Her expression was captivated, rather than concerned or frightened. The brute of a guard who had been prepared to stab Kelp in the back, now stood beside Shifra, intent on protecting the false queen.

The Tri-Alanth followed his gaze to where Shifra squatted on Hellenor's throne. "Is that your pretty princesss? She truly is beautiful. Her hair is like fire, and her skin is as smooth as velvet, and unburnt."

The monster sounded so sinister that Bayerd had an idea. It was not a nice idea, but he was not feeling in a particularly nice or forgiving frame of mind. Nor should he be.

"She really is gloriously beautiful, isn't she? I love her with all my heart, especially all that fiery red hair, so you leave her be," Bayerd shouted, of Shifra. "Don't you dare burn one hair on her lovely head!"

The Tri-Alanth focused again on him, her eyes fixed on his chest. The flames on his skin had died. The glow in his heart was easy to see, since he was shirtless and the vast hall was not brightly lit.

"The heaven stone of fire burns inside you ssstill," she hissed, distracted.

She had not reacted as he had hoped to his order not to burn Shifra, and he said, "Well, it's not like I want it inside me, or even want the damn thing anymore. It doesn't share any heavenly wonders with me. Instead, it has stolen my voice and made my life a living hell. If I could get it out of me without dying, I would do so, believe me." It was so nice to be understood and not have to mime everything, even if it was by a murderous monster.

"Why don't we ssstrike a bargain. You will allow me to cut the heaven stone out of you. I will take it back to my mountain and your people will never trespass there again. In exchange, I won't incinerate everyone in this room, including your precious princess," she hissed.

"And before you answer, know thisss—now that I have traced the pathway to your castle, I can come out of any fire that burns within these walls, at any time. No-one will be safe inside these walls ever again."

And a people needed fire for heat in the cold of winter, and to cook their meat and boil their water. A people could not live without fire. Even a fool knew that. "How is that possible?" Bayerd asked.

"Fire is kin to fire. I followed the scent of your fire, it is unique because it comes from the heaven stone, and now I know the pathway here." The Tri-Alanth smiled nastily, showing her long fangs. "Let me take the stone out of you now, and you have my word I will never trespass here again. As long as your people stay away from my mountain, your precious princess will be safe."

She finally gave him the opening he had been waiting for. And perhaps it was time to speak plainly. The enemy of your enemy is reputed to be your friend, after all. "Here is my deal. I will let you take the heaven stone out of me willingly, if and only if you incinerate that beautiful woman sitting on the throne, and no-one else. Although, if that big ugly guard beside her gets a little burnt, I won't be too upset."

Her eyes narrowed. "Fallen out of love already? Men are so fickle."

"You don't need to know the whys and wherefores. Just do it and I will let you take the stone without putting up a fight—but I do need a bit of time to complete some important tasks before I breathe my last. Two days—forty-eight hours should suffice, and then the heaven stone will be yours."

"Why do you want the princess killed? And why would you willingly sacrifice yourself?" The Tri-Alanth was curious.

Bayerd considered how to answer her. "I have lost everything worth living for. I have lost my love, who is sleeping with my best friend. I have lost my truest friend because he is sleeping with my love. I have lost my voice, and even my home. I have not even the smallest speck of dignity left to comfort me."

The Tri-Alanth laughed, enjoying his misery. "Now I understand why you want your princess dead. And we have a deal." With no more warning than that, the Tri-Alanth surged out of the fire and across the hall toward Shifra, who froze like a bunny cornered by a fox. There was no way for her to avoid the blast of fire that targeted her. And it was such a ferocious amount, the false queen did not even have a chance to scream. One second she was sitting there, the next second she was one of two pyres of fire. Her guard had also taken the brunt of the flames. Hellenor's throne fared no better. Bayerd hoped the true queen would not hold that against him when she ruled again.

All around the grand hall, people gave into panic, running amok and screaming like banshees.

The Tri-Alanth darted back toward the hearth, and Bayerd, who simply stood there, rooted. In truth, he was too shocked to move. Shifra had been evil, but it is still no easy thing to watch another person go up in flames, especially when you are the one responsible. 'At least it was quick,' he thought, hoping for the same for himself, when his time came.

The Tri-Alanth slithered into the fireplace. Her return to the hearth had a calming effect on the crowd. They stopped screaming and running amok, for the most part. "Did you like watching your princess burn?" the Tri-Alanth asked.

"No, but it had to be done," he said.

"Well, I enjoyed it ssso much."

"I'm sure you did."

"I will enjoy slicing you opened even more, when you lie willingly before me, and then the heaven ssstone will be mine," she hissed.

Before he could respond to that, Kelp shouted, "No, he will not be giving up his life!"

Bayerd swung around to gape at her, wondering how on earth she could understand their fire conversation. And then he saw the small lick of flame she was holding in her upturned palm—the Tri-Alanth's fire, taken from one of the many fires the monster had set. Gerald and Orson didn't look at all happy about this development.

"Put it out," Bayerd ordered, not wanting her to suffer. His words accidentally set one of the long wooden tables ablaze.

Kelp skirted around it, toward Bayerd and the Tri-Alanth, her face taut with pain, yet resolute. "No. You will not leave me again, husband. You will not die again. We will find a way to remove the stone without killing you, and I'll have a dragon deliver it to the mountain. That is the deal, Tri-Alanth. You will leave us in peace and I will see the stone delivered to you."

"By dragon? You are the princesss who is kin to dragonsss?"

"Yes," Kelp gasped.

Bayerd could not bear to see Kelp in pain. He pressed his hand over hers, smothering the flame.

196

The Tri-Alanth said, "So the dragon princesss is your true princesss. Who was the other one?"

He angled away from Kelp, so his fire would not be near her, and said, "A murderous, traitorous despot." He did not add 'like you', he only thought it.

"And your princesss wants to amend our deal."

"There is no need. Come for me in two days, at this hour, as we agreed. The bargain we struck stands," he said.

"If you do not present me with the stone, or yourself, when I return, I will burn everyone in the castle to ash, including your true princesss," the Tri-Alanth hissed.

"There is no need to burn anyone. If I can't get the stone out, I will let you take it out. I won't fight you. You have my word. And I stand by my word, which cannot be said for every creature in this room," he alluded.

"Then our pact stands."

"A pact you will keep this time." Bayerd glared hard at her.

"Of coursssse." She retreated deeper into the hearth and vanished into the flames. The hall was totally silent for a charged moment before everyone began talking at once.

Bayerd ushered Kelp to the nearest jug of water. Her palm was red and blistered, and his heart ached to see her injured. He knew the pain she must be feeling, firsthand, yet she did not moan or complain. He guided her hand into the pitcher, wondering how much of his conversation with the Tri-Alanth that Kelp had overheard.

Around them, people put out fires and righted benches and talked excitedly about the monster that had visited them.

Kelp dropped onto a bench, hand soaking in the pitcher. "I can't believe you were going to die again, when you have just returned to me," Kelp whispered, her voice pitched too high with suppressed tears. If so much evidence had not supported Jabalot's claim, Bayerd would have believed her still in love with him. "Oh, I wish you could speak. There is so much we have to say to each other. Did you have a hand in Shifra's demise?"

He nodded, a bit guiltily.

"Brilliant idea," she said with a sweet smile, just for him. "And what about the monster, will she wait for us to deliver the stone to her mountain?"

Without a voice, Bayerd could not answer that question in detail, so he simply shrugged. And there was something more important that she needed to know without delay. Queen Hellenor should not be left to endure the dungeon for a minute longer than necessary.

Bayerd tilted his head at the door. Kelp did not ask questions. She rose and followed him when he walked that way. Orson joined them without an invitation. "How's the hand, Kelp?" he said.

"It shall be fine."

"And where are we going?" Orson asked curiously.

"I have no idea. Bayerd knows, but of course he cannot say."

"The less talking he does, the better, now that he talks in fire," Orson said, stating the obvious.

Bayerd rolled his eyes and walked faster. It was not easy to spend time with the two people he most loved, knowing what they were getting up to behind his back, and in his bed.

They accompanied him to the entrance of the dungeon. Two guards were posted there. Bayerd didn't know if the pair was loyal to Shifra or Hellenor. He pointed to the door, indicating that he wanted to enter. The two oversized sentries did not step aside to grant him entrance. They looked at each other.

"What?" said the balding guard.

"That's a door," said the big-eared guard, too loudly.

Bayerd pointed at himself, then at the door, more emphatically, indicating that he wanted to enter the dungeon.

"Huh?" said the balding guard.

"You are Prince Bayerd, returned from the dead, and that is a door," said the big-eared guard, very loudly, over-annunciating his words. Did he think that Bayerd had lost his hearing and his brain along with his voice?

Bayerd almost growled, until he remembered that he should not start any more fires. There had already been enough burning for one night. He thought for a moment, then pointed to himself, pointed to the door, and walked his fingers through the air in the direction of the door, mimicking walking into the dungeon.

The balding guard looked to the big-eared guard for guidance, even though none was likely to be forthcoming, given what Bayerd had already witnessed. The big-eared guard said, "I don't want to dance, especially with you. Not even if you put on one of those lady dresses you like to wear."

"He'd probably set you on fire, if you did dance with him," the balding guard added.

Bayerd stomped his foot in frustration and surged forward, trying to push his way past the two guards, who were easily twice his size.

"Move aside, now," Kelp ordered, finally intervening. He wasn't sure why she hadn't done so earlier, unless his attempt to enter the dungeon had simply been too entertaining to stop.

Bayerd led the way down, down, down, into the bowels of the foul dungeon. Whenever a door got in the way, he simply melted the lock with his dragon-breath. Given his druthers, he would have turned the whole damn dungeon to ash, so that no more poor souls would have to suffer the place.

His blasts of fire also helped to warm the air and dispel the damp. When he reached the door to the queen's cell, he melted that lock too. He flung the door wide, arms triumphantly raised. Finding and saving the queen would certainly enhance his reputation, and perhaps elevate him to the rank of true hero.

Alas, the cell was empty. Only the queen's ball and chain, with the melted links, proved that Bayerd had the right cell.

"Why are we here?" Kelp asked, at something of a loss.

"Not the nicest place to visit," Orson added.

Bayerd scowled at him and pointed at the ball and chain, and remnants of a fire.

"This is where Shifra kept you?" Kelp guessed.

Bayerd nodded and raised two fingers, indicating that there had been two in the cell, then he mimed a crown, using his hands to form a circle over his head.

"You believed you would die down here?" Kelp guessed.

"I don't think you'll turn into an angel if you die," Orson said. "You're not very angelic. And you don't die, do you?"

So his mimed crown was being perceived as a halo. Bayerd shook his head vigorously and stomped for the door. He stomped all the way up the long stone steps. He surged out of the dungeon into the courtyard. It was an unexpected hive of activity and noise—joyous noise.

In front of the stables, Queen Hellenor was surrounded by her subjects, who were cheering and whooping. Without the ball and chain, she had managed to escape the dungeon herself. Well, after plotting with her, Bayerd knew firsthand how keenly her mind worked, and how sly she could be. He should not have been surprised, but he was deeply disappointed that he did not get to free Hellenor and wear the mantle of hero.

Kelp gave a joyous cry and rushed toward her aunt. Hellenor opened her arms and embraced her. "Auntie, you're alive!" Kelp said, tears of joy filling her eyes.

"Shifra had me locked up, but I managed to escape. I am unharmed, merely a little worse for wear." The queen shot Bayerd an apologetic look. Did she feel bad for not allowing him some credit in her escape? Alas, he understood. A queen had to be seen as a ruler, not a victim. By escaping on her own, the queen proved that she was not someone to be trifled with.

"I have been told that Shifra met a fiery end," she added.

"She did, by a monster that came out of the fire." Kelp gripped the queen's elbow when she swayed. "We shall talk in your rooms, auntie. A little sit-down and a meal will do you the world of good."

The queen nodded and allowed Kelp to shepherd her toward the castle. She was slow and shaky, weaker than she wanted to admit. Orson moved to take her other arm and assist her to walk. As the three moved together, they looked like they belonged together somehow. And Bayerd was still a dragon-man without a voice, a man who likely had a mere two days to live, unless by some miracle he survived the stone's extraction from his heart.

Feeling like an outsider, he slipped deeper into the boisterous crowd. The castle folk were so focused on celebrating Hellenor's return and Shifra's dramatic downfall, that he went unnoticed as he stumbled through the press of bodies, head down. He was exhausted into his bones after his performance and confronting the Tri-Alanth—and all the hardship that had come before that.

On impulse, he ducked into the knights' quarters. He crawled into a bunk that looked unused. Maybe it had belonged to one of the knights who had died on the quest, under his charge. He pulled a blanket over his head and fell instantly asleep.

When he awoke, the waning light informed him that it was the latter half of the afternoon. He had slept for almost an entire day. The room was empty and he was hungry—very, very hungry. He helped himself to a plain cotton shirt that belonged to one of the knights, He donned it and entered the courtyard, head down, again hoping to go unnoticed.

And he did, probably because he no longer resembled his former self, in dress or stature.

He entered the castle and started toward the kitchen, then halted. He wished to be remembered with dignity, not as a beggarman. At the moment, his borrowed shirt was so overlarge, it was in danger of falling off his shoulders. And the fire had done fair damage to the leather of his trousers. It was so compromised, it was ripping apart as he walked. His boots were in even worse shape.

Alas, his remaining clothes were in the tower rooms he had shared with Kelp, once upon a time and not so long ago. Now, Kelp and Orson and a babe were probably calling the rooms their home. Bayerd supposed he should meet his son at least once before he departed, or became one of the dearly departed. He just hoped the child did not resemble its mother to any degree.

'Get the ordeal over with,' he thought. He made his way through the castle and up the long winding staircase, each step seeming heavier than the one that came before. When he reached the door at the top, he knocked as if he was a visitor, which he was now.

No-one answered the door. He knocked louder. Still no-one answered. He opened the door and stepped inside. The outer room was quiet and empty, and he didn't hear any noise from the bed chamber. The last thing in the world he wanted to witness was Kelp and Orson naked together. If he saw that sight, he would have to throw himself out the tower window headfirst to end his torment.

He crossed the room on quiet feet and took a cautious peek into his former bed chamber. It was blessedly empty. He would not have to face Kelp and Orson quite yet.

Bayerd quickly located a pair of leather riding trousers and a plain dark blue tunic. They had not been worn in almost a year. In truth, they had not fit in almost a year. He stripped and donned the new garments. They were loose, to be sure, but not disgracefully so. They weren't likely to fall off and leave him bare-assed. He stepped into his old leather boots. They fit like old friends.

He gave his hair a cursory brushing and tied it back with a plain strap, not a bow. He never wanted to wear a bow again as long as he lived. 'That should do,' he thought, and glanced in the looking glass. He was surprised to see that he looked like himself again—thinner and rather beaten, but still like himself. If only he could sound like himself again. He missed his voice, not as much as he would miss Kelp and

Orson when he left the Golden Kingdom, or died, but close. He yearned to wield his voice again—the blade for his tales.

He scooped up the clothes he had shed and shoved them into the bottom of his trunk. Something rattled and he reached into the pocket of his ruined trousers. His fingers knew Kelp's locket as soon as he touched it, for he had removed it from her neck too many times to count, not wanting it to get in the way of their skin-to-skin contact.

The locket was a tangible reminder of both the love they had once shared, and his acute failure as a husband, which had resulted in Kelp ordering his assassination, and taking up with Orson. He held the locket in his palm for a long moment before he decided to keep it as a reminder of both the best of times, and the worst of times—which were his own damn fault.

His old travelling pack was in his trunk. He removed it, shook it out, and tucked the locket inside it. The pack would do to carry what little he needed to take with him, if he survived the Tri-Alanth. But until matters were resolved, he would continue to stay in the knights' barracks.

He added his parchment and quill and ink, and one change of clothes. It was the way he used to travel. He hoisted the small pack over his shoulder, then stopped.

After their marriage ceremony, when he and Kelp had spent the day in bed together with the door barred to the rest of the world, Kelp had braided a lock of her long dark hair with a lock of Bayerd's golden hair. She had turned it into a bracelet with a strand of ribbon running through it. It had encircled a post of their bed, declaring them united. Was it still there, or had Orson and Kelp removed it and tossed in into the fire?

Bayerd set down the pack and moved to the head of the bed. No, the circle of braid was still there. He carefully untied it from the post and retied it to the strap of his pack. He smiled, to know a small part of Kelp would always be with him, along with the memory of that most wonderful day.

He hoisted the pack again and left the bed chamber. He was about to open the outer door to the corridor when he heard voices. Clearly, he had trespassed a little too long. Not ready to face Kelp and Orson, he ducked behind the upholstered couch before the door opened.

"But where can he be, Orson? We've searched high and low, and found not hide nor hair of him," Kelp said, walking into the room.

202

"You know Bayerd, he's probably off sulking somewhere, hiding and licking his wounds," Orson said. "I told you, he's been all grumpy and moody since he lost his voice. He even punched me in the nose. It's still sore." He shut the door too hard, rattling the more fragile things in the room, and Bayerd's nerves.

"Not so loud, Orson. I just got little Darton to sleep," Kelp said softly.

Bayerd's jaw dropped. It was lucky he didn't set the couch on fire when he cursed. Only a hand clapped over his mouth stopped the flames from coming out. Kelp had named his son Darton? After her evil, murderous cousin, the one who had taken great pleasure in torturing Bayerd? Why would she do such a thing? Unless she had grown to hate Bayerd rather than love him, or perhaps she loathed the babe that had been foisted upon her—her husband's bastard, with a harpy no less. Bayerd dropped his head into his hands in despair. He needed to get the hell out of that room unseen.

Something was laid on the couch. Kelp and Orson sat, close enough for Bayerd to touch. They were probably cuddling and canoodling. His ragged breath sounded loud to his ears and he tried to calm himself.

"Where can he have gotten to? And why has he disappeared?" Kelp repeated.

Orson sighed loudly. "Listen, Kelp, I didn't want to tell you this, but Bayerd has heard a certain rumour," he said leadingly.

"Oh lord," Kelp groaned.

"He has heard that you and I are sharing a bed. Well, after we were caught rolling around in your bed together in the middle of the night, everyone has heard, haven't they?"

"Yes," Kelp said. "No wonder he punched you in the nose."

"I punched him back. Think I broke his nose again."

A soft rustling sound drew Bayerd's attention. He peaked under the couch and could see Orson's boots and Kelp's slippers on the other side, and … a babe was crawling around. A cute little tyke with curly sunny locks and sky blue eyes. Bayerd's boy did not look at all like his harpy mother. He was quite beautiful.

He spotted Bayerd and his eyes widened. His rosy little mouth opened and he gurgled in laughter. Bayerd held a finger in front of his own lips, signaling silence. The baby gurgled again. He probably didn't understand Bayerd's message—probably too young and stupid. He began crawling under the couch toward Bayerd. Bayerd motioned him back. The baby didn't understand that either, and kept crawling. He reached Bayerd and chortled in laughter. Bayerd tried to shove him back under the couch, but he rolled onto his back and started waving his arms and legs as if he wanted to be tickled. Bayerd frowned at him. He grabbed Bayerd's tender nose in a sticky little fist. He had surprisingly strong hands and Bayerd had a hard time not crying out in pain, which would have given him away, and set his child on fire.

Bayerd picked up the babe and tickled him, hoping his nose would be released. Instead, the child grabbed onto Bayerd's hair with his other hand. He pulled hard. Bayerd shook his head. The babe released Bayerd's nose, leaned in, and bit it. He only had about four teeth, but they were sharp little things and Bayerd whimpered. The babe thought that was funny and started laughing very loudly. Bayerd hadn't known that babes could laugh like that. He studied the child in amazement, and then he became aware of how quiet the room was. When had Kelp and Orson stopped talking?

He glanced upward and two faces were peering down at him over the high back of the couch.

22. An Affair of the Heart

There once was a man whose heart
Was so broken it cracked apart
It could beat no more
Pieces fell to the floor
And they get run over by a cart

-Bayerd the Storyteller, Limerick

"Bayerd, we've been looking everywhere for you," Orson said. "I see you've met your son."

Bayerd nodded, and still holding the babe, he stood up.

Kelp leapt to her feet and circled around the couch, her eyes teary. "Oh Bayerd, isn't he beautiful, and so sweet-natured," she said, of the babe. "I love him dearly. He reminds me of you. When I believed you and Orson both dead, he was all that kept me from sinking into despair."

Bayerd scowled at her. He wanted to ask why the hell she had named his son Darton then, but he could not. Wait! Yes, he could. He had parchment and a quill now, and Kelp was of the upper caste and knew how to read.

He picked up his pack, stomped over to the table where they used to share tea, and pulled out his writing implements with one hand, whilst trying not to drop his squirming son on his head. With no finesse to his letters, he scribbled, '*Why did you name my son Darton?*'

Kelp read over his shoulder. "I did no such thing. Your son is named Bayerd, after you. Although we call him Bay for short. Darton is the cat, your son's favourite playmate." She pointed toward the couch.

He went to have a look. An extremely ugly, scrawny black kitten was curled up, sound asleep on the upholstery. So that was Darton. The name suited the runty thing. Bayerd nodded his head approvingly.

"See how easy it is to misunderstand what you hear," Kelp said pointedly.

Bayerd looked back and forth between her and Orson, one eyebrow raised, significantly. He had not misunderstood the affair they were having. Bayerd tucked his son under one arm, stuffed his possessions back in his pack, tossed it over his other shoulder, and started for the door.

"Where do you think you're going?" Kelp cried.

Bayerd pointed at the door. Surely it was obvious.

"No, you can't take Bay. He is my son now, too."

Bayerd turned around, marched back to the table, dropped his pack on the chair, almost dropped his son on his head, and pulled out his writing implements. The ink had spilled all over his spare suit of clothes, but he didn't care. Using the dregs of the ink that remained, he wrote '*Kelp and Orson*', and drew a big heart around the two names.

Kelp glanced at the sheet and her mouth tightened until it was ringed with white. "You of all people should know better than to believe gossip," she cried.

He scribbled, '*I never believed the gossip.*'

"Then what has changed your opinion?"

Bayerd pointed an accusing finger at Orson. He put his son down on the chair so he could use both hands to mime a pair of big flapping lips—Orson's lips. His son patted at the spilt ink, splashing it everywhere, then he fell off the chair. It was not a great distance and he didn't even cry. He was a brave little lad from the look of it.

Kelp, meanwhile, was trying to figure out his message. "Orson quacks like a duck?" she guessed.

Bayerd scooped up his son, who was leaving inky handprints all over the finely woven carpet. He picked up his quill again and wrote, '*Orson told me*'.

Kelp gasped and planted her hands on her hips. Orson was on the receiving end of a very accusing glare. "You told Bayerd we were … intimate?" she sputtered.

"Uh," Orson scratched his head, "no, I don't think so. I mean, why would I? In truth, I can't remember weeks of my life, got whacked on the head, more than once. But I wouldn't tell Bayerd a lie, unless I was confused. I must have been confused."

Bayerd shook his head, and pointed to Kelp's chest.

"What?" Kelp said, confused herself.

Bayerd put his son down on the couch to wake up the cat, and picked up his quill. He tried to write, '*Orson spoke about your birthmark*'.

206

Alas, there was no more ink left, so he undid the top tie of his tunic, parted it and squeezed his meager chest together, trying to create breasts. There was hardly any spare flesh to speak of, but he tapped the exact spot on his tunic where Kelp's birthmark was located, and pointed at Orson.

Orson guessed, "You want to be a lady?"

Kelp guessed, "You used to be so fat you had breasts?"

Bayerd shook his head, then rubbed it. He was getting a headache.

Orson said, "I've got it. You have a broken heart."

Bayerd shook his head, then nodded because he did. His mixed message was not helping to clarify matters.

The cat yowled when his son pulled on its tail. Bayerd picked up the boy, saving the poor cat from more abuse. He pointed to his parchment and mimicked writing, hoping someone would produce more ink. He also wanted to broach the topic of Kelp ordering his assassination. He wished the truth from her lips before he breathed his last, or departed the kingdom, whichever came first.

The babe was squirming so Bayerd put him on the floor. He couldn't fall off the floor. Orson guessed, "You want to write down your new tale?"

Kelp said, "Surely this isn't the time to script a tale." She stepped closer and looked deep into his eyes. "Husband, I don't know what Orson said to you when he was knocked senseless, but I have never been unfaithful to you." She took his hands in hers and rubbed her thumbs across his scarred palms. "I know that we had some difficulties before you left on your quest, but I never stopped loving you. I have never been unfaithful to you. You must believe me."

Bayerd wanted to believe her with all his heart, so that it wouldn't be broken anymore, but there was no denying that Orson had seen his wife in a state of undress. And the conversation he had just overheard had made mention of them being caught abed together in the middle of the night. Even a man with his head in the sand would have a hard time ignoring such blatant truths.

He took her uninjured hand in his and led her into the bed chamber with a dark glare in Orson's direction, letting him know he was not welcome to join them. He shut the door firmly and turned to face his wife. Now that they were alone, he boldly unlaced and unbuttoned the front of her gown. She allowed it. He parted the lace, baring her breasts. His eyes drank in the sight of their creamy pale perfection. He bent down and kissed the moon-shaped birthmark that nestled against her left nipple. She murmured in pleasure when his lips lingered there, and she stroked his hair.

As soon as her hands stilled, he straightened. Bayerd held her gaze and touched the birthmark.

Her brow furrowed. "That is what you were trying to explain by showing your chest? Orson spoke about my birthmark? He described it?" she guessed. Well, she was smarter than your average princess.

Bayerd nodded sadly.

"Orson may have seen the birthmark accidentally one night, but I have never lain with him. I have never parted my legs for him. I have never even kissed him on the lips," she said.

Her words sounded so sincere, if only they were truth. Bayerd did not want to argue with her, well, he couldn't since he had no voice. He simply did up her gown. Before he could open the bedroom door, she cupped his face with her soft hand, the uninjured one. She leaned in and tenderly kissed his lips. He kissed her back—a farewell kiss, although she did not know it.

Before he left the kingdom, or died at the Tri-Alanth's claws, he wanted so badly to apologize for the man he had become when fear ruled him, driving Kelp to want to do away with him and seek comfort in another's arms, but he could not, so he simply kept kissing her, deeply and hungrily. When the pleasure of her touch became too much to bear, because he knew he would never feel it again, he released her lips, opened the door, and left the bedchamber.

Kelp trailed him out and Orson was waiting, playing with the babe. Kelp said, "Sit down, Bayerd. We shall share a goblet of wine and I will tell you the story of how Orson saw my birthmark."

Orson blushed red all the way up to his hairline. "It was an accident. How does Bayerd know I saw it?"

"Apparently you told him."

"I didn't, I wouldn't, unless I told him when I'd been bonked on the head. I honestly don't have a clue what I said then."

"Be quiet, Orson." Kelp poured three goblets of wine. Bayerd did not sit, he stood with his arms crossed, waiting. Kelp took a sip before she said, "Not long after you left the castle on your quest, Orson and I learned of a rumour going around, that he and I were keeping company—close company," she said significantly. "And Orson, in his wisdom, decided we needed to discuss it privately, so no-one would see us talking, I suppose. So he waited until the castle was quiet and everyone was asleep, then he snuck into my bedchamber to talk about the rumour."

It did sound like something Orson would do. Bayerd glared at Orson.

Orson said, "Stop being so bloody grumpy. I was just trying to be discreet, nip the rumour in the bud, you know. So I snuck into Kelp's bedchamber and it was dark. I couldn't see. And when I went to shake Kelp awake, well, I grabbed something I shouldn't, if you know what I mean. I thought I was shaking her shoulder, only it wasn't her shoulder."

Bayerd rolled his eyes.

"Yes," said Kelp primly. "And then Orson sat down to talk, on what he thought was the edge of the bed."

"Only it wasn't the edge of the bed," Orson interjected. "I sat on Kelp, and she began thrashing about, and then I fell over onto her and we got all tangled up together in the blankets, and I couldn't get up. It could have happened to anyone."

Bayerd doubted that very much.

"To make a short story even shorter," Kelp said, "we were discovered like that by my ladies and a couple of guards."

"And Sir Stalwart," Orson added

"Oh, yes, and Sir Stalwart, he turned up a little after the fact," Kelp agreed.

"And when everyone ran in with the lanterns, Kelp's nightdress had shifted around a bit, and that's when I saw the … the birthmark," Orson said, the hot blush staining his ears, making them look like overripe misshapen tomatoes.

It was the most ludicrous tale Bayerd had ever heard, which meant it could only be the truth. He felt such profound relief, he started to laugh, which was not a wise thing to do given his condition and present location. He clapped a hand over his mouth and hurried over to the fireplace until he could control his mirth. It took several minutes and by then, a roaring hot fire was burning.

He returned to sit with Kelp and Orson. Kelp said, "I take it you believe us?"

Bayerd nodded, shamefaced.

"Good. And might I remind you, the whole kingdom has seen all you have to offer, husband, on more than one occasion," Kelp pointed out.

He nodded and took a sip of wine. The whole kingdom certainly had.

If he'd had a voice, he would have been forthright, and simply asked then and there, if she had commanded Jabalot to assassinate him, or if that too had been a huge misunderstanding. He now believed Kelp had been true to him, and she seemed to love him still, so maybe, just maybe, she had not wished him dead. Perhaps he was grasping at straws, but he preferred to believe she had not ordered his assassination, despite all the damning evidence to the contrary.

Alas, he had no voice or ink, so he could not ask.

And Kelp had another matter of import that she wanted to discuss. She said, "We do need to figure out how to get that magical stone out of you, so that it can be delivered to the monster. I don't want her to return here, she is far too dangerous to my people."

Bayerd was simply glad she didn't know that the Tri-Alanth would be returning to the castle the next day, for him or the stone. The Tri-Alanth had said that extracting it would kill him, unless she was wrong, or lying. He didn't trust her any farther than he could toss her great hulking bulk, so she might be lying. But if there was a way to get the stone out, he didn't know what it was. The stone was lodged in his heart, and a man could not live without a beating heart. His heart might feel rejuvenated now that he knew Kelp had been true to him, but that did not supernaturally excise the stone.

Well, if he only had one day with his wife, he intended to make the very most of it. He swallowed his wine in one gulp and stood up, tilting his head toward the bedchamber. He wanted nothing more than to fall into bed, and simply hold Kelp on what might well be their last night together.

Kelp smiled and said, "Orson, can you take Bay to Irvette for the evening."

"Happy to. I'll even help her look after the little troublemaker, if she'll have me." He scooped up the lad, tucked him under one arm, and departed quickly. When you had servants to take care of them, babes weren't nearly as inconvenient as Bayerd had expected them to be.

Alone, Kelp kissed him sweetly on the mouth, her lips as soft and velvety as a fresh-picked peach, and more delicious than nectar. "I cannot wait to share a bed with you again, my husband," she said, and slipped her tongue into his mouth. He almost moaned, until he realized that would burn Kelp's face. He jerked away from her and clamped his lips together, trying to contain the fire that welled up inside him.

"What's wrong?" she asked.

He mimed fire shooting out of his mouth and her going up in flames, with a lot of flapping hands and pained expressions.

"You are about to be sick? Because you've eaten some rotten meat?" she guessed.

Bayerd shook his head, and pointed at the fire that burned merrily in their hearth.

"You think the Tri-Alanth was lying and is going to attack you tonight through that fire, and bite you in half to get the heaven stone?" Kelp said, sounding very alarmed indeed.

Bayerd shook his head, then wondered if she could be right. Would the Tri-Alanth attack while their defenses were down? He strode over to the fire, closed the damper, and shut the fire-guard, hoping to extinguish the flames. Kelp picked up a pitcher of water, opened the fire-guard, and doused the flames completely.

"That should do it," she said, shutting the fire-guard tight. She smiled and stepped close, kissing him once again, intimately, hotly, lustfully. Bayerd willed himself not to make any sounds of passion that might produce flames, and that was not an easy thing to do. Being a storyteller, he was inclined to be verbose and rather noisy, even in the throes of passion.

Kelp drew back, and gazed into his eyes. "What is wrong, Bayerd? Are you not looking forward to our reunion as much as I am?"

He nodded emphatically, then spotted his parchment and ink still on the table. He linked their hands and drew her to the table. He picked up his quill and dipped it in the dry inkwell repeatedly, emphasizing the need for more ink, so he could communicate in written words.

"I, too, am looking forward to our reunion, my love. Your fire-show was magnificent, and highly arousing." Kelp pressed against him and nuzzled his neck. "I want to count every one of your new scars, and kiss them better," she murmured breathlessly.

A man had never needed control more than Bayerd did at that moment. He held his breath, and bit his tongue, and thought about the Tri-Alanth trying to have her way with him. He even thought about harpies, and their foul stench. That dampened his passion most effectively, yet it did not cause the debilitating dread that it would have before his quest.

He stepped back from Kelp and clasped her shoulders. He shook his head. Her brow furrowed. "Why not?"

211

Bayerd scanned the room and spotted a lit candle. He fetched it, and brought it to Kelp. He pointed at the flame and then at her, moving the candle closer, but not too close.

"You are worried that you will light me on fire? Burn me?" she guessed, finally getting it right. He nodded and kissed her cheek. Her face fell with disappointment. "Oh. Yes, I suppose it could happen, couldn't it. You do tend to shout a lot when we make love."

He nodded. They gazed at each other sadly, and then Kelp smiled. "I have an idea."

Bayerd raised one eyebrow hopefully.

"Fire cannot burn in water, can it?" She pointed to their ridiculously large bathing tub.

He shook his head and grinned back at her.

"I'll have the servants fill our bathing tub, and to hell with the inappropriateness of the hour," she declared, and rang her handbell. When Maiga turned up, Kelp issued her instructions. Before an hour had passed, the bathing tub was full of heated water, carried bucket by steaming bucket up the long winding staircase to their tower rooms. Kelp shut the door behind the last of the servants, and barred it.

Bayerd began to undo his trousers. Kelp brushed his hands aside and took over, removing his clothing slowly and examining his new collection of scars, and kissing each one, as she had promised. He had to stop her from doing that when she discovered the fang marks in his upper thigh. His control was already sorely taxed.

When he wore nothing but his own skin, he returned the favour, which took much longer with a woman's clothing, what with all the layers and buttons and bows and ties and hooks and ribbons and lace. Kelp had no new scars, only the burn on her palm. Her body was perfect.

Bayerd climbed into the tub first and blasted fire at the surface, heating the water that much more. Kelp lit the candles that ringed the tub, and doused the lanterns, creating a subdued romantic atmosphere. She sank gracefully into the water, with her hair floating all around her. His mermaid. He had never seen a lovelier sight. She kissed Bayerd, nibbling his lower lip and slipping her tongue into his mouth. He had to duck under the surface to groan and moan a bit.

When he was in control, he surfaced and hauled in a breath. He kissed Kelp like a starving man and pressed their flesh together. It was agony and ecstasy, because he had to keep such a tight rein on himself.

212

He ducked under the water to groan again. When he surfaced, Kelp straddled him, wrapping her legs around him, joining them together in the most intimate and pleasurable way imaginable.

He was so overcome, he sank under the rippling surface where he could do no harm with his fire, taking Kelp with him. They made love in the buoyant world under the water, and loving his wife after so long apart was all that mattered. Kelp, as a half-mermaid, could stay under the water without breathing for an uncommonly long time, and that certainly came in handy. Bayerd surfaced periodically to haul in air, in-between kissing Kelp and stroking her, pleasuring her until she shook and clawed at him, and finally went limp, holding him tight enough to strangle him, but in the best way.

She was on top of him at that point and Bayerd found his own release, sending Kelp into mindless ecstasy one more time. The intense sensations were so overwhelming, and the waves of pleasure that flooded him went on and on, as if they would never end. The world seemed to fade away. Only then did he realize that he had not breathed for a very long time. No wonder his head was spinning and his vision was going dark around the edges. And the glowing light in his heart was almost extinguished. He felt a painful cutting pressure there, and tried to surface for air. Alas, Kelp was still in the clutches of rapture on top of him, and seemed unaware that he was drowning. His thrashing only seemed to excite her more, and she pushed him deeper under the water. His vision went black before he could reach the air.

Bayerd returned to awareness to find himself being hauled over the side of the tub by Orson, who dropped him on the floor. He had a blinding headache and couldn't breathe. Hitting the floor made the water that filled his lungs come spewing out. Only then could he breathe to some degree. He groaned weakly, and no more than a small stream of fire was produced. Orson bellowed and backed off. Bayerd lifted heavy lids and squinted. Orson's sleeve was on fire. His friend stuck his arm in the bathing tub, cursing all the while.

"Bayerd, you're alive. I was so afraid you had drowned," Kelp said, her voice shaking. "I had to summon Orson to help get you out of the water." She had also taken the time to don a robe, for modesty's sake, although it was clinging to her damp body quite scandalously.

He struggled to sit up. She helped him. He blinked around in confusion, trying to recall his last conscious moments. Orson tossed him a towel, saying, "Cover yourself, man. I already had to haul your naked ass out of the tub. I can't believe you drowned in a bathtub. I know you can't swim a stroke, but who drowns in a bathtub?" Orson shook his head at Bayerd in disgust.

"I might have held him under," Kelp admitted, her cheeks turning painfully pink.

Orson grimaced. "You decided to assassinate him yourself then? Rather than have Jabalot do it? I admit, I thought you'd given up on the idea now that Bayerd is more himself, cured of his cowardice, but I suppose since he can't talk, and keeps lighting everything on fire, well, guess he's still not much good as a husband."

Orson was only able to ramble on as long as he did, because Kelp was quite speechless. Her mouth opened and closed, but no words were coming out.

"What?" she finally managed. "What are you on about, Orson?"

"I'm talking about you hiring Jabalot to assassinate Bayerd, on the quest. I found out about it from Gerald. Or maybe I knew about it before, but couldn't remember, since I've got those big gaping holes in my memory." He looked at Bayerd, who in spite of being more than half-drowned, was doing his utmost to pay attention to the conversation. "Did I know about Jabalot? Oh, wait, did you know about Jabalot? Maybe I shouldn't have said anything, if you didn't know Kelp had arranged for Jabalot to do away with you."

Kelp didn't give him a chance to answer. "Enough nonsense, Orson! We need to get Bayerd into bed before we discuss this foolishness any further. Help him to his feet."

"Not until he puts that towel on, I won't. And he better not set me on fire again," Orson declared.

Kelp wrapped the towel around Bayerd's middle, when he couldn't, and tucked it in place. Only then did Orson haul him to his feet, although in truth, he simply lifted Bayerd.

Bayerd nodded his thanks and noticed that the glow in his heart was bright again. To his relief, the stone was no longer causing him pain. He touched the spot thoughtfully, remembering how the glow had dimmed both times he had almost drowned, and the pressure and pain, as if the heaven stone wanted out of him—needed out of him. Perhaps the magic heaven stone required the air as much as Bayerd, to sustain itself. And when Bayerd was deprived of life-giving air, so too was the stone. Maybe there was even a way to force the stone to leave him of its own accord.

Orson dropped him on his bed. Bayerd was so exhausted, and half-drowned, that he fell instantly asleep, or perhaps he fainted. He probably fainted.

23. In Knight's Armour

Rub-a-dub-dub, two men in a tub,
and who do you think they be?
The jester as fool, a'drowning in the pool
The swordsman as friend, to bring about his end
One quick stab, perhaps a second jab
Rub-a-dub-dub, two men in a bloody tub,
and who do you think they be?

-Bayerd the Storyteller, Rub-a-dub-dub

Bayerd awoke to find himself in a bed that was going up in flames. He cried out another stream of fire, which only made matters worse. He rolled over and checked that the bed was empty, save for himself. Thank the stars, it was.

He scrambled out of the burning bed, clad in nothing but a damp towel. He raced to the door and there was Kelp, seated with Orson, who was holding Bay on his lap. They were sharing breakfast, or perhaps lunch. The sun did seem to be quite high. Bayerd smacked his palm on the wall to get their attention. They glanced up, startled.

He waved his arms wildly and pointed into the bedroom, not quite sure how to mime 'fire'. His towel wasn't securely tucked and dropped off. Orson covered the babe's eyes. Kelp blushed. "You're certainly eager this morning, husband. Just let me finish my breakfast, then Orson can watch Bay."

Bayerd shook his head wildly, replaced his towel, and noticed that the bathing tub hadn't yet been drained. He dashed over to it, snatched up a handy bucket, scooped it full of water, and raced back into the bedroom. He tossed the water on the fire and ran for more.

Kelp and Orson watched him run back and forth. It took about five buckets of water to douse the flames. Fire out, he donned pants and a cotton shirt and went to sit with them.

His son chortled at him, showing two little teeth. Bayerd plucked the babe off Orson's lap, and set him on his own. Bayerd's parchment was still on the table and the lad smacked at it, leaving jammy little handprints all over it, which gave Bayerd an idea. He dipped his finger in the raspberry jam and wrote, '*Bed was burning, set it afire in my sleep.*' He had to dip his finger in jam four times to complete the message.

Kelp read it and said, "I smelled smoke, but I thought it was just you." She went to have a look and returned, saying, "Yes, it is quite burnt, and soaked now. I'll have the servants cart it away and bring a new palette. But that can wait. You must be hungry, and there are matters to discuss, once you have eaten." Her voice had turned grave. Did those matters include Jabalot's role as assassin? Bayerd had a hazy memory of Orson running off at the mouth about Jabalot, the night before, before he had passed out from drowning.

He nodded and helped himself to sausage and eggs. His son helped him to eat them. It was a cozy breakfast, and Bayerd thoroughly enjoyed the company even though he couldn't speak a word and could only listen to those who could talk. When he was sated, he pushed his platter aside and dipped his finger in jam again. He wrote, '*Ink better than jam for writing*'. If they were going to be discussing Jabalot, Bayerd needed to be able to express himself.

Kelp read the message and smiled. "But not nearly as tasty." She took his hand and suckled the jam off his finger. He whimpered in pleasure, keeping his lips firmly pressed together. A small lick of flame shot out of his nose and set Orson's toast on fire.

Orson scowled and poured tea on his toast, dousing the flames. "Enough of that, you two. There's a babe at the table."

Kelp nodded and left the room, presumably to find ink. Bayerd was glad for the moment alone with Orson. He was fast running out of time and needed to talk, or mime, to his friend. He needed to enlist Orson's aid, for he did not want to distress Kelp with the truth—that he only had about half a day left to get the heaven stone out of his body before the Tri-Alanth returned for it—or him. Even the issue of Jabalot as assassin took a backseat to that.

He tapped Orson's arm, pointed to himself, opened and closed his hand like a talking mouth, and pointed to Orson, miming that he needed to talk to Orson.

Orson said, "I don't really like puppets, they're kind of creepy, but Bay likes to play puppets."

Bayerd shook his head 'no', telling Orson that he had gotten the message all wrong.

"Yes, he really does like puppets. I'll prove it." Before Bayerd could stop him, Orson pulled off his big smelly sock and inserted his hand into it. He opened and closed his hand, as Bayerd had done, making it appear as if the sock had a mouth and was talking. In a singsong squeaky voice, he said, "I am a snake and I like cake." He darted his finger in and out of a hole in the toe, like a snaky tongue, before he picked up a pastry with his smelly sock and pretended the sock was eating it. Little Bay began to laugh so hard, he spit out the pastry he had been gumming.

Bayerd scowled at Orson and dipped his finger in jam. He wrote, '*I need to speak with you, now, privately.*' He tapped the parchment urgently, his finger not unlike an irate woodpecker's beak.

Orson squinted at the jammy letters. "You know I don't read so good, especially after all those blows to my head, and those letters aren't written very clearly." He picked the parchment up with his sock and pretended to eat that, too. The babe had a fit of giggles that would have had him falling off the chair, if Bayerd hadn't been holding him securely.

And Kelp might be back at any moment. Bayerd set his son on the floor and wondered how else he could communicate with Orson. And then he thought of a way. He beckoned Orson to follow him, and approached the bathing tub. When they stood beside it, he took Orson's free hand and gripped his friend's fingers tight. He breathed a tiny flame into Orson's palm, hoping it would allow them to communicate. It had worked for the Tri-Alanth after all, so why not him?

Orson cried out and jerked his hand away, smothering the fire with his sock-puppet hand.

Bayerd scowled, pointed a warning finger at Orson, and grabbed his hand again. He tried to blow another flame into Orson's palm. Orson was having none of it. He yanked his hand away, and facts were facts, when it came to brawn, Orson had Bayerd soundly beaten. Yet, Bayerd could not give up, he had to enlist his friend's aid. He could not carry out his plan alone. He leapt forward and grabbed Orson's hand, at the same time twisting around so his back was to Orson. He locked Orson's arm between his side and his own arm, then blew a flame into Orson's palm.

"We have to talk," Bayerd said, aiming his flames at the bathwater before Orson could wrestle free.

"Ow, ow, ow," Orson screamed, fighting and lifting Bayerd right off his feet in the process.

"Do you understand me?" Bayerd roared in frustration, making the surface of the water boil.

"Yes," Orson moaned.

"Then listen -" But Bayerd got no further. Orson yanked on his arm and shoved Bayerd forward in the same motion. Bayerd went tumbling over the edge of the tub and splashed into the water headfirst, sending waves cascading over the lip of the tub. When he surfaced, Orson's hand was submerged in the water and he was whimpering. Bayerd had thought his friend made of sterner stuff. Kelp had been far braver than Orson when holding fire.

Alas, there had been no chance to explain his plan. Before he could attempt to set Orson's palm on fire again and outline the details of his half-formed plan, Kelp returned with ink. "Did you set yourself ablaze, husband?" she said, giggling at the sight of him, fully clothed and bobbing in the bathing tub.

He scowled and pointed an accusing finger at Orson, who said, "He was trying to light my hand on fire. I pushed him in by accident."

"Did you? If you would like to pass Orson a message, husband, I've brought the ink. You can write it down and I will read it to him," Kelp suggested. Bayerd shook his head and avoided her keen gaze. "Are you sure?" Her eyes narrowed with suspicion.

Bayerd nodded his head. Kelp set the writing supplies on the table. She picked up the babe, who was quite wet, as was the floor. "I'll have the servants mop this up and empty the tub, and replace our bedding," she said, allowing the matter to drop.

Bayerd pointed at the tub of water and shook his head emphatically. He needed the water. It was a key element of his plan. And there was no denying that it came in handy to douse the fires he kept setting. He proceeded to splash water around, miming putting out a fire, so Kelp would know not to empty the tub.

She said, "If you want to keep playing in the tub, it can be emptied later. Your son likes playing in the water, too."

She stripped off Bay's soaked clothes and handed the squirming boy to Bayerd, saying, "Hellenor has summoned me, so we will have our discussion when I return." She sighed. "There is so much to be put to rights after Shifra's time on the throne. I shouldn't be too long, I hope."

So Bayerd stayed in the tub and played with his son until they were both quite pruned. It was great fun. The lad thought it was hilarious whenever Bayerd blew flames to keep the water warm.

When Irvette came to take charge of the babe, Bayerd was relieved that she carried him from the tower room. Orson made to follow her, a besotted expression on his face. Bayerd had no choice but to blast a stream of fire to stop him leaving, which Orson did not appreciate one bit, nor did the carpet, but Bayerd needed some private time with Orson, to explain and carry out his plan. He had had a lot of time to think, while playing in the tub.

Bayerd was quite convinced that he had to drown, to be so close to death that the magical heaven stone would—hopefully—push out through his skin, and he fully expected the exit wound to seal shut, cauterized by the stone's peculiar properties. And then Bayerd would have to be hauled from the water and revived. Bayerd had drowned many times, and he had always revived, so he didn't anticipate any trouble there, as long as Orson was at the ready to haul him from the water. And when all was said and done, he would be alive and the stone could be presented to the Tri-Alanth when she returned for it. A straightforward but effective plan, he thought.

It shouldn't have been difficult to explain, even without words, yet Orson's skull was proving uncommonly thick in more ways than one. He was useless at interpreting the simplest pantomimes, and he could barely read, and he was frightened of getting even the teeniest bit burnt.

As soon as Orson finished stomping out the burning carpet, he scowled at Bayerd and said, "What do you want now?"

Bayerd rolled his eyes and beckoned Orson closer.

"Oh no," Orson said. "I'm not letting you burn me again. My hand stings like the dickens, I tell you."

Bayerd shook his head, indicating that he would not burn Orson again. Well, not unless he had to.

Orson said, "It does so sting. Don't you tell me it doesn't."

Bayerd groaned in frustration, since he was in the water. His flames made the surface simmer, as if he was stewing in a pot. Orson backed away. "See, you are going to burn me."

Once again, Bayerd shook his head. He even laid a hand on his heart, pledging his word.

"Well, okay then. What do you want?" Orson said grudgingly.

What Bayerd wanted, at that moment, was a cleverer and more amenable friend, but Orson was all he had. Hoping Orson would understand, Bayerd ducked under the water, then he surfaced, pretending to be dead by keeping his eyes shut and sticking out his tongue, letting it loll to the side like a dead cow's. Still mimicking a drowned man, he parted his shirt, tapped the spot that was glowing, and drew a line across it with his finger. He then pretended to pull the heaven stone out with his hand, since he didn't know how else to mime the stone coming out by itself.

Explanation complete, he opened his eyes and found Orson gazing down at him with an extremely alarmed expression on his face. "You truly think that's the best way to get the stone out," Orson gasped. Bayerd nodded. "But ... but that will kill you."

Bayerd shook his head and smiled reassuringly. He tapped his temple to indicate that he had it all figured out.

"Yes, I think you're bonkers," Orson said. "And your idea to get the stone out is nuts. It will kill you."

Once more, Bayerd shook his head. He floated to the edge of the tub, needing to write one word. With a wet finger, he traced '*Now*' on the stone tiles. Orson sounded out the letters, moving his mouth. He deciphered the word and his jaw dropped.

"Now? You want to do it right now?" he cried.

Bayerd nodded. He took Orson's hands, and tried to pull him into the tub. Orson jerked back. "No, I'm not ready to do this."

Feeling ever more desperate, Bayerd clasped his hands together beseechingly and mouthed, "Please."

Orson said, "No. I can't do it. I'm not ready."

In a fit of pique, Bayerd rose out of the tub and stomped across the room, soaking everything in his wake. If Orson would not hold him under the water so he could drown, he would just have to do it himself, and that required weight—heavy weight. And hopefully Orson would be willing to pull him from the water and revive him once he had drowned—once the heaven stone was out.

In the corner of the room, a polished suit of armour stood like a lifeless sentry. It had been Kelp's father's, and served no purpose now, other than decoration. But it was plenty heavy enough to drown a man—especially a man of Bayerd's reduced stature.

It was so heavy, he struggled to remove the helmet. He placed it on his head, with the face-guard opened, then strained to lift the chest-plate up and off the wooden mount that displayed it. Since it was buckled to the smaller back-plate with a row of ancient rusted buckles and dried leather straps, lifting it was the only way to get it off.

Orson watched him, head tilted quizzically. He did not offer to help.

When Bayerd lacked the strength to raise the armour up and off, he took a different approach. He simply knocked the support frame over. The display clattered loudly to the ground, almost landing on his toe. He removed the helmet from his head when it threatened to tip him over, and slid the chest armour off the wood. He tried to lift it over his own head to wear it, yet lacked the strength to do even that. With a resentful glare at Orson, who was simply standing about like an idiot, he lay down on the ground and tried to crawl into the armour, feeling rather like a worm squirming into a too-small hole. He got a bit stuck, and would have cursed in frustration if he could have done so without setting the carpet on fire, again. He was kicking his legs, trying to squirm back out of the armour trap, when Orson finally deigned to help.

He picked Bayerd and the armour up together, gave the armour a few good tugs, and Bayerd's head popped out the neck hole like a turtle emerging from its shell. Bayerd contorted his arm joints until his arms were in the right place, sticking out through the armholes in the armour.

Clearly, Kelp's father had been a much more robust man than Bayerd. The armour was far too big and loose on his frame. It was actually ideal in regards to his plan, for it hung so low on Bayerd's shoulders, he could see his upper chest. He could see the heaven stone that glowed within his skin. He would be able to see when the glow died—unless he died first.

He tried to bend over, to pick up the helmet. Alas, the weight of the metal toppled him over and he fell to the floor. As hard as he tried, he could not get up again or even turn over. He gave up trying and lay there like a dead turtle.

Orson heaved a mighty sigh and lifted Bayerd to stand for a second time. He also retrieved the helmet and dropped it on Bayerd's head, almost giving him a concussion. "I don't know why you want to dress as a knight now, unless it's to fight that three-headed monster," Orson griped. "But I think the armour will be more of a hindrance than a help since it's so heavy, you can barely move in it. And you know you can't fight to save your life."

Bayerd glared at Orson, slammed down the helmet's visor, and stalked toward the bathing tub. He tripped and tipped forward again, and lay there unable to get up, again. Orson picked him up, again, saying, "See, the armour is going to get you killed for sure."

That was the plan—more or less. He shoved Orson away and his friend said, "That's not very nice when I'm only helping you."

Staggering under the burden of the armour, Bayerd made his way more carefully to the edge of the tub. Orson planted his hands on his hips and shook his head at Bayerd. "What the heck do you think you're doing now?" demanded Orson.

Bayerd tapped his glowing heart, and drew a slashed line across it, repeating his mimed instructions to Orson. He wanted no misunderstanding between them.

"I hope you know what you're doing," Orson groaned, his face one big frown.

Bayerd nodded, although in truth, he did have some doubts. Leaning on the edge of the tub, he stepped one leg over it and into the water. He meant to sink gently down. Alas, his foot slipped and he fell with a tremendous splash. It probably drenched the room as if there had been a deluge inside the tower.

He managed to twist as he fell, and landed on his back, with the weight of the armour trapping him there. He truly could not surface to save his life. Events were unfolding faster than expected. He hoped Orson was ready to do his part—and was clear on what that part was. You could never be too sure with Orson.

When Bayerd began to run out of air, panic welled up in him. He fought to get free of the armour, even though he knew he had to drown a little longer. It is no easy task to fight one's instinct to survive, which is the strongest instinct a man has.

He stopped struggling when his muscles grew too limp to move. He looked at his chest. As before, the glow was dimming, yet it was still there. Bayerd's vision began to fail. He felt the water surge around him when someone joined him in the tub. Through the ripples, he could just make out Orson standing tall over him, his sword in hand and raised high over Bayerd, its tip targeting his heart. Why did Orson have his sword out? And pointed at Bayerd's heart? His brain had gotten too fuzzy to puzzle out that mystery, or feel any true alarm.

He squinted at the stone and its glow was now as faint as the last little ember on the wick of a snuffed candle. Just a little longer he thought, right before Orson's blade stabbed him in the heart. The water turned blood red, from his blood. He must have screamed, but since he was under water, Orson did not get incinerated.

Above the water, there was the sound of a door banging and a woman screaming and a baby crying. Orson's sword jerked up and out of Bayerd's chest, lifting him momentarily clear of the water, which hurt even more than when the sword had stabbed into his flesh. And then he died, although perhaps he merely fainted, since he did revive, eventually.

The armour was off him and he was comfortably installed in his bed, or as comfortably installed as he could be given the most recent indignities to his fragile mortal coil. All was quiet—no shouting or stomping or crying. Just how much time had passed since Orson had stabbed him in the heart? Bayerd rolled onto his back and couldn't suppress a groan.

Kelp moved into view. "Lie still," she said and settled on the edge of the bed. She smiled and touched his cold chest with her warm hand. His body felt as weak as a drowned worm and his head as foggy as a cloud.

He glanced down and to his profound relief, his chest no longer glowed, and his heart was still beating. There was a third gruesome scar over his heart, which was every bit as healed as the two older scars. His theory had been correct—on exiting, the stone had sealed his wound. He just hadn't expected the stone to leave his body on the end of Orson's sword. Clearly, Orson had not understood his clever plan at all.

"The stone is out of you," Kelp said in a voice that trembled.

Bayerd smiled up at her and wanted to tell her he loved her, yet he was too afraid to speak lest fire still spew out of him. He would not test his voice when Kelp's beautiful face was close enough to singe.

He struggled to sit up. Kelp helped him. He spotted Orson, hanging back guiltily. Well, Kelp had done a lot of shouting at him, not at all pleased that he had stabbed Bayerd.

"Can you speak now?" Kelp asked, studying his face.

He shrugged, then motioned her back. He gave one little groan and no fire came out. Feeling braver, he whispered, "Kelp." There was still no fire, only his love's name. He smiled. "I think I can talk. Yes, I can."

"Yes, you can." Kelp threw her arms around him.

"And you'll probably never shut up," Orson muttered under his breath, loudly enough for all to hear the quiver in his voice.

Bayerd pulled Kelp against his chest and hugged her tight, blinking away tears of joy and relief. Then Orson hopped aboard and wrapped his arms around the pair of them. He hugged them both so tight, he almost crushed them together into one person.

"I thought I killed you," he mumbled, sounding quite overcome and not at all like Orson.

He released them and leaned back on a pillow, crossing his ankles, making himself right at home in their bed. "I don't know where you came up with that crazy idea, Bayerd, to drown yourself and get stabbed in the heart to get the stone out, but it worked. Stone came out on the end of my sword, so it worked like a charm. And that big gaping hole in your chest sealed right up."

Bayerd chuckled, since he could. "My plan did not include getting stabbed in the heart. That was your contribution. My plan was simply for you to hold me under the water until I drowned and the stone came out of its own accord, and sealed the exit wound. At that point, you were to haul me out of the water so I could revive."

"Oh, really? So I wasn't supposed to stab you? Huh, imagine that. You really aren't very good at miming, Bayerd. T'is lucky you have your voice back."

"Yes, and lucky the stone is out. The Tri-Alanth is most impatient for its return. She claims it speaks to her about all the stars in the heavens and the great fire that warms our land. She believes the stone came down to earth on her mountain, just for her." Bayerd relaxed back against the headboard, an arm around Kelp, as happy as a man could be that everything was working out perfectly. Or almost as happy as a man could be. The Tri-Alanth still had to be dealt with.

"Orson, aren't you supposed to be watching Bay?" Kelp said, a worried little frown between her eyebrows. "He is awfully quiet, and that usually means he is getting into trouble."

"Like father like son," Orson said, and looked around. "Where did the little scamp get to? He's getting to be a real fast crawler. I hope he don't roll down the tower stairs. I'm going to start putting a leash on him."

He left the bedchamber to find the babe and Kelp called, "Close the door."

225

Orson did, and Bayerd was alone with his wife, his love, after what felt like a lifetime of hardship. He leaned close and brushed her velvety lips softly with his. She moaned and would have deepened the kiss if Bayerd had not pulled back.

"What now, husband? Does our new palette not suit you?" Kelp asked playfully, patting the fresh bedding.

"Oh, it does, most assuredly." He nibbled her ear. "And I need no palette when I have you, I need nothing but you."

"Will you whisper words of love in my ear? All night long?" Her hand traced the scars over his chest, and she leaned down to kiss the newest one. Her tongue and teeth took over, toying with his nipple, which, thank heavens, had survived all three wounds intact.

He groaned in pleasure. "I will, and I will do anything and everything else you wish, all night long." He shuddered when her hand stroked down his ribs. "Or we could test the bed now," he gasped. Passion had a most invigorating effect on a man, far more effective than any tonic. Everything faded into unimportance when searing desire reared its ravenous head.

"I do so love hearing your voice again." Kelp's moist mouth nibbled his neck. "And as tempting as that suggestion is, my love, I doubt there is time enough at the moment. And I don't want to rush a good thing."

"No," he agreed. "And I have new tales to tell you, unbelievable tales of the quest for the heaven stone." His hands roamed over her body, hoping to convince her to change her mind.

"I am eager to hear all about your adventures and hardships, husband. Both the truth and the tales," she added, suddenly looking rather sad.

"What upsets you?" Bayerd asked.

"My own actions. I have a confession to make."

"You did hire Jabalot to kill me?" Bayerd guessed, since that was the one volatile topic they had yet to address.

"You don't believe that rubbish, do you?" Kelp asked, drawing back.

"I don't really believe it," he stressed, "but Jabalot did confess all when he thought we were about to die in the mountain, and he had no reason to lie then. He said you had hired him to make sure I never returned from the quest. And if you did, I can certainly understand why ..."

She leapt from the bed so quickly, it might have been swarmed by irate porcupines. "How can you accuse me of such a dastardly deed? How can you believe I would ever want you dead?" she cried.

"I didn't really believe it," he repeated, "but I can understand it. I was a terrible husband and an embarrassment to you. I was cowardly and ridiculous and … well, if I had been married to me, I would have wanted me dead. And you are a royal, kill or be killed, you know. Since Jabalot still walks free after killing three knights, someone of royal standing had to speak on his behalf."

Kelp's brow furrowed. "You're right. I hadn't thought of that, but it was not me. I did not order Jabalot to kill you. Even when you were not yourself, I still loved you. I wanted to help you rather than kill you. That is my confession. It was I who sent you on the quest, not Queen Hellenor. I sent you from the castle, hoping the time away would restore you to the man you once were. But I had no idea the quest would be so dangerous. I did not mean for you to suffer so, or be gone so long." Her lip trembled. "And I did not order Jabalot to kill you. Why would he tell such a vile lie?"

Bayerd pointed to his pack, which someone had brought into the bedroom while he lay unawares. Kelp picked it up and handed it to him. He reached in and found the locket. He showed it to Kelp. "Jabalot had this on him. He claimed you gave it to him in gratitude, for making sure I did not return from my quest."

"My locket," Kelp said. "I discovered it was gone soon after you left. I thought you had taken it with you, so you would have my portrait to gaze upon while you were away."

Bayerd shook his head. "Jabalot had it. He claimed you gave it to him."

"Well I did not." Kelp slipped the locket on.

Bayerd believed her. His Kelp was forthright, not a liar, and he felt ashamed for doubting her. He rose and clasped her hands, guiding them to his mouth to kiss them. "Forgive me for being an ass, yet again. Now that my voice is restored to me, I will find out why Jabalot is lying. Perhaps he was tricked into believing it was you who had ordered my assassination, when it was another. He is as blind as a worm, you know. Well, he did mistake Revel for me, and Revel had curly ginger hair. Perhaps Jabalot thought it was you when it was someone else entirely."

"Shifra," Kelp said, as if the thought had just struck her.

But it made complete sense. "Shifra," he said with a nod.

"It wouldn't have been too difficult for her to have the locket removed from my room, probably by a servant." A thought struck them at the same time.

"The buxom wench that almost drowned you," Kelp said.

"She did slip into our bedchamber while I was in the bath, and too drunk to stop her," Bayerd admitted, his cheeks colouring at that embarrassing memory.

"Shifra. I'm glad she is gone," Kelp declared, although her mouth remained downturned.

Trying to coax her sad frown away, Bayerd kissed both corners of her mouth, and then the middle. He said, "I will spend the rest of my days being the man you deserve, if you can forgive me for … for everything."

"Let us hope this three-headed monster will leave us in peace once the stone is returned to her, and that we have many many days and nights together, for you do have much to atone for, husband."

Her words sounded forgiving and Bayerd grinned. "That I do, and my worst crime was not having faith in you. It will never happen again."

"See that it doesn't." She looked him up and down. He was tattered, scarred, bone-thin and beaten. He was not a vision to behold, yet Kelp looked at him with such love in her eyes, it was as if she was drinking in the sight of him.

"Come back to bed, my love," he said, and tugged her that way. She allowed it until an anguished cry from outside the bedchamber stopped them both in their tracks. In all their years together, Bayerd had never heard Orson sound quite so panicked.

Both he and Kelp dashed for the door. She flung it opened and they could see for themselves why Orson was so distressed. Little Bay was sitting atop the dining table. He was happy enough, trying to stick his hand in Orson's large smelly sock, yet his little belly glowed as if a coal burned inside it.

"He swallowed the stone," Orson cried. "We were playing puppets, making them eat the stone. I only looked away for a minute, and he'd swallowed it right down."

Kelp clapped a hand over her mouth and said, "Oh no."

Bayerd felt decisive action was called for. He scooped up his son, gripped the babe by the ankles and shook him upside-down, hoping the stone would be instantly regurgitated. The lad waved his arms about in delight and squirmed like a fish on a line. He was a born daredevil.

"Stop that," Kelp ordered Bayerd in her steeliest tone.

"But he likes it," Bayerd said, "and it might dislodge the stone." He shook a bit more vigorously and the lad squealed with delight. The blast of flame that came out of him targeted Orson, since the babe was facing the big oaf directly.

Orson screamed when his shirt went up in flames. He leapt into the bathing tub, which was no longer filled with blood-red water. Kelp must have had it refilled with fresh as a precaution, whilst Bayerd was recovering in his bed. The fire had also been relit and Bayerd wondered if he should put his son in the hearth, since he was bound to be every bit as fireproof as Bayerd had been when the stone resided in him. Before he could decide, the baby turned his head, trying to look at Bayerd, and shot another stream of fire sideways, scorching Bayerd's arm, which was no longer even the least bit fireproof.

Alarmed to be holding a dragon-baby, he put his son down rather abruptly. In truth, he dropped him on his head, but only from a foot or so above the ground.

Before Kelp could give Bayerd the dressing down that he probably deserved, Bay started wailing in earnest, shooting more flames out of his mouth. Bayerd and Kelp backed away. Orson stayed safely in the tub, up to his neck in water, ready to duck under if more flames should target him.

Kelp's ladies must have been curious about all the screaming, for both appeared in the door. "Stay back," Kelp warned Maiga and Irvette. "Bay has swallowed the heaven stone."

They could probably figure that out for themselves since the babe was glowing and spewing fire.

"What now?" Bayerd asked, at a loss.

"We need to make him sick so he spits up the stone." Kelp looked around the room frantically.

"Too many sweets make babes sick," Maiga called from the doorway.

"He likes sweets," Irvette said.

"And eating sweets will make him stop crying," Kelp agreed.

It sounded promising to Bayerd. Certainly better than shaking his son upside-down or tossing him into the fire, or into the tub to drown since he couldn't swim any better than Bayerd. "Have you any sweets handy, my love?" he asked.

She nodded and edged toward the sideboard, skirting carefully around the babe's flames. She slid open a drawer and removed a waxed-paper package. She unwrapped it and extended the tempting treat toward the babe. "Chocolate. Look Bay, chocolate," she said.

He stopped crying and his little mouth puckered. While he wasn't producing flames, Kelp moved closer. Bay reached out a wet fist and took the square of chocolate. He began to suckle messily on it, and he smiled.

Everyone breathed a sigh of relief, until a hissing noise from the fire filled the room, and it was not the normal hissing a damp log might make. It was far more sinister and threatening than that. The five adults turned as one to face the hearth—and the monster slithering out of it.

"But it is not yet night!" Bayerd cried angrily. "You've come before the appointed hour." Perhaps he should not have been surprised, since he knew the Tri-Alanth was inclined to break her word.

The eldest head simply hissed at him and he could not understand her any longer. She looked exhausted; the scales under her eyes were dark bruised circles. The two baby heads were crying in an annoying hissy, whiny pitch, as if they never stopped.

Kelp picked up Bay and hugged him protectively against her chest. She stepped back, trying to conceal his glowing middle with her arms. Bayerd stepped forward, doing his best to keep the monster's attention on him. "Come back tonight, as agreed, and you will get the heaven stone," he said.

She narrowed her slitted eyes on him—on his chest. He was no longer speaking in flame and she drew her own conclusion. She hissed angrily, sending a narrow stream of fire directly at him. Its heat licked his already burnt arm and he gasped in pain. His reaction simply confirmed what she already knew, that the stone no longer resided inside him.

She hissed questioningly, her head tilted in puzzlement.

"The stone is out of me, and still, I live," Bayerd declared. "It will be presented to you tonight, as agreed upon. Come back then. Return when the sky is dark."

She shook her head, proving she understood his words. Her mouth pulled into a viperous smile, and her eyes focused on Kelp, or more precisely, on the babe in Kelp's arms. Could she sense the stone in his little belly?

"Run, Kelp," Bayerd said, stepping between her and the Tri-Alanth. Orson splashed out of the tub and moved to Kelp's side, to hustle her toward the door. Bayerd was surprised that she went along without protest, then realized that she was, first and foremost, protecting his son. If he could have loved her more, he would have done so then.

They almost made it out the door.

The Tri-Alanth surged from the fire so fast, it was as if she had been launched from a catapult. Her scaly length brushed past Bayerd, knocking him flat. And he had no sword to stop her, as if he could have accomplished such a lofty feat. Her extended neck blocked the only exit from the tower room, before anyone could escape. Even Kelp's two ladies were trapped.

The Tri-Alanth and Kelp faced off. Kelp said, "We will get the stone out of the babe and present it to you tonight, as Bayerd told you. He is a man of his word."

The Tri-Alanth simply shook her head. Orson's wide eyes were darting all about the room quite frantically, and Bayerd realized his valiant friend was looking for his sword. Bayerd spotted it first, propped against the side of the tub. He dashed toward it and scooped it up.

"Toss it," Orson shouted.

And Bayerd did, since the sword would be put to much better use in Orson's hand. Alas, Bayerd was still lacking strength and Orson's sword was uncommonly heavy. It clattered to the floor halfway between them, out of range of either.

The Tri-Alanth did not stand about twiddling her claws, waiting for one of them to retrieve it. Her long snaky neck wrapped around Kelp, trapping both her and the babe Kelp held in her arms.

"No!" Bayerd cried. "There is no need to harm anyone. You will get your stone. Let them go, I beg of you."

Kelp was turning rather red in the face, as if she was being squeezed too tight, which she undoubtedly was. Orson lunged for the sword. The Tri-Alanth swatted him to the ground with one of her other necks. Bayerd dove toward his friend's blade, and got swept off his feet by the monster's tail. With her three necks, her long tail, and her talent with fire, she was a formidable foe. And she had Kelp and the babe. If she abducted them through the fire with her, Kelp would be burnt to a crisp.

231

Bayerd eyed the contained blaze and knew it had to be doused, or blocked, or something. He backed toward the fireplace, sealed the damper with a quick hard yank on the chain, and slammed the fireguard shut, almost in the same motion.

He planted himself in front of the dying fire, arms crossed like one of the queen's sentries. "There is no need for this. The babe will spit up the heaven stone and we will give it to you. We don't want it!" he stated, appealing to her reason.

In answer, she hissed a stream of fire at him. He fully expected to get fried then and there. Instead, water flew through the air, dousing her flames and soaking Bayerd. Kelp's two ladies stood by the tub, already scooping more water into buckets.

The Tri-Alanth cast them a resentful glance before she lunged toward the window, taking Kelp and Bay with her. Bayerd had completely forgotten that she had wings, not that he could have blocked both the fireplace and the window, and the fire had been the greater threat to Kelp.

The monster moved as fast as a lizard, darting for the opened tower window. Bayerd took off after her, alas, only as fast as a man. He snatched up Orson's sword in passing as she slithered out the window. As snakish as her body was, she had no trouble fitting through the opening.

Her ten-foot long tail was disappearing as Bayerd reached the window. He knew he could not let her get away with Kelp and his son, for she would do them terrible harm and he might never see them again.

As desperate as a man can get, he latched onto the end of the Tri-Alanth's tail as it tumbled out the window.

24. Three Heads are so Much Worse than One

The monster is dead, every last head!
One, two, three, fiddle dee dee
The monster is dead, every last head!
One, two, three, fiddle dee dee

-unknown, Untitled

Bayerd was yanked out through the tower window on the Tri-Alanth's tail. Alas, he only had one free hand, since the other was still clutching Orson's sword. One hand was not enough to grip the monster's thick tail. He needed something more secure to hold onto. All he had was Orson's sword. He plunged the blade deep into her muscular tail, planting it like a stake. Then he was hanging on for dear life as she screamed in rage and contorted violently, trying to dislodge him.

The Tri-Alanth lurched in a downward direction and turned her head backwards to spit fire at Bayerd. When the ball of flames surged toward him, he gripped the sword with both hands and swung out of the fire's path. Its passing heat was enough to singe his hair as he avoided the blue flames by the skin of his teeth. His actions caused the sword to cut partway through the monster's tail as if he was slicing off the end of a gigantic sausage.

The Tri-Alanth keened in pain, in a pitch so high and loud, it must have ruptured the eardrums of all the angels in heaven. She dropped out of the sky almost as fast is if she was falling. Bayerd barely had time to wonder if his actions were helping his wife and son, or hastening their demise, when the sword slid slickly out of the monster's bloody tail, and then he was falling toward the moat, which, in spite of his tendency to drown, was preferable to the rocky ground.

He landed with a loud thud on the edge of the drawbridge, rather than in the water. Wood is more forgiving than stone, yet the impact felt like it cracked every bone in his already battered body.

There were cries of alarm from the castle folk as the Tri-Alanth came down to earth in the courtyard, at the end of the drawbridge.

Perhaps the damage he had done to her tail had compromised her ability to fly, and she could not simply fly away. Or maybe she was simply hanging around because she wanted to fry him alive—that was certainly a possibility since she had nothing but hatred for him in her cold heart.

Bayerd tried to stand and managed a sagging kneel. To his profound relief, Kelp and his son appeared surprisingly healthy, all things considered. After a fortifying breath, he staggered to his feet and limped in their direction, gripping Orson's heavy sword in a sweaty hand and using it as a cane to keep himself upright. The Tri-Alanth waited for him at the end of the drawbridge, her eyes narrowed to slits, her neck coils tight around Kelp and Bay.

When he stood before the monster, he raised the sword in challenge, hoping he looked brave and threatening, in spite of the fact that he had to use two hands. He had quite an audience. Every last man, woman and child in the Golden Kingdom must have stayed to watch the show instead of running for their lives. Most of them sighed with gusto, some groaned, and a few merely chuckled. Bayerd's recent reputation as a coward and fool did not inspire confidence, to be sure.

He set his jaw, determined to save his loved ones, and at the same time prove to Kelp, and everyone else, that he was no longer the pitiful creature who had cringed inside the castle walls for a year, afraid of his own shadow.

The Tri-Alanth glared at Bayerd with such intense loathing, he should have turned to ash on the spot, and still she did not release Kelp and Bay from her coiled neck. At least Bay was not crying, he looked to have a mouthful of chocolate that he was gumming still. Kelp's face was bloodless white, yet resolute. The archers on the battlements were surely notching their arrows, yet they could not shoot with Kelp and the babe acting as a shield for the monster. Add to that, the Tri-Alanth's scales looked as tough as a dragon's. They were surely impenetrable to arrows.

"Release them," Bayerd ordered. "Release them and fly away, and I will still give you the heaven stone." He was lying. The Tri-Alanth had proven herself too dangerous and vengeful to be allowed to leave. He had no doubt that she would simply return through a fire and murder everyone in the kingdom, first chance she got.

In answer, she hissed a stream of fire in his direction and spread her wings, launching off the ground awkwardly, her tail dangling crookedly behind. Her wingspan was an impressive forty feet, if not more.

"Bayerd, catch," Kelp screamed. She tossed the babe down through the air toward him.

What was she thinking? Clearly, she had far more faith in him than he deserved. Bayerd dropped the sword, since he certainly didn't want to skewer his son upon it like a ripe melon. He stepped forth, reaching out with both arms as if he was indeed catching a ripe melon. The babe dropped into them and Bayerd squeezed him tight against his chest, against his furiously beating heart.

Perhaps he squeezed too tight, for the baby vomited out a great deal of chocolate—and the heaven stone. It splatted onto the edge of the drawbridge and glowed brightly in the dusky light. "What a good little boy you are," Bayerd said, kissing his son on the forehead.

The Tri-Alanth stopped flapping her wings and settled back to the ground. Alas, Bayerd was in no position to battle her, having exchanged the sword for a sticky, squirming, and fragile infant.

He glanced around for someone to take charge of his son now that the lad no longer breathed fire. Orson and Kelp's ladies must have hurtled down the stairs at top speeds for they were already in the courtyard. Orson was in the lead, barreling toward Bayerd with all the grace and subtlety of a wounded warthog.

"Orson," Bayerd bellowed, his voice like thunder, and as Kelp had done, he tossed his son in Orson's general direction, trusting that his friend would catch the boy—which he did. Orson was nothing if not trustworthy.

Bayerd immediately plucked up both the sword, and the sticky heaven stone. It was his best hope to bargain for Kelp's life—perhaps for all their lives. He clenched his fist tight around the little stone, wondering how to accomplish the goal without ending up as a pyre of fire, like Shifra.

The Tri-Alanth didn't like him manhandling her precious crystal. She blasted a thick, sizzling stream of flame right at him. Before he could think twice about it, he shoved the heaven stone into his mouth and swallowed. He preferred to lose his voice over going up in flame and burning alive. There really was no choice to make. The stone tasted like chocolate and went down easily.

When the Tri-Alanth's fire hit him, he was already fireproof. Her flames bathed him instead of burning him alive. A chorus of alarmed cries filled the air. Everyone thought him incinerated until the monster's fire was snuffed when she snapped her jaws shut.

Bayerd was revealed, standing triumphantly, feet planted and sword raised, its blade glowing orange from the heat of the fire. He brushed off the smoldering remains of his tunic, simply glad he was wearing leather trousers. He bowed gracefully to his audience and to his princess, milking the moment. How could he not?

A cheer went up from the crowd and Bayerd's heart swelled to grand proportions. For a lovely moment, he felt like a hero, even though he knew he was no such thing. Yet he could play the part of hero, since he was first and foremost, a performer. And whilst he might not be a true hero, he was no longer a coward. There is a great deal of middling ground between the qualities of bravery and cowardice, after all. Most men are not wholly brave-hearted or lily-livered, and neither was Bayerd.

A few of the castle folk even shouted out requests for a fire-show. It was not the time or place for that. The Tri-Alanth hissed furiously at him and squeezed Kelp even tighter.

Bayerd froze as if turned to stone, his glorious moment doused. "Don't do that! I will not trade the heaven stone for a dead princess," he declared in his steeliest tone, although all that came out of his mouth now was a stream of fire, which he directed at the moat water. "That would be a poor bargain indeed. I will only exchange the stone for a living and breathing princess," he added.

The Tri-Alanth's neck coils loosened grudgingly, until Kelp could draw in a gasping breath.

"I'm delighted we understand each other," he said in flame. "Now, let us complete our bargain—I will exchange the heaven stone for my brave and beautiful wife. And I will instruct the archers to let you fly away freely, an accord that will be most beneficial to both of us." He motioned for the archers to lower their arrows, and they did, if only by a meager inch or two.

He risked one more sliding step closer to the Tri-Alanth and Kelp. Two pairs of eyes narrowed suspiciously on him. Both were wondering what he was about. He was wondering that himself, since he was rather unclear on what his next move should be.

Over the monster's shoulder, Bayerd noticed Orson passing the babe to Kelp's ladies. A nearby knight handed Orson a sword. Orson began to sneak closer. Bayerd didn't want to share his heroic limelight with anyone, especially Orson, but perhaps he did need a bit of help to dispatch the three-headed monster. As long as Orson filled merely a small supporting role and did not steal his thunder, Bayerd could accept his friend's helping hand, or helping sword as it were.

Possibilities flitted through his mind as he thought hard to come up with a plan. The damage to the Tri-Alanth's tail did seem to have compromised her ability to fly—perhaps he could use that to his advantage. He doubted that she could swim, since she was more dragon-lizard-snake than fish, and Kelp could hold her breath for an uncommonly long time. That factor could certainly work to their benefit.

And then events began to unfold around him at lightning speed— events that were completely beyond his control.

The Tri-Alanth stomped forward, onto the drawbridge. The wood creaked and groaned under her tremendous weight. Bayerd retreated to the middle of the drawbridge. Orson gave a lusty battle cry and rushed forward, sword leading the way. His intent to attack the Tri-Alanth was blatantly clear. A crowd of knights followed his lead and charged with him. And some fool at the gate thought it a good idea to start cranking up the drawbridge as fast as he possibly could. In the fool's defense, perhaps he merely wished to stop the monster from making off with the princess.

Bayerd lurched and staggered, trying to stay on his feet when the slant of the drawbridge threatened to toss him right into the monster's jaws, or the coils of one of her free necks.

With the attacking knights at her rear, Bayerd lurching toward her in front, and the ground shifting beneath her feet, the Tri-Alanth must have felt besieged on all sides. She tried to turn around, since there were a lot more attackers behind her, and they weren't fireproof. Alas, the drawbridge was only as wide as it needed to be for a wagon to cross, and she was much longer than a mere wagon. Add to that, the planking was slippery and tilting more with each passing second. She began to slide toward the crowd of attacking knights and blasted fire at them. Most simply raised their shields to block the flames and kept coming. And Kelp remained trapped in her neck coils—helpless.

With a hiss of frustration, the Tri-Alanth raised her wings and tried to take to the air. Bayerd had the high ground, so to speak, and since he was sliding down the drawbridge toward her raised wing anyway, he leapt onto it when it almost knocked him into the moat.

The Tri-Alanth screamed and her wings whipped back and forth wildly, yet she did not rise. With her damaged tail and Bayerd's weight on her wing, she truly could not fly. Since he had a sword in hand, he tried to stab her wing, to ensure she couldn't take off. Alas, she beat her wings even harder and he lost his grip on the slippery scales. He went flying through the air and plummeted toward the water to a chorus of 'not again' from the audience of castle folk, as if he splashed into the moat every other day and twice on Sunday. He landed in the filthy water and sank like a suit of armour, as was his wont.

Overhead, the Tri-Alanth slid right off the drawbridge and splashed into the water on top of him. They sank down, down, down, all the way to the silty bottom.

Bayerd tried to spot Kelp. He knew she was down there with him because she had still been a captive of the monster when it entered the water. Alas, he couldn't see a damn thing except murky froth. The Tri-Alanth was thrashing about in a frenzy and making no progress toward the surface. Clearly, she couldn't swim any better that Bayerd himself. But as long as they drowned together and Kelp escaped, Bayerd could live with that—or die with that, as it were.

He just hoped he would be remembered as a hero rather than a coward, despite the fact that he hadn't actually defeated the three-headed monster. He had simply fallen into the moat and drowned. At least he had seen Kelp one last time, and loved her well. And he had given her a son, although it had not been done in the traditional way.

As he drowned, the strength left his limbs and the cohesion left his thoughts. He was swept up in thick coils and pulled in two different directions, as if he was being rack-tortured, yet he felt no pain. With one foot already firmly planted in Death's kingdom, he felt very little. Blackness swarmed him and Death's door opened wide. He didn't even have to knock. Perhaps he was a much anticipated guest. Given how many times he had already stood before Death's door, perhaps he was.

He was about to step through the doorway when he realized the sword was still clutched in his fist, in a Deadman's grip. He should keep fighting Death, since he had a sword. He jabbed weakly at Death, and Death presented itself as one of the coils that bound him. His jab was little more than a nudge since his limbs felt as weak as kittens. The sword slipped from his grasp—no, it was being drawn from his grasp. Was Death disarming him?

Bayerd blinked hard, trying to see through the thick fog in his head and the silt in the stirred up water. A pale face floated there for just a moment, Kelp's pale face, then it was gone. There was a dull glint as the blade slashed toward him—no, toward the coils that bound him. He was released in a wash of warm red that was more blood than water. The blade flashed again and again. The thrashing monster went still. Bayerd thought a decapitated head floated by him, but that was probably a hallucination, like everything that was happening around him and to him.

A hand gripped his wrist and he was being pulled up, up, up. Before his head broke through the surface of the water, the hilt of the sword was pressed into his slack hand. His fingers closed around it, and he was not the one controlling them. Another's hand squeezed his fingers around the hilt and held them there. His dying brain was as imaginative as his tales, he thought, before the world faded to blackness.

He awoke on solid land, facedown, with hands pounding him on his back. It made no sense at all, unless it was true that he did not die like a normal man. The pounding on his back made him retch up a tremendous amount of foul water and whatever else was inside him.

He fought to stay conscious, to know that he did live … to see Kelp. He strained to push back the darkness that still threatened to claim him. It took a Herculean effort, but he kept that darkness at bay. He panted air, not water, and slowly, slowly, the world began to solidify around him.

As his abused hide was dragged up and over the lip of the moat, he strained to recall what had happened in the water. His memory of events was confused, to say the least.

He was distracted when he began to feel things again—things like the jagged stones that scraped his tender flesh. He cried out in pain and protest and no flames came out of his mouth, only rather embarrassing whimpers that a man should not make, especially a heroic man, which he was trying very hard to be. He swallowed down the whimpers and breathed a bit deeper, which led to spewing out another wash of water. The world got even more substantial after that and his head stopped spinning like a top.

He sat up and looked around. He was on the edge of the moat. Kelp knelt beside him, as wet and bedraggled as he had ever seen her, and all the more beautiful for it.

A cheering crowd encircled them. There were chants of, "The monster is dead, every last head! One, two, three, fiddle dee dee. The monster is dead, every last head!" Some quick thinker had come up with the rhyme.

"Kelp," Bayerd whispered, "my Kelp." He took her hand and kissed her fingers. "You … we … how …" He gave his head a rub, as if that would bring missing memories back. "I admit, I don't recall all of what happened in the moat. Drowning will do that, I suppose."

"Yes, it will. Well, I recall everything," she declared, loudly enough to be heard by their audience, who fell silent.

Bayerd felt at a disadvantage sitting on the ground when surrounded by those who loomed over him. He staggered to his feet and drew Kelp closer. "What happened down there?" he asked, tilting his head at the cursed moat. Now that he had a better view, he could see three decapitated heads bobbing on the stirred up water.

"Why, you slay the beast, my husband. You fought as bravely as a knight and lopped off all three heads, ending the monster's destructive rampage. We are safe now, thanks to your valiant actions."

Orson snorted in disbelief.

Kelp silenced him with a glare. Bayerd frowned, trying to remember. He'd had a sword, he knew that much. Maybe he had somehow slayed the beast. Or had Kelp done the deed? And gifted him the title of hero? Well, such a generous gift must be accepted with good grace.

He cleared his throat and declared, "What transpired in the dark waters of the moat is a tale worthy of the telling, but it should not be told when we stand here shivering in the cold wind. It should be properly told when we are seated before a warm fire with full cups and fuller bellies. I will tell the tale when we next gather to feast!" His voice rose and crested, filling even the expansive courtyard with its presence.

"And will you perform a fire-show, too?" someone shouted, which started a chorus of voices clamouring for the same.

"I no longer breathe fire," he said, with an affronted sniff.

To a man, their faces fell with disappointment.

"No more fire-shows?" they cried.

"No, but my voice is restored to me, and I have many new tales to tell," Bayerd said.

"But no more fire-shows?" the crowd repeated.

"No, no more fire-shows," he snapped, put out. He didn't even know where the heaven stone had ended up after he vomited it up with the moat water, well, not until Kelp pressed a small stone into his palm. He glanced down and saw the glow of the heaven stone. "Oh, fine. Perhaps I will perform a fire-show, if my audience is truly appreciative of my new tales," he said grudgingly.

Resounding cheers almost deafened Bayerd.

He linked his hand with Kelp's. The crowd parted and they walked across the courtyard, into the castle and up the long stairs to reach the peace and quiet of their tower. Since they were closely followed by Orson, the babe, and Kelp's two ladies, their tower rooms were not quiet for long. And there was some celebrating to be done, although Bayerd lacked the stamina to revel with any true enthusiasm.

It wasn't until much later that night, when Bayerd and Kelp were finally tucked up together in their bed, cocooned and alone, that they had a chance to talk privately. And the talking had to wait until Bayerd had loved his wife quite thoroughly. He found he had plenty of stamina for that. When they were finally sated, he kissed her cheek tenderly and said, "I am not convinced I slay the monster."

She linked their fingers. "Of course you did, my husband. You are everyone's hero now, not just mine."

He smiled at her in the candlelight. "I should be. I saved the queen, you know."

"So you have told me. Queen Hellenor disagrees."

Bayerd leaned on his elbow and gazed down at her. "I truly slay the monster?"

In answer, she nibbled his earlobe, which was no answer at all, although it was delightfully diverting.

"You wouldn't lie to me, would you?" he asked.

"Never," she whispered in his tingling ear, "unless it was for your own good."

Kelp's sweet mouth found his lips, distracting him from questioning her further. She distracted him so thoroughly, he forgot what they had been discussing. And after he had loved her again, he was simply too exhausted to do anything but sleep like the dead, his dreams filled with all the new tales he couldn't wait to perform. And he might have dreamed a little bit about fire-shows.

THE END

If you want more dragons, you can find them in FIRE-SCAPE.

241

www.ingramcontent.com/pod-product-compliance
Lightning Source LLC
Chambersburg PA
CBHW020728210626
46807CB00016B/474